The *Silent*

BANTAM BOOKS BY JACK ĐANN

THE SILENT

THE MEMORY CATHEDRAL
A Secret History of Leonardo da Vinci

JACK ÐANN

The $\mathscr{S}$ILENT

BANTAM BOOKS

New York   Toronto   London   Sydney   Auckland

THE SILENT
A Bantam Book / July 1998

BOOK DESIGN BY SUSAN YURAN.

Library of Congress Cataloging-in-Publication Data

Dann, Jack.
The silent / Jack Dann.
p.   cm.
ISBN 0-553-09716-4
1. United States—History—Civil War, 1861–1865—Fiction.   I. Title.
PS3554.A574S5   1998
813'.54—dc21   98-4815   CIP

Published simultaneously in the United States and Canada

Bantam Books are published by Bantam Books, a division of Bantam
Doubleday Dell Publishing Group, Inc. Its trademark, consisting of the
words "Bantam Books" and the portrayal of a rooster, is Registered in
U.S. Patent and Trademark Office and in other countries. Marca
Registrada. Bantam Books, 1540 Broadway, New York, New York 10036.

PRINTED IN THE UNITED STATES OF AMERICA

BVG   10   9   8   7   6   5   4   3   2   1

FOR JANEEN WEBB . . .

FOR TRUE RECOGNITION

Contents

	Acknowledgments	*ix*
	An Author's Note of a Sort	*xi*
1	Seeing the Spirit Dog and Forgetting How to Talk	1
2	Piling Up Dem Bones	21
3	Private Newton's War in the Air	47
4	Jimmadasin Rises Up from the Dead	59
5	The Walkin' Boy	75
6	The Cave of the Baby Jesus	91
7	When Dixie Died	115
8	In Heaven with General Jackson and Abe Lincoln	131
9	Losin' Things	163
10	Listenin' to the Spirits Fight	189
11	Followin' the Spirits through the Smoke	209
12	The Power of Roots	221
13	Puttin' Money in the Bank	247
14	The Portals of Heaven	269
	Afterword	*281*
	A Note from Jack Dann	*283*

Acknowledgments

The author would like to thank the following people for their support, aid, and inspiration:

Irwyn Applebaum, Lou Boxer, Norm and Paddy Broberg, Susan Casper, Edith Dann, Lorne Dann, Terry Dowling, Gardner Dozois, Sue Drakeford, Harlan and Susan Ellison, Andrew Enstice (who introduced me to Lieut.-Col. G. F. R. Henderson, C.B.!), Keith Ferrell, Greg Frost, William Gibson, Robert Harris (whose research was invaluable), Ron and Louise Harris, David Hartwell, Merrilee Heifetz, Charlie and Betty Kochis, Chris Lawson, Pat Lyons, Race and Iola Mathews, Sean McMullen, Maja Nikolic, Steve Paulsen, Pamela Sargent, Tracey Schatvet, Thomas Schlück, the staffs of the Hupp's Hill Battlefield Park & Study Center and the Cedar Creek Battlefield Foundation, the staff of the Wayside Inn, Lucius Shepard, Jonathan Strahan, Nick Stathopoulos, Nita Taublib, Dena Taylor, Christine Valada, Janeen Webb, Stewart Wieck, George Zebrowski, and special thanks to Jennifer Hershey and Tom Dupree; and, of course, to my editor Pat LoBrutto, who knows why.

An author's note of a sort

I wrote this, and then Uncle Randolph went over it and fixed my sentences and punctuation and broke everything up into sections and put in some of the quotations and fixed whatever else could be fixed. Uncle Randolph and Doctor Keys think it's "therapeutical" for me to write down what happened. They think if I can just write about all the terrible things that happened, they'll sort of go away or something and I won't think they were all my fault.

I think that Uncle Randolph shouldn't listen to doctors.

Anyway, I tried to write like everybody talked, but with some of the colored dialect it was hard to write it down, so I just did the best I could. Uncle Randolph went over that too. And he took out some of the swear words, which he said wouldn't read well because he said I had too many of them, but he left some in so you could get a feel for the truth. He didn't take out anything important, though, even though he said it made his heart sick to read it.

I don't know about that.

It's done now, and if anything's wrong it's probably my fault.

Anyway, it's mostly true.

EDMUND "MUNDY" MCDOWELL
NOVEMBER 16, 1864
SCRANTON, PENNSYLVANIA

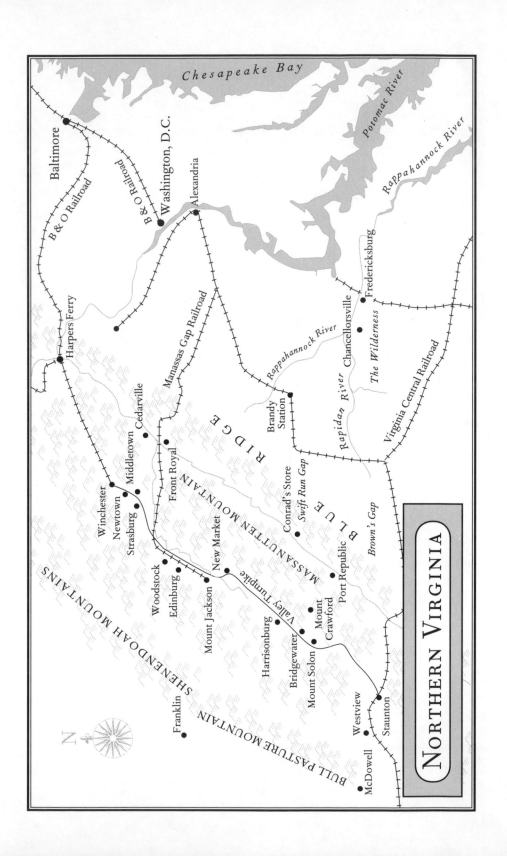

Chesapeake Bay

Potomac River

Rappahannock River

Baltimore

B & O Railroad

B & O Railroad

Washington, D.C.

Alexandria

Fredericksburg

Harpers Ferry

Manassas Gap Railroad

Rappahannock River

Chancellorsville

The Wilderness

Rapidan River

Virginia Central Railroad

Brandy Station

B L U E   R I D G E

Cedarville

Middletown

Front Royal

Conrad's Store

Swift Run Gap

Brown's Gap

Winchester

Newtown

Strasburg

M A S S A N U T T E N   M O U N T A I N

New Market

Port Republic

Woodstock

Edinburg

Mount Jackson

Valley Turnpike

Mount Crawford

Harrisonburg

Bridgewater

Mount Solon

Westview

Staunton

S H E N E N D O A H   M O U N T A I N S

B U L L   P A S T U R E   M O U N T A I N

Franklin

McDowell

N

NORTHERN VIRGINIA

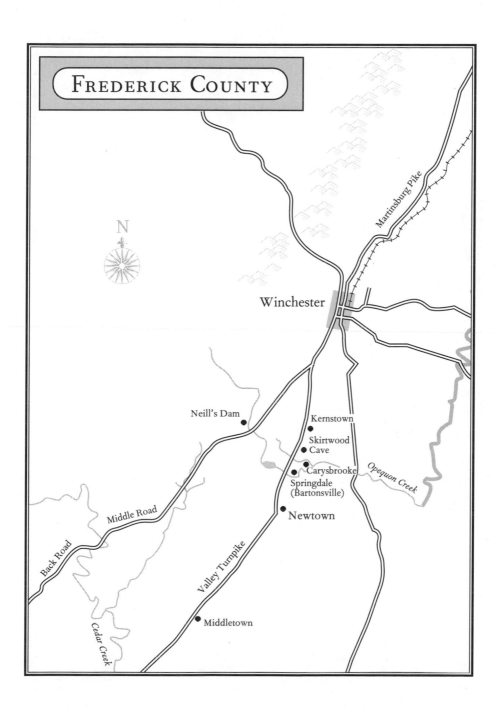

The $\mathscr{S}$ILENT

SEEING THE SPIRIT ÐOG AND FORGETTING HOW TO TALK

Oh yes! Oh yes!
I been conjurin'
Oh yes! Oh yes! Oh yes!
I been killin',
No cause, no cause, no cause,
In de worl'.

CONJURIN' SONG

*I*T WAS AROUND THE TIME I SAW THE SPIRIT DOG AND BECAME INVISI-
ble that I forgot how to talk. I can think the words in my head and write them
down on paper (well, you can see that!), but when I open my mouth to try to talk,
I just seem to choke. Doctor Keys had a word for it, but I forget what it was.
Naming it seemed to make everybody feel better, though. That's more than I've
seen most doctors do anyway—except to cut the arms and legs off soldiers. I
sure as hell saw a lot of that! I think those goddamn doctors killed more soldiers
than all the guns and artillery put together. But I'm getting ahead of myself
here. Uncle Randolph says I'm always getting ahead of myself, but I'll tell you
the whole story for whatever it's worth.

I could start anywhere, I suppose, but that would take too long, so I'll start
right out on March 23rd, 1862. It was a Sunday, cold and miserable and cloudy.

Come to think of it, though, the only real *sunny* day I can remember around then was ten days before General Jackson pulled our army out of Winchester because General Banks had brought his Federals down from Harper's Ferry to invade us. Not even him and Colonel Ashby's "Six Hundred" could've held out against Banks's blue-ass bucktails. Seemed like there was a million of them. And boy, was there a commotion in Winchester! Poppa took me to town to see General Jackson, although I met him later on my own and wished I didn't. As our army started off toward the Valley Pike, all the girls and old ladies were crying and wailing that they were being left to godless tyrants, and some of the soldiers were even crying, just like their mothers, and then suddenly the soldiers just starting singing "Yes, in the sweet by and by," and pretty soon everybody was singing it, until they left. Then the town was quiet as death, I can tell you. Well, maybe not *that* quiet, but pretty close to it. Nobody wanted to talk. Everybody just felt like crying, I guess.

But there I go digressin' away from my story . . .

Anyway, on the Sunday I originally started off talking about, the people in Winchester had damned good reason to be caterwauling and crying because that was what they now call the battle of Kernstown, which you all know about. It was when Jackson came right back up the pike to fight the Federals, who outnumbered him two to one. And it was bad! But I'm going to write about it, no matter how much it hurts me.

Now, Poppa used to insist on going to church every Sunday morning. Although he never had a church of his own, he was still a proper minister. Usually Episcopalian. And as we also had the farm and the day school, we made do well enough. We'd usually go to country churches and prayer meetings at people's houses, where Poppa could preach the skin off the snakes, as Mother used to say when he wanted her to do something. But Poppa had friends in Winchester too, and was invited by Mr. Williams (he was the rector) to preach at the Episcopal Church on Kent Street. Mother was all excited because she loved going into town and seeing everybody, especially Mrs. McSherry, who was her best friend, but I never did like Mrs. McSherry's boys. Not much, anyhow.

Of course, I wasn't going to church with them on account of the ringworm. I had the 'ruption all over my scalp, and it itched like a sonovabitch. My father attributed my malady to hanging around with the nigger kids—he would never say "nigger," even though we had two of our own before they ran away to the Federals. He only allowed us to call them "colored people" or "darkies" or "servants." Like everybody else, I called the old ones aunts and uncles, just like I did my real aunt and uncle, those I knew like family, anyway. I never understood him about that. Christ, the niggers called themselves niggers. So he thought I caught the eruption from the niggers who lived on the next farm—we'd borrow them sometimes to help with the farm work—but I reckon that I got it from David Steward's dog. David was one of Poppa's students, and his half-dead Irish setter had a terrible case of the mange, but I felt sorry for the damned thing and petted it. David had the ringworm too, so it had to be the dog. Course, so did the niggers. Seemed like everyone but Mother and Poppa had it that season.

Mother didn't care how I'd caught it. She'd been doing her best to cure it by rubbing my head with silver nitrate medication that burned like fire and another potion she'd made up by dropping a copper penny into vinegar; and part of my hair fell out because of it and hasn't grown back even yet. And as a further humiliation, I had to wear a turban around my head "so as not to scratch the worms and infect everybody else."

"I can't go out like this," I said to Poppa when he called me out of my room, expecting me to be all shined up and dressed for church. I was in my night drawers, and I left my turban off. My hair was mussed and greasy and itchy. Poppa was wearing his best black suit and a shiny cravat, and Mother was wearing her Sunday dress and a brooch and a bonnet with a white bow.

He turned to Mother and said, "If you were conspiring with him to stay home on the Lord's Day, you could have at least told me. I would have made provisions. We could have borrowed Eliza from Arthur Allen. She'd look after him while we're gone and make sure he had a decent Bible lesson." Poppa shook his head, as if he was telling somebody "No," and said, "At least his darkies didn't run off to the Yankees."

"You *know* why ours left," Mother said sharply. That stopped Poppa pretty cold, and then she looked at me and said, "And how do you suppose we'd look taking Mundy with his head looking all encrustated like that? Mr. McDowell, sometimes I wonder about—" Mother would always get started and then stop just like that. Now *she* was the one looking guilty. She talked low now, as if she was being introduced to someone important. "Mundy will be fine here alone. I've prepared his Bible lessons to study while we're at church. Everything's all laid out on your desk. You might want to approve it, of course. And we can stop at Mr. Allen's farm on the way to church. I'm sure he won't mind sending one of the servants over to look after Mundy." She looked at me and nodded, as if to say "I told you so."

But I knew they wouldn't do any such thing. They always used to threaten me with Eliza. All she ever did though was tell me to read the "Raising of Lazarus" or "Daniel in the Lions' Den," and then she would put on all of Mother's dresses and bonnets and jewellery and twirl around like she was at a ball. But she never did steal anything.

I heard a real good blast of cannonading in the distance; and Mother got the funny look on her face that she always gets when she's concerned and said, "Perhaps we should all stay here with Mundy."

But Poppa said, "It's just the usual annoyance of the enemy," and that was that.

He limped out onto the porch to listen, though. I should have probably told you that Poppa had served in the militia as a chaplain until he got an inflammation in the bone of his leg. He almost died from the blood poisoning and brain fever, and he had to use a cane after that, and sometimes his words would get all mixed up—but never when he was preaching the skin off the snakes.

"It's just skirmishing, like yesterday, and the day before that," he said, sniffing, as if he could smell the noise. He used to do that in the schoolhouse back behind the barn, lift up his head and take a sniff, and then he'd take the switch to whoever was passing notes or whispering or not paying proper attention. "But it might just come to something. Your Colonel Ashby, God bless him, must be biting off General Shields's toes again. And I hear that Jackson's coming north. But that's all gossip. I hear the same thing most every day." He sniffed again, and sure enough the cracking of muskets started, then died, and it seemed like it would just be an ordinary Sunday, except I wouldn't have to go to church.

Mother finally came out on the porch and said, "I do fear leaving Mundy alone."

"Well, I gave my solemn promise to Mr. Williams that I'd deliver a sermon, and a man's word is his bond. You can come with me or stay, as you will."

You see, Mother would always turn everything around on Poppa. And there just wasn't any way she was going to stay with me and not go to town, even if she would have to worry about me a little. We were used to the cannonading and the skirmishing. It was nothing more, I suppose, than having thunderstorms every day. Only that wasn't true. Everybody was fearful, just nobody cared to show it.

I watched my folks go off in their carriage, but I didn't know that I was only going to see them once more in my life. Or that Sunday was going to bring more than thunder.

It was going to bring the dogs right out of hell.

I LISTENED FOR A WHILE TO THE CANNON VOLLEYS AND MUSKET FIRE echoing across the hills and waited for them to stop. They always did. But then they'd start right up again like rain falling hard on a tin roof. I knew something more than skirmishing was going to happen—I could *feel* it—and I knew that Mother might talk Poppa into turning the carriage around, so I went out beyond the old corn house that had burned down. I went past the garden and lumber house by the edge of the woods to check the gums, which was what Poppa called our rabbit traps. I don't know why we called them that. I'd asked Poppa about it once, and he just said that's what they're called. We used boxes about two feet long baited with pieces of apple, and they worked better than noose snares, that's for sure. Poppa wasn't much with a rifle and never had time for it, so we ate a lot of rabbit during the winter. I'd catch fifty, maybe more before summer, and that was more than enough to fill out what we had of bacon, sausage, pigs' feet, and ham. It was against the rules to kill rabbits on the Sabbath, but I usually did anyway. I'd leave them hanging in the smoke house because it wasn't fair to leave them in the gums until Monday.

I knew I was fooling myself with all this business of going out to the woods to check the gums. I knew I was going to see about the skirmishing, but I just felt better fooling myself. Maybe I might change my mind and go back to the house and study the Bible.

I found only one rabbit; it was in the gum by our stone fence. It was a big one with brown spots; and as I grabbed its hind legs with my left hand, it shook like it was vibrating. I know how to kill rabbits quickly and efficiently, just hit it sharp on the back of the neck and drop it before it dies. Bad luck if it dies in your hands. Aunt Hanna—she was our servant who ran away to be with Uncle Isaac—told me that if an animal dies in your hands it's bad luck and you'll surely die before your next birthday. So I always dropped them quick.

Anyway, I was ready to hack this fat rabbit right behind the ears and drop it next to the gum when something strange came over me, and instead of killing it, I threw it right over the stone fence and let it escape into the woods. To this day I don't know why I did that. It wasn't like I felt sorry for the rabbit. Maybe it was because I knew I was going to break my word to Poppa and go out to watch the skirmishing. Maybe I didn't want to commit two sins right after the other. Angry with myself for being so stupid, I climbed over the fence and left the farm. But you know, something felt different, not right, as if just then something had changed; and yet I couldn't tell you what.

It wasn't difficult to figure where the fighting was. I just had to follow my ears, which, of course, led me just about to Mr. Joseph Barton's farm. I knew this country pretty well and cut through the woods and over Sandy Ridge. No sense walking big as life through the fields and getting your foolish ass shot off. The woods were empty because the fighting was concentrated pretty much along the pike, and it was just skirmishing, nothing much more than that from what I could tell. But I couldn't see anything much, not even from the ridge, which is pretty high and starts to the west of Winchester and runs some six miles down to the Opequon Creek. The pike's not far and runs along to the side of it.

I guessed that the Yankee guns were firing somewhere around Pritchard's Hill, and that our own were returning fire from Hodge Run or maybe below. If General Jackson and his army were around, they certainly weren't *here*.

Course, soon as I figured that, I heard twigs snapping all over. Then I heard what seemed like a thousand muskets firing all around me, and there seemed to be a whirlwind of balls suddenly flying around and hissing just like snakes. I could almost feel the whomp of a minié ball as it hit a tree trunk to my right. Somebody shouted and I heard the thud of a ball hitting something soft, and a noise such like someone just had his breath knocked out of him. And then I heard a heartbreaking wailing like a mother who'd just lost her son. "Come on, boys," someone shouted in a bluebelly dialect, and more twigs cracked as men ran through the woods.

I stayed close to the ground. It was cold and damp, and I could smell the moss on the birch and, I swear, I could also smell the sour-apple sweat of the soldiers even though I couldn't see much of them. I did see several men through the trees, and I thought they might have been our own, but I couldn't tell; they could just as easily have been Yankees. I crouched even harder against that birch tree as if I could squeeze myself right into the bark when the muskets started firing again. It was hard to tell where the balls were coming from. It didn't seem like there could be that many soldiers out here. Most of the Yanks were at least a half-mile away. Then I heard someone stepping through the woods near me calling and crying over and over in the most plaintive voice you ever heard, "Whey is my boys? Whey is my marsters?" And that voice sounded just like Jimmadasin, the McSherrys' house servant. You couldn't miss it; he had a voice that was so high and reedy, it sounded just like a woman's. But I always thought he was having it up on all of us, because when he sang his voice would suddenly get deep and full. He was responsible for minding Allan and Harry McSherry, who were twelve and fourteen, respectively. (I told you about them before; their mother, Cornelia, was my mother's best friend.)

Well, the shooting stopped, and someone said, "Get the hell outa here, you crazy nigger. Yer gonna get yourself killed." That sounded like one of our boys, but I guess it didn't much matter to the nigger who it was because he just kept on walking until he was right beside me.

And just as I'd thought, it *was* Jimmadasin right there in the flesh. He was wearing the filthy felt hat he always wore, pulled down right on his forehead, and though he was old, he was no bigger than me. His face was wrinkled up like a dried prune with bushy white eyebrows, and he was shaking like he was going to have a convulsion. But he wasn't hiding or ducking down to get out of the way of those minié balls. "Lord, please, dey just chillen, bofh a dem," he whined, spreading out his arms like a preacher calling to God. "Please, marsters, don' kill dem." Then he turned and saw me, and his head nearly cracked backward with surprise. "Lord Lord, yes indeed I foun' one a my boys, see? It's a miracle."

I didn't make a sound. I wasn't going to say a thing to this crazy nigger who seemed determined to get himself—and me—killed. But no one was paying any attention to us. Someone shouted, "Forward." There was another explosion of musket shot that just about shook the trees. There was shouting and crying and then it was just quiet except for cannon being fired near the pike. I suddenly realized how scared I was, and I was probably shaking as much as Jimmadasin because he suddenly started hugging me and cooing like a bird and saying, "Dem soldiers gone, young marster's safe wid me," and I suppose we just sat there against the tree, rocking each other like babies until the shaking stopped and I realized that I was humiliating myself. But Jimmadasin must have read my mind, or was just thinking the same thing, because he let go of me gently and stood up, slapping at his legs as if he was cold, and looking around, as if he were suddenly curious and impatient. "We got to get goin', more soldiers gonna be comin'."

"What're you doing here?" I asked like I had just woke up and found him standing over me, his face big as the moon.

"I thought for da minute you'se young Harry," he said, extending his hand out for me to take hold. "Das da honest truth. Come on now, it's dangerous here."

I let him pull me up, but before we went running off to safety I wanted my question answered to my satisfaction. And I know this sounds crazy, what with muskets exploding and soldiers running around all over here just seconds before, yet I felt safe here in the woods. There weren't any birds singing, and there were cannons and muskets firing, but right here felt sacred or something. I told you it didn't make any sense. "I ain't going noplace," I told him, "until you give me an explanation of what you're doing here."

"What *you* doin' here?"

"I asked *you*," I said.

"You ain' mah marster, but I'll tell you again jes like I tol' dem soldiers, I'se lookin' for mah marsters, mah chillen, an' mah mistress is jus 'bout half crazy wid worry."

"Then Mrs. McSherry sent you," I said; and believe me, it didn't escape my notice that he was talking in a low, deep voice now that almost was scaring me.

"*I* sen' me," Jimmadasin said, and started pulling me away, but I wanted to investigate because I heard moaning not far off. "I gotta find mah marsters, an' you're goin' to help me. I goin' to save you for your folk, an' you ain't goin' to fight me or pull away to sneak 'round dose dead an' dyin' soldiers."

"And what are you going to do if I do?" I said, feeling the humiliation burn around my ears.

"Whump your arse is what I gonna do," Jimmadasin said, and when he said that in a low rumble full of meanness and menace, I felt like I was six years old again. I probably didn't mention this before, but when I was a baby, Poppa used to threaten me by saying that if I didn't do what Mother asked me to, he'd call Mrs. McSherry and have her send Jimmadasin over with his stealin' bag to steal me away and get me out of her hair. I'd seen Jimmadasin walking home once with a bag slung over his shoulder, so I knew it was true. Anyway, Poppa had turned him into the bogey monster, and I used to have dreams that Jimmadasin was coming right through my window, even though it was on the second floor, to throw me into his bag. Then he'd take me somewhere dark and dirty, and when he'd pull me out of that bag I'd be somehow turned into a girl. And I'd wake up screaming. I didn't find out until later that his real name was James Madison, after the old president. But when he talked in that low voice I'd heard him use when singing, I knew he'd do just what he said. He was my size, but everyone knew how strong he was. So I went along with him until I could escape. We kept inside the woods for a while, then went across a field with broken stone walls here and there. We were between the Cedar Creek Road and the

Middle Road, and way up ahead was the tollgate and the white tents of the Yankee camp and, of course, Winchester town. The sky looked gray like it was promising to rain, and I suddenly felt the cold, maybe because I wasn't wearing any shoes, but unless there was snow on the ground that would freeze your toes off, I didn't usually wear them. I had so many calluses that I could step on stones and briars just like I was wearing shoes. I was wearing a short coat, though, which was warm enough.

Then out of the blue, after not talking, just walking, Jimmadasin said, "I 'pologize for bein' harsh. I wasn't goin' to whump ya, just p'otectin' ya." His voice was still soft and low and grumbly.

"I know," I said.

He nodded and said, "Den show me whey is my marsters."

"How would I know where they are?"

"You know."

"No, I don't."

"You plays wid dem."

"Only once in a while, not today."

He looked down at the ground. I could see he was disappointed. "Den I'm taking you home to be safe, an I'll find 'em myself. Don' stop here, we got to keep walkin'. The soldiers behin' us, we just saw a few a dem, but der's an army comin'." And he whispered, like under his breath but so as I could hear, "A 'ntire fuckin' army."

"Whose?" I asked.

"Gen'l Jackson."

"Did you see him?"

"I jus' know, dat's all. Now are you gonna tell me whey is my marsters, or am I gonna take you home? I should prob'ly do dat anyhow."

He took hold of my arm, gently but tight, and I figured I'd better appease him, so I said, "I'll take you to the places I know, but it's gonna be like finding a needle in a haystack."

"We can do dat."

And so I really did try; I took him to all the places I knew around here that Harry and Allan liked best. As they always got everything they wanted, and had their own muskets, I used to go hunting with them. (Of course, their muskets overshot everything, but once you got used to them you'd have a fair chance at hitting something.) Sometimes they'd let me shoot wild pigeons or doves or partridges, and I used to like their dogs that would always go along. So I took old Jimmadasin to Neil's Dam and to the woods where we always had good luck and a few other places with pretty good views, where they'd probably be if they were anywhere; and Jimmadasin started getting nervous, as he thought we were getting too close to danger, and started to talk to himself in a tiny, high voice like he was his own mother scolding him.

I asked him about that.

"You think I'se a dumb nigger fuck, don' you, but I ain't. You'se white an' don't got to worry 'bout nuthin'. If you was colored, you'd understan' quick, believe me." He laughed, but he was talking mean and quiet. "An' you also thought I mus' be a dumb crazy fuck, Marster Mundy, when I was lookin' for my boys in the woods. But dem soldiers ain't goin' to shoot what dey think is a dumb nigger wid a mamma's voice, now ain't dey? Nidder da 'Federate or da Yankee soldier. I 'ready proves 'dat to you. If I was hidin', an' dey caught me, dey'd shoot Jimmadasin's ass dead. An' maybe shoot you wid me just for good measure or by mistake."

I owned that was possible.

"So maybe come a time when Marster Mundy learn dis nigger's tricks," Jimmadasin said, and we both started laughing because now we knew something nobody else did. And as we walked all over hell looking for Harry and Allan McSherry, the fighting got worse and worse, and we had to back off and keep going up toward Cedar Creek Road near where it meets the Valley Turnpike by the tollgate, which was near Abraham's Creek. I knew the creek, and so did Harry and Allan, but I knew that if they were here, they wouldn't be that far away from the fighting, which was behind us in the woods and fields between Cedar Creek Road—the lower part—and the Valley Pike near the Opequon Church. Damned if Jimmadasin wasn't right; we saw our 'Federate boys marching across from the pike along two routes. We were above it, but this wasn't no skirmishing; it was war. We could hear so many volleys of cannon that it just turned into one continuous roll, like the kind of thunder that seems to keep going on and getting louder after each flash of lightning. Seemed that now there were soldiers all around us, Yankee soldiers, and without saying a word we just ran, and I must admit I was glad to have Jimmadasin holding on to my hand. Everything seemed to go fast and slow at the same time. I know that sounds crazy, but that's how it was. Everything was happening inside of a second, yet it was slow too. Ah, I don't know, that's just how it was. There was smoke everywhere like there was a fire, and I could smell powder—it was sharp and hurt my nose like I had breathed in pepper and iron filings—and there was an explosion nearby that nearly knocked us down and pieces of metal and trees were flying through the air, and Jesus Christ I thought I saw a bloody hand falling with all the dirt and debris; and there were men screaming for help and calling for their mothers and then sonovabitch if another shell didn't explode like lightning striking the same place twice, and clots of earth and leaves and branches were flying, it was like the whole world was flying up in the air, and there were more screams—probably our own too—and I stepped on something that seemed to burst under my foot. It was part of somebody because my foot was bloody and sticky, and I remember screaming then, I don't know why because in a way I wasn't scared, it was like I was off to the distance watching Jimmadasin and myself running like fools, and everything got dark and cloudy and everyone was shouting and shooting, and Jimmadasin was pulling me along and we were both shouting, and then suddenly it was over and we just sat in a field together breathing heavy and I was so exhausted that I upchucked a little before I could even catch my breath. I could still feel whatever it was that I had stepped on, and I rubbed off what I could of the blood with dirt and leaves. "Get the hell outa here, boy," shouted a Yank soldier up ahead of us, and I couldn't tell if he was yelling at me or Jimmadasin, and behind him ran a standard bearer, who didn't look like he was much older than me. I should have been fighting the Yanks, but Poppa wouldn't have none of that, and maybe I should have run away to join the militia, but I figured he would have stopped it anyway. Mother would cry that I was a baby every time I brought it up. I was old enough to be a drummer at least. You could be twelve and be a drummer, and fourteen and be a soldier. "Move it out," someone shouted, and again, I didn't know if he was talking to the soldiers or to us, but Jimmadasin and I moved. More Yanks were moving down to meet our boys, thousands it looked like, marching down a mud road that wasn't much more than a path; and they were moving everything, including cannon. I thought we were safe hereabouts, but then we came upon a bluebelly who looked like he was asleep against a tree. One leg was stretched out straight and the other one was pulled up to his chest, which was a good comfortable way to sleep. Except he had a mess on his lap that looked like sausages.

"'Testines," Jim said, pulling me along. "Musta been from dis mornin' 'cause dey so swollen. Big guns do dat, just 'splode all over like we seen."

I was feeling a little sick, but once we walked right through the Yankee ranks, as if we were passing them on the street in town, I felt relieved and ashamed. Relieved because I could see town people around here on the hills who came to watch General Jackson shoot the asses off these Yankee invaders. Ashamed because now we were behind Yankee lines, under the protection of General Shields, who was the enemy, and I figured that was only a coward's reason to be comfortable.

I can't remember how long we remained just standing around, as if we were lost and trying to get our direction back, but it seems that it must have been a while because I was hungry, which was probably what was making me sick all along. Still, the sound of cannon and musket fire echoing around the hills was a continuous roll, and I thought then that there must be thousands getting shot and blown up and killed. It wasn't that many, but I learned quick that once you've been right there with all the dead and dying soldiers, Confederate or Yank, you feel the same if it's two or two hundred. I didn't know that then, though. I was jittery-nervous, like I was in a dream where one minute you're here and one minute you're somewhere else, and I had a metal taste that sometimes almost choked me whenever I swallowed; and something else. Everything seemed pressed together somehow, and maybe because it was exciting, but even with all the dying and screaming I felt a strange and horrible sort of happiness.

Once I saw those people from Winchester standing around, people who I'd seen before but didn't really know—like Mr. Rosenberger, who was on the town council and knew Poppa, and Doctor Baldwin, and the dentist whose name I can't remember—I knew where we'd probably find the McSherry boys. The fighting was all going on in the woods and fields on and around Sandy Ridge, mostly where we'd been, and I pointed out some likely places to Jimmadasin. Most of them were taken up by spectators trying to get a good view, but Harry and Allan were nowhere to be found. I told Jimmadasin we had to go back down a ways closer to the fighting if we were going to find them. He said no but went anyway—he sure as hell loved those two boys—but he scolded himself in his high, scared voice all the way back. I didn't expect to find them; I just wanted to get close to where I could see and get away from the other spectators, but we found them anyway sitting on a stone fence with a near perfect view of the Federal regiments.

"Hey Mundy, you come to the right place to see the fight," Harry McSherry said, ignoring Jimmadasin but looking uncomfortable nevertheless.

Jimmadasin screamed for them to come down from there because of how dangerous it was. He ran right up to both of them, pulled them down from the stone fence, nearly breaking their bones, and hugged them. They tried to escape, but, as I said, old Jimmadasin was strong; and it didn't seem that he'd ever let go of them again.

"Yo' mamma's sick wid worry o'er you, both of you."

"Lemme go," Harry said. His brother Allan didn't struggle; he just looked scared of everything, but he was only twelve, more than a year younger than me. "Momma knows we're watching the battle," Harry said. "We went early this morning. She gave us permission, you ken go an' ask her."

"I don' hafta ask nobody, 'cause she tole' me to bring you home safe an' soun', dat's 'xactly what she say. An' dat's what I'm goin' to do right now." Jimmadasin started marching them around the side of the fence and turned to me, expecting me to follow, but Harry begged to stay just for a few minutes more and explained that it was safe here and Jimmadasin could see that, for there were no dead bodies here or nothing.

Jimmadasin allowed five minutes.

We could see the Federals hiding behind stone fences, and between them and General Jackson's army were trees and small brush and more fences. There were woods down a ways to the right and a ravine, but there was nothing straight ahead beyond that stone fence but empty field, and our Confederates throwing everything they had at the line of Federal soldiers. The Federals were shooting back, of course, mostly cannon somewhere off to our left, but mostly they were getting shot at and shelled. It was loud, and much of the time that we all sat there together on the fence, we couldn't hear ourselves talk. Harry was wrong about one thing, though: There were dead soldiers all around here. I could see them when I looked hard. They were covered with dirt and filth and blood that looked black, and they blended right into the ground and woods and brush, which were all torn up anyhow. Even though I don't care a wet shit about Federal soldiers, it half made me sick to see them dead and lying around all over. Course, I just figured they were Yanks. They could've been our own men. . . .

Well, then all hell broke loose, and we almost got killed by our own 'Federate shells, which exploded in the trees right behind us; and it suddenly seemed that you couldn't be safe nowhere. A head torn right off at the neck rolled right in front of Allan's foot, as if it was a pumpkin or something; and Allan screamed. Course, I don't blame him for that, especially since I could swear that the lips moved. Jimmadasin made some sort of a sacred sign with his hands, then there was another explosion, and Jimmadasin and Harry and Allan McSherry were gone.

It was like I woke up and they were gone, but I remembered what happened only afterward. Jimmadasin had grabbed Harry and Allan with those big hands of his and tried to do the same with me, but I was running before I could even think about it, not necessarily away from Jimmadasin but running just the same, and I didn't stop until I was in a little grove of brush and young trees. There was noise all around me, and I could hear men groaning and breathing and reloading their muskets. I got to know the rattle a ramrod makes when it's pushed down into the barrel.

I had run the wrong way, and I didn't dare move, and how I wished that Jimmadasin had grabbed me, damn him, because I was right in the thick of the fighting. I could see pretty good too, and then even more bluebellies came running into the battle, replacing the Federals who had been killed—and they were lying everywhere, like it was a game and couldn't be real, and when I didn't see pieces of flesh and smears of blood, that's the way I was thinking it was. The fire from both sides was devastating. Not even the stone wall could protect the Federals from that terrible hail of shot and shell, and I imagine our own boys were dying just the same on the other side of the wall. There were more Federals to my left, and they were the Eighty-fourth Pennsylvania. One of their officers waved his sword and shouted like he was giving a speech: "Hold your ground; stand solid; keep cool; remember your homes, and your country; don't waste your powder," and the damn fool was standing right out there in front of his men, leading them forward until someone called him to fall back because he was exposing himself unnecessarily. But he didn't pay any attention and advanced with his men right into the fire of our boys. More bluebellies were falling than advancing, it seemed; but when I saw that officer fall, even though I felt sorry for the poor bastard, I thought right then that, yes, we were going to win, that General Jackson was going to kill so many Yanks that General Banks would have to retire back to where he came from and get the hell out of Winchester for good.

I crawled forward, emboldened by the killing, I guess, although I wasn't being smart, just curious, and I've learned better since then.

Now I could see our army down below what was a hill or maybe more like a ravine, and the bluebellies were charging right down there through galling fire; and you had to hand it to the Yankees, they were determined. I watched two of their color bearers fall, and saw the flag lifted up again each time. But our guns were too much for them, and the right side of what looked like a thousand Yanks just gave way, and the bluebellies were running right back in the direction they came; but like flies around honey, more soldiers just seemed to swarm in, then the Yanks let out a terrific shout, something like a wolf howl; and Yankee and Reb were killing each other with bayonet and fighting hand to hand and getting all mixed up with each other. But the Yankees got past the stone fence, and sonova*bitch* if they didn't turn our own boys, rout them, and I remember saying to myself that this was only one little tiny piece of the fight, that our boys were pushing the Yankee soldiers back everywhere else, but I could feel that wasn't true. I just felt sick and sort of paralyzed, and suddenly I wanted to get home, even though I would be in big trouble. If you want the truth, and I'm ashamed to admit this, but I wanted my mother. I wanted to smell rabbit stew and all the fixings. I wanted to feel the warmth of the hearth and all that. And all this would just be sort of like a dream I would forget, or just remember like you remember a good story.

I could tell by where the sun was, or the smear that was the sun behind the clouds, that it must be close to twilight. As I probably said already, everything seemed to be going fast and slow at the same time, even though I know that's impossible; and somehow the whole day had gotten swallowed up in a few minutes. But I was going home, that's all I knew; and so I just walked in the opposite direction of the fighting, back up toward where Jimmadasin and I had gone to get out of danger before. I didn't know better then, but I thought that nothing could be worse than seeing all those dead and wounded soldiers laying all around like they were dolls or something. I had to keep my eyes open and be alert, but I found I could ignore seeing the dead soldiers and the wounded ones too; only thing I couldn't ignore was their cries, and so I gave some of them water, which they all begged for; and even now that I think of it I'm ashamed I didn't try to do more for them. But I just left them.

Well, I couldn't have done anything much for them anyway, except keep them company when they cried for their mothers and give them a little water.

I should've stayed with them.

But I wanted *my* mother.

So I pretended it was all going to be all right and took the straightest route home, not even thinking that I might step into more fighting. I just figured if I ran straight ahead, big as life like old Jimmadasin taught me, I'd get home safe and sound. Which I did. It was just before dusk, when everything looks bluish and pretty, and the fields and woods were all shadowy like they were sunk in dark pools of water or something, but if you looked out at the mountains you could sometimes see parts that were sunlit, and you could sometimes see rays coming right out of the sky like a painting in the Bible. That's how it looked when I reached our farm; but even before I could see the family house, I knew something was wrong because I could smell burning and hear terrible screaming and crying, and I could tell Mother's voice, and Poppa's. Poppa was screaming more than anyone, and then he stopped and there were other voices I didn't recognize. I ran right through the woods to get to the front yard of "the Big House," as we called it, as if we had a hundred slaves like the Bartons from Springdale, who Poppa knew. But that doesn't matter, and I'm just keeping away from telling you what happened.

But I'm going to tell you. . . .

Anyway, there was our house with its big chimney and porch with columns and the red sandstone flags that made a pavement through the lawn between the shade trees and stopped by the board fence that Poppa and I had whitewashed. And there was the sunlight just going over the mountains. And the smell of smoke. The entire farm except for the Big House seemed like it was on fire, the barn and lumber house and schoolhouse. I was behind a big tree, and I could see every little detail of everything, it seemed, and even though I wish I couldn't, I remember it all: I remember the rotten trunk of a cherry tree that was just beside me, I remember the white fungus growing on its gray bark; and I remember the smell of the woods and the smell of the smoke, and the screaming, although as I think about it I still want to close my eyes, but I didn't, although I wish I did because two men came riding out from the back of the house; and they were hooting and shouting and laughing like they were drunk or probably crazy; and they were both wearing cheap butternut coats and pants and those funny-looking Federal hats that had enough fittings on them to make a copper kettle. One had a pine torch, and he was leaning low on the side of his horse, almost falling out of his saddle, to touch that torch to everything he fancied. The other was just riding behind him, pulling along two other horses.

"C'mon outa there," shouted the one with the torch. "Gonna get hot, an' it's our turn, ya greedy bastards."

And the house started smoking. He had started the fire in the back of the house, and suddenly I could see flames licking the roof, and I could hear terrible cracking noises like bones were being broken or something, and then someone ran out of the house and shot the horse right out from under the soldier with the torch, and someone else came out of the house, and he was pulling Mother, and she was naked and full of blood, and I wondered where was Poppa, where was Poppa, I remember thinking that over and over like a song; and I was watching when I should have been running right out there and killing them, burning them and shooting those sonovabitches, but then the soldier that had been pulling Mother just dropped her outside the door on the porch. She wasn't making any noise, but I saw her move, and then the soldier whose horse was shot out from under him ran over to the porch, and all the men started fighting with each other, and they fell right over Mother, and I heard a keening, a noise like Jimmadasin would've made, and I realized I was hearing myself, hearing the inside of my head, and I blinked, that's all it was, I blinked—and then one of the men must have dragged Mother off the porch and onto pavement, and he was on top of her and his pants were down, and another one, another one was—

Looking straight at me. I know he saw me. He must've. He just looked right at me, and I didn't move, and I didn't breathe, and then he looked away like he never saw me, and I remember thinking then that I was invisible like air or like a tree in a huge forest.

And then he was gone, as if *he* had disappeared, and so had the other men, but maybe it was me, maybe I just went blind or something, because all I remember from then on, for I don't know how long I was watching that man hurting my mother, I was remembering nice things and terrible things, as if I had escaped from that tree and the time and what I was seeing, and was only seeing things in my mind.

I had to go in and save Mother I had to find Poppa, for the house was burning, burning, catching fire in a hundred places, and I could feel the heat, but I was thinking remembering couldn't move and then I was touching the bark, feeling the slimy moss remembering remembering how at the start of spring Poppa and I always made piles of brush and dead leaves and vegetation and anything else burnable that we could gather in our fields. Then Poppa would check that the wind was just right, so that the fire didn't get out of control, and then with a pine torch he'd light those piles, poking them here and there with a long pole, going from one pile to another, while I ran around gathering everything that would burn to keep the hungry fires going; and I remembered and remembered so well I could see it right before me, so well that I could blank out what was happening right in front of me, and I saw me and Ishrael Moble and three of his darkie children that Poppa had borrowed from Arthur Allen, who owned the next farm down the road from us, and Ishrael was ploughing a furrow around our field of broom sedge, and when he was done Poppa would light the sedge on the windward side, and it would blaze like a sonovabitch, and Ishrael and his kids and me and Poppa would beat out the fire with green cedar branches whenever it escaped over the furrow, and once it did and we lost a rail fence and burned a field and—

They were gone.

I found myself standing on the edge of the woods, holding my breath, being invisible, looking at the house burning, feeling the heat on my face like waves coming over me, and I had seen everything, I knew that I had seen what the men did, what they did to my mother, and I could see Mother there yet, lying on the red sandstone flags, and I just ran across the lawn to her. It was as if I had just gotten here. Like I hadn't been watching, hadn't been invisible, hadn't held my breath for . . . how long? Five minutes? Ten minutes? Uncle Randolph says it's impossible to hold your breath longer than a minute, but I know I could have held it forever that day.

I heard that keening and knew I was making strange noises and sobbing and crying, but as soon as I knelt beside Mother I saw that she was staring off and not blinking. But it wasn't even so much that. It was like she had been turned into a doll or something. She looked like porcelain, like all the stuff had gone out of her, and I knew she was dead.

Poppa . . .

I tried to go into the house, but the fire was bad inside, and so I came out and dragged Mother away from the house, but I saw that it was hopeless, that everything was hopeless because I knew that Poppa had been in the house and was killed too, just as Uncle Randolph later told me.

It was when I was guarding Mother that I saw the dog. He came running from the direction of the meat house, where I figured he had gotten in. He was the biggest dog I ever saw, more like the size of a horse, and he was black, and he smelled like burning, and he was running right toward me with his mouth open and his eyes were on fire. They were big as saucers and looked like balls of fire.

No one is ever going to tell me that dog wasn't real, because I saw him, and like before, when the men burned down the house, I became invisible. I kneeled there beside Mother like I was frozen. I didn't breathe. I didn't make a sound. And that dog stopped so near to me that I could smell his sour-rotten breath and damp, sweaty fur. And I could feel the heat of him.

He sniffed at Mother, looked at me a real long time like he knew me, and then he ran off to the edge of the woods, where he watched me with his eyes that were burning in the dark because it had gotten dark while I had been sitting there with Mother.

I stayed with Mother while the house burned. I held her hand, which was like ice.

Until I heard people coming.

I guess the dog heard them too, because he disappeared.

But I saw him after that.

I guess I mostly traveled with him after that.

PILING UP ÐEM BONES

Are you all dead? Are you all dead?
No, thank the Lord, there's a few left yet,
There's a few—left—yet!

YANK SICK CALL
CHORUS

*I*KNOW I SHOULD'VE BURIED EVERYONE PROPER AND SAID PRAYERS, especially over my mother. I should have stayed by the Big House when I heard neighbors coming, and maybe I could have helped them put the fire out and then gone inside to find Poppa's remains and bury him too. But I just couldn't stand to see anyone, and I couldn't stand to be near anything that had been comfortable and part of my old life. It was like there was a fence between me and everything that had been. Didn't matter anyway because everything was burning up, and I felt . . . I felt *free*. I know that sounds bad, but there you are. I felt all emptied out, and I heard the thunder in my ears that always comes before I start crying. Course, I wasn't crying. I was invisible now and wasn't part of the world anymore, and I remember feeling that nothing could hurt me but maybe the spirit dog, and I knew he was waiting for me in the dark shadows of the woods, though I figured he could be invisible wherever and whenever he wanted to.

And maybe not even the spirit dog could hurt me.

Maybe *nothing* could anymore.

Well, that's how I was thinking as I was running away from the Big House that was howling as it burned like it was some sort of animal. I found out fast that pretty much anything and everything could hurt me—but not the same way they seemed to hurt other people. Just differently, I guess. So anyway, I ran through the woods back to where we'd fought the battle of Kernstown. You're probably wondering why I didn't stay by the house if I knew that there was that spirit dog ghosting around in the woods. Well, I guess I just wasn't scared anymore like I had been when I was . . . different, before I became invisible. (I don't care what Uncle Randolph or Dr. What'shisface thinks, I was pretty hard to see.) I knew I could be safe by just staying put where I was by the house. But I couldn't, and that was that. If that spirit dog was going to get me, then so be it. God's will be done, as Poppa would say.

But as I was running through those woods that looked like they were sunk in some pale fog from the moonlight—wasn't more than a sliver of moon buried in the dark, cloudy sky—I figured that I had the spirit dog wrong.

It was like I first thought: He knew me.

Maybe he was a ghost just like me.

Maybe he wasn't *my* dog, but I started taking a certain comfort in him, like he was protecting me; and though I couldn't see him, I could feel him running with me just out of eyesight. So I ran like a sonovabitch. I ran like the spirit dog was after me. I ran like the Yanks or Confederates—or whoever they were that killed Poppa and my mother—were after me, right behind me with their knives and muskets and torches, killing anything that got in their way and burning down the entire state of Virginia.

Once I broke out of the woods and was in the fields, I stopped. I had to because I could hardly breathe. My heart was beating so hard I could feel it trying to crawl right up my throat, and I could feel it pounding in my temples, and I just stood there in the open, breathing and looking out into the distance. Believe it or not, I could see pretty well. The clouds had rolled back from the moon like the sea had for Moses, and there was this big clear space filled with the bit of moon, and further away were hard, twinkling stars, then the heavy, ugly edges of storm clouds. It was raining—not a hard rain, but more like a mist that just made you all wet all over; and I could smell the rain and the storm. It was sharp like the taste you get when you put your tongue on a piece of metal, but the rain carried other smells on it, the bitter smells of powder and the sweet vomit smell of death that made you want to gag. I knew the smell would get stronger if I kept going, if I crossed over to Sandy Ridge by the stone wall where our boys lost the battle. Once I got my breathing under control, I listened hard. I could hear some bats that were flying around behind me in the woods, and I could hear, ever so faint, the groans and calls of the wounded up above on the ridge, and I had to go there, as if they were calling to me, as if somehow by going back there I could undo everything that had happened at the farm, like the night and the rain would wipe everything clean again, and I would help some of the soldiers and then leave them and go back to the farm, and everything would be okay. I would have just lost a day, but everything would be all right, and nobody would know but me.

I looked around, as if I had just spooked myself; and there was the spirit dog off to my left and ahead of me, standing like he was in his own pool of moonlight. I could see his eyes were red, I was sure of that, but I didn't have the urge to run away from him. I had stared him down once, I guess, and now he wasn't going to hurt me. Or that's what I thought, anyway. He was . . . waiting for me. Like I was supposed to follow him, and so I nodded at him, figuring he would understand, which he did, and he ran across the fields off toward the ridge, which was lost in the darkness. I was breathing easy now, and suddenly everything seemed to be clear to me. Maybe I couldn't undo everything by going back there. But if the spirit dog was running toward the ridge, he had a reason. And I was supposed to follow him. Where else was I going to get enough food to keep me going? And one other thing: I knew I was going to need some kind of shoes. I could stand it tonight, but the cold surely wasn't over yet, and I couldn't depend anymore on being someplace where I could keep warm. I'd need things if I were going to be on my own; probably money too.

I'd find what I needed up on the ridge, and maybe I could help make it easier for our soldiers that were wounded and thirsty and dying out there. The Yanks sure as hell wouldn't help our people.

But I would make the bluebellies pay some little bit. That's what I told myself, anyway. So I started walking again, and the stink got so rank I thought I was going to have to turn around; and I suddenly remembered Hog Day, which we had every year in early December. I remembered sitting out by the nigger house on the farm with our own niggers and some that Poppa had borrowed from our neighbor Arthur Allen.

Poppa always borrowed because you needed a lot of hands to slaughter hogs.

Our own Uncle Isaac was always in charge of all the other niggers, and his wife, Aunt Hanna, would be there right with him. She'd be smoking her pipe, looking around with her head at a strange tilt because she was blind in one eye, but nobody'd laugh at her or give her any guff. She'd got respect because she used to play cards like she was a witch; she could shuffle a deck with one hand and throw the cards up in the air, and they'd all come down one after the other in a line like they were sewed to her fingers. No one would talk about that, though, because Uncle Isaac wouldn't allow it, but Aunt Hanna told me and showed me everything when we were alone. She even told me how she got her other name, Mammy Jack, which was what everybody called her outside of our family. I love her, I must admit, even though she ran away to be with the blue-bellies and gave up her own people. I suppose she did it for Uncle Isaac, who always said he was no slave, even though Poppa treated him like family. Still and all, I'd give anything right now to be alone with her in her cottage and have her show me how to play blackjack and shuffle with one hand. Since I'm going on about her, I should tell you she was fat and pretty and her skin was lighter than Uncle Isaac's; she would get burned if she stayed out in the sun too long. Uncle Isaac was a skinny rail. But there was a meanness in Uncle Isaac that would come out of him when he got protective over Aunt Hanna or even me, for that matter. He'd just say "Don' fuck wid me" real low, like it was one long word, and nobody ever would, not even the "paddyrollers," as we called them—those were the patrolers that roamed around to catch niggers that didn't have passes from their masters to be running around on their own.

I kept walking along in the moonlight across the fields and into the woods beside Sandy Ridge, thinking and remembering like I was in two places at once; and I put the handkerchief that Mother always made me carry right up against my mouth, but after a while I guess I got used to the smell of dying and dropped the handkerchief along the way because I wouldn't have use for such things anymore. The groaning of the wounded soldiers was getting louder; and I couldn't stop thinking about slaughtering the hogs, which I loved when I was younger because I would always get my own pig tail, once the hog's 'testines were thrown into the tub and the liver and lungs hung up on ridge poles. There was always a lot of hog killing on that day, I can tell you, but much as I always wanted that pig tail, and long as I had to wait for it, I never enjoyed it much when Mother finally got around to cooking it up for me. All the kids that were there, even the nigger kids, would get something: a pig tail if there were enough to go around, which there usually were, or a slice of liver. Hog liver, just cut out and fresh and put right away on the coals, was the best eating in the world. I could feel my mouth water, even with all the stink around me, just thinking about it. And I remember how it took all of us to throw one of the hogs down so Uncle Isaac could slit its throat and then ever so quick push that knife down right into its heart. You had to be an expert to do that, and use a special two-edged knife. It was my job to make sure the water barrels were ready to scald the hogs. Poppa'd give me the nod, and I'd carry the stones we'd been heating up in the fire into those barrels, and they would steam and bubble, and you'd think all the water was going to lift right out in a cloud. That's how hot the stones were. After that came the butchering and roasting the livers and cutting off our pig tails, and the part I hated most: riddin' the guts for the lard. Aunt Hanna would take all the chitlins and hand them out to all the nigger families, and then after all was said and done, the corpses would be taken over to the smoke house to hang until they could be cured and cut up into hams and middlings and shoulders and sausage and feet and all the rest, and then—

I almost fell over him. Gave me as big a fright as seeing the spirit dog for the first time. He was kneeling behind a tree, and didn't move even when I accidentally pushed against him, which confused me even more because he was all primed like he was going to fire a musket. Only his musket was lying on the ground beside him. I couldn't see him real well, but I could see him; the light was milky and dim. He was a bluebelly, I could tell that much, and he was froze completely in that position. I don't know why I did it, but I touched his face, maybe like a blind person does to see what he looked like, because as I said it was just moonlight and not a lot of it, what with shadows and everything; and when I touched his forehead, I felt something wet and moving, and I can't tell you how much that frightened and revolted me, like I was seeing my mother again lying out there on the red sandstone flags. This soldier had been shot right through his forehead, probably while he was aiming and about to pull the trigger of his own musket, and probably early in the battle because the maggots had time to get to him. I wiped my hands off on leaves, and I started shaking all over again and had to calm myself down by thinking that I didn't want the spirit dog to see me in such a condition and that he was probably watching me right now from the shadows.

I picked up the soldier's musket. It was a Springfield; I could tell by the weight. I knew something about this because I tried one out once. It can shoot fifteen hundred yards with considerable certainty, which is about the same as an Enfield. Most everybody preferred the Springfield, though, because it was lighter to carry. I never had the chance to shoot an Enfield, so I couldn't speak from experience; but anyway, here I finally had a musket in my hands, and a dead soldier who had to have a cap and cartridge box and boots and a blanket—I could see the blanket—and probably a rubber poncho too, and shoes, and . . . greenback money, which Poppa always said was better than our own Confederate shin plasters. But now that I had my chance, I didn't want that musket, like it was a pig tail or something. I had thoughts of using that musket to kill those soldiers or renegades or Indians or paddyrollers or deserters or whatever they were that killed Mother and Poppa, but I was thinking different now because I was already a spirit. That musket wasn't going to do me enough good, wasn't going to kill enough Yank soldiers to make a difference, and if anybody could see me carrying it, they'd think I was a soldier and probably try to shoot my ass off. Maybe they could see me, maybe they couldn't. I wasn't taking any chances. So I left the gun alone. I just wasn't going to need it. But I did rifle through that dead soldier's pockets, keeping away from him in case he fell over, but he was dried up and frozen stiff in that position, except for the spot being eaten by the maggots. I wasn't going to look at that—they were certainly in the eyes too, and I thanked heaven it was dark and I couldn't see well enough. Funny thing, though, is that he didn't smell that bad. I thought maybe it was because I was used to the stink now, but it wasn't that, I can tell you, because I know the difference. He'd just sort of dried up instead of bloating out and rotting away.

I carefully pulled off his shoes like he was asleep or something and I was afraid of waking him. I was right about him being dried up and frozen in that position, but when I tried pulling off his shoes, he fell over with a thump; and his arms and legs and everything stayed in the same position. Only he was lying on his side now. I jumped back and felt terrible about disturbing him, like maybe I would wake him up or something. But I had to keep going, and so I pulled those shoes off anyway. They were canvas, probably store bought. I put them on; they were a little big, but that didn't matter. Then I pulled off his blanket and rubber poncho, which wasn't so easy because he was lying on them. They wouldn't do me much good right now; I was already soaked through and through. But I found some money and enough bacon and hardtack so I wouldn't starve. I discovered just then how hungry I was, and without even waiting to get a respectable distance away from there, I bit off a piece of the bacon and ate it raw. The hardtack cracker wasn't so easy to eat, but I managed, and then, weighted down, I got moving again. But not before I said a prayer over the dead Yankee like I didn't for my folks. I don't know why I did that, over a bluebelly, but it just came over me. I couldn't believe in religion the way Poppa did. I'm more like my mother was, I suppose. Anyway, that was the last prayer I ever said for *anybody*. But I had to do something after stealing the soldier's gear and money, and knocking him down. It was like he was being vigilant for his country even after he died, and I had desecrated something holy. (I'd done worse later and didn't need any prayers. But there you are, that prayer just came over me the one time. Like crying.)

I made my way along Sandy Ridge and planned to come up behind the stone walls where our Confederate lines had broke so I could help our own wounded. From what I heard about how the bluebellies went about it, they would just take care of their own, and by the time they'd let our own people onto the field, most of the Confederate men would be dead and ready to bury. But it didn't matter, because I ended up on the high side of the stone fences. I could tell I was on the Yank side just by the way the soldiers called out. They didn't sound like us— course, most of them weren't calling out at all, but just groaning; and all I could think of was that I was in some sort of terrible forest like you'd read about in a fairy story, and all this groaning and gurgling and coughing and farting and wheezing and calling and everything were like animal or maybe insect sounds like chitterin', or maybe like strange birds in a jungle. Altogether it's a sound like nothing else; and I kept hearing those grown men calling for their mammas like they were little boys, and I didn't listen to that because I understood how they felt and wasn't going to think about it. Anyway, I just didn't feel right about leaving them like that to suffer and all—not that I would go out of my way to help any of them—but the bodies got so thick that I couldn't help but step on one or another, no matter how careful I was. Most of those that were wounded and could talk wanted water. They'd all drank their canteens dry and still had a terrible thirst, but I could always find canteens with some water left in them; the dead soldiers hadn't had time to get thirsty, I guess. In fact, I could have collected enough Yank canteens in this dead place to open up a store if I'd wanted to.

All the while, I was trying to get down to our own soldiers.

I told myself I was collecting water for them from the Yanks, but after a time I just couldn't stand to stay there and help any more of those soldiers. It was like I suddenly couldn't breathe, like all these moaning and groaning and mumbling bluebellies were lying on top of me or something, like I was being suffocated by the dead, bloated bodies, and all I could think of was maggots and blood and touching that soldier who was shot through the forehead, and I wanted to scream, but of course, all I could do was open my mouth and the only thing that came out was a breath sound like a "ha" without any voice, like I was laughing at all of this; and I bolted like a horse from a fire, running, I suppose, with my eyes closed, I can't remember, but I kept running until I was away from that mound of the dead and dying, until I was on real ground where the bodies were only scattered around, and I would have kept running if it weren't for the spirit dog.

He appeared just ahead of me, so close I could have run right into him, just like I ran into the dead bluebelly soldier. He had appeared to tell me there was danger about, I knew that, and his red eyes were like lanterns, only they didn't move or flicker. Sure enough, not more than five seconds later, I heard voices and branches breaking, and I could see two bluebellies walking around big as life with torches. For one hot second I felt anger and I was scared all over again because I thought they might be some of the ones who killed my folks and were now back to burn everything down; but then I realized I was thinking crazy, that these were just ordinary Yankee soldiers. I stayed put, didn't hardly breathe, got as invisible as I could, and listened.

One of the torches moved back and forth, and somebody said, "Shit, they're scattered hell to breakfast." He sounded like he was talking right through his nose.

"They're our boys," said the other, and he sounded like he could've been from the South. "Some of 'em are alive, listen."

"I tol' ya, I need to find somethin' ta read."

"What yer doin' ain't right, just ain't."

"Ain't wrong, either. No man goin' to be readin' when he's dead, 'cept maybe the Bible."

"But I can hear men groaning, we're supposed to be attendin' them."

"They're probably secesh, an' if they're our boys they're better off dying here nice an' clean than bein' sawed up by that quack sawbones in the church. So stop your fretting, we're doin' them a favor. We gonna be here all night anyway, an' once we're back at the goddamn church you can bet your ass they'll have somethin' disgusting for us to do, and it won't be walking around by ourselves in the fields, thank you ma'am, so just cool your heels, or else you can go on and be Jesus Christ Himself on your own."

They were stumbling around some, but didn't say anything for a minute;

then one of them laughed, the one who'd been doing most of the talking, the one who talked through his nose. Maybe he had a cold, I don't know. I just listened, and every once in a while I'd glance over to see if the spirit dog was still where he'd been, and he was. The bluebellies weren't coming toward me *yet;* if they did I suppose I shouldn't move or breathe or anything. That would be safest. But, as I was going to learn over and over, you never know just quite what you're going to do, no matter how much you plan things out in your mind.

"Shit, you're scared of the goddamn dark."

"Am not."

"Well, I ain't goin' to believe it's because of the bodies, we seen more than enough of that."

"I guess."

"Well, then?"

"You ain't goin' ta find books on these men."

"Then money, or buttons or stamps or somethin' we can sell," said the one who talked through his nose. The other one must have said something I didn't hear because the first one went on, "Harry, they're *dead*. Might be us who might get dead tomorrow, or who knows when. So who's goin' to give a shit if we take a little something? What do you think the officers are doin'? Same goddamn thing, 'cept *they're* gettin' rich while you and me are standin' around here in the dark." There was some more shuffling around, and I thought they'd gone out of earshot; all I could hear was groaning and "Mamma" and whispering, and behind all that every once in a while regular night sounds from the wind and the like. The night air seemed to carry every sound like it was next to you, which worried me because if I could hear them, then they might be able to hear me, even if I was a spirit now; and I found myself counting my breaths to make them quiet, so I wouldn't breathe so much, and I didn't move, like I was a statue or that poor dead bluebelly that was aiming his invisible musket at an army that was now all safe in their tents. After a minute (although it could've been longer because everything still seemed to be happening either real fast or real slow and nothing in between), I heard the soldier who spoke through his nose say to Harry, the other one, "You see, right here, gener'l, I found a book, and it ain't a Bible, it's a genuine yellow Beadle. *The Gold Fiend.* I ain't the only one who carries around novelette stories. I was supposed to borrow this one from —"

Then he went quiet. I could see the light from his torch, and I could see the other torch coming closer like they were giant fireflies, but that was all; and I wondered what stopped him from talking. I didn't have to wonder long because

Harry said, "Yeah, it's Jake Yeager. Poor bastard. Just leave him be, come on now. Let's do what we're supposed to and get outa here."

"Coupl'a hours ago in the fight, he could've been shot right next to me, and I wouldn't've thought nothin' of it. I don't care about seeing dead men no more than if they were cows or hogs or dead horses. But shit, seeing Jake . . ."

"You hardly knew him," Harry said. "So he lent you a book."

"I know. I know. It don't make no sense. I shouldn't give a shit 'bout him any more than this dead nigger over here."

Dead nigger?

Of course, I thought it had to be Jimmadasin, and I knew I was going to have to take a look for myself and find out. What could he have been doing around here again? Looking for me, probably. I'd find out soon enough, I thought, because as soon as the soldiers were done robbing the dead, I intended to see for myself; and after about fifteen minutes or an hour of them crashing around in the forest and that field and me breathing as quiet as I could, they left. Well, they stopped making noise, and I just thought I was there alone with the groaning men and the dead men and the wet air that was giving me the chills and carrying the smells of shit and death and powder; and every once in a while I could hear a noise from down yonder in Kernstown or maybe as far away as Winchester. I felt alone, like I was paralyzed and killed like the soldiers scattered around me; and I figured that even though they were dead they'd have smelled the dirt just like I was doing, and the rain; and they were probably spirits now, still smelling and hearing, but, like me, not being able to talk. And they'd be more invisible than me.

I had, I guess, a vision just then of all those dead soldiers, Yank and our own alike. I imagined they'd be walking around here like Harry and the one who talked through his nose, except nobody could see them, not even me. I wondered just then if they could see each other like I could see the spirit dog. Maybe they could see the spirit dog. Maybe that's why he came up here.

I looked around for the spirit dog, but he wasn't here anymore.

That's when everything happened.

I heard something move behind me, so I stopped breathing or moving or anything; I just lay with the side of my face on the ground, smelling that black wet earth, which smelled like it had just been turned, and I blocked out all the other smells of shit and death; and as I smelled the grass and dirt, I kept thinking crazy things like my thoughts were just falling in front of me, and I remembered a hot day in June right near where I was now, only closer to the turnpike, and I guess I was wishing so hard that somehow I could see it in my mind like it was bright and hot and dry. I had been hunting with Harry and Allan Mc-Sherry, but they wouldn't let me do any shooting—I told you I didn't much like them, they were selfish about everything—so I had gone off to explore on my own and that's when I saw a locomotive going right down the pike under a clear blue sky like that ghost train engine didn't need to be on tracks or anything. I can still remember it was engine number 199, and its front wheels had been replaced with huge wooden ones, and it was being pulled by teams of horses and men—must've been fifty horses at least and two hundred men, all in teams, all pulling that shiny engine. I knew they were going to Strasburg because those men, mostly soldiers, were singing "On to Strasburg" at the top of their lungs. Poppa told me later the Confederacy was going to put it on the tracks of the Manassas Gap Railway and send it down south. It was one of the locomotives General Jackson captured when he raided the B&O Railroad at Harpers Ferry.

But right now, it all seemed like a dream (especially now, I guess, as I was scared out of my skin and lying out in this stinking field of dead soldiers); and then when I thought of Mother and Poppa, they too seemed like they were from a dream. And I thought about poor old Jimmadasin and wondered if he was lying dead right near me in this field.

But I wasn't in a dream now because I heard someone fart real close to me; and it was so loud and unexpected that I jumped. It was like the cracking of a musket. Or I must've moved because next thing I knew someone shouted something and I knew whoever it was had seen me and was after me, and I found myself running before I could even think about it, but not for very long probably because the next thing I knew I was flying through the air and then I smelled the stink of a bluebelly soldier's armpit as he grabbed me like I was a sack of meal. They probably thought I was a rebel soldier that got left behind, and now I was their prisoner, and they'd probably shoot my ass off or buck and gag me and torture me to death or send me to Fort Delaware where everybody died anyway.

"I told you he was just a kid," said the soldier who was holding me tight so I couldn't move my arms or kick him. "But from the look of him, I'd say the little bastard was stealing from our dead. Is that what you were doing, is it?" he asked me, shaking me around hard and squeezing my arms so hard they went numb. "Is that where you got that poncho, you little thief?" I couldn't see much of his face, but I knew he was big; and I could see the soldier who was with him, a sergeant. I could see the three upside-down chevrons on his sleeves and brass buttons on his coat because he was holding a lantern that was splashing light all around like he was going to swing it in circles and do tricks; and speaking of tricks, I figured I had just been tricked by that spirit dog, who had been sitting there away from me like everything was all right and didn't give me no warning at all and just plain disappeared to save his own ass, which was a damn good lesson because I shouldn't have trusted him or anybody.

"All right, Eurastus, stop hurting the boy." The sergeant came closer with his lantern. He was heavyset and had a beard and mustache; that's all I noticed because I was concentrating on pulling away from the soldier who was holding me, which was probably stupid, but I wasn't thinking, I just wanted to get away and be invisible. . . .

That was it, of course, so when I thought of that I stopped pulling and struggling and thought that just maybe if he let go of me for a second he wouldn't be able to find me again in the drizzling dark. You couldn't even see the moon now, except for a thin smear on the edge of the sky; that's how heavy the clouds were, but it had stopped raining. Nevertheless, I was soaked through, and the rubber poncho I had tied around myself made the damp and the wet sticky. I was shivering with the cold, or maybe I was just afraid, I don't know.

"That's better," said Eurastus, and he let go of me just a little, but he had big hands and was strong and had a good, hurtful grip on both my arms, so I couldn't get away, at least not yet.

"Don't worry, we're not goin' to hurt you, little feller," the sergeant said. He held his lantern steady now. "Now what in God's name are you doin' out here? An' wearing one of our boys' ponchos to boot. You from Kernstown or Winchester? You know you ain't supposed to be anywhere 'round here—it's off limits 'cept for the United States Army."

I didn't have anything to say to him, of course, but I wasn't going to look scared and stare down at the ground like I usually did when Poppa scolded me. I looked straight up at him and waited until Eurastus relaxed so I could make my move; and even right now I was thinking about Jimmadasin probably laying out just beyond the lantern light, maybe dead or dying and maybe wanting a little water, and I listened, as if the Yanks weren't even there. I listened for Jimmadasin's high voice calling for help or something. It wasn't until the sergeant started talking to me again that I looked around for the spirit dog too, but he was still disappeared.

"You hear what I'm saying to you, lad?" asked the sergeant.

I must admit there was something gentle about this fat sergeant, like he somehow had no business being in the army, but Private Eurastus would've liked nothing better than to bash my face in first chance he got. I knew that because he was hurting my arms and my chest again, doing it sort of in secret so the sergeant wouldn't see. Anyway, I knew he was a private because I saw that he didn't have any chevrons on the sleeve of his frock coat, which smelled like fish. I don't know how, but it did.

"Well . . . ?"

I nodded my head to the sergeant, but just once, just to show him that I understood.

"Maybe he's deaf and dumb," said Private Eurastus.

I didn't want to look at him. I figured that somehow if I looked at Private Eurastus, it would give him some sort of power over me or something, but I couldn't help it; and it surprised me that he wasn't big, just tall and reedy. He had those big hands, but he looked skinnier than most 'Federate soldiers, like he hadn't been fed for months. That just made it worse: It was humiliating to be captured by what looked to me like a weakling. Maybe it was just that I was weaker than him, or more probably that looks can fool you because he had a grip as strong as Uncle Isaac's; and just about now I didn't feel anything but exhausted and humiliated and sick that everybody was stronger than me.

"Is that it?" the sergeant asked me. "You can't talk?"

I nodded again.

"So he ain't deaf, just dumb," the sergeant said to Eurastus. "You hungry?" he asked, and I shook my head, but only once, which was enough. I knew I shouldn't be having anything to do with them at all, and that if I did I'd never be able to get away, so I just swallowed and looked down at the ground and concentrated on disappearing, which is what I should've been doing all along.

"All right, Eurastus, let him *go*. I can see you're hurtin' his arms."

"If I do, he's going to run, sure as I'm standing here," Eurastus said. He loosened up his grip a bit and I could feel my arms again, but he wasn't going to let me go completely, even for the sergeant. "What do you want to do?"

"Shit, he found his way here, I'm sure he can find his way home."

I could feel that the sergeant was looking at me while he talked, but I didn't look up.

"No, I don't feel right about that," the sergeant continued after a time, like he was talking to himself. "We'll take him over to the church and let the sawbones decide—he's got the rank, after all. Maybe the little shit is a secesh spy. You never know with these people. They'd stoop to use their own children to do their dirty work."

I concentrated on the ground, concentrated on making myself invisible, because for a second there things seemed like they were starting to go my way. The bluebellies had at least considered letting me go.

Then I got my chance. . . .

There were cracking noises like twigs breaking, and I could see torches off to the right. I knew it must be Harry and his friend who talked through his nose, but it seemed like the Yanks who had captured me didn't know that.

"Halt, who goes there?" shouted the sergeant. "Identify yourselves."

They waited long enough to answer. . . . "Private Harry Beem, sir. Eighth Ohio Volunteer Infantry, United States Army."

"And who else is with you? I know there's more than one of you out there. Identify yourselves."

"Private John Smith, same," came the reply after a good long while.

"Show yourselves and state your business," the sergeant said.

"Who the hell are *you*?" Private John Smith asked in his nasty nasal voice like there was going to be trouble.

"Hospital Steward Theodore Dunean, Fifth Army Corps, United States Army, or Sergeant Theodore Dunean, Fourteenth Indiana Infantry, which-ever you prefer. But either way I outrank your ass. Show yourselves *now!*"

The sergeant certainly had a loud voice and authority, which must have shook up Harry and his thieving friend, who probably knew who he was, because I could hear branches crunching and all kinds of rustling, which I figured meant they were going to make a proper appearance and explain themselves.

But the torches disappeared, and those two bluebellies weren't hurrying to show themselves and be saluted.

They were running away.

Which is what I should have been doing. . . .

"Sonovabitches!" shouted Private Eurastus. He let go of me just then and fired his musket in the direction of Smith and Beem. Here was my chance on a stick. I picked up and ran for everything I was worth; and I felt like I had just bro-ken out of jail or something—I mean, I was scared out of my socks, but I felt real joy because I was free and wasn't ever going back into human company again, I swear; and I was going deep into the woods where I knew my way with everything in there, and I remembered just how stupid I had been not to have taken the musket from the dead soldier, and then I thought, maybe I wasn't so stupid because if I was caught like I was with the musket, the private would've probably had an excuse to shoot me. But I would need a musket, that's the thought that slid back and forth in the front of my mind while I ran through the darkness, getting whipped once right in the face with a branch, but I could see a little now that I was away from the sergeant's lantern that was stuck so close to my face that it blinded me in the dark and—

I felt something heavy and wet bang into me, and it knocked the wind right out of me, I can tell you, and for a second I just couldn't figure what happened; I thought maybe somehow I had run smack into a tree, but then the tree moved and caught me around the chest, even though I was pulling and punching for all I was worth. But it was Harry who caught me—and to this day I don't know how the hell he did it, but he did—and he held on to me like I was the Grail, as Poppa would say, and I was still wiggling and fighting him hard enough that I probably could've gotten away if I had a few more seconds even, but he shouted for the sergeant, shouted that he had got me and that he was a loyal Yank and was surrendering and wanted to know what to do.

Eurastus didn't waste any time getting back over to me. He was holding me now, and hurting my arms and chest terrible. Maybe he expected me to scream or something, but I just stood there and felt myself getting sick like I was going to upchuck or faint like fat Mrs. Routzann did when Poppa was preaching about sin being like a maggot or something; and then when I didn't struggle or anything, Eurastus loosened his hold on me, but only a little. I knew it was time to quit because it was just a matter of time before he would have enough excuse to bash me good or kill me or run me around with a rail or torture me until I was dead anyway. In fact, if he could figure a way to get me away from the sergeant, he was going to hurt me bad or kill me, no matter what. I was as sure of that as Poppa was about God. But I remembered something about patience being a virtue, so I just stood there like all my bones had gone soft and smelled Eurastus's fishy frock coat while Sergeant Dunean interrogated Harry about who his commanding officer was and what happened to his partner, Private Smith.

And one, two, three, Harry spilled his guts and told them that "Private Smith" was a made-up name, that the other soldier's name was really Joseph Catterson and he was a private too, and that he lied about everything and was from the 110th Pennsylvania, though he came from Boston, and the sergeant said how it sounded like he had a baked bean accent, whatever that was. Then

Harry went on to tell how he and Catterson were supposed to be picking up the wounded and bringing them back to the church for the sawbones, and that Catterson was malingering, and how much it upset Harry. He said he thought that Catterson had got himself into some sort of trouble with his unit and was trying to stay away from them until everything passed over, and Harry thought that Catterson really wasn't so much, come to think of it, and that he got scared and panicked and that's why he ran away.

"He didn't seem scared to me," Sergeant Dunean said. "Sounded like he was achin' for a fight to me."

"He gets mean when he's scared," Harry said. "I've seen him before . . . before we started fightin' here."

"So he's your friend," Sergeant Dunean said.

"No, I just know him," Harry said, hanging his head like there was no use of anything and he was going to get punished no matter that he was innocent.

I think you would've needed a shovel big as a plough to get through that man's bullshit, even if part of it was true—I 'spect that the name was true because Catterson sounded more like a real name than Smith, although I'd heard of a family by the name of Smith who had all their horses impressed by Captain Bob Clarke, who was a Confederate officer who used to come by for dinner on Sunday nights. But old Harry wasn't as bad as Catterson, who was probably on his way over the hill right now, deserting. So I guess Harry wasn't entirely wrong to expose that bastard to save his own ass. And Harry had been properly assigned to this duty, or it seemed so, anyway. I sort of liked Harry. He was probably a saint alongside of Catterson. Even if he said that he had been trying to get away from Catterson all the while and was afraid Catterson would shoot him dead. I knew *that* was bullshit. In fact, he said Catterson even threatened him when they were watching us through the bush. That's when they saw me, he said, and Harry probably saw his chance to be a hero by catching me.

"Where's your litter?" Sergeant Dunean asked him.

"Back where we were when you challenged us," Harry said. "I could show you. Catterson doused both torches and then ran off. But I could find my way back with your lantern."

"There was enough light for you to catch the boy here."

Harry nodded and looked hangdog again. He certainly had that expression down pat. "I could find the litter for you, just have to search around in the dark a little is all." He had a long face that looked rather sad even though just now it was looking hopeful, like maybe he wasn't going to be bucked and gagged and paraded around in front of his company.

"Eurastus, you go with this malingerer and gather up his gear, pick up the wounded, and report back to the church," Sergeant Dunean said. "And I don't want you fuckin' the dog. Get your wounded and your prisoner back to the church before me or *you'll* be answerin' charges." Then the sergeant directed himself to me and said, "Boy, I don't know if you're deaf and dumb or what, but if you try to break away again, I'll shoot your ass off like you're a deserter. You understand that? I need you, so you'd better stand right there like a man."

I figured I'd be smart to nod, which I did quick.

"Okay, Eurastus, let go of him, he'll be all right."

"No, he won't. The little dungshit is goin' to run off again."

"I just told you to let him go."

Eurastus finally did let me loose, and of course I did think about dashing into the dark, but thought better of it. I couldn't see the spirit dog anywhere around, which probably meant I was still bad luck, so I just stood there watching the sergeant.

"You see?" Sergeant Dunean said.

"I still think he's a goddamn spy or somethin'," Eurastus said, and you could tell he was riled that I was free and he hadn't got the chance to break my arms and kick my ass.

"Well, then, we'll find that out. Meantime, you're in charge of Private Beem. I'll take the boy with me and bring back one of our soldiers for the sawbones to cut up. Where's *our* litter?"

"Right behind you," Eurastus said.

"You take the lamp, I'll take my chances with the boy," and then we just started walking around, looking for wounded soldiers to carry, and the sergeant was real close to me all the time, leading me where he wanted to go, but I wanted to go back over to where Jimmadasin possibly was and find out if he was dead or wounded or what. The sergeant wasn't having any of it and in no time we found a soldier who was groaning, and the sergeant examined him like he was a doctor, all the while giving me orders and telling me what to do, and then we had to carry the soldier. Now that I think back on it, I'm sure the sergeant picked a small, skinny bluebelly, so I'd be able to help carry him, and we rolled the poor bastard onto the litter, which folded out, although it was as big as a regular stretcher. He groaned and was talking nonsense about how bugs were eating him alive and that his mother was watching, and O God, he wasn't supposed to die here, it was written in a book and he saw it, and that minié balls and grape or canister or nothing was supposed to be able to hurt him, and that we should listen, listen, and we would be able to hear God with our own ears, and then we would believe him. Well, he was heavier than a skinny guy ought to be, and I dropped my end of the litter and felt bad about that, especially when the sergeant tied the wounded Yank somehow into the litter and dragged him along all by himself. I walked beside the litter and patted the soldier and gave him a little water now and then, and I listened hard so I could hear God, but there was nothing out there now but wind and stink and a dirty-looking sliver of moon that kept disappearing. Then it started raining and maybe a minute later it stopped, then started. Crazy.

Of course, I could have run away. I had plenty of chances. I could've slipped right into the dirty dark, which was steaming although it was cold because a fog had settled right down on the ground over all the dead and wounded soldiers, and the wounded ones probably thought they'd already died and were in Heaven waiting for Saint Peter to count them up and bring them in. But anyway, a sort of listlessness came over me like you get when you wake up and are about to fall back to sleep again, like that. I felt heavy and tired and just didn't care about anything. It's difficult to explain exactly, but I sort of felt as if I were looking at everything from the end of a long tunnel or something, and I could see what was up ahead, which seemed like it was . . . far away; and I was having enough trouble just dealing with that. Or maybe it was like I was dead and walking around looking for Saint Peter myself, and so I just kept walking along with the sergeant, who kept ordering me to stay alongside him until we'd dragged that poor wounded soldier to the brick church that had been right in the middle of the early skirmishing that went on east of the pike. Of course, we had to cross the pike, which was littered with clothes, ponchos, blankets, shelter halves, Bibles, photographs, cards, songbooks, cooking utensils, haversacks, cartridge boxes, empty canteens, and even muskets, although mostly smooth-bores. There was probably more, but the bluebottles would have already taken anything valuable. I felt sorry to see all that mess, as it was left by our own soldiers who were being chased by General Banks, and I felt ashamed, but I was sure that none of it was left by Colonel Ashby and his riders; they would've been killing just as many Yanks while retreating as when they were advancing. But, as I said before, nothing much mattered to me while I was walking with the sergeant to the church because I was mostly dead for that time. Then Sergeant

Dunean asked me if I thought I could pull my weight, as he said it, and help him with the litter, which I did.

I wouldn't've cared if the litter broke my arms or the moon fell out of the sky. Sergeant Dunean kept talking to me and asking me questions, as if he figured that at any moment I was going to start to talk; but I didn't, and even if I could've, I wouldn't've.

I felt like I was waking up or something when I saw the church. Like my thoughts started going faster, and life was coming into me.

Maybe it was because seeing the flickery yellow light in the windows reminded me of something, but I can tell you I was better off staying dead because once we got up close I could see all the corpses or wounded soldiers— mostly you couldn't tell them apart. There was a constant groaning, just like in the woods. Someone was crying, sobbing like a little kid who couldn't catch his breath, and someone was swearing that if he died here the doctors and their wives and children and nephews and even their dogs would be cursed, and so would everyone else, which I suppose included me, although that wouldn't matter much now. The bodies were neatly stacked in rows on either side of the front door, which was open, and the hospital smell was even worse than anything I had smelled out in the woods. And in the quivery light from the church, I could see the soldiers lying outside that big old door real good; and I could see that some of their wounds were moving. At first I couldn't understand that, and figured it must have been my eyes; but it wasn't. It was maggots, and those little bastards must procreate in no time at all because it was like a swarm of bees had settled down on the hot wounds of those Yank soldiers, only the maggots didn't make any buzzing noises.

Sergeant Dunean and I put our soldier down at the end of a row and didn't bother trying to pull the litter out from under him; at least he was covered up—that's more than the rest got. Then the sergeant pushed me into the church ahead of him. He was still talking to me, as if he were talking to a baby, and I was expecting him to start making googoo noises any time now. Maybe he was thinking about his own children or something. I didn't much care, as long as I didn't have to see Private Eurastus, but he would be waiting for me there in the church; that's what Sergeant Dunean had told him to do. Sonovabitch if I didn't come to attention and turn around to bolt right out of that church, but it was too late and the sergeant was blocking the door, and anyway, Eurastus wasn't there.

I would've been truly relieved, if it wasn't that I just found myself in Hell.

When I first looked inside that church, that's just what it looked like; it's what I'll always think of as Hell, no matter what Doctor Keys tries to tell me different. And I still wake up dreaming about it, maybe because I came out of there and killed that sonovabitch, that sonovabitch who—

But I'll tell you about that by and by.

What I saw when we stepped into that church was a large room with high ceilings all lit up with nothing but candles, which were flickering and guttering everywhere—all over the floor, in the aisles; and in the places where there'd been neat rows of pews for Sunday church, there were wounded bluebellies, and there was the groaning just like outside, but more than that: These soldiers were shrieking and cursing and kicking up a fuss like if they didn't get enough attention now they were going to drop dead and then rise right up again and haunt this place forever.

I listened hard, although I couldn't hear God outside like the soldier we brought in. But I could certainly learn some new ways to curse in here. And I thought for a second that these soldiers should consider themselves lucky that they weren't lying in the rain and dying with their asses sucking in the mud. But then again I thought that this was worse because at least the others could look up at the sky and maybe see a star or the bit of moon riding through the clouds before they died. The soldiers in here probably figured they were in Hell too, just like I did, and so they acted appropriately. Now, you've got to understand that everything I'm describing I saw in a second, sort of like when you turn your head around because it wasn't more than a second before I was looking at what Poppa would have surely called fiends. Two men covered with blood were standing around the church's Communion table, which had a bluebelly soldier on top of it. I figured that the one with the thick gray side whiskers was the sawbones because he looked older than the other one, who had a wispy beard and didn't seem to be at all sure of what he was about. There was blood spattered and pooling all over the table and the floor, and behind the doctor with the whiskers was a pile of arms and legs, and most of the legs still had on their shoes and stockings, like they were still ready to go walking around by themselves. And there were church pews all helter-skelter with soldiers lying on them. It sounded like insects buzzing around in here with all the soldiers breathing and groaning and swearing. There were some soldiers sitting on pews; they were the lucky ones who weren't hurt so bad and could walk around on their own. One of the soldiers was sitting on a pew next to another and holding the other soldier's hand, which was wrapped up in a bloody ball of what looked like a woman's skirt

material. The wounded soldier looked all pasty-faced, and the other one called
to Sergeant Dunean and asked, "'Scuse me, sir, but could you tend to my brother here? He's had all his fingers 'cept the thumb shot off, and he's awful weak."

Sergeant Dunean nodded to him and held up his hand as if to stop him, and
then pulled me over to the other end of the room; and we stepped over the soldiers lying everywhere and had to go around the mess of pews, so that now if I
wanted to escape, I'd have to get around that Communion table and the doctors
and all the pews, thank you. I saw a pile of books on a chair next to where we
were standing; some of the pages had bloody fingerprints all over them. One of
the covers read *Principles of Practice of Surgery, by F. W. Sargent, M. D.*, and
there were two volumes of something called *Smith's Operative Surgery* set
together like they were on a library shelf. I suppose I was looking hard at those
books because I was afraid of looking at the soldier on the Communion table;
but I couldn't help myself. I had to see what was going to happen to him. His leg
was wounded terrible, and you could see the hole in it right above the knee.

"You took your sweet time getting back here, Dunean," the doctor with
the chops said. His voice sounded slurred, like he'd been drinking. "So I'm
making do with Doctor Foye here, but Doctor Foye doesn't seem to be able to
keep this main artery from bleeding," he said, speaking now to Doctor Foye.
"It's enough that I've got to work without an assistant to hold the limb and support the flap. Compress it, man, unless you've got something against this poor
soldier! There, that's not difficult if you're paying attention."

"Did Eurastus come back, Doctor Zearing?" the sergeant asked the older
doctor. Sergeant Dunean looked tired, but not at all nervous about being in the
presence of these doctors, who also had to be officers.

"Does it look like he came back?" Doctor Zearing asked. "Though it
doesn't matter, 'cause he's got shit for brains, just like those other two idiots Surgeon King at Five Corps sent me. Wait'll you meet *them.*"

Sergeant Dunean said, "I think I already have. Both of them are malingerers, one of 'em ran away when I challenged him. I'll write up a full report.
Private Eurastus is overseeing one of them. They should've been here by
now. . . ."

But Doctor Zearing didn't seem interested, or wasn't paying attention.
"Who's the boy?" he asked.

"Found him in the woods robbin' our dead. Figured it would be best to just
follow orders and bring him in. He's certainly secesh, but he can't—or won't—
talk."

"So you brought him back *here*?" Doctor Zearing said, laughing.

"With your permission, I'll take him over to regiment for interrogation."

The doctor glanced over at me like I was another one of his patients and said, "We'll tend to him later; he doesn't look like a terribly dangerous criminal. In the meantime, Sergeant, take care of that soldier's fingers. . . . And you, boy, can make yourself useful and wash out the wounds of the soldier beside you. You see him there, his face is all covered? Sergeant, show the boy what to do. I'm going to get to that soldier next. He's a captain, one of Colonel Kimball's boys. I knew his father."

I looked over to my right and saw a man hunched over on a pew with his back against the wall. He had a brown, bloody cloth hanging over his head, and I couldn't help but think that there was something awful and funny about that, like he would suddenly tear off the cloth, jump up, cry "Surprise!" and wave a flag or something.

Doctor Zearing called to the soldier, asking him if he was all right. The soldier made a grunting noise. "There you are," Doctor Zearing said to his assistant doctor. "And I'll explain when I start working on him why I think he can be saved. We'll teach you how to be a surgeon yet, George, if you can manage not to faint dead away on me again." He smiled at George, asked him for the Catlin knife, which was longer than a bowie knife and had a long yellowish-white handle, probably ivory; and then, like it was nothing out of the ordinary, he just cut around that leg and pulled the skin back. Sergeant Dunean was talking to me, but I couldn't take my eyes away from what was going on because next thing you know the doctor was sawing right through the bone, and then he was tossing the leg over where the others were, and then he was shouting at George for a "tenaculum," or some word like that, and then he was calling Sergeant Dunean to help out too with tying off the blood vessels quick while he filed down the bone. "Now, you see, George, the way I cover the head of the bone here? You've got to leave ample flap after you divide the skin or the poor bastard's going to feel like he's wearing tight pants forever." But George was getting flustered about something. "Don't worry," Doctor Zearing said. "We're almost finished. You've given him enough natural air. The chloroform's not going to kill him."

"His pulse is sinking," George said.

"We're almost closed."

"I think we should give him some liquor of ammonia."

"Then go ahead."

I watched all this like I was fascinated and couldn't move, although what I should have been doing was thinking of a way of getting to the door before Eurastus arrived. I'd have to get by Sergeant Dunean and the doctors and step over and around the pews and soldiers.

I started moving through the pews, natural-like, as if I was looking for something, and I was being all relaxed, getting invisible as I could, though it didn't feel right—it was as if I'd lost the knack somehow. I saw George put a red glass bottle up to the soldier's nose, and then I could feel myself getting invisible again, like I hadn't been since I first saw the spirit dog, and I forgot about everything except getting out of the church. I was moving real good and quiet when Sergeant Dunean came out from around the Communion table and called to me. Now, right there and then I should have run for the door, but I just stood where I was like I had forgotten how to walk. I just stood there looking at the pile of legs and arms by the Communion table, and for a second I thought that *my* legs were in that pile.

Sergeant Dunean came over to me, took my arm (but without hurting me), and led me over to the soldier with the cloth over his face.

I felt my face get hot like I'd just been caught playing with myself; and I heard Doctor Zearing swear—I guess because whatever George stuck up that poor legless soldier's nose didn't work; and then Doctor Zearing said, "All right, George, let's just finish this and I'll show you a trick. Give me that bottle of chloroform and watch that stump; I still need to finish closing and wrap it." Then Doctor Zearing shook the chloroform over the sleeping soldier's crotch, and sonovabitch if he didn't sit right up like someone had throwed cold water over him. George held on to him, so he wouldn't tear off his stump, I guess, and the soldier just looked around surprised, and then when he saw that he didn't have a leg anymore, he screamed and fell right back on the table like someone had hit him on the head.

"Chloroform feels cold on the skin," Sergeant Dunean told me as he carefully peeled the cloth away from the face of the soldier who was hunched over on the pew. I've got to admit I jumped at what I saw, but the sergeant just kept chattering away like there was nothing at all wrong. "Now, reach over there and get that basin of water—it looks clean enough." Then, after telling me to stow my poncho lest I sweat to death, he walked over to another pew where there was a pile of what looked like dirty laundry, and he brought back a torn piece of linen; but meanwhile I thought I was going to be sick just looking at that poor man. It looked as if his eyes and his nose had just been scooped out, and he must've felt that I was standing there over him because he smiled and slowly pointed to the side of his head with his finger; and he said in a voice so low and husky as to be nothing more than a whisper, "If the ball would have struck me here, I wouldn't be troubling you right now, young sir."

He was a Southerner.

I could tell by his accent, and I looked at his clothes and saw he wasn't wearing a bluebelly uniform. Maybe Doctor Zearing had him mixed up with somebody else. Or maybe he was letting Sergeant Dunean know that this Confederate was a family friend, and he was going to be treated just like a bluebelly. I hadn't seen any other Confederate soldiers in here, or maybe I just hadn't looked close enough; right then though I looked around hard, but I couldn't see any others.

Sergeant Dunean came back and said to the soldier, "Don't you worry, sir. If Doctor Zearing says he can fix you, then that's that. I understand you know each other from before the war."

The soldier nodded, and all I could think of was that his face looked like a piece of meat, but Sergeant Dunean showed me how to clean him up and then, without saying a word, gave me the towel after he rinsed it in the basin. So I washed the soldier's face, and emptied the bloody water from the basin and went out to fill it; and that would have ordinarily been my chance to escape, but I went back inside to finish up the 'Federate soldier who just kept talking to me as if nothing was wrong. It was pitiful, especially since every once in a while his head would jerk back like somebody'd slapped him hard. I finished washing him, and he asked me to put a cloth back over his face; he said there wasn't any need to sicken the other patients. I did what he asked and made up my mind I was going to leave, no matter what. I was going to get away from everything but the woods.

Sergeant Dunean was on the other side of the room, and he was operating just like he was a doctor: giving the patients chloroform to put them to sleep, cutting off fingers, suturing, bandaging, putting morphine powder into their wounds, administering chloroform and ether, and sometimes sprinkling chloroform on their balls if they didn't wake proper; but he was especially good at pushing his fingers into wounds to locate bullets—or at least that's what Doctor Zearing said. He didn't need to use the bullet forceps like the doctors. So he was kept pretty busy, especially as he had to bring the soldiers in from outside the church. I helped him some, and so did Doctor Foye, and even Doctor Zearing, who would get winded every time. I got close to Doctor Zearing once, and could smell liquor on his breath; but, still, that didn't stop him from operating and cutting up those soldiers one after the other without a break—except to take a sip from a metal flask that he said was filled with black tea. After a while the doctors and Sergeant Dunean called me whenever one of the soldiers had to be put to sleep. It got so I just kept a funnel and a blue bottle of ether in my pocket. Everyone was shouting all the time. I'd start doing one thing, and someone would call me to do something else until it seemed I was doing everything at once.

While Doctor Zearing was drilling a hole into the head of the Southern soldier I had washed and tended—as if the poor bastard needed another piece taken out of him—he ordered me to take the pile of arms and legs away and throw all the parts into a pit behind the church. He called me "Little Sandman" because I was administering the ether, and he didn't know my name. I guess he forgot that I'd try to escape, and maybe Sergeant Dunean didn't hear or wasn't paying attention, or maybe he wasn't there just then; I don't remember. I do remember that the sergeant was cussing while he was sawing through the arm bone of some poor unconscious soldier; he was just calling out one swear word after another like it was a roll call; and that's when I disappeared.

I just walked out, big as day, stepped over the wounded and the corpses we hadn't carried out to the back to be buried with the arms and legs, zigzagged around the pews and the soldiers laying and sitting everywhere, past all the candles standing everywhere and guttering and sputtering, and some of them were blowed out by gusts of wind coming in from the door and the windows (but Doctor Zearing insisted on the healthful free flow of atmospheric air); and then I was out in that atmospheric air, which was cold and full of moisture. I got away from the rows of wounded soldiers and that church as quick as I could so as not to be seen, but my eyes weren't adjusted to the dark yet, and everything looked darker than it should, and somebody said "Hey" in a low voice, as if he was hiding out and didn't want to be seen either. I ignored it and kept going, figuring the faster I get out of here, the better off I was going to be; but someone was behind me, and when I made a run for it, so did he, and sonovabitch I knew—I knew soon as I was running that it was Private Eurastus, that that malingerer had been hiding out here and taking it easy and probably drinking, and he had probably killed Private Beem. I wished for the spirit dog to save me because Eurastus was running hard and catching up, and then he tackled me and started slapping me and punching me just like I knew he would, and there wasn't anything I could do but curl up and protect my face and balls, and all the while I was thinking that I had to make a smart move and push myself away from him and run away; and in my thoughts I could've made one kick and gotten away from him, but that was just in my thoughts because he was beating me all over and I couldn't do anything but try to protect myself. After a time he began cooing to me like Sergeant Dunean, and I thought that maybe he had heard Sergeant Dunean talking baby talk like that.

Eurastus was cooing away like a bastard when he started tearing away at my pants. At first I couldn't understand why he'd want my clothes, as they'd be too small for him. Then he held me so tight I could hardly breathe, and I felt a terrible pain right in my ass. I would've screamed if I could. Everything seemed to go red behind my eyes, which were closed, as if I could just shut everything out, like pulling the sheets over your head after a nightmare; and then I don't know how I thought of it—in fact, I did it without even thinking; it was like somebody *else* did it—but I managed to reach into my pants' pocket and pull out the bottle of chloroform, and I gave a jerk like I'd wished I could have done before to escape Eurastus when he was beating me, and twisted just enough to smash that blue bottle into his head. It wasn't being struck by the bottle that stopped him but the chloroform that spilled onto his face and into his nose and eyes. He gagged and wheezed, and I got to my knees and shook that bottle and held it right under his nose. My hand was bleeding and felt like I'd been holding it in snow, but Eurastus was just lying there like he was just taking a nap, and I covered his face with his own poncho and pushed as hard as I could. I can't tell you how long I smothered him, but I didn't stop because he was dead or anything, but because I suddenly saw the spirit dog; and I admit I couldn't help myself but I just couldn't think of anything but to run.

To run through the night like a spirit, like the dead soldiers whose souls were just blowing around, light as feathers.

I don't know if I was invisible or quiet or noisy. I just knew I was probably a murderer. And that I wasn't never going back there.

Ever.

PRIVATE NEWTON'S WAR

IN THE AIR

Run nigger run, run nigger run,
Don' let de paddyrollers catch you,
Run run nigger run.

A BANJO PLAYER'S
DANCE SONG

WELL, I DID. GO BACK THERE, THAT IS.

I was going to head out in the opposite direction and go east and keep to the woods and never come out again like I told you, but I couldn't help it, I just had to find out if Jimmadasin was dead or wounded or was even there in that field. Maybe I went back because I felt cold and dirty from what Eurastus had tried to do to me, but I didn't feel bad about killing him, if I killed him. I suppose I did, but maybe I didn't, and I'm never going to know anyway. As I said, I just felt cold and dirty, and I needed to find Jimmadasin. Not that he could make anything better. Well, maybe he could. I just felt I couldn't leave him like I left everybody else, so there I was heading back to the battlefield when I had promised myself not to.

But I should tell you that I robbed Eurastus. I don't feel bad about that

either. He deserved it more than the soldier with the maggots in his eyes. I took
Eurastus's poncho because I had left mine all folded nice and neat in the
church, and I took what hardtack and pork he had, and, sonovabitch, if he
didn't have an officer's revolver stuffed in his blanket along with a pouch of
caps and paper cartridges, so I took that. It felt like a Colt .44 revolver. I also
took his haversack and a stash of money he had picked off the dead bluebellies,
but I left all the pocket watches and rings and buttons and tobacco. I could see
a little in the moonlight, but mostly I was feeling my way through his plunder.
Another thing I took was a book. I couldn't read what it was, but it was about
the size of a small hymnal or something. I couldn't figure Eurastus carrying a
Bible, so I thought it must be something he stole that was interesting, like those
Beadle books I had overheard Harry and Private Catterson talking about.
Eurastus probably took this book from Harry, probably after he killed him.
Maybe he even found Catterson and killed him. Seemed to me that Eurastus
would have liked to kill everybody. Anyway, I dumped everything out of his
haversack and just took what I told you. I wasn't going to take his blanket
because it smelled like fish, but at the last minute I took it anyway. I figured it
was better to smell like a fish than freeze my ass off. Even without the wind,
it was cold out. I wondered what time it was, how long until morning, and I
left Eurastus there in the moonlight looking like one of the statues in the
library, except he had his booty dumped all around him and his pants around
his knees.

I ran back to the battleground like that was the only safe place, and I knew
the way, and branches didn't snap under my feet, nor did they slap me in the face;
and I knew that I'd figured out how to be invisible again, like I suddenly remembered. Maybe all I needed was practice, and I had been practicing in the church
and when I was running away from Eurastus and all, but at least it came back to
me now, although I had to stop and go to the bathroom because my ass hurt so
much. Maybe it was the pain that made me remember how to keep invisible, or
maybe it was being alone. That was probably it, being alone. Maybe if I pretended to be alone all the time, I'd be able to stay invisible, and that's what I
determined to do. Not even Jimmadasin would be able to see me. Not even the
spirit dog. . . .

I looked around, but I couldn't see the red eyes of the spirit dog anywhere.
I kept my eyes peeled, though, because I was expecting to find that spirit dog
ghosting around the battlefield; I knew now that he liked to be around dead

people. I was alone in the dark and the moonlight and the shadows, and I wasn't scared, and I wondered if the Colt was loaded. I knew how to load it, and tear the cartridge, and empty the powder into the chamber, all that. I knew because I had watched a demonstration at a meeting of the Seventh Regiment where Poppa had presided to say the prayers; that was in June of '61. Colonel Ashby was there and had bowed his head when Poppa spoke the Scripture, and I even remembered the prayers Poppa said, which made everybody feel that we were certainly going to smite the oppressor's hand:

> *"These Southern states at Thy command*
> *Rose from dependence and distress;*
> *And 'stablished by Thy mighty hand,*
> *Millions shall join Thy name to bless."*

Well, Poppa's dead, so none of that came to much, except to make everybody feel good; and I suppose it made me feel good even now just thinking about Poppa and Colonel Ashby . . . and thinking about Mother standing way back with the other women and somehow scowling and looking proud at the same time. I recited that hymn of Poppa's while I sneaked through the night back to the ridge where I'd find Jimmadasin, if he was there. When I got there, the sky was getting gray, and the fog was rolling on the ground. I could see better now, but it was dangerous being out here without the protection of the night. Then I saw the spirit dog. I didn't trust him because he would take just as much pleasure getting me killed as showing me where Jimmadasin was, but I followed him anyway. I didn't have much time, and I imagined that pretty soon the battlefield would be crawling with newspaper correspondents and generals and sightseers and people from the town who were allowed to come for the 'Federate dead and wounded, so I followed the spirit dog, who wasn't much more than just another hazy, foggy shape ahead of me. Could've been anything, I suppose, like bushes or trees or shadows, but I knew what he was, and I followed him, and he led me right to Jimmadasin. Sonovabitch if it wasn't him. I'd've known even in the moonlight, but I could see him laying there, his clothes stiff from dried blood, and the flies buzzing around where he'd gotten shot right in the chest. That must've been a hard way to die; I could tell because his face was all pulled out of shape like he had stuffed his mouth full of food and had choked on it. Funny thing, though, was that one eye was open and the other closed. I couldn't understand that, and I thought I'd better close the other one, but then I remembered touching the soldier's face with the maggots, and even though it was Jimmadasin I just couldn't bring myself to do it. Even though I couldn't see maggots in the one eye that was open.

Well, I knew that he was probably dead, but I was disappointed because I had it in my mind that if he was only wounded, I'd help him away from here and take care of him from what I'd learned helping the doctors out in the church, and we'd live in the woods and trap and never come out, not even when the South won the war. He'd know places to go because he told me there were lots of niggers who'd run away and lived in the woods and even had families. He even said he knew a good place in Massanutten, which is a mountain, and he winked at me like it was a secret. (Course, he couldn't say the name properly and called it "Massah's Nuddem," but I figured out what he meant.) And I know he probably wasn't bullshitting me because the paddyrollers were always hunting for cave niggers, as they called them.

But too late for all that now.

I'd done right by him by going back, but he was going to have to get himself buried; it was morning now, and as I looked around the battlefield, I could see all the bodies strewn about, and some of the soldiers were still alive and moaning; and I knew I had to get out of there right away. Seeing them so clear was like waking up from a dream, and I just couldn't look at them. I apologized to Jimmadasin and got out of there. I wondered if he had come back after me, trying to save me or something. I guess I'll always think that. What the hell else would he be doing out in that field? He'd most likely got his Harry and Allan back home safe to Mrs. McSherry, and that's where he should've stayed. Dumb sonovabitch.

I guess I owe you, Jimmadasin.

But I still couldn't stay to bury you.

It took me a while to cross the Valley Pike because there were thousands of bluebellies marching down toward Middletown and Strasburg, and there were bluebellies coming back after skirmishing with Colonel Ashby, and there were sutlers with their wagons probably full of canned meat and butter and pies and molasses cakes six for a quarter (it made my mouth water just to think of that), and mule teams pulling artillery carriages, limbers, and caissons; I never saw so many cannons and ammunition. Of course, I could've probably crossed at any time and nobody would take any notice, but if I learned anything from the spirit dog and the soldiers it was to be careful and not trust anything, including yourself. Just because I felt invisible didn't mean a thing.

I crossed the pike and just kept going, walking through the fields above Skirtwood Curve, then down past Carysbrooke and Springdale and Bartonsville, not realizing until I was almost asleep on my feet and numb from the cold that I was heading toward the Massanutten. It seemed like even after he was dead, old Jimmadasin was giving me directions.

I had meant to get over to the Martinsburg Pike and then into the Blue Ridge Mountains, where I figured I'd be far enough away from the Yanks and our own 'Federates to be safe. But here I was now going south, not exactly following our army along the Valley Pike, but keeping to the fields and woods and out of the way, although I had to hide from Yank cavalry once and skirmishers another time. Still and all, I was mostly away from all human kin, as Poppa'd say. I probably should have turned around and gone east like I'd intended, but instead I found some woods that were dark and seemed safe. It probably sounds crazy, but when I stopped there I smelled hayfern, which smells just like new-mown hay, and before I could even think about anything I started crying, but I stopped myself by imagining that the spirit dog was watching me, even though he seemed long gone. Course, there was no hayfern, just dead leaves every-where and rotting logs and moss, and everything looked dead, or asleep, and it didn't seem like spring was ever going to show up around here. The trees were bare, and there were patches of snow.

I couldn't keep my eyes open any longer; so I lay down on top of Eurastus's rubber poncho, which I put up against an old chestnut tree. I could see my breath, and I remember thinking how glad I was to have the Yankee soldier's canvas shoes before I fell asleep.

It's funny because it's only now that I'm writing this that I remember what I dreamed then. I dreamed about Hog Day and Poppa and Mother and Uncle Isaac and Aunt Hanna, and she let me call her Mammy Jack like all the others did, and I smoked cigars and shuffled the cards just like she did, and everybody was impressed, and they started calling *me* Mammy Jack, and then me and Private Eurastus started slaughtering the hogs right in front of the Big House on the pavement of red sandstone flags. I remember that instead of blood from all the slaughtering, there were flowers all over, flowers like I'd only find in the woods in spring and summer—laurel and azalea and dogwood and Indian pipe;

and there were all sorts of wild creatures watching, like they had no fear at all: black bears and deer and foxes and elk, and every kind of bird you could think of.

I had Uncle Isaac's long knife and I knew every one of the hogs because they all had names, only they weren't hogs—

I WOKE UP LIKE I HAD SPILLED CHLOROFORM ALL OVER MY CROTCH.

It was a good thing that that dream woke me up, or I probably would've froze right there under that old chestnut tree. I was so cold I was numb, and all the trees were coated with the kind of sparkly snow that's like ice. For a minute I didn't know where I was; nothing looked real, although it was beautiful, like everything ugly was hiding under the snow. It was like waking up cold and wet up in the clouds, like somehow I'd gotten up there and was looking around at their shapes. But once I got up and made myself keep walking, once I got out of there and walked through fields and followed streams that weren't even frozen, there wasn't any more snow, except in patches here and there. It was as if it had just snowed on me, like that was the only place that froze up; and I was glad to get out of there.

Although I'd probably only slept a few hours—and maybe less than that—I was starving. I ate some more of the pork and a hardtack cracker that almost broke my teeth. But now I was sweating with the poncho and blanket around my shoulders. It wasn't warm, but it wasn't cold either; and it was still early. The sun was high and the sky full of storm clouds, and although I had miles and miles to go, I felt dizzy and feverish and I ached all over. I figured I had caught the ague back in the church, and I heard what that could do to you. Pretty soon I'd be shaking and out of my head, and I'd be shouting things that didn't make any sense, or seeing God and talking to Him like that bluebelly soldier Sergeant Dunean and I had dragged to the church. Well, maybe seeing God wouldn't be such a bad thing, but truth to tell—and I know Poppa would call me blasphemous—I didn't really much care about seeing God. And when I thought about Poppa and Mother, and tried to think how it would feel to be back home like nothing bad had happened, I didn't feel anything. I wondered if I'd want to talk to them if I could, like the soldier who could talk to God, but I didn't feel no yearning to do it or anything. I figured I must be suffering from the ague of sorts because just walking around in the fields and meadows and around the hills alone, with nothing but the wind and creeks and dead grass and white trees, made me feel better than I could ever remember. It was like I'd just walked out here and was going to be free, and it wasn't going to hurt anybody, and nothing bad had happened yesterday, and Poppa and Mother wouldn't mind—

But those were crazy thoughts, so I just kept walking until I got tired again, and I slept pretty warm with the poncho and the blanket, although I couldn't bear to bring the blanket all the way up to my neck where I could smell it, and the poncho made me sweat. I thought I'd wake up shaking because I was shaking when I laid down, but I was all right. I did think I was seeing things, though, because when I woke up everything seemed like it was lit by moonlight, only it was brighter, and mist was sliding through the trees like ghosts or something, and I could see where the moon was, but it was behind clouds that filled up the sky. I got up and packed up, and I was starving—it seemed I was always hungry now—but I wasn't going to eat there because everything looked too strange, and I felt scared. I looked around for the spirit dog, but there was only me and the trees and the leaves that swirled around like they were alive and wanted to get out of here too. So I packed up quick, like this place had suddenly become dangerous, and my blanket was soaked through, and when I got moving and got out of the woods the mist turned to rain, and it was pretty warm out; and I discovered that it wasn't moonlight I was seeing but morning daylight. I had slept through mostly the entire day and the night too and woke up the next day just after dawn.

For a while it was hard to walk; I'd given myself a charley horse from sleeping all twisted up under Eurastus's blanket for all that time, and I kept shivering like I was cold, and then I'd feel warm. But as I walked through fields and meadows, which got sharper and clearer as the morning light got stronger, I remembered how Eurastus beat and kicked me. That's probably why I slept all twisted up, just like I was, to protect myself from him. I had probably been dreaming about him too, and I wondered whether he was dead; and just then I remembered the book I had taken off of him.

It was all of a sudden like that book was the most important thing in the world, even though I hadn't looked at it but in the dark.

So I walked until I got to a place where I wouldn't be standing out like a scarecrow in a field. I found a little valley where it would be hard to see me unless you'd been there all along. There wasn't any woods hereabouts, just hills and fields with the biggest stones I've ever seen standing here and there like they'd been dropped, and some of them were taller than a man. I sat down against the

north edge of one of those rocks, and right there in the rain I opened up Eurastus's haversack and took out the book, which had a yellow paper cover and a
drawing of a cigar-shaped balloon with an evil-looking man with a mustache
leaning out of what looked like a carved wooden basket. But looking at that picture made me feel like I was right in the basket and looking straight down; and
there were rods sticking out from all over the basket, and hanging on ropes from
the rods were huge globes all lit up; and in the middle of those rods and ropes
and globes was a boy who didn't look to be much older than me hanging from a
rope ladder and climbing up to get into the balloon, and way below that was a
city that was so far down that the buildings looked like toys. The boy climbing
the ladder wore a Union uniform and looked real determined, not scared at all.
I finished reading that picture for I don't know how long before I read the title,
called *Private Newton's War in the Air*. Underneath the picture was written "A
True Flag Adventure Book by R. A. Riley."

I opened the book to the first page and read the first line. I was shaking and
shivering like I was reading the Bible for the first time or something. It started:
"As Frederick C. Small, spy and traitor to his country, chewed on a cocaine
lozenge, he contemplated how he would steal the United States of America's
most secret weapon and drop bombs from the atmosphere upon the sleeping
city of Washington."

I could have stayed there and probably read the whole thing—it wasn't
very long, just thirty-odd pages—but I was going to find myself a safe, dry
place in a cave or something in Massanutten Mountain where nobody'd find me,
and there I'd probably read this book a hundred times until I knew it backwards
and forwards. So I put it back in the haversack to protect it like it was the Bible
itself. I'd have it to look forward to. I knew about books like these, but Poppa
was adamant that all books except Christian tracts and the Bible were scurrilous
trash. I remember asking him about newspapers because he loved to read newspapers, and he told me that as far as I was concerned it was all trash, even the *Virginia Free Press*, unless he told me there was something special in there that I
could read. Never was any use in arguing with him, but I could feel him watching me like he was the spirit dog. I looked around, just in case, then got back on
my way until I was out of those fields with the rocks, and the land got rougher.

The sun burned away the rain, and if it weren't for everything looking
brown, you'd think it was a spring morning. There was a sweet smell to it, and
in the distance on both sides of me, beyond the miles of fields and hills, were the
Shenandoah and Blue Ridge looking a grayish blue, like they always did in the

morning. And ahead was the Massanutten. I used to like looking at the mountains and could see them from the porch of the Big House. So I guess that's why I started thinking about Poppa and Mother, and though it wasn't raining anymore, I could hear a thunder sound in my ears. I remember sometimes hearing that sound when I was a kid, usually when I was sad and about to start crying.

But I didn't . . . cry.

Instead I remembered something Aunt Hanna said about spirits. She told me that she had found 'ligion, as she called it, when she was my age, except she didn't know how old she was. I'm just about fourteen, or pretty close, give or take. That's when she had her first vision, which she said was the same as a dream, except sometimes, if she was having a holy day, she didn't need to be asleep to have a vision, she'd see it right there like it was real. Now, Aunt Hanna told me that her vision came to her while she was sleeping, but she'd had plenty after that while she was awake, but it was from that first vision that she became so good at cards, and she always said that she was playing cards for the Lord, and that the Lord works in funny ways, and that she wasn't smart enough to figure it out, but just to follow in the Lord's way. She always used to ask me when *I* was goin' to get 'ligion, and course I didn't know, until maybe just now out here walking to the Massanutten. You see, I was thinking about what Aunt Hanna said, and remembering most of it because I don't forget too much usually, and I remember that she'd told me that when she had her first vision it was about the Ship of Zion that was coming for her, and it was loaded up with angels and what she called seraphs and the like. According to her, that ship was floating right in the heavens, right in the sky under the sun, and it came for her, and she jumped into it, and she said that everyone was singing this song, which she used to sing to me sometimes:

> *"Oh, sister, has you got yo' counts conceal?*
> *No man ken hinder.*
> *I has my counts conceal 'fo I lef' de fiel',*
> *No man ken hinder.*
> *Ridin' on de conquerin' king.*
> *No man ken hinder."*

She told me that she learned to play cards on that ship while she was sailing around Heaven. The angels also told her that her 'ligious name would be Mammy Jack because it was God's will that she be the Queen of Blackjack; and if she abused her gift, the angels would take it right away from her. She also learned that half of everything she won was supposed to go directly to God, which she said meant the church and niggers who needed some help. So she always had a stash, and she called it her vision money.

Well, I guess I got my vision from that book that was now safely stashed away in Eurastus's haversack around my middle. I got it after I left the fields with all the scattered rocks, but not long after that. I was following a stream and getting closer to the spur of the mountain when I heard whispering. I stopped and looked around, but there wasn't anyone here but me. I remember that when I first heard the whispering and determined to my satisfaction that I was alone, I just stood still listening and looking at my feet, which were pretty muddy because the ground had gotten soft now that it was warmer. And I heard Frederick C. Small, spy and traitor, calling to me clear as day. He had a high-pitched voice, almost like Jimmadasin's. I felt dizzy all of a sudden, and then I imagined I was climbing up that rope ladder to that steam balloon, or whatever it was, and I was in Heaven floating and hanging, and above me was Frederick C. Small, who was going to try to kill me; but in that vision I wasn't scared at all, and I could feel the air around me just like I was on the ground, and the wind was blowing, and I felt that I didn't have to read that book because right there in that vision I already knew what was going to happen.

The next thing I remember I was back in the field, on the ground, and Mother was asking me, clear as day and not in a whisper, if I had got my counts conceal. I didn't quite know what she meant, but I knew it was Mother talking, and I later figured out that that vision was telling me how to stay invisible and that I was going to help serve God and that Poppa and Mother dying and me escaping was for a reason to help save the nation.

My vision also corrected the book by showing me that Frederick C. Small was a hero, and not a spy and a traitor. But there was something that nagged away at me, although I figured it had to be foolishness because it wouldn't make sense. And that was that Frederick C. Small wanted to kill me because I was the traitor.

Course, maybe my vision wasn't like Aunt Hanna's.

Maybe it was something else.

IT TOOK ME ABOUT FOUR MORE DAYS TO GET TO MASSANUTTEN, EVEN though I was practically right on it, probably because of the ague. I did have the chills and hot spells. Now, ordinarily Mother would've steeped some hazel-brush and blackberry roots into a tea, but I didn't even have an oyster can like most of the soldiers to brew up coffee or anything, and I wasn't good at picking roots, even if I knew where they'd be. All I had left was a bit of pork and hard-tack biscuit, which I ate as slow as I could, but it wasn't easy going down, especially that hardtack without anything to drink, and my mouth was as dry as dust. I should've taken Eurastus's canteen, but I didn't. I was drinking from streams, but they were muddy, and so I complicated the ague with probably dysentery. I could've avoided that if I'd've listened to Sergeant Dunean because he told me that wearing flannel around my stomach would prevent the shits. But I didn't have time to get any; I was lucky enough to escape from the church and Eurastus.

So I guess I laid out in a field somewhere for a while—I can't remember—until I started having visions again; and it was Jimmadasin who came up to me and told me to get up. He said he knew where to find clean water, and that was the only thing that would cure me, 'specially since I didn't have any flannel or was likely to get any. I dreamed that I followed him, and I remember him talk-ing to me like it was real, which probably means it was a true vision that had come to pass, like Aunt Hanna said, except there was none of that Lorday, Lor-day singin', spring of all my joy, hallelujah stuff.

Jimmadasin asked, "Why you dress uped like dat, you ain't in da army."

Jimmadasin was right. In my vision I was wearing a 'Federate uniform like I was an officer: a gray dress coat with two rows of brass buttons and a cap with stripes of gold lace. I even had a saber, which didn't seem to get in the way when I was walking, although it was long; and it had a gold tassel knotted on the pom-mel. I explained that I couldn't talk, and we both laughed at that because, of course, I was talking now. So I explained that all this was from a book called *Private Newton's War in the Air*, which had once belonged to Private Eurastus, who had tried to kill me, and that I was a character in the book, only the book was wrong about me being a Yank because I was Southern true, and Jimmadasin could see that from my uniform. Then Jimmadasin asked me if I were dead too, and I thought no, but then again maybe I was; but he figured I wasn't or he wouldn't have to be here as part of my vision to help me out. I wondered if dead people had visions, and he said, "Nah, you dead you dead, an' den when you good an' dead, you get into other people's visions. Only na'chal."

I guess it was a waking vision because old Jimmadasin kept pushing at me to keep going, and every time I'd feel so weak I had to lay down, he'd whistle and talk to himself for a while, and then start picking at me to get up "an' walk in da sunshine," and I remember yelling at him and telling him to leave me be, that I needed to sleep and my bowels had sickened, and if he'd just let me alone I could die and get it over with, and then I'd be just like him, and we could go off and wander around and do whatever it was spirits did with themselves. But he wasn't having any of that, and he kept pushing and prodding me along and telling me about how everything was going to be wonderful in Massah's Nuddem. After a while I could even hear people who weren't spirits whispering to me. Mammy Jack told me I was having a vision and that I should be both proud and humble before the Lord; and Uncle Isaac, who was married to Mammy Jack, kept saying, "Don' fuck wid me" in that low, scratchy voice of his. I remember shivering and shaking and being sick and vomiting and being hungry and sleepy and my bowels ached like Private Eurastus was squeezing me and sticking himself into my behind, and I remember seeing the spirit dog following us, probably because we were all dead. But everything was also happening ever so slowly, like cold water getting up to a boil, yet all the while I was walking, walking because Jimmadasin wouldn't let me be, and he'd push me to walk and walk and walk, and he'd look into my thoughts and laugh at them, and make me walk another step, and another step, and then he'd laugh in that high voice of his until we finally got right into the Massanutten Mountain, which opened right up like the biggest mouth you could ever imagine and swallowed me and Jimmadasin and Uncle Isaac and Mammy Jack and the spirit dog that was following us.

Just swallowed us into stone-cold darkness.

JIMMADASIN RISES UP FROM
THE ĐEAD

Done caught de rogue!
Ha! Ha! Ha!
Done caught de rogue!
Ha! Ha! Ha!

RING GAME
SONG

I woke up with a jolt, like I had fallen off my bed in the Big
House, and for some reason I was breathing hard like I had been running. I had
blisters all over me, but my fever was gone. The first thing I did, though, even
as I was looking around to see where I was, was to get hold of Eurastus's Colt
.44 revolver. I was still breathing hard, though I don't know why, but I was
scared anyway, and I had it in my head that before I did anything else I was going
to make sure I was protected.

I felt better as soon as I had that piece in my hand.

It was a six-shot, single-action, percussion revolver, but I probably
already told you that. I checked, and, of course, it wasn't loaded, so I loaded it.
I suppose any cavalry officer would have laughed and laughed watching me trying to load that pistol, but I got it done. I half cocked it, tore off the paper of a

cartridge with my teeth—and that tasted bitter, a little like dirt, but I'd done it once before and knew what it would taste like—and dumped the powder into the chamber, then tore off the paper from a ball, put that into the chamber and pressed it hard with my thumb, then turned the cylinder, rammed the ball with the pistol lever, and I did that six times; and I wasn't done even yet because I had to cap the cones before I could let the hammer down real gentle onto the safety notch. And then I just sat there, with my back against cold rock, and aimed that pistol toward the light. I must've been pretty weak because that pistol felt heavy, and after a minute, or maybe it was a few seconds only, I had to let it down. But I could've held it up there long enough to fire a few shots into anybody who wanted to come in here and kill me.

It was daytime, and it looked bright, like maybe it was noon.

I was in a cave and looking out.

It wasn't a deep cave with icicles and caverns where you could get lost and die; it was just a sort of a hole naturally dug out of the rise next to the stream. That stream was almost a river, and I could see the water washing over two gray rocks that stood up together like a couple holding hands, and the water sparkled and threw real fast sparkles of light through the cave; and I could hear the water gurgling away, and now I remember, I remember that just listening to that water was like listening to voices, and if I held my breath and listened right now I could hear voices, only I couldn't make them out very good. But I remember hearing Jimmadasin and Poppa and Mother and Aunt Hanna, only she was more Mammy Jack than Aunt Hanna, like she was in the guise of the Lord or something; and I realized that the spirits had led me here and kept me alive, even the spirit dog; and just then, but only for a second, I realized that everybody was dead, and I wanted Poppa and my mother, but if I thought about them, I'd see them back at the house before it burned, and I couldn't stand to do that, so I turned my thoughts away from them and figured that even if I was dead and a spirit too, I'd have to attend to my business.

First I looked around, just to make sure that there wasn't something in the cave that could surprise me, like when I touched the maggots in the soldier's head or something. The cave had long cracks in it, like mud that had dried, and it went back only about five or six feet. Someone had been here before me, though, because there was burnt wood from an old fire near the front edge of the cave. Close enough to the front so the smoke wouldn't choke you, but far enough in so the fire wouldn't be seen so easily. But I figured it'd be seen if someone was looking, but you'd have to be right down here and know what to be looking for. Jimmadasin knew what he was doing when he led me out here; and I remember him pushing and cajoling me along like he was a real person and not a spirit, although I also know that I'd probably just been feverish and out of my head, and that's why I heard words coming from the stream. It was sort of like seeing shapes in the clouds that seem like real things and places even though you know they're just clouds. Course, sometimes I believed the spirits were real and sometimes I didn't. I suppose I mostly believed they were real at night, and when there were dead people around.

I got up then but found I was too dizzy to stand. Still, I had business to take care of, which was protecting myself, and so I crawled to the lip of the cave and leaned against the cool stone and looked out to check that I was safe . . . and alone. This could probably be the most dangerous place in the world, even though it was quiet and peaceful. I looked out and saw hills that looked quite steep, but mostly everything was woods: great big hemlocks and oaks and brush and leaves swirling around like devils; and the ground was brown and looked like it was moving because of the leaves, like they were a comforter that was being shook to get flat on the bed. I felt the sun on my face, and for that second it was the most delicious thing I ever felt, and I just wanted to sit there and feel that sun heating up my face like I was coming back to life; but nevertheless, I forced myself to keep a sharp eye, and when I was finally contented that I was alone, I crawled back to where I'd been and thoroughly checked my gear. I should tell you that even though that sun felt good, it was a cold day . . . just the direct light of the sun felt good on my face. As soon as I was out of its light, I started shivering again.

Anyway, I still had my short coat, which was filthy and stiff from mud, and Private Eurastus's stinking blanket and his haversack and my pistol, of course. I dumped the haversack and counted twenty-two dollars in greenback cash; a brass button that must've stayed in there when I shook everything out after I killed Eurastus; a box of matches; my book, which I told myself I'd better not read until I had everything under control; a handful of paper-wrapped cartridges and a tin of caps for the Colt; a small pocket knife with a cracked pearl handle; a piece of pork not even the size of my thumb; and two hardtack crackers that were infested with a few weevils, or maybe they were maggots. But I wasn't going to think about that. I brushed away the webs and set the hardtack biscuits down beside the pork and the rest of the stuff. I figured that I could build a fire and wave the hardtack over it . . . that should kill them. I thought that maybe I just wouldn't eat the hardtack, but that and the pork was all the food I had. And the pork was rancid, but I could probably eat it anyway, even though it was crusted over black as tar. If I had a frying pan, I could soak the biscuits in water from the stream and fry them up in the pork fat. That's how the soldiers did it, and they called it skillygalee. Jimmadasin told me about that. But I didn't have a frying pan. I thought that if I'd had an ax and a few nails, I could make my own gums and catch rabbits. Course, I still didn't have a frying pan, but I figured I could hang them over the fire. But I didn't have an ax, so time would have to come soon when I'd chance making myself visible and shoot something for my supper. Maybe a possum or a wild pigeon or a dove, or rabbit, after all.

But not today. I was too weak to do anything but make do.

About all I could manage was to crawl out of the cave—as I said, it really wasn't a cave, more like an opening is all—and get some firewood.

I wondered how far I was from General Jackson's troops, and how far I was from farms and human habitation and stuff; but I was too weak and tired to investigate. I made my fire. Then I burned out as many of the weevils as I could, but I almost burnt one of the biscuits when I dropped it. I cut up the pork into two pieces—they were a little yellowish on the inside—and held them over the fire with a forked stick I'd found, and the fat jumped and sizzled in the flames, and just smelling that pork burning made me homesick and terribly hungry. I ate the pork and one cracker. Even if that pork was a little off, it still tasted good to me. None of it filled me up, but I figured it was smart to save the other cracker.

So I huddled there by the fire and smelled the pork fat even after it was all gone, and I slept a little and looked at the cover of *Private Newton's War in the Air*, but I wasn't strong enough to read it. I dreamed some more about it, and woke up feeling a little sick, and then I slept some more, and then it was dark, and I felt all right; and I wrapped myself up as best I could in Eurastus's blanket because I didn't want to keep a fire going at night. Too dangerous. I leaned my head close to where I'd made the fire, so I'd smell the char rather than the blanket.

But I smelled something else during the night, and, of course, I thought I'd been dreaming or something because I smelled onions. Raw onions. I had a whiff, and then I woke up, and I was holding that Colt so tight it's a wonder I didn't send off a round and wake up the world. Everything looked milky outside the cave, and it was like I was looking out from a tunnel. Every once in a while the trees and branches would shake and shiver in the wind like they were skeletons dancing and convulsing everywhere they stood. But the gurgly, whispering stream noises were comforting, and even though I kept sniffing, I couldn't smell the onions anymore.

More than anything, I wished I was home; but I didn't think about that.

I watched for the spirit dog because I remember hearing howling, but, to tell you the truth, I couldn't remember if I heard the howling or barking or whatever it was when I was walking around with the spirits or whether I had dreamed it while I was here in the cave recovering from the fever. But it sounded like bloodhounds. I know their bark because I've seen the paddyrollers use them to smell out and catch niggers.

Just thinking about that seemed to start my fever back up.

But everything was quiet . . . and stayed quiet; and the spirit dog wasn't anywhere to be seen; and neither was Jimmadasin or any other spirits. So I guessed I was done with spirits now that I was getting my strength back and my fever was gone.

But I should have paid attention to that onion smell. . . .

THIS IS THE PART THAT I WAS HESITATING TO WRITE ABOUT, EVEN though I already told you I'd probably killed Private Eurastus and saw the spirit dog and Jimmadasin, so you probably think I'm crazy, anyway. But I figure if I'm going to tell the story, I might as well just tell all of it, even if it's embarrassing and humiliating.

Anyway, I spent the next day just laying in the cave and being quiet and listening to the stream and getting my strength back. It was sunny and warmer still, so I moved right out to the lip of the cave and let the sun cure me. I ate the last of my stores, which was that one hardtack biscuit, and I crawled down to the stream afterward and drank probably half of it; it was cold and fresh and delicious, and it made me think of fresh strawberries and blueberries and biting into green apples. I stuck my whole head in, letting the cleanness enter me. I washed up as best I could, then sat for a while on the bank right next to the water while the sun dried me off . . . and I started to worry a bit because I suddenly realized that I was probably going to live, that I wasn't a spirit, that it was daylight, that tomorrow would be coming right after tonight, and I was already hungry again. I looked around—but I wasn't walking around much yet because I was still all weak and light-headed—and although there were probably a thousand roots and bugs or something I could eat, I couldn't see anything; and I remember Mother telling me not to eat anything, no matter how good it looked, unless I knew exactly what it was, or it'd most likely kill me. I probably wouldn't've cared much about that last night or the night before, but I suddenly felt like I was part of the sun and the heat baking down on me. I know this probably doesn't make much sense, but even though everybody had died, and it was my fault I didn't save Poppa and Mother and maybe Jimmadasin too, I didn't care; I wanted to live and feel the sun and eat so many pies and molasses cakes and ham steaks and drink so much milk and cider that I would explode; and it would be like the dream I remembered about Hog Day, except instead of flowers splashing all over the place, there would be sunlight, just like it was on the stream, like it was shiny pieces of gold that you could hold and roll in your hands. But I got jolted out of those thoughts when I remembered that one of the hogs to get slaughtered was Mother and—and I just stopped thinking about all of that, but still, as I lay out there in the warmth and the fever had left me and I was feeling my strength return even though I didn't have enough food and didn't know where I was going to get any more, I felt suddenly hot and flushed and, truth to tell, my cock just all of a sudden got so stiff that it was hurting me. And my head was pounding, and I could feel my throat get all tight, and then, suddenly, I didn't much care about anything except relieving myself. I just couldn't help it, even though I knew, right as soon as I grabbed hold of myself and started polluting myself, that I was sinning, that this was probably just about the worst sin anyone could do, with the exception probably of murder; but, then, I've already done that, so it didn't make much difference.

But I did stop myself, at least long enough to get back to the cave where I thought I could sin in the dark (although you really couldn't say it was dark in the cave, maybe a little shadowy is all), but I knew that God was watchin', or maybe not. I always figured that there was so much for Him to watch that He'd have to miss some of the small stuff like this. He probably was watching a battle somewhere, where everybody was getting wounded and killed, and He was probably more interested in that than watching me pollute myself here on Massanutten Mountain. Then again, maybe this was a real bad place for sinning because God gave Moses the commandments up on a mountain, so maybe all mountains were sacred to him. Didn't matter, I guess, even though I tried to leave myself alone. I sat as far back in the cave as I could get and looked out into the light. I didn't pray or anything like that. I just told myself I could be strong, that the ague had just left me and I could weaken myself and even die if I continued touching myself, and I told myself that even if God wasn't seeing me, the spirit dog or Jimmadasin or Poppa's spirit probably was.

It still didn't matter because I was rubbing myself like I was infected with poison ivy, and like I said my head was pounding, and it felt like everything was pounding along with it, and I wasn't even thinking about any particular girl or anything; I wasn't thinking about seeing Katie Cartmell's tits—or her behind, which she'd showed me once right in her dining room when her folks were out, but the servants saw her too, and they just smiled like she was showing off a new dress or something. Worst of all, even while I was playing with myself, I was remembering one of Poppa's sermons; and I could hear the words, like they were all pushed together into one terrible sound; and there was Poppa raising his arms like he was someone from the Bible standing right in front of me, and shouting, "Among the hapless inmates of the lunatic asylum, none is more incorrigible nor more incurable than the wretched victim of this odious vice." And he was going on, even as I felt myself getting hot and prickly around my groin, and in just an instant, just a second more, I was going to get relief. But Poppa just kept going on. "With the fragments of his shattered reason that he is still capable of gathering up from the sexual wreck, he craftily exercises in devising means and securing opportunities to elude the vigilance of his keepers and to indulge his despotic lust and—"

And it was just then that I saw the girl.

And smelled that onion smell.

And I was caught, right there with my self-abusing—and there was nothing nothing in the whole wide world that could be more humiliating—and my dick just shriveled up in my hand until I could hardly feel it, and I pushed it into my pants in a flash, without thinking; and at the same time, at the very same time, it occurred to me that I was surely in some sort of danger, and so I went for that .44 Colt, which was on top of Eurastus's haversack. She was about as close to the Colt as I was, and she jumped for it too; she probably figured I'd kill her if I got to it first because she'd caught me in the act of abusing myself; and who the hell knows, in the terrible state of lust or whatever it was that I was in, maybe I would've.

We wrestled each other, and I'll admit she was probably stronger than me; but that was because she was older than me—maybe sixteen or even older than that—and I was still weak as a kitten from the fever and the shits. Her hair was long and black and kinked, almost like a nigger's, but her face was white, though darker than mine, and looked . . . thin; and I couldn't've told you just then if she was pretty or not. She was wearing what looked like old rags because I noticed that her dress, which was dirty, was torn in all different places; and while we were wrestling I could smell the onions, and I smelled her sweat, which smelled wild, like an animal or something; and the Colt got pushed or kicked away from both of us while we were fighting to get it; and suddenly she stopped. She had my arms locked, and she was on top of me with her legs on either side, and she said, "Had 'nough yet?"

I kept fighting until she said, "Truce?" and I nodded. She got off of me—and I was relieved because my arms felt like they had when Private Eurastus had been holding on to me so tight—but she didn't go away. She was kneeling right beside me. I sat up and moved back a little; but she was still between me and the Colt, though I could see it, of course. It was clear over on the other side of the cave, close to the opening. I considered my chances of getting to that pistol but figured I'd bide my time and catch my breath and wait for the light-headed feeling to go away, and maybe by then she'd move out of my way so I could make my move.

"I been watchin' you," she said, "but everybody's left here. 'Cause of you, prob'ly." She stopped talking and just looked at me, as if she was waiting for me to say something to her, like tell her my name or something; and for maybe a second I forgot that I couldn't talk, and I wanted to ask her questions—like who was here, and why they left because of me—but though I could hear the words in my head, I couldn't . . . find them to say. It was like I'd think of the words and then before they could get out of my mouth, I'd lose them, so that I'd open my mouth and all that would come out usually would be "ha," which was just a breathing sound. That's what came out then.

She looked at me funny and said, "You goin' to tell me your name?"

Her eyes got narrow when she looked at me, like she was thinking of something serious, but all I could do was look right back at her, and finally I shook my head and sort of shrugged and looked down for a second at the ground. I did that without thinking and realized it was probably dangerous to look away from her even for a flash. I was still thinking about getting that Colt pistol, but I knew better than to look around at it because that would tip her off.

"Don' worry 'bout your gun," she said. "It ain' goin' to move." She waited for me to say something, I guess, because she was quiet for a while. Then she said, "S'all right, you can talk to me. I know how long you been here and everything. I won' hurt you, you're safe with me. Look!" And she raised her hands to show me she didn't have anything in them.

I knew she was making fun of me, and so I didn't shake my head or nod or anything; but she kept looking at me and smiling—not a big smile, but the kind that was devilish and made you feel like a fool; and I could see that two of her front teeth were chipped. Probably someone had hit her.

"Hey, did you hear what I just said?"

I nodded at that, which seemed to make her happy, and she moved closer to me, looking at me as if she were studying a bug. Her knees were right up against mine. My face suddenly felt hot again, but I was afraid to touch it, lest it make me appear weak. But I knew it was still the humiliation of getting caught, which wasn't going away, and my heart was still beating hard, but that was probably because it got weak from the fever. I couldn't help but see that she had a mole on her cheek, and it looked sore; and her eyes were brown. I could see that her face was all streaked with charcoal, probably because we'd been wrestling near the fire ashes. I had it on me too. She looked like some sort of combination white girl and nigger and Indian.

"Can't you talk?"

I shook my head and tried not to look at her breasts.

"So you're just dumb is all," she said. "Like somebody cut off your tongue or somethin', huh?" I could hear the mocking in her voice.

I nodded anyway.

"'Cer'nly didn' cut your pecker off, huh?"

She was still kneeling over me and smiling like she didn't have a care or a fear in the world, and the way she was holding herself, I couldn't help but see into her dress a little and see that she had big breasts; and like I said I tried not to look at them, but it was obvious she was showing them to me, big as life. None of that fooled me because I figured she probably had a mind to rob me, and she wasn't going to catch me out again.

I just had to get to my pistol. Then I could pick up my belongings and get out of here.

She touched my leg and shook it, like she was trying to get my attention, and said, "Yeah, there was soldiers or somebody roamin' around, but they're gone now. The niggers left at the first bark of the dogs—dogs spook 'em worse 'n anything." Although I tried not to, I looked at her breasts again. I just couldn't imagine about tits. It was somehow like they were such perfect things that you could hardly think about them. I figured that just touching them would almost be like coming. I remember how I used to think about Lorena Keller's tits all day in Poppa's schoolhouse, and how I would look across the room at her and try to imagine what they would look like under her dress; but Poppa would always catch me thinking polluted thoughts and slap me for daydreaming.

But right now, even with being able to see this girl's breasts, I was still thinking about how to get away from here.

"They was after you, huh?" she said. "You run away from your folks, I'll bet. Or else you're probably a crim'nal, maybe a deserter from the army. They're all over hereabouts. But I don't think so. You're too young for that. Shit, you ain't much more than a baby." Then she smiled at me again, but differently, sort of like she was in her own room and about to go to sleep and have sweet dreams, and said, "You're safe here now 'til the niggers get back. Course, they might walk right in here while we're talkin'. But I know the marster, and he's smart. He'll prob'ly hide out for a couple've days." She looked at me and waited, like she was expecting me to answer or suddenly start laughing or something. "You don' get it, do you?" she said. "The marster's a nigger. He always used to tell me not to wriggle my ass 'til I was sure it was safe . . . and then wait some more for good measure." She laughed at that and said, "Boy, but he didn't know what kind of advice he was givin' me." She just went quiet, like she was suddenly embarrassed; I had the feeling, though, that she had some affection for the nigger marster, whoever he was. Then she leaned away from me a little, like she was afraid of what I was going to do, and said, "So now tell me, you always play with yourself right in the open for everybody to see? I saw what you were doin' by the creek. I guess you came in here to finish up, huh?"

That caught me by surprise, and I could feel my face burning; and she laughed like she had caught me doing it all over again. I was going to go for that Colt now, but she must've read my mind or something because she grabbed my arm to hold me there. She was strong, but I felt the humiliation burning on my face like the fever; and suddenly it didn't matter if she was stronger than me, I was going to get away from her no matter what. I surprised her by knocking her off balance with my shoulder, but she grabbed me before I could get to my feet.

And then we were wrestling again.

And then we weren't.

I don't know how it happened, but we got locked together so that neither one of us could get out of it, and I was smelling her sweat all mixed up with the onion smell, and then we were rubbing up against each other, and then we were kissing, and my hands were under her dress, and I was feeling her up, and she was doing the same to me; and I figured nothing mattered anyway because Mother and Poppa were dead and for all I knew I was a spirit just like Jimmadasin, and maybe this girl was too, although she felt strong and soft, and then she was pulling at my pants, and her dress was open; and as soon as she got hold of me and started pulling so smoothly, I felt my groin become warm and I felt embarrassed and wanted her to stop, but it was too late because I could feel myself coming all over her hand and myself, and then we were just laying there together. She didn't say anything about what happened. I'd never done anything to a girl. I just knew what was supposed to happen, but after a while, she took my hand and put it between her legs and showed me how to press a certain place, which was like a knob, and I just kept squeezing my hand on it until she was shivering like she had the fever, and she'd keep looking over at me—not smiling or nodding or anything, just watching me with this real gentle look on her face, like she was looking at a picture, or like my mother used to look at me sometimes, but her whole body seemed to be shaking—and then I couldn't help myself; and I started getting excited and stiff all over again, and I wondered what I should do next, whether I should try to get on top of her or let her show me what she wanted when she was ready—if she was going to be ready, because it felt strange just watching each other like we were while I rubbed her. It occurred to me that girls do the same thing I had been doing, and I felt better about even getting caught because it probably wasn't as bad a sin as I'd thought. Poppa had talked it up worse than it was, probably; and I felt humiliated that I could even think it, but I thought just then that Mother probably used to rub herself like I was doing to this girl; and while I was doing it and looking right back at her and feeling comfortable and maybe safe or something like that, I was also hearing all the noises of the stream and the wind, and everything seemed to be louder and closer, and she started shivering even harder and moaning and saying "oh, oh," and my hand was hurting from rubbing her, but it wouldn't be fair to her to stop because she was breathing hard and making terrible but beautiful faces, and then she clenched her hand and pressed her face against my neck like she was nuzzling me—or was going to bite me—and she went into convulsions, maybe two, and I held her tight like she was going to be sick, and then it was all over, and we just laid there together. I was still excited, though, and she saw that, but all it took was for her to touch me and rub her fingers along my cock again, and I came, not even getting near to doing it the right way. But maybe that would happen later, and I didn't care. We were half naked. My pants were down around my knees, and she still had her dress on around her stomach, and I remember playing with her breasts, exploring them. I had never been able to touch a girl like this and take my time, and then I guess I just fell asleep.

When I woke up she was just sitting beside me and watching me.

She was all dressed, although I could still see into her dress a little, not that

I really cared to just now; it was sort of like being all calm, although I was still thinking about how it would feel to put my cock inside her, what it would feel like. That sounds bad, I know, but I liked being close to her, even with the onion smell that hung on her—but it was mostly on her feet—and although I was still maybe a little worried that she would still try to rob me and maybe kill me, I felt quiet and gentle with her.

Then I noticed that the Colt wasn't near the front end of the cave where it was kicked; and I guess I must've jumped up or something because she said, "Here, I ain't goin' to take your gun," and she gave me the Colt, which was right on top of Eurastus's haversack; she didn't seem at all worried that I might just shoot her dead. "Though it's mine by right. I earned it. You think I just fuck aroun' with people for nothin'?"

I held on to the gun and just watched her. She was standing right beside me, and I guess I sniffed at her without even thinking about it. But the onion smell was probably as much on me now as it was on her.

"You really *can't* talk." She said that like she was astonished and finally believed me.

I put the pistol back on top of Eurastus's haversack and got dressed.

"Well, if you can't tell me your name, I'll just have to make one up for you. How's that?"

I thought about using a piece of charred wood from the fire and writing "Mundy" on the ground for her. She didn't talk like a nigger, but that didn't mean she could read. But I just couldn't get up the gumption to try to write or anything like that for her. It was like when I forgot how to talk, I changed from being Mundy to being someone else. Even though people might be able to see me, like this girl, I was still invisible. It just wasn't complete. She'd be able to see something about me, maybe, but not much.

I wondered about her, though: where she came from, and what she was, whether she had run away from her family, or, maybe, she was half and half and ran away from her master to live out here free. Maybe that's what she was getting at with all that talk about her "marster." I looked at her close, and as I told you, her skin wasn't much darker than mine. She had freckles too, like me, which probably would burn bad in the first hot day of summer. (Mother always had to put salve on my face and arms, which burned worse than the sunburn.) Her hair, though, was kinked, like I said, but I've seen white girls with hair curly as a nigger's, so that didn't mean anything, either. (And I've seen niggers like Aunt

Hanna who had more freckles than God.) From what Jimmadasin and Uncle
Isaac told me, whites were always making babies with niggers, so it didn't matter if she was colored or white anyway. I wasn't worried that I'd given her a baby
because all we did was touch each other. I didn't think anything could happen
that way, although there were a lot of things nobody talked about. So maybe I
could've. . . .

"Maybe I'll call you Dan'l like in the Bible, 'cause he was in a cave too."
Then she started laughing and walking around me like she was dancing, and she
put her bare foot in my face. When I pulled my head away from the onion smell,
she laughed even harder. "So that's what you was sniffin'. Onion. Ain' that
right?"

I nodded, and she started laughing again.

When she was done, she said, "Maybe I'll call you Onions. You *got* to be a
city boy. From Richmond prob'ly, or like that. Must be, 'cause you don' know
nothin' about the country or you'd of knowed that onions keeps away dogs—
makes 'em lose the scent, just like they can't scent you over the creek here. And
if you would've knowed anything, you wouldn't be burnin' your fire with that
wood you used, you'd of used oak bark 'cause it don't give off much smoke. You
prob'ly brought the dogs by lightin' your fires all over the place. It's a wonder
you didn't get caught." She shrugged and said, "Maybe it wasn't you anyway.
You hungry? I'm starvin'."

I could feel my stomach roll when I heard those words.

"Well anyway, Dan'l Onions, you wait here and I'll be back," she continued, looking very pleased with herself for inventing those names for me. Then
she kissed me and stepped out of the cave; but even though we'd done things
together I hadn't ever done with anyone else, I still wasn't going to allow her to
go and maybe bring back those niggers or whoever she was talking about before
to rob me, although she didn't try to get at the Colt or anything. I wouldn't trust
her any more than I would the spirit dog, although I wanted to.

So I followed her out the few steps down to the stream, and she stopped
and said, "No, Onions. You wait back at the cave." It was as though she was talking to a child . . . or a dog. Like she thought that once she gave me a name it would
give her some sort of power over me. But it didn't.

"If anybody's at the camp, they'll sooner shoot your ass off than look at
you 'cause you could tell the paddyrollers 'bout them, and they won't allow
that." She laughed at herself. "Course, you couldn't tell *nobody* about them,

anyway, but they don' know that. So just calm yourself and wait for me in the cave. Worse that'll happen if the marster's back early is I won't be able to come back for a while. Whatever, you just stay here."

But I just followed along anyway.

"Didn' you hear me?" she said. "If you're goin' to be stupid, you can starve your dumb ass off. I ain't takin' the chance that the marster's come back, 'cause if he's back and catches me with you, he's goin' to beat my ass and put me in the ground. And prob'ly kill you, to boot. It's dangerous enough that I'm goin' there to steal food for you. So you can trust me or eat some of those rocks you're standin' on. Well . . . ?"

I nodded, and since she kept looking at me to do something, I turned and went back to the cave.

And then I followed along after her.

After all, I had the Colt.

She walked along the stream until the bank got high, and then she climbed up to higher ground. I waited a good bit, then followed. Came to some thick woods, and then after a while came back to the stream again, or maybe it was another one. The stream formed a cascade here with little waterfalls gurgling and foaming in their own wriggly path inside of the stream itself. You could easily walk across the rocks, and on the other side was good loamy ground, covered with leaves, and even with the stream spraying here and there, it smelled . . . dry. Crisp, like nothing was rotting. Like there were no bodies perfuming the air. And there was the Christmas smell of pine.

I followed her along the stream, which got wider. The water was crashing and breaking over all the rocks and stones, and I imagined that the stream was getting strong and would turn into a river down a few miles. She walked across the stream on the rocks and stood on the other side of the bank. She looked around, and I stayed hidden. Just because I didn't know about onions didn't mean I was from the city. I could probably hunt and keep out of sight better than she could. Probably. Anyway, when I figured it was safe, I crossed the stream. The stones and rocks were slippery as hell, but when I got to the other side and climbed up the bank, I couldn't find her anywhere, but I looked all around, then just followed the stream, keeping it to my left, and after a while it turned into a waterfall. Mist hung over the falls, and the trees all around were thick and naked except for some brown leaves that managed to stay stuck to the branches over the winter. I made noises with every step because of the leaves. This place seemed to glow in the sunlight. I was on the edge of a clearing and I had a good view of the falls and everything. I rested against the thick trunk of a tree that had dead vines all over it.

And then I saw her.

She was coming right out of the ground near the waterfall. Like she was rising up from the grave or something.

I couldn't believe my eyes. But that wasn't the half of it. . . .

Something hit me hard from behind.

I imagined that maybe the tree had come alive, even though that seems crazy. But everything just exploded, and I guess all the stories I'd heard were true because I saw stars, or maybe flashes or sparks.

And when I woke up I saw Jimmadasin standing over me, big as life.

He was wearing the damnedest clothes, which probably proved he was a spirit. He had on a gray frock coat that was threadbare and a gentleman's hat that matched the coat, but it wasn't a top hat; it was soft and mashed in; and he was wearing tight blue trousers that had a green stripe, and they were torn out at the knees; and he had on a frilly high-collar shirt that was probably once white but was greasy-gray now, and though it was buttoned up to the top, he wasn't wearing a cravat. And he had shoes.

I wouldn't have thought spirits would need shoes, but then I remembered Jimmadasin walking with me when I had the ague and was having all my visions, and I figured that he'd probably need shoes, same as me. And it also made perfect sense that I was probably having another vision, which would also explain why I'd seen the girl rising up from the ground. That was just part of the vision. I looked around to see if the spirit dog was watching this, but he wasn't, and then I looked at myself quick to see if I was wearing the uniform from my last vision—the gray dress coat with two rows of brass buttons and a cap with stripes of gold lace. But I wasn't, and I didn't have a saber either, just the clothes I was wearing when I left home.

I tried talking to Jimmadasin, of course, because I remembered that I could talk in visions, just as Mammy Jack could travel around Heaven when the Ship of Zion would come for her; but when I tried to talk, all that came out was the same old "ha" sound like I was laughing or choking.

Jimmadasin just stood there in front of me. He was scowling terrible, and his face was wrinkled up and mean, like he'd suddenly become a king or Moses or something and had the wrath of God all loosed up in him.

And I knew he wasn't going to show *me* any mercy.

THE WALKIN' BOY

Oh, yes! Oh yes!
I conjured you,
I conjured you,
No cause in de worl',
No cause in de worl',
Give me yo' han' . . .

CONJURIN' SONG

*I*FIGURED THAT THERE WAS SOMETHING WRONG ABOUT JIMMADASIN AS soon as he opened his mouth. I remember how Jimmadasin talked, even when he was a spirit; and *this* Jimmadasin didn't talk like him. This spirit talked just like Poppa, like he was a preacher and had learned English from white people. But then I figured that maybe that's just the funny way God works. If He can make animals talk, He can surely make Jimmadasin's spirit talk like Jesus or Jefferson Davis or anybody else.

But this Jimmadasin also looked different.

His lips were pulled back more and he was missing a tooth right in the front, and he smelled like perfume instead of sweat. And his eyes seemed meaner and closer together. Now, maybe this wasn't Jimmadasin's spirit at all. I remembered how when he was alive Jimmadasin had told me to come here and then how his spirit had guided me here like one of Mammy Jack's seraphs of the Lord. Maybe this Jimmadasin was a demon meant to interrupt God's will. Or maybe . . . maybe he was just a nigger who talked like Poppa and looked like Jimmadasin.

That thought seemed funny to me then, maybe because I was scared seeing this spirit with his face hanging in front of me; more likely it was because I still wasn't in my right senses after being hit behind the head.

"Do we amuse you, son?" Jimmadasin's spirit asked. "Is that it, you little white maggot sumbitch shit?" He said that brightly, as if he were inviting me over to dinner, but before I could shake my head or anything, he slapped me hard in the face; and I saw blood behind my eyes, but no sparks or flashes, just red; and, of course, I knew right then that this couldn't be Jimmadasin 'cause the real Jimmadasin would never hit me like that. Not when he was alive or when he got to be a spirit. I fell backward and curled up, figuring this nigger minister spirit was just like Eurastus, only he could talk better.

"Come on now, son, you're not hurt. That wasn't nothing but a love slap," and the others standing around laughed at that. I should have told you about the niggers standing around him because I'm trying to be consecutive, which is what Uncle Randolph told me is the best way to write; but although I probably saw all those niggers who were with this spirit that looked like Jimmadasin, they didn't make any impression on me until they started laughing and humiliating me. That's what got me to uncurl and face the spirit. I moved away from it but didn't stand up, and when I moved, one of the niggers kicked me in the back. Or maybe it was one of the white kids; there was one standing right beside the spirit. There were two old women, maybe forty or sixty years old, who probably belonged to the spirit, and younger girls and teenage boys and older ones too; and they all wore rags of one kind or another. Some wore skins like Indians, or butternut, which even Mother called nigger cloth, and parts of soldiers' uniforms: frock coats, pants, like that, and one of the women was wearing a Union dress coat with brass shoulder scales and blue braid across the chest. It was torn, of course, and dirty, but pretty impressive nevertheless. She clucked at me the way Aunt Hanna used to when I was a baby and got into trouble, and she had wrinkles in her neck and a thin, sort of dried-up face like skinny old ladies sometimes have, but she certainly wasn't skinny; she would've made up about two Jimmadasins.

"Lucy told us how you were chasin' her to discredit her virginity and do her bodily harm," the spirit said. "But it makes you wonder how she come to know you can't talk. Course, I believe you *can* talk."

I glanced around, trying to figure if I could surprise them and make a run for it, and I looked around for Lucy—at least now I knew her name. She'd turned me right in to save her own ass, but, of course, that's what I expected. She wasn't anywhere to be seen. And there wasn't any way I was going to get past the spirit and his congregation. So I figured the safest course would be just to look down at the ground.

"And unless you talk, we're going to bury you alive. Now what do you have to say to that? Well . . . ?" The spirit waited a bit and then said, "Meantime, we'll find out for certain what you're up to. We'll find out if you're the enemy, and where you come from, and if you got to do with the Lord or with Satan."

Everybody around me made noise when he said that, like they were agreeing with him. "And if what Lucy says is true, and the walkin' boy agrees with all of it, then the Lord is going to make you weaken and sicken and pine away and die for all that, and I ain't going to have to slap you ever again for the truth, 'cause it will all be writ, right there where you're sitting, in the dirt and in the air, and there—" And he pushed his finger hard into my chest.

Everybody standing around me was quiet now, and they sat down on the ground, everybody watching, but nobody looked relaxed. In fact, they all looked scared; and you could have heard a pin drop when the spirit asked for a deck of cards and the walkin' boy, like everybody was holding their breaths lest *they* get into trouble. The woman wearing the Union coat with blue braid walked away and came right back with a pack of greasy red and white playing cards in one hand and a big green bottle with a string tied around it in the other. I got real nervous then because I saw something moving in the bottle. It was the biggest damn spider I'd ever seen. I wonder how they shoved it through the neck of the bottle. Anyway, she gave it to the spirit, who put the bottle down right in front of me, and I could see it was a crab spider, the kind you sometimes find in thistle blossoms in summer. Only I've never seen one even half that big. And even though it don't make sense, I've got a terrible fear of spiders.

"Now we can let the walkin' boy tell us about you," said the spirit, who was kneeling behind the bottle like it was sacred, and he shuffled the cards. It didn't take much to figure that the walkin' boy was in that bottle. "Or you can come right with us and the Lord and tell us the truth. Are you ready to talk now and make everything easy? I promise no harm will come 'pon you if you witness yourself before God and His followers here. You afraid of this spider here? You don't have to be if you're walking in the way of the Lord . . . if you're talking the truth." He looked hard at me, like he could look the words right out of my throat, and if I could've talked I would've, believe me.

But since I couldn't, I just watched the spirit.

If he was a spirit he should know I couldn't talk. Course, he probably did know and was just torturing me.

Jimmadasin never would have done that.

But then this wasn't Jimmadasin.

I thought about Mammy Jack and wished she was here because she'd know what to do, she'd have the Lord dismiss the spirit or something and get me away from here. And she'd show him a thing or two about shuffling cards. I kept as far back as I could from that crab spider, which was walking sideways up the glass. It almost filled up that bottle, which had raised letters on it: C.S.A. It would walk up the side of the bottle, then fall down. There was gravel or something on the bottom because the spider would get all distressed when the spirit gave the bottle a shake. I guessed he was getting the spider upset enough to poison me at the right time. I considered just making a run for it, but I knew it would be useless. Still, if he opened that bottle, I figured I might as well try; maybe they'd lose the spider in the grass or something. "Georgina, go get Lucy," the spirit said to the woman in the braid jacket. "She should be a witness."

The woman shook her head like she was saying no before she spoke. "She sick, an' Armarci's lookin' after her."

"I don't care," the spirit said. "She has to be here for this. She's play-acting anyway, most likely."

The woman shrugged and walked away, but she came back alone. She shook her head again, as if she always said no to everything. "Ain't nobody down dere, I looked all 'roun. I tol' you a pig slut don' change."

"Armarci will be back, and you can beat her ass when she does," the spirit said. Then he looked around and asked, "Who's seen Cow? I swear he was here."

But nobody had seen Cow.

"So they *all* run off together," the spirit said, looking angrily at me. "What'd you do to them? Or maybe you're all doin' it together. Well, we'll find out now." He looked around at the niggers in the circle and said, "You ready to go after them?" The boys nodded. The girls just looked down at the ground, as if everything was their fault and they weren't looking up lest they get blamed. Then he slapped the pack of cards down in front of me. "Cut those cards."

Everybody pushed in closer around me and the spirit. There was hardly room to move, and I wasn't comfortable with that spider right by my leg. I was terrified, but I wasn't going to let them know that.

I cut the cards like I was told.

Ten of diamonds.

The spirit picked up the card, then held it over the bottle and watched the bug. When it moved, he pulled the string so the bottle would point in the same direction as the bug. Then he made me cut the deck again: jack of clubs; and he kept shuffling while I kept cutting, and each time he'd hold the card over the bottle and watch the bug and pull the string to spin the bottle; and when the spider wasn't moving around enough, the spirit would shake the bottle hard and you could hear the gravel—or whatever it was inside there with the spider—hitting the inside of the glass, and that would make the walkin' boy wake up and move quick.

Everybody just watched, and it was as if we were all in a certain rhythm, like everything was this certain rhythm—Mother and Poppa dying, Eurastus talking baby talk and putting his thing into me, Doctor Zearing drilling into the head of the soldier who didn't have a face, the farm burning, the spirit dog appearing and disappearing, me cutting the cards, the spirit shuffling the cards, then spinning the bottle; and it was like everyone was breathing together, and the sun came out from behind the clouds, and I could feel the warmth of the sun on my face, shuffle, cut, spin, and my head was aching, pounding in the same breathing rhythm of shuffle, cut, spin, and then the spirit suddenly grabbed my hands and held them so tight I thought my fingers were going to break, and he closed his eyes yet his face was right in front of me as if he was still looking at me from behind those closed lids; and I felt something, I don't know what, but something went through me like happens sometimes when I touch metal, like sparks; and even though this Jimmadasin was made out of flesh—I was surely feeling his grasp—I was sure he was a spirit after that.

Probably a demon.

Or something like the spirit dog.

Then he opened his eyes, and I knew I was in trouble, that whatever he'd seen behind his eyes when he was looking at that bug or at me or at whatever he was looking at . . . was bad; so I took my shot and made a run for it, but I didn't even get out of the circle. Two of the niggers held me down. One was taller than Jimmadasin and the other one was skinny and had red hair, and he was hurting me worse than the tall one. And while they were holding me down, the spirit said, "You all saw where the walkin' boy walked, and you can see right there where the bottle points." Everyone agreed and made a lot of noise, and it sounded like they were in church saying "Amen!" and "Hallelujah!" after everything the minister said. "The walkin' boy gwine lead us right to the runagate apostates. See where the bottle points? That's where they ran, that's where they're hiding! That's where we'll find the whoremaster and his whores." Everybody hosanna'd, and they were all standing up and excited now. Then the spirit told the boys who were holding me down to hurry up and put me away, so they could all search and find Lucy . . . and find Armarci and Cow, whoever they were.

I figured they were going to murder me right then and there, but instead they dragged me away.

AND DROPPED ME DOWN A HOLE IN THE GROUND.

It wasn't the same hole I'd seen Lucy rising out of like a corpse or a seraph; this one was down past the waterfall, which I could hear booming like far-away thunder. One minute I was looking at the ground and over at the stream, which was sparkling in the sun and frothing around rocks and sounding bigger than it was, and then one of the niggers let me go so he could pick up a pile of leaves and dirt and twigs that were laying on top of something; and next thing I knew both of them were throwing me down, and I grabbed at the sides of the hole, which was dirt of course, and caught the rail and rungs of a ladder and broke my fall before I landed at the bottom, which probably wasn't as far down as I'd expected; but it was far enough so I couldn't get myself out. They pulled up the ladder, pulling it away from me, and then everything went dark when they covered up the pit, and although I could see a glimmer of light up at the top, that was all. It was dark, and I smelled damp clay like you'd smell when someone was getting buried, and I was crying and thinking, O God, O God, I'm buried alive, and I tried to call out to Mother and Poppa and even Jimmadasin to save me, but all I could hear was a shuffling noise above, probably the wind, and my own "ha," like I was the Devil himself who was laughing at me. Then, I don't know . . . I might have gotten dizzy and dropped dead for a while like I did when I got hit on the back of the head, but the next thing I remember was being able to see a little, even though most everything was shadows, except for ghost-light from above, like I was in the woods at dusk, except that's too good a thing to compare this place with. I was surely in the grave, but if this was a grave it was certainly fixed up. I was in a room that looked like around ten foot square. There was no bed, just a mattress stuffed with what looked like old dresses and stuff; it was damp and smelled bad. Only other thing was a sawed-off block that could serve as a chair; and there was a place where a fire had been laid. There was a smoke hole in the wall, and I started digging, thinking that maybe that would be a way out. But my hands hurt—they were full of slivers from sliding down the ladder—and I got tired before I got far enough to even figure out if I could escape that way. I guess it was from not eating, but I felt sick, like the ague had come upon me again; and so I waited it out, waited for spirits to maybe come and tell me how I could get myself out of this mess, and I sat there shivering in the cold and damp and dark. I heard something scurrying around, figured it was a rat, and jumped to my feet; and then the noise stopped, and I knew that there had to be another way out of here. I felt around, looked as hard as I could, but it was hard to see. A plank covered the top of the hole, where they had thrown me in, and it was only around the edges of that plank, which itself was probably cov-ered with dirt and leaves and garbage of sorts, that a little light could come through. But I felt around anyway, then gave up and sat down on the block until I got sleepy and almost fell off it. Just after that, I heard the spirits, or what I thought were the spirits. I guess I have to thank Mammy Jack because I fig-ure that what happened next was because of my vision, and she told me about visions and showed me how to have them. I guess I also have to thank Jimmadasin—not the spirit that had me thrown in here but the *real* Jimmadasin, the one who told me about Massanutten Mountain, and showed me how to escape to it. I was thinking a lot about the spirit that looked like Jimmadasin, and in my vision I imagined that it wasn't a spirit at all.

If he was a spirit, he wouldn't have needed a spider in a bottle to tell him things.

He would have known everything all along.

Of course, I wasn't sure about any of that; and I figured I'd just ask the real Jimmadasin once I started having my vision. I could feel it coming over me. I could feel it through my shivering and the heat I was feeling all over my face, and all the while I was thinking about how I wanted something to eat, although the longer I went, the easier it got not to eat. I could imagine that after a while you wouldn't be hungry at all, and you could just slip out from being a person right into being a spirit. I don't think it would have taken anything to do that, and I considered it, but, as I'll tell you, it didn't work out that way. So anyway, I was sitting on the block, and I remember exactly what I was thinking when I went into my vision and got saved. I was thinking about being hungry, and I was thinking about Mother and Poppa, and I realized that when I was feeling bad about them, when I heard that thunder sound in my head like I was about to cry, the bad feeling was in my stomach, and it was sort of the same as being hungry. I figured that grief was just another way of being hungry; and I imagined that I was looking up and up and up like you could only do in visions, and I could see the steam balloon hanging right up there, and I could see its ropes and rods and huge globes all lit up, and the balloon was huge, covering the entire sky, which was probably Heaven, and I was climbing up the rope ladder again, and I was wearing my vision uniform—my dress coat with the brass buttons, and my saber was hanging from my belt and weighing me down—and there wasn't any wind, just that big shadow over me, and I could see Frederick C. Small hanging over the carved wooden basket, and it was me. He was wearing the same uniform I was and calling down to me ever so soft, like he was the wind calling and whispering and blowing past the rods and ropes and globes. . . . "Onions? Onions? Dan'l Onions, are you dead or what?"

But the voice wasn't calling me from above.

It was behind me.

Lucy.

She'd appeared like a spirit, and then it seemed like I was floating, floating right up to Heaven, floating right up the ladder to the basket of the steam balloon; only after a second, I guess, did I realize that somebody had picked me up; and I was being pushed and prodded into the earth through a tunnel that came out on the side of the hill over the stream, which was probably the proper entrance; but I hadn't thought to search around for another entrance on the floor of the tomb, or whatever it was.

And then like an explosion there was light all around me.

Surely I had just come into Heaven. . . .

I DON'T REMEMBER MUCH ABOUT HOW WE GOT AWAY.

I was going in and out of consciousness, seeing flickers of light against the darkness like fireflies on a hot August night; and I imagined that each flicker was a second a minute an hour a day; and all the days were careening forward, turning into weeks and months and years, until so many would go by before I woke up that I'd have no hope of ever getting back.

But then all those flickers came together until all I could see was light.

I remember looking out of the cold, dark, whispery woods and seeing the mountains and hills and meadows and fields that were pocked up with snow and browned over and scattered with rocks and broken-up stone walls like on the field at Kernstown. The sun was shining so hard that it hurt my eyes just to look out, which was probably why, unless you were dead, you couldn't look upon Heaven because it was too bright and it would burn your eyes right out of your head. That's what it felt like to me.

Then the light faded.

We'd probably gone deeper into the woods. I remember tree trunks and roots that looked like huge, sleeping snakes. I remember fungus, and the smell of rot mixed with the dry smells of leaf and winter, and I remember how I yearned for Heaven, for the brightness that would melt out my eyes and would let me see Mother and Poppa and the house and Mammy Jack and her playing cards. All burning. But there in that heavenly fire nothing would be destroyed, and we'd all become fire and light ourselves, and nothing in the whole wide world or in Hell or anywhere could hurt us.

I guess I was sick again with the ague.

I looked for the spirit dog. I looked for Jimmadasin, but I don't know what I would've done if I saw him because I'd be afraid it was the marster Jimmadasin, who I'd be happy never to be acquainted with again. Cow and Lucy were dragging me along, helping me just like Jimmadasin did when he brought me here to Massanutten Mountain, and if I'm going to keep consecutive, I should tell you about Cow, who I figured out was the boyfriend of Armarci. I hadn't seen her, just heard about her. I felt like somehow I had put Cow together like a puzzle; it was like seeing the trunks of trees, and a leaf here and there, and little by little putting everything into a picture. That's how it was with Cow. I remember his face looking huge and right in front of me, like the marster Jimmadasin's, only Cow had good straight features: a thin and long nose and eyes that didn't seem to hardly ever blink, and his kinked hair was cut so short it looked shaved, and he had a high forehead, so I guess he was getting bald, although he wasn't old. He was wearing a homespun shirt and a vest that had once been full of loud colors but had faded into the colors of autumn leaves; and he kept scratching himself, so I figured he had crabs or lice like all the soldiers;

and I wondered how come I wasn't itching. I probably would be soon, though. Anyway, Cow wore brown trousers that could have come off a Confederate soldier, but I couldn't tell—they didn't have a stripe or anything—and he wasn't wearing any shoes. I remember looking at my feet to see if I was wearing shoes, and sure enough I still had the canvas shoes I'd taken off that poor Yank soldier who died taking aim with his musket. I was surprised that Cow hadn't taken my shoes.

I remember stopping and sitting against a tree while Cow and Lucy talked about the marster Jimmadasin just like Uncle Isaac used to talk about Poppa; and I could hardly tell if they loved that spirit or hated him, but they certainly enjoyed laughing about him. I was cold and shivering, but Lucy wouldn't allow a fire—not yet, she said; and then we were walking again, and Cow was pulling me and pushing me, and I think I was dreaming even while I was walking, or was having a vision, although I don't think so . . . and in my dream I could talk again, and I told Cow to leave me alone and asked him why he was called Cow; and he told me, but suddenly I couldn't hear him; I could just see his lips moving, so to this day I don't know why he was called that.

But he could talk, and I remembered bits and pieces as we escaped, sort of like you remember dreams; his voice was low and scratchy until he'd get excited and then it would get higher, but not like Jimmadasin's voice.

"I'se only doin' 'dis foah you."

"Lemme alone," Lucy says. It's night, and we're not far enough away from wherever the marster Jimmadasin might be to have a fire. It's cold and dark, and even though we don't have a fire it smells like smoke. I hear the wind blowing through the trees and I hear Cow and Lucy moving around, scrunching leaves, and I shiver in the damp cold.

"You ain' no bedder'n me."

"I ain't no nigger," Lucy says.

"You'se a nigger fo' sure."

"Get your hands off me—I'll tell Armarci, sure as shit I will. You think she'll marry you after that?"

"We ain' doin' dat anyway."

"She thinks you are."

"Now we jus' ain't!" Cow's voice is loud in the darkness. Surely anybody could hear that. *"She back at da camp waitin' for da marster, put all yer money on dat. We both at fault, neither of us got her from da woods."*

"She wasn't waitin' where she was supposed to," Lucy says, her voice low like

she's talking to herself. *"She didn't want to get to any soldiers. She just wanted to be with you, so you're prob'ly right, she's prob'ly waitin' for you back with the marster."*

"I ain't goin' back dere, even fo' Armarci. Stayin' wid you."

"Well, I'm goin' to the soldiers, where the money is, and I'm goin' to buy clothes and eat right and then maybe go to Richmond or someplace and have a bright life."

"Nigger white life." Cow laughs, and I think of water filling up in a basin; but when he's not laughing there's a meanness in his voice, a slow, considered meanness, like he can't talk fast because he's angry and holding it all in.

"Well, you are *a nigger, and you can't come."*

"I goes where I want."

"You'd be nothin' but contraband to the Federals. They'd send you North and work you to death. Worse'n Alabama."

"Whadabout you?"

"I am goin' to sell my *ass right here,"* Lucy says, and they both laugh like that's the funniest thing they ever heard.

"Dey's other niggers 'round here. I gonna be my own marster jus' like da marster, an' den get Armarci back from him. Meantime . . ."

"Stop it! Can't you see Dan'l's right there?"

"How come you knows his name if he so dumb he can' talk?"

"'Cause I named him."

"Like you'se his mamma. His missy." They giggle like they're drunk or something, and then Cow asks, *"How come we gone back to get 'im?"* I feel myself get tense like I'm ready to fight, and I hold my breath, lest I miss them saying something; and it seems that every rustling and wind noise is so loud like crashing, getting in the way of my hearing the answer to the most important question.

"'Cause the marster would've killed him."

"Nah, he wouldn' do dat, an' so what if he did? You think he so special jus' 'cause he white? Willy white an' so is Darryl, an' you calls dem trash."

"Marster would've killed him dead." Lucy says it just like that, soft, like she's saying it over to see if she believes it.

"Didn't never kill nobody long as I been wid him. Wouldn't never kill you 'cause you fucked him, didn't ya."

"Fuck you an' the horse you rode in on," Lucy says, and they start laughing again, and I can't figure out if Cow's meanness in his voice is just made up, like Jimmadasin talking in a squeaky voice to look like he was just a dumb nigger.

"Ain' never had a horse," Cow says, and as if that's really funny, they start laughing crazy again; and when they stop, Cow says, *"Marster ain' so bad. Takes care of everybody. Even white niggers like you. An' he bein' a conjureman help everybody, 'cludin' you."*

"That's all nigger bullshit."

"Ain't, an' you knows it," Cow says. *"I seen how he conjured on you, I seen dat wid my own eyes how when you come back da las' time an' you'se sick wid dem things like boils, 'member dat? You was one sick pussy, full a clap an' eve'ything else terrible."*

"You don't know squat 'bout anything," Lucy says. *"Wasn't clap."*

"Was worse, was boils, 'cause you was conjured by bad men, by dose soldiers you want to go back an' fuck, 'an da marster conjured da sickness right outa you. I seen what come outa dose boils."

"Nothin' came out of nowhere, 'cept your mind."

"Live things come out and crawl aroun', I seen dem," Cow says. *"An' you was havin' fever and jus' about died. Wasn't for da marster you be dead now."*

"I'll allow how he took care of me. He takes care of everybody. But you ain't free 'cause he owns your black ass. Only a matter of time before you go crawlin' back. Ain't it? . . . Ain't it?"

"You ain' no different."

"Maybe," Lucy says.

I can barely hear her, but then I hear her slap Cow. *"I told you not to touch me. Ain't you afraid those live things might be inside me?"* She laughs, but it's quiet, as if maybe she believes that she had things crawling inside her.

"Marster cured you."

"Maybe he conjured me."

After a while Cow says, *"Maybe he did. An' me. An' da boy. Everybody."*

Everything's quiet, except for the whispering and sometimes the howling of the wind; and it's so dark now that I feel like I'm blind. Long minutes pass; and I suddenly have a desire to hear a clock ticking, as if that would arrange everything back to right. I hear breathing and dark sounds, like the woods are breathing too. No moon and no stars, just black sky, probably clouds, thunderheads, and it smells like it's going to rain; there's a sharp, uncompromising smell to the air.

"Don' go," Cow says.

"I thought you're goin' with me."

"You knows what I mean."

Then comes what I fear, the clockless minutes or hours, and I don't want to hear the wind, and I don't want to hear them jostling each other and rolling on the leaves; and I don't want to hear I don't want to hear, and then they're breathing like they're out of breath, and I can tell they're trying to be quiet so as not to wake me, and that somehow makes it worse, and now she's whispering to him, and it sounds like they're saying *"Hey yah hey yah"* over and over and over to each other; and I try to close it all out by looking hard into the darkness, by trying to conjure up the spirit dog, by trying to leap or fall back into my vision so I can climb up that rope ladder into the steam balloon and float away to Washington; and I can see shapes moving toward me, then disappearing, and I imagine I'm falling sideways into the Massanutten Mountain, but I'm still lying here listening and feeling more alone than if I *was* alone, like I'm laying in the field with the other soldiers, with Jimmadasin, and I'm dead, but I can hear everything; just stop it stop it, and I can see the man laying on top of Mother outside the Big House, but now I'm thinking only of getting away, getting out of here, but I don't have food or the Colt or Eurastus's haversack or a knife or money—the marster Jimmadasin got everything of value, and it would be too dangerous to go back to the cave, and I wouldn't find it anyway—and then in my humiliation I hear myself making noises along with Lucy and Cow, my "ha" sound; and Jesus they can hear me and they stop and she calls to me, like she's afraid or something, but now I'm gone, hardly breathing, invisible like a spirit slipping out of a corpse; I'm counting fast and passing through the shapes in the dark, through the seconds and minutes, which seem like flickering shadows, getting away from Lucy and Cow, getting away from the spirit dog and Mother and Poppa and Eurastus and Mammy Jack and Sergeant Dunean who's covered in everybody's blood, getting away from Jimmadasin who's dead down on Kernstown field, getting away from the marster Jimmadasin with his walkin' boy, passing through the spirits and spiders and everything else, until finally, I guess, I passed right into the nightmares that come with sleep.

I DREAMED ABOUT THE WALKIN' BOY, ONLY HE WASN'T A SPIDER ANYmore, he was Jimmadasin, the real Jimmadasin, and he was laughing and looking just like himself and walking around me sideways like we were both in a bottle; and he told me that the preacher and conjurer wasn't him and wasn't no spirit either, but he didn't know who he was—maybe his brother or cousin or something, or probably no relation at all; but what was important, Jimmadasin said, was that he misdirected the preacher and his minions, which is what he called them; he misdirected them so they'd never find me and Lucy and Cow.

"You needs to go visit da baby Jesus 'cause you's close now, Marster Mundy." When I didn't answer him in my dream, he asked, "Whassimatter, cain't you talk?"

I shook my head, and he laughed because he knew I could talk, but even though I wanted to, I couldn't. I tried, and he just laughed and danced around me, wriggling his arms and legs like he really was a spider and telling me if I don't start talking soon he was going to turn himself back into a spider and bite and poison me 'til I died; and I wanted to ask him about the baby Jesus, but even if I could talk, it would be hard to talk to him because he was crawling around so fast.

But he knew what I wanted to say without me even saying it, and he said, "Baby Jesus in da cave, he black like night an' in da cave jus' like in da song."

I didn't know the song, so he sang it in his highest marster-don'-shoot-me voice.

> "Eye in de cave
> Eye in de cave
> Keep yo' eye in de cave.
> You gwine fine Jesus
> P'otectin' de night
> P'otectin' lil' white Mundy dere in de night.
> So eat yo' meat an' chaw yo' bone,
> 'Cause all dese spiders dey comin' home."

And then I saw everything moving all around me like wind blowing the leaves, only it was all spiders, and I jumped up, trying to scream, but only saying "ha" and expecting Jimmadasin to save me, but he disappeared, and all I could hear was his voice, only it wasn't his voice anymore.

It was Cow's.

And Lucy's.

And I was awake now and listening to them arguing in the dark.

"You're nothin' but a goddamn liar," Lucy said. "Well, you got your prick into me, so you're a happy nigger, ain'tcha."

After a time Cow said, "Ain'."

"Ain't what?"

"Dunno. Fo'give me, Lucy."

"Why'd you do it?"

"Dunno. Jus' wasn't thinkin' right or somethin' I forget."

"Forget?" Lucy asked. "What you forget?"

"'Bout whad I tole you, the baby Jesus."

"Shit! And you and the horse you came in on," Lucy said.

I didn't understand what she meant, but she talked about horses coming in a lot. I shivered in the cold. Mammy Jack would call this spirit weather, I guess, because everything would be quiet and still like a painting, except for some rustling and sneaky leaf noises, but then the wind would come up all of a sudden, blowing everything around, and it seemed like it was the coldest wind I ever felt; and then it would stop, all of a sudden again, like you'd imagined it all. And it would get so quiet you were afraid to breathe.

"I 'pologize dat I was wrong, but when Armarci weren't dere, I jus' didn' figure to—shit, I didn' figure her comin' to no harm way or nothin'. I didn' lie 'bout dat, like I says she prob'ly wid da marster right now. I think she gone back, I swear on eve'thing, but den I 'member 'bout the cave wid da baby Jesus. Da one you always goes to."

"You're talkin' crazy."

"I followed you dere, an' it was far, an' I knows who livin' dere too. An' you tole me 'bout a secret cave where the baby Jesus live."

"Did not."

"Did too, an I looked when you fucked other chillun dere."

"I don't fuck children."

"An' 'member when you screamed 'cause dey was after you? I killed dat cuntlicker an' you never knowed nothin' 'bout it. Saved your ass, an' you owes me to help me find Armarci."

There was just night noise for a while, no wind, just rustling leaves and maybe an animal scampering through the brush, probably deer. Then Lucy said, "So that was you. I never stopped to look back."

"Are dey your family or are you wid da marster?" Cow asked.

"So you took Armarci there," Lucy said, as if she didn't hear what Cow had just asked.

"But she was scared to death to go in dere," Cow said.

"How come?"

"'Cause she say da baby Jesus mus' be in Hell an' I had to save Him."

"And . . . ?"

"She wasn't goin' in dere, an' wasn't lettin' me go in dere."

"Then why do you think she's there now?" Lucy asked.

"She know you been dere, an' dat you da one dat can save the baby Jesus. She thinks dat's why we 'scaping da marster an' savin' yo' white boy. All for to save the baby Jesus, amen. She thinks we's dere now, prob'ly. Somewhere dere."

"But she was *supposed* to meet us in the woods by the rocks," Lucy said.

"I knows dat, but she didn't. Maybe I mixed everything up, an'—"

"And you'd waste time with me while Armarci was heading for the caves."

"Wasn't wastin'. We headed in da right direction. I figured dat's where we goin' anyway."

"Liar!"

"Is da right direction."

Lucy started laughing at that, and then Cow laughed too, but he didn't seem sure of himself; and then I heard some more moving around, and I figured that they were going to go at it again; but Cow said, "Can we go an' save da baby Jesus an' Armarci?"

"Ain't no baby Jesus, and Armarci will never be able to find that cave."

"She find anything."

"You're crazy, you know that?" Lucy said.

"Yah, I guess."

"And you'd fuck me instead of saving the baby Jesus."

"Was on da way."

They started laughing after that, and we left the camp in the woods at dawn.

It was snowing, but there wasn't any wind at all; and those snowflakes were as big as the walkin' boy and as white as Heaven.

THE CAVE OF THE
BABY JESUS

I want to hear my Jesus,
When the world is on fire,
Don't you want to hear my Jesus,
When they all consumed?

VIRGINIA SLAVE
PRAYER

A S I SAID, IT WAS SPIRIT WEATHER BECAUSE WHEN WE WERE UP AT dawn and getting ourselves ready to go to the caves and save Armarci and the baby Jesus, or whatever, we couldn't see anything but fog and mist; and when that burned off, it only seemed like it rose up some because the sky was gray and heavy-looking and right on top of us. I was wet and shivery and hungry, but I was used to all that by now; I could hardly tell the difference between just being tired and having the ague. I learned that Mammy Jack was right about being able to have visions while being awake because I figured I'd been having so many of them, it was hard to tell which were visions and which weren't.

We had a little bacon for breakfast, but we had to eat it raw while we walked because Lucy said that if Armarci was stupid enough to try to get to the caves, she'd probably be dead or half froze by now anyway; and if we were

going to save her we didn't have time to be dilly-dallying around like house servants. It was bad enough that we didn't keep going at night; but without even a
little moonlight, it was darker than sitting in an outhouse at midnight with your
eyes closed. But we were going now, and Lucy was complaining and swearing
like a field hand at poor Cow who just walked alongside her or behind her and
looked hangdog. I guess he figured that she had the right of it, but I figured if
she kept it up and he got mad enough, he could kill her like slapping a gnat. He
was big and when he turned this way and that, I could see the muscles in his neck,
so I just figured he had muscles everywhere else too. There was something I
liked about Cow, and something that scared me about him. He seemed so quiet,
obedient as most any slave, yet there was a sort of anger that kept flashing in his
eyes, and he didn't seem to care to hide it; or maybe it was just something I could
see now that I was changed and almost a spirit myself.

I practiced being invisible as we walked to find the baby Jesus. Being
invisible had failed me as much as it had worked, but I wasn't giving up on it. I
practiced as we walked around and down the mountain, and sometimes I felt like
I was as cold and ghostly as the air; it was like walking in clouds, but when the
fog settled or cleared, I could see right into the valley like God, and I could see
mountains and hills and woods and rocky fields and snow-spotted meadows,
and I saw a town that seemed to just appear out of the fog. And I could hear what
was thunder or skirmishing, probably skirmishing, echoing real faint around
the mountains, but that was probably because we were on the wrong side at the
time to hear it good. So we walked like spirits through the spirit weather, we
walked right around that Massanutten Mountain and then we kept to the woods
along a long gap—I don't know which one, maybe Short Mountain Gap—and
we came out of that mountain like the Hebrews or something. I kept looking
around for the spirit dog too, but there was nothing but woods and hills and
fields. No spirit dog. I couldn't tell if we were out of the spirit weather, though.
It was just gray and cloudy, but it wasn't raining or snowing, and there wasn't
any mist hanging in the trees. We just kept out of sight as best we could now, and
kept away from farmhouses.

Everything around here looked desolate, which was understandable
because of the long, hard winter. I don't think the war had much effect on how
things looked in most places—only where there was fighting or where the
armies had been, and they hadn't been right here where we were walking, at
least. I could hear the skirmishing clear now, the crack-crack of muskets and the
explosions of artillery; but it was all pretty far away, most of it just echoing

around. It was almost comforting to hear it, though, as long as it was distant. But we were heading toward the fighting because we were heading back toward the pike, which runs all the way down to Staunton, where it meets the Virginia Central Railroad. I was there once with Poppa at a revival meeting; and there had been so many tents in one corner cornfield where they were all celebrating that it could have been an entire army. Poppa was only there to sell these special Bibles he had come by. He thought it was all right for me to come along, even if all those people at the convention were a different denomination. Sold all those special Bibles too, although I couldn't ever figure out why they were special, except that they smelled like smoke, like they'd been in a fire or something. Maybe Poppa was getting rid of other denominations by selling them cursed Bibles. I asked Mammy Jack about that, but she got angry and threatened to tell Poppa what I told her. Still, she did a lot of exorcising the spirit, or whatever she called it, for the rest of the week.

As we walked along frozen ground and through snow patches and grass frosted stiff with ice, it started to hail; not big pieces that could crack your skull open but little bits that would bounce if they landed on anything flat; and pretty soon they were flying everywhere like bits of sugar candy. So I guess it was still spirit weather, but then the hail just suddenly stopped, and the clouds started to disappear, and before an hour was up it was sunny and warm. I still shivered, but I forgot about the cold and imagined that this was a little piece of spring that had been stirred up by the spirit weather. I enjoyed it, and it felt good seeing the mountains blue and shimmery in the distance and behind us and all around us, like they were clouds or dreams or something.

But I was hungry again; and it was hours—or seemed like hours, anyway—before Cow started complaining and asking Lucy for some lunch, but I guess they didn't do much preparing because she told him that all we had was the bacon, and we ate all of it for breakfast, and that we weren't so far from the caves anyway. Cow wasn't having any of that, and they started arguing about whose job it was to look after the provisions; and it didn't seem to me after all the fuss about hurrying to get to the caves that Cow—or Lucy, for that matter—cared much about finding Armarci and the baby Jesus right quick because they decided to go on a foraging expedition.

Maybe they just forgot about the cave for a while.

But when we came upon a nice farm with an old stone-chimneyed big house, Cow said he wouldn't go near there even if we were starving because that was the farm that he had originally run away from. He said every Sunday

afternoon his marster used to take him all the way to town, where they had a special machine to beat the shit out of slaves. He explained that his marster used
Cow to demonstrate how good that machine worked, but Cow said that the missus was sweet and juicy and would always bring him table scraps after he had the
shit beat out of him and was washed down with pickle water or just plain salt to
make the beating burn better and was finally dragged back home in special
handcuffs that had scrollwork all over them like they were made out of the finest
silver.

"You makin' that up," Lucy said. "You can tell that to Armarci and all the
other niggers and make them believe it, but it's bullshit and you know it."

"I shows you da welts."

"I seen them, 'member?" And she looked at Cow like she knew everything about him. "Just means you got whipped bad. . . . What'd that machine
look like, anyway?"

"Belong to Marse John Archer Wilson, I never forget dat man's name.
From New Market, an' he jus' sit in a big chair an' smokes his pipe an reads his
paper and jus' paddle a liddle bit wid his foot, an' da machine does all da beatin'
by itself. An eve'ybody else gets all excited. Dey pays to see it."

"You believe that?" Lucy asked me, which was the first time either one of
them had talked to me all day; I figured it was because of being invisible. But
now Lucy was looking at me big as day, expecting an answer because even if I
couldn't talk she probably figured I could nod. Well, I wasn't going to nod or
shake my head because I didn't know anything about whipping machines,
although it certainly sounded like bullshit to me, even though Cow was coming
up with names and places and certainly made it sound real enough probably to
fool a nigger.

"You see, he believe me," Cow said, although I hadn't nodded or
anything.

"Just stop the bullshit and go see about foraging some food."

"Tole you, I ain' goin' dere ever again."

"Then we'll just keep goin' until we get to the caves," Lucy said. "We're
wastin' time with all this bullshit, and your Armarci's probably already dead by
now, or froze, or back with the marster or something. If she comes to harm, it's
all on you."

"Den let da chile do the foraging," Cow said, like he wasn't listening to
most of what she said. He turned to me, looking straight at me with those deep
brown eyes and humiliating me.

Just then I realized what it was about him that was different—different than Uncle Isaac or Mammy Jack or even Jimmadasin—and that was he always looked straight at me, right into my eyes; and it shocked me. Not even the marster Jimmadasin looked me in the eye directly. That mean bastard spirit just looked at me sideways, like he couldn't bear to look upon my face for more than a second; he probably thought I'd turn his hair white or something, like Moses, but I looked square at him and could tell the meanness in his eyes. I couldn't see meanness in Cow's eyes, though. They looked sleepy, like he'd just woke up and was still seeing whatever he'd been dreaming about, but then in the next second they'd look angry. Probably doesn't make a whole lot of sense, but that's how they appeared to me.

Anyway, as I said, he humiliated me by calling me a child; and I figured this was as good a time as any to get away. I could forage for food on my own. I didn't need them. But Lucy and Cow had rescued me from the marster Jimmadasin's hole in the ground, so when Lucy asked me if I wanted to get the food, I nodded; and Cow pointed out where everything was and what to watch for and said that he'd be going around nearby foraging too; and Lucy told me not to try to steal a pig or anything that we'd have to take apart or that could make noise and give us away. She told me to get any kind of smoked meat I could find, and Cow pointed out the smoke houses and the hen house where I could forage some fresh eggs and the log cabins where the slaves lived, probably six people to each house; and maybe if I knew what I was about I'd be able to snitch a pie from the big house and maybe something edible from the nigger quarters. Better that I went, even if I got caught, because I was white.

I figured Lucy would have had a good chance too, but maybe they wouldn't think she was white enough or something.

THE FARM WHERE COW HAD BEEN A SLAVE WAS NEATLY KEPT; NOT RICH like the Bartons' plantation in Springdale, but there were six slave cabins, a couple of tobacco-drying houses, a corn barn, hay rick, and the smoke houses, which I told you about. It was better than what Poppa and Mother had by a long sight, and just looking at that farm, crusted here and there from the snow that hadn't melted yet, made me feel sick. I didn't want to see another farm ever again, or a town, or a street or a church or anyplace with people; and when I saw the shade trees near the big house I half expected to be coming upon red sand-stone flags and the same board fence we had at home, and then I suddenly thought of Mother laying on the red flags and the spirit dog staring at me with his red eyes and I couldn't get them out of my mind no matter what else I was thinking about; they just seemed to be stuck there, even while I was thinking about other things like Cow, how there was something about him that made me feel safe, even though he'd probably've killed me for a chaw of tobacco, which was what he'd gone on and on about, saying he was sick of "rabbit tobacker," and I knew what that was because I chewed it myself to practice spitting; it was made out of dried Life Everlasting, and I figured that a weed with a name like that couldn't be bad for you; and I had to show Cow that I wasn't a child, no mother's child, and I thought about Lucy fucking him while I lay awake and remembered Lucy catching me polluting myself, and then there was Mother laying on the sandstone flags dead, and I saw the man on top of her, and I saw he was wearing canvas shoes like mine and I could see his ass, and it was white as maggots; and then I was crossing from a stone fence over to the corn barn and past that to the hay rick and right past the chicken coop and then to the barn until I could see the big house right ahead of me and the neat line of nigger cabins about a half-mile down a hill to my left; and all I could think about was that.

Lucy was right: I was white. I could walk around all I wanted, wherever I wanted, for as long as I wanted, as long as I wasn't stealing, and I wasn't stealing yet, just looking, looking, looking, and I felt like I was seeing everything for the first time, like everything was new; and I figured that I was just having another vision or something, but I was going to go along with it. I practiced being invisible, just walking along, although I didn't see anybody, which was unusual on a farm except maybe on a Sunday afternoon; and I looked all around the fields, but nobody was around. It was as if this was a dead place like Kernstown field, but when I stood quiet and listened, I could hear something like maybe singing, although I couldn't be sure, but I thought it was coming from the direction of the cabins. Well, here I was, probably all alone on the farm—or at least alone enough to steal everything I wanted—and God knows I was hungry, but the hunger felt distant all of a sudden, like the skirmishing; and I felt a wonderful kind of power, sort of, like I was the only one in the world, and I figured I was surely invisible, surely now, so I started walking down to the cabins and looking around like I was big as day and invisible as a spirit. I know that I should have been stealing eggs from the chicken coop and checking the barn too, and finding all the bacon and ham and jowl and sausage and pig's feet I could find in the smoke houses; and just thinking about meat made my jaw ache and get tight, and then I started thinking about pickles and preserves, and my stomach rolled, yet it still felt like somebody *else* was hungry; and I found myself walk-ing between cart tracks in the field, walking down toward the singing, which became louder as I came upon the log shacks, which were in fine condition; the marster was good to his niggers here.

I came to the cabins that were all lined up in a row, and I heard singing com-ing from one of the cabins—the one on the end; all the others were empty. I should have been going through the empty cabins, looking for anything I could find; but instead I went to that last cabin and stood looking in past the door, which was wide open. The room was so crowded with niggers that it took a while before anyone even noticed me. But I could see an old door sitting on top of two big flour barrels, and on top of the door was a woman covered with a sheet, all but her head and shoulders. Her hair was white, and her skin looked like black crepe pulled tight over her bones. I could see just where those bones were, and their outlines, and her mouth looked puckered, probably because she didn't have any teeth, but a red and blue bandanna was tied under her jaw and knotted on top of her head, probably to keep her mouth closed. But what scared me were the two copper pennies laying over her eyes; and I couldn't help but imagine that those copper pennies were the dead eyes of the spirit dog, all dull instead of fiery.

Then one of the tallest and skinniest niggers I ever saw came out of that door before I could even think to run away and patted my shoulder and bowed and called me "young massah Benjamin," and I didn't know who young massah Benjamin could be—maybe from the big house, or from an even bigger house down the way or something; but then I was inside the room, and the tall man was patting me and talking about how wonderful it was I could be here, that it was an honor and a privilege and everything else; and I figured he had to be the min-ister because he was all dressed in black, except for his shirt, which was white. He wore a threadbare frock coat and trousers that were too big for him. He had blacked his shoes so you'd forget to notice how torn up they were. He was bald and ugly, but for all that, he looked like one powerful preacher; and his breath smelled sweet, like fruit that had gone a little rotten. I felt the heat of the room, the heat and the smells of all the people. The women and girls were mostly sit-ting in chairs and on boxes and rough stools all against the walls, and, standing all around, and even up on the loft which could only be reached by a ladder, were men and boys; and the preacher made a fuss over me until he told everyone to hush up and take their seats, and in the most beautiful voice I ever heard he began singing and preaching and hallelujahing and circling around the dead old lady laying on the door; it was like he couldn't tear himself away from her. I was sitting in a chair with the girls, right in front of the dead woman in the place of honor, and everyone was smiling at me and then crying out "Amen!" or "Lord Lord!" or "Yas, Lord!" and "Hallelujah!" and all that; and that preacher was good because he was calling everybody up into a frenzy of crying and shouting "Lord!" and he gave such a sermon that I couldn't help but listen and I started feeling like I had known the dead lady, who everybody loved and called "Sweet Grandy," and I just figured she was probably like Mammy Jack, even though you could have put four of her into one of Mammy Jack's dresses; and then everybody was singing and standing up. I didn't feel like I was being suffocated, even though I could smell all that sweat mixed with the smells of food and tobacco and hoe perfume, and at first it made me feel a little sick, but then I found myself liking it, feeling like this was what it was really like to be invisible, that this was how spirits or angels felt. I stood up with everybody else, and smiled back at everybody, and I walked around and looked around and I've got to say that I've never seen so much food. (I should have said this before, probably, to be consecutive, but to tell the truth, I didn't even see all that food until I started walking around.) And then I felt hungry, starving, and there on boxes were chitlins and chine and pig's feet, all in saucers that were cracked and broken, and there were dried cherries and pickled cherries and preserved cherries, and other preserves and meats, most likely sent over from the big house; and I just picked up what I wanted like I was the marster or God or the spirit—I picked up a handful of the dried cherries and a bottle of preserves—and walked right out into the sun, out of the sweat and bodies and humming and all the Lordying and singing and talking, right into the snap of the cold bright afternoon. But before I left I paid my respects to the old Sweet Grandy lady by stopping and watching her to see if there were any spirits or anything hanging around her. There weren't, but I had a terrible inclination to lift up those big copper pennies off her eyes and see what was in there.

I imagine they were just holes, and I shivered, thinking about the soldier with the maggots in his eyes; and I thought that this old lady was enjoying a pretty good death, with all the food and people and the minister with his beautiful voice; and the soldier, who was dried out just like the nigger lady, except for his eyes, was probably still laying there in that field alone, probably not even realizing that he was dead and didn't have his musket anymore.

But as I watched the Sweet Grandy lady laying dead on that door, I could almost see the maggots crawling around under those pennies; and suddenly I wasn't invisible anymore. I wasn't the young marster or the spirit or God or anybody, and I ran until I was breathing so hard I felt sick. I stopped under some plane trees and ate some of those dried cherries, which were probably the most delicious thing I've ever eaten, and I almost finished all that I had—but not the preserves—and then I went directly to the smoke house and sure enough there was everything you could ever want: rabbit, bacon, ham, jowl, sausage. I took what I could carry, but I had the feeling that everyone would be about, that they'd be looking for me, that I'd get caught, and I didn't know what they'd do—maybe take me off to town and put me on Cow's whipping machine or in jail; but it didn't make sense that the owner would be that bad and have such a nice farm and nice, well-fed niggers; fact, those niggers had more than some white people. I remembered the smell of all those people pressed up close together and for a second I wished I was back there, but they'd discover me and take me to the big house and that would be the end of it. Although I wanted to get away, I stole into the barn and the chicken coop and got some eggs, and I even sneaked up on the big house to see if there was anything worth taking, but there wasn't.

I'd done better than Cow, probably, and didn't feel bad about leaving, but I couldn't help feeling that everybody but those niggers were dead, and that's why it was quiet as Sunday; and I imagined that maybe the nigger cabins were Heaven or something, and I just got to be in there for a little while.

After that I considered that maybe the baby Jesus could be in a cave.

Jimmadasin thought so.

But I stopped thinking about Jesus and Heaven and food and Jimmadasin and everything else when two scraggly, half-starved mongrels came running through the fields. They were barking and running after me, and they looked mean and sick. I stopped and stood stock-still, just like I did the first time I saw the spirit dog. These weren't spirit dogs, of course—I could see that because they stank of wet and dog, and their eyes were white and runny—but they were showing me their fangs and growling and barking deep and sharp like they'd like to take me apart. One of them was brown and spotted white; the other was black, but he was spotted too. I could feel my heart beating hard. Surely they'd be able to smell my fear, and the next thing I knew I was breathing out of my mouth and making the "ha" sound like I was an animal, or like *I* was the spirit dog now. They kept their distance, but I knew for certain they were going to attack me for some of the meat I'd stolen. I tore off a piece of the ham and threw it far as I could. They both ran for it. I threw another piece at them and then ran like a sonovabitch for the woods to find Lucy and Cow.

After that I didn't feel like that farm was a dead place anymore, or some kind of nigger Heaven, or anything like that. I kept thinking that maybe those dogs had something to do with the spirit dog, but I knew better. They weren't spirits. They were just mongrels.

And Jimmadasin was dead.

And there probably wasn't any baby Jesus.

And the spirit dog was long gone.

WE ARRIVED AT THE CAVE OF THE BABY JESUS IN THE EARLY AFTERNOON. The sky was clear, like it had never had a cloud in it, and the sun was burning down and giving off the kind of light you get in hot summer when everything looks like it's caught up in pollen or gold dust or something out of a fairy tale. I always used to love that, especially when I was alone, because it was then that everything looked like it should . . . the way I remember seeing things when I was a baby. But I forgot all about the yellow sunlight and how the day looked and everything else when I heard the screaming. At first I didn't know where it was coming from: It was a girl's voice, or a woman's—I couldn't tell which—and it sounded far away and hollow like it was echoing around the mountains.

"You hear dat?" Cow asked, like he wasn't sure that he was hearing things. We had stopped by a line of misshaped oak trees that looked onto a hill, and somewhere in there, where the screaming seemed to be coming from, was the cave of the baby Jesus. I was looking straight out across the field to another line of trees that ran along in a half circle from where we were down a ways to the hill where the cave was supposed to be, but I couldn't see anything but what I told you.

"Could be anything," Lucy said. "Prob'ly an animal or somethin'."

"Ain' no animal," Cow said, in a low, growly voice; and then I heard the crying, screaming sound again, distant and hollow sort of and scary, and it didn't sound like an animal to me either. Cow shouted something about that scream coming from Armarci, and even though Lucy shouted at him to come back, he just suddenly got up and ran straight across the field toward the line of oak trees in front of the hill, which wasn't far away, and sonovabitch if he didn't just disappear into those trees or the hill or maybe into thin air. I must have blinked my eyes or something because I didn't see exactly how he disappeared, but Lucy did and said, "He's goin' to be one dead nigger, one dumb asshole of a dead nigger. Damn diarrhea sonova*bitch*. Come on, Dan'l, we're going to find the Federals and get away from stupid niggers once and for all." She looked at me for a while—not long, but it felt like a long time—and asked, "You think I'm a nigger?"

I shook my head, figuring that was what she wanted me to do. She probably wasn't a nigger. She didn't look like one, except for her hair, but Poppa used to say that Jews have kinked hair, so she could have been that. (I never in my life saw a Jew, so I couldn't say.)

"So you wanna go with me or not?"

I nodded.

"Then let's get outa here. Stupid goddamn Cow. I don't care how strong he thinks he is, he's gonna get killed in there. You ever meet deserters?" she asked me. "Well, they're bad and dumb and mean is what they are, every dick-lickin' one of 'em; and I'll bet anything they're holed up in there, don't matter if they're our own boys or bluebellies or what, they're all the same. Kill you for a button. Every single one. Oh, they prob'ly got Armarci, or somebody just like her, you can bet your skinny ass on that, Dan'l. Sonova*bitch*!" She kept looking where Cow had gone like she could still see him. "You goddamn nigger. There's another way in there. I could've told him that if he'd of kept his pants on for two goddamn seconds. Sonovabitch bastard, he doesn't have a torch or a musket or anything. But he's too goddamn stupid to think of that. An' even if he *had* a torch, the deserters goin' to see him first thing anyway 'cause they gonna be lookin' right out at that entrance. But Cow's too stupid to know the secret way in." And then she said, "You wait here, Dan'l. I'll be back, you just stay here quiet, and don't let anybody see you, or, I'm tellin' you, they'll kill your ass dead too." She mumbled some more swear words about Cow, about what a dumb nigger he was, and then she went off after him.

And I followed her.

I don't know why, and I've thought about it a lot, but when she told me about the deserters hiding out in the cave of the baby Jesus, I thought about Mother and Poppa and the Big House burning and the sonovabitch bastards who burned it; and then suddenly it was like I was watching Mother being raped and killed all over again, and I knew—I *knew* now that the man who was doing it was a deserter. But all I could do was listen to Poppa screaming Mother's name "Mina, Mina!" inside the burning house; and here I was looking and listening to it all over again; and I watched for the spirit dog; and sure enough, he appeared right in the field before me, big as life, his eyes burning like banked embers. He just walked out there behind Lucy, who couldn't see him, of course. Lucy kept to the safety of those twisted oak trees—not like Cow, who just ran straight through the fields like nothing could hurt him.

I could see that the spirit dog was waiting for me, and I wondered where he'd been and how come he hadn't revealed himself since I got to the cave where I wrestled with Lucy; and I knew that if the spirit dog was revealing himself, it meant trouble. That's why I should have left Cow and Lucy to find Armarci and the deserters and the baby Jesus by themselves.

But I followed Lucy anyway and kept to the cover of the trees.

I felt a burning, frightful feeling in my chest and stomach, and the spirit dog just watched me like he'd done the first time I ever saw him; but just as I got near him, he disappeared. There was a sudden chill as the clouds covered up the sun, and the leaves and the air smelled as dry as old Sweet Grandy or probably Jesus. All kinds of thoughts entered my mind, and I imagined that when Jesus was hanging up there on the cross dying for all our sins, He didn't smell like the soldiers in Kernstown field. I'd sniffed at Sweet Grandy back there in the nigger cabin, and she didn't have any rotten smell to her either. I figured that she was all dried up like a gourd on the inside, except maybe for some maggots that had probably got into her eyes; and I figured that Jesus must've been the same, except the maggots probably would have left Him alone because He was the Son of God. But Poppa always said Jesus was a man too, so the maggots probably did get Him after all; but only for a little while, until He rose up from being dead. So He probably got new eyes. I wondered whether when Jesus was lying there dead before He arose whether the apostles put pennies over His eyes too. I supposed they did, and that's probably where the niggers got it all from. I wondered about how Jesus, after being dead and then arising all those thousands of years ago, could turn into a baby right here in Virginia; but I figured that if Jimmadasin could be dead in Kernstown field and still walk around as a spirit, then the baby Jesus could probably be waiting for all of us in the cave.

And then I was right behind Lucy around on the other side of the hill.

"You're just as stupid as Cow," she said in a real low voice as she stepped through brush and leaves, and looked around like she had lost something. "Just get the hell outa here." She looked at me, then shrugged and said, "Well, it's your ass." She laughed softly. "My ass too. I guess we're both stupid. You afraid to be alone?"

I nodded.

"That's what I figured. Tell you what. You can wait in the woods, right over there, and you can see where I'm going to go into the cave, and if you get into trouble you can go into the cave same way I'm goin' to. What about that?"

I didn't look at her. It didn't make much sense to me that if I waited in the woods I wouldn't be alone. But I wasn't afraid of being alone. I was afraid of—

I couldn't find that thought—it was like trying to talk—and then Lucy said, "We ain't goin' to find Armarci or prob'ly Cow either. I'm as dumb as he is . . . comin' over here, but you know what, I owe him, and I always pay back what I owe; but I'll tell you somethin', I ain't going to put my head in a noose for him or anybody. If I can't help that stupid nigger out, then he'll just have to be another dead nigger, and that's his problem, ain't mine." While she was digging through a pile of leaves and twigs, she asked, "Dan'l, you know why I like you?"

Well, I was ready to find out, but she forgot about telling me, I guess, when she found the pine boards that made up a cover over what looked like a decent-sized hole in the ground, maybe three feet wide. I don't know how she ever figured exactly where to be digging, with all those weeds and twigs and dead leaves laying everywhere like they were all dumped there all at once. Anyway, she pulled the cover over to the side, arranged leaves and twigs over it again, so no one could tell it was a cover, and then looked up at me like she wanted to know if I was going to go into the woods and wait for her or whether I was going down into the cave with her. I figured I knew what the cave would look like because I'd become an expert on caves after hiding in the shallow cave by the stream and then being dropped into a hole by Marster Jimmadasin's niggers. That hole was larger than this one that Lucy had covered with her pine boards and camou-flaged with leaves and branches; she must have learned that trick from Marster Jimmadasin. So I figured this cave was probably like the one I had been buried in, about the size of a room in the Big House—but no, that couldn't be: All those deserters and the baby Jesus and whoever else was in there would need more room than that.

"Well, you comin' or not?" Lucy asked. "Cow's gonna be one dead nig-ger 'fore you make up your mind, and I ain't got the time to be your mamma . . . or his, neither, for that matter."

I pointed to the hole, and she told me not to explore anything when I got to the bottom or I might fall into a pit that was deep as Hades and die. Then she said, "Well, if you're going, go on," and so I climbed down a rough-hewn ladder that was in the cave. I had to step carefully because the pegs weren't evenly spaced, and I didn't know how far down it would be to the bottom; but there was light coming in from the opening above me, and so I could see a little. . . . I could see a cloud of dust swirling around me like a big halo, like what you see when the sun comes through a window, except the light was the color of tin; and below me I could make out strange-looking cones like I imagined would be at the bottom of the sea or something. I wanted to go right back up, but Lucy was on the ladder above me. She pulled the cover back across the hole and adjusted it, and it became pitch dark. All I could see were purple shapes like I sometimes saw when I closed my eyes. I reached bottom, but then I had trouble keeping my balance because the ground was all just bumps and rises. Lucy came down right after me and told me it was all right for me to move over; there was enough room, and we just stood there close together in the dampness and the dark and listened. I could hear the drip-drip of water and every once in a while a splash like there were fishes swimming around or something, and I thought I heard insect noises, a buzzing like locusts or something flying around, only far away, but I couldn't be sure about that. Then I heard something that sounded like whimpering, or maybe crying, but it was so low and echoey that I couldn't tell what it was or where it was coming from. I thought for a second that maybe Jimmadasin was right about the baby Jesus, that He was here and crying in the dark, like this was the manger built out of stone, and that those cries were trying to come right up out of the stones, but then I imagined maybe I was hearing somebody talking, but I couldn't make out any of the words; and then everything got so quiet I felt I was probably dead and then I heard something that sounded like a rock falling or an explosion—like cannon fire, maybe—that was far, far away; and it came up from the rocks, I was sure of that this time.

"Shit!" Lucy whispered, and I figured that whoever else was in the cave, in the next room or whatever, could probably hear anything Lucy said out loud, and that's why she was whispering. "Sounds like a musket. . . . Goddamn stupid nigger just got kilt, I knew it, I *knew* it was gonna be." And after she said that we just stood there close together and breathed, and I felt myself getting scared because it was so dark that I imagined I was going to suffocate on the darkness, like it was heavy and would drown me, and I took deep breaths, but I could still breathe. I thought about Cow, about how he always looked straight at me and would sometimes nod to me—and once he even smiled at me like we were just two white people greeting each other—and I wondered if he was dead; but even if he was, even if he'd just been shot and that's what that explosion was, it didn't really matter because he could just be a spirit if he wanted to, like Jimmadasin, and he could stay here with Armarci—that's who he was looking for anyway—and if he was a spirit he could probably see in the dark.

"Least nobody's 'round this end," Lucy said. "That's somethin'. Stupid goddamn niggers, both of 'em. I can't see Armarci findin' her way out of the camp, much less gettin' here. And Cow, he ain't much different. Stupid piss-drinkin' deserters an' stupid niggers, they're all the same," and Lucy went on like that like she was so angry she'd kill everybody, and I imagined she was crying too; but she was only talking to herself, sort of like praying, just swearing and feeling bad and thinking things out; and while she was doing that, I felt like everything was so close I could hardly breathe; and then she touched my neck and rubbed me and said, "Don' you worry, just stay put an' I'll get my stash, if it ain't been stoled." She struck a match, and the yellow, flickery light lit up her hands and a little bit of the cones and things that looked like icicles sticking out of the ground and the ceiling too. I felt that darkness let go of me a little. She went through a few matches while she walked around, and I know it sounds silly, but seeing the matches cupped in her hands made me think of how I used to catch lightning bugs in a pasteboard box and feed them to the frogs. The throats of those frogs would light up and glow like lanterns—you could see the glow right through their skin, and you could even see into them when they jumped into the pond. But even though I was remembering about frogs and could see some light, my heart was still pounding, and I was feeling all sweaty, like it was hot and everything was pushing close against me again, suffocating me, but it wasn't hot. It was cool, but warmer than outside.

I just wished I had stayed in the woods like Lucy had told me to . . . but I forgot about breathing and everything else when Lucy lit a torch.

I was so surprised that I took a step backwards and almost fell.

This place was huge, and the only thing I could think of was that I was inside of some huge mouth, like inside a whale or something. Those icicles and cones all over the ceiling could have been teeth or fangs, and also, when I looked I could see all these rocks that looked like they'd been a waterfall and got frozen. And there were rocks that looked like grapes, rocks that were all hollowed out like saucers, rocks that looked like lily pads and ledges and folds of drapery; and maybe it was because of the torchlight and the shadows, but some of the rocks looked just like bacon. As Lucy walked back toward me, and the shadows were jumping all over the place, I felt like I was froze just where I was standing; I just wanted to climb back up the ladder, and I imagined how it would be to get lost in here without a light. But when I followed Lucy like she directed, I found it was worse than I thought. There were tunnels and rooms and corridors, and if you got too far lost you'd never, never find your way out, and I wondered if Lucy knew her way around that well; after all, she had trouble finding the entrance, and it took her three matches to find the torch; and as I followed her, the ceiling just kept getting lower and lower, until we were bent over, and I cut myself on one of the rock fangs that I didn't see because I was looking at the ground, and I felt the walls and the ceiling and everything getting narrower and closer, and I started feeling like I couldn't breathe again, only now it was worse, and I was choking on the smoke, which smelled like tar and something rotten; and Lucy said, "Dan'l, stop it, what the hell's wrong with you? Christ, you'd think you'd been running a hundred miles the way you're carryin' on. You wanna stop for a while? Ain't nothin' to be scared of or out of breath for. I been in here a hundred times, I even lived in here once, but I know how people get scared in here. You feel like you're chokin'? That's what sometimes happens. I saw that once—a big strappin' boy who started cryin' and beggin' to get out." She laughed, but it was more like she just breathed out hard. "Was bad on him 'cause we just put out the torches and let him scream, but you got me right here, although we're gonna have to put out the torch in just a minute. You gonna be all right if I do that?"

I nodded, but I felt sick and imagined that all the millions of tons of rocks above were going to cave in on top of me, and I'd be buried here forever in the darkness. Like poor Cow. I felt shivers and couldn't swallow just thinking about him probably dying in the dark, feeling the way I did about all that rock and knowing he wasn't ever going to see the sun or stars or trees or Armarci or anything but this cave ever again—unless, of course, he had quick-changed into a spirit and gotten out. But I couldn't imagine a worse way to die; it would be worse than Mother being killed on the red flags or Poppa burning and calling for Mother, it would be worse than swelling up on Kernstown field, or having your arms and legs cut off by the sawbones, or having Eurastus put his thing up my ass and—

Then we heard voices again, only this time I could make out what they were saying; and Lucy snuffed out the torch, leaving us standing in the dark with purple and yellow swatches and ribbons swirling around in the blackness like fireflies leaving trails. I smelled the tar from the torch; it was strong and I could taste it in back of my mouth. But Lucy put her arms around me, and I told myself not to be scared, that I was used to the dark now. I thought about Lucy's breasts, which I could feel pushing against me, and I remembered how they looked and felt, but nothing was helping; I was trembling, or maybe both of us were, and I heard those voices like they were whispering right in my ear, like they were spirits telling me what to do, but I knew they weren't spirits because spirits don't usually whine. . . .

"*You sure this is far enough?*"

There was laughter, like a sharp crack of musket. "*You worried that Captain Bridgeford's comin' in here lookin' for these niggers, that it? Now maybe he's bringin' the whole First Virginia jus' to find your ass an' shoot it off.*"

"*I think we been here too goddamn long is what I think.*"

"*If you could think you'd never enlisted.*"

"You *did.*"

"*Ain't talkin' about me an' what I did.*"

"*We got to get out of here.*"

"*This is the safest place in the worl'.*"

"*Ain't.*"

"*Why, 'cause you kilt the nigger? Shit, it's only a nigger for Christ's sake. Nobody's never goin' to find us or anything else in here, an' here you are goin' on like you kilt the old man hisself in front of the entire mess. We're safe as houses in here.*"

"*I didn' kill her.*"

And then I heard a wailing sound, but it was soft like it might have been wind blowing through tunnels or something; and it took me a bit to realize that it was someone crying. Then I figured maybe that's the sound I heard before and thought was the baby Jesus.

"*Frank, you stupid crazy sonovabitch, stop it, it ain't nothin'. You didn't kill nobody. So cut it out. Let's just get out of here.*"

"*I ain't never kilt a girl, nigger or no.*"

Nigger or no nigger or no, it was like the sparks and ribbons of light when Lucy snuffed out the torch, and that was the end of it, and the only thing I could hear was a watery sound like a splashing far away, and then even that stopped, and all I knew was that Lucy had her arms around me. She was taking even, short breaths like she was counting, and I waited and waited, as the darkness became heavier and closer, and it was harder to breathe, and then Lucy said, "They're gone. I think I know about where they were, and that's farther away than you think 'cause sometimes you can hear things real close in here that are far away, but I wasn't about to go and light a match and give us away, just in case I figured 'em wrong." And she let go of me and lit the torch. It was so bright it seemed to burn my eyes, and she said, almost in a whisper, "I'm goin' to find out what happened, and I'm afraid you ain't got no choice but to come along, unless you wanna wait here in the dark, but I think you'd get too spooked, right? Well, I warned you, didn' I? If I turn around and leave, I'm always gonna wonder what happened. Same for you, though you prob'ly wouldn't give a shit about Cow. But *I* gotta find out, understand?"

I nodded, and without waiting Lucy started walking deeper in the caves, and in some places we had to crawl through tunnels, and we'd come out in rooms and walk down what looked like corridors, and once we passed a pool that reflected the torchlight, and I saw white bugs without any eyes, and we went through another huge room filled up with columns and fangs on the floor and ceiling, and after that we walked and crawled through more corridors and tunnels until Lucy whispered, "We're close now, so get ready, 'cause I'm puttin' out the torch, so grab on to me so you won't get scared."

She put out the torch, and I looked around, through the yellow swirls and purple ribbons that turned into cloud shapes and then were swallowed into the dark. "I know where we are by heart," she whispered. "I'll light a match maybe, but from now on I ain't goin' to be doin' much talkin'."

I held on to her dress, and we walked slowly through the dark. "Dan'l, if those cocksuckers killed Cow, I'm gonna kill them, just so you know. Ain't much you can do now—I told you to stay back, didn' I? I damn well did, Marster Dan'l Onions." I guess she didn't mean what she said about not talking because she kept whispering like she was praying, and I don't even know if I heard everything she said because the darkness seemed to pull everything into itself, but I remember she said she had my Colt .44 revolver, and she was sorry, but she went and stole it back and it was hers now, and what did I think I was going to do about it in here?

She was right, so I just held on to her, feeling around for the Colt but not finding it, and then the ceiling got low again until we were crawling, and I felt something squash under my hand. I couldn't see what it was—probably a bug or something worse—and I remembered that soldier's head rolling right in front of Allan McSherry's foot, and I remembered stepping on something that burst under my foot when I was with Jimmadasin . . . and feeling maggots squirming around in the dead soldier's eyes . . . and seeing the walkin' boy crawling around the bits of dirt and grass in that greasy green bottle; and everything seemed to be rolling in front of my eyes like I was looking through one of those boxes and seeing pictures; and I heard myself making the "ha" sound. Lucy must have heard it, and maybe it scared her too, maybe the dark was suffocating her and she was fighting it too, because she just stopped and whispered, "You dirty diarrhea sons of bitches, you damn dirty fuckers," and then suddenly I could see what she meant because she lit a match.

It was Cow, laying right in front of us with his face mostly blowed away, probably by musket. His shirt and the faded vest with all the colors were splashed with blood, like it was all part of a design. I couldn't look, but I couldn't stop looking either, and I felt bad for him because he didn't have his eyes left to put pennies on, and I wondered if his spirit could have gotten out of him, what with his face like that, but I suppose it didn't matter; then the match went out like a little red eye, and I felt myself shaking and crying in the dark; but this was the funny thing about it: Even though I knew it was me, it wasn't. The real me was just inside myself and watching all this fuss and waiting for Cow's spirit to arrive; but it didn't. Probably too narrow in this place, even for spirits.

If I could find a place to put two pennies, though, I would've.

If I had two pennies. . . .

"Dan'l, that's what we heard, isn't it," Lucy said, but it didn't seem like she was talking to me, more like to herself. "Those cocksuckers was draggin' Cow in here, and they're dumb, dumb as doors is what they are—they prob'ly think this place here is all closed off, like those stone places where they bury rich people." She laughed, softly. "So Cow, you stupid asshole of a nigger, you got buried like the rich people. Marster Cow, now—that's what all the angels can call you." Once she started talking to Cow, it didn't seem she could stop; and I started wondering if maybe he was talking back to her or something because she seemed calm, and she'd pause and listen and then go on, so she must have been hearing something.

"So what'd they do with Armarci?" she asked him, and then she lit another match. "I figure she's gotta be close by, don't you, Dan'l?" And it was a good thing I was still holding on to her because she just bolted out of that crypt space or whatever it was, and the match went out, and then she said, "Fuck it!" and lit the torch. The light hurt my eyes, but we were out of that tunnel where they'd buried Cow and in a room with a ceiling that was high enough so you could walk under it without bending, but I had to watch for the stone icicles, which could crack open your head or put your eye out; and, sure enough, Lucy found another tunnel like the one we had crawled through, and there was a girl laying in there with her dress all pulled up around her. I could tell she was a nigger, but not much more, and I wasn't looking too hard, anyway; I'd seen enough dead people to know what they look like. One thing, though: I was surprised I couldn't smell them a while back, but the air must've sucked up all the dead smells. It just smelled wet in here. Like the damp had gotten into everything. I supposed they'd start smelling in a day or so, unless they got dried out and hollow like the Sweet Grandy lady or the soldier whose shoes I was wearing.

"And here she is," Lucy whispered, although she'd been looking at her for probably a minute. She turned and looked at me, as if *I'd* killed them both. Then she just nodded at me, like Cow did after I was done foraging, like it was a sign of respect or something; and I figured we were going to kill the deserters dead, although I didn't know how I was going to accomplish that without my Colt or a musket or a knife; but Lucy would only need me if she couldn't kill them all herself. I guess I didn't worry about it much, even after Lucy put the torch out; after seeing Cow and Armarci—I suppose it was Armarci—all the fear went out of me. It was like being back with the spirits, going back to the battlefield . . . it was as if nobody was alive here in the cave, we were all just spirits. I expected to see the spirit dog in here somewhere—he'd surely be easy to spot with those eyes of his—but he was probably waiting outside.

It took us about ten minutes walking in the dark to come out near where the deserters were encamped. I could smell bacon and the woody smoke from a fire, and just like I was a dog or something, my mouth started watering. I could see some light, but it wasn't much; it looked like fog moving around on the cave walls. We'd reached the entrance where Cow had probably gone in.

We could also hear the deserters.

> *Jackson's got more recruits than muskets*
> *wid all those regiments from Augusta County*
> *an' we're legal anyway*
> *You killed the niggers*
> *Fine make you feel better*
> *I tol' you that four hundred times already*
> *He can shove his furloughs up his ass*
> *An' you fucked the nigger*
> *an' they can shove that conscription where the sun don't shine too*
> *We're goin' home let 'em come after us*
> *Nothin' would happen if we jus' went back*

Could do that but tomorrow got to go back in the mornin'
Let 'em face Daddy
an' say we just got lost
Captain Bridgeford eat that comin'-in-in-the-mornin'
shit up wid a spoon.

I followed right behind Lucy until we could see the two deserters from behind a ledge that was grooved and looked like bacon and came down from the ceiling at an angle. They were pretty far away, but there was enough light coming in from the entrance so that we could see; everything around them looked gray and dusty, and there was smoke from a small fire that surely needed to be stoked up some. But those men seemed like they were just about asleep, even though they were still talking. One of them was stretched out by the side of the fire with his feet facing in our direction, and the other one was sitting right beside him with his back against the wall. The one sitting up was wearing a homespun butternut jacket; he was clean-shaven and had some fat on him, and it was probably the dim light and the flickering of the fire, but it looked like there was something wrong with his chin, like it was divided up in two or something, and his face looked like he was concentrating hard on something, like it would always be in a frown. He had long hair, though, and it was thick. The other one didn't look like he was much bigger than me, and he kept shifting around on the ground like he couldn't get comfortable, and he'd moan and make funny noises every once in a while, but for all that I couldn't get a good look at his face; and Lucy pulled me away, and we got a good ways away from them in the dark and sat with our backs against the cold stone wall of a corridor and listened to them talk, which was like listening to water in a stream, it was so faint, and then it would be quiet as a grave, and then there would be water sounds, and maybe an hour passed or maybe more, I couldn't tell in the dark, but finally the deserters stopped talking, although I could hear snorting every once in a while, and maybe I fell asleep for a while, maybe a minute, I don't know, but Lucy was gone.

I heard a shot, and before I knew anything I was running and stumbling and feeling my way along the corridors or tunnels or whatever they were, and I was so scared being alone in the dark and everything that I forget all about direction, and I thought that I was surely lost and I'd never get out of the cave alive, and I imagined that I'd fall into a crevice or Hades and die there, or that I'd step on Cow or Armarci, and I'd have to die with them alone in the dark, and all I could see were purple spots that seemed to float a few feet in front of me like fog, and I figured maybe they were spirits, and maybe they would help me, but I knew better than that after my experience with the spirit dog, but I would have given anything to see the spirit dog, to see his eyes glowing in the dark ahead of me instead of those spots of fog, and I felt the cold wall, and suddenly there was flapping and I smelled a terrible stink like ammonia, and I was stepping in mud but I knew it wasn't mud, and I was making the "ha" sound and there were things flapping above me, and then something flew into me, and I turned around, running and touching the slimy wall, almost slipping on the dung, and it was purple dark and I knew I was going to die and my chest was going to explode I'd taken the wrong way again I was lost and I was going to fall and the rocks were going to crush me and I was going to drown and I came around a corner and—

I could see a little, and then in no time—all of this seemed long, but it was probably only a few seconds—I was watching everything happen and trying not to breathe too hard. There was Lucy standing against the wall and pointing my .44 Colt at the deserter whose feet had been pointing toward me before, but now I could see him full, and he looked young and had a peach-fuzz beard and dirty blond hair, and he looked a little like the other deserter, the stocky one, who was laying near the entrance. He had been shot in the chest, and the blood must have been coming down his arm under his shirt because it was dripping down his finger and making a little pool on the ground. Everything was going so slow now and I could see everything like God or Jimmadasin; but Lucy was hesitating about killing the other deserter, who looked a little like the dead one—maybe they were brothers, which would explain why one of them had said "Let 'em face Daddy."

The deserter was almost kneeling in the fire, and he wasn't much of anything because he was begging Lucy not to shoot him, that he believed in God and he was sorry, and how he was scared and saying "Jesus Christ, Sweet Jesus," like that over and over real low, and Lucy was calling him a fucking murderer real low too, like they were afraid of disturbing anybody. Lucy was holding that Colt and shaking, and then the deserter saw me, looked right at me, and even though I didn't make a face at him or anything, he closed his eyes and said "Jesus Christ" again, and the next thing I knew there was an explosion and Lucy must have shot the poor bastard just like that because he seemed to fall right onto the fire, and then something shattered like maybe glass—I don't know what he had in his pocket, maybe a bottle of corn juice or something—but suddenly the fire was wild all over his legs and his crotch, and he was crying for Jesus and then he was running toward me like *I* was going to save him, and I think Lucy shot him again, but he still came rushing toward me all with that fire all over him, burning and glowing and smelling like hay and burnt leather and chicken, and I got over to the other side of the cave in a hurry. I must've had a vision right there because the only thing I remember were explosions, which must have been that Colt, but those explosions seemed to be going off inside my head, and then I felt like I was on fire, and I was breathing cold air that held the scent of burning and green wood, and I was running through leaves and brush and weed and snow, and I could see the sun behind the hills, lighting them and making shadows dark as midnight, and everything looked so clear and sharp like the whole world was cut into little shiny pieces, like I could see every stone and branch, and I was outside and the woods were ahead of me and Jimmadasin was behind me, shouting at me, following me right into the woods and telling me that I was leaving the baby Jesus. "Yes, yes, you was right by da Son of God, an' too dumb to see Him, but d'others seein' Him, sure as shit dey do, remember dey's yellin' 'Jesus, Jesus,' " but everybody yells for Jesus and their mother when they're dying.

I stopped because I could hardly catch my breath. It was cold in the woods, and the piny smells and patches of snow and ice made me think of gums and rabbits.

"You left Jesus, you'se on you' own now, don' deserve nobody," Jimmadasin said; and I wanted to go back to Lucy, but I couldn't, even though I could hear her calling for me, and she sounded desperate, like she was weak and I'd left her all alone, and then she sounded angry and shouted at me and called me names like I was Cow.

I waited to see if Cow was going to appear.

I waited to see if the deserter who was on fire was going to appear.

I waited for the spirit dog and Jimmadasin and maybe even for the baby Jesus.

But Jimmadasin was right: I was on my own now.

He was probably right about the baby Jesus too.

When Đixie Đied

He give you a vision,
He give you a sign,
He at de door.
He at de door.

Bright mansion above,
An' fire below,
He give you a vision.
He give you a sign.

A PRAYER FROM
MAMMY JACK'S SHIP
OF ZION VISION

I HAD A FEW DAYS OF SUMMER AND RESTING UP BEFORE I FOUND MY-
self right in the middle of skirmishing and saw how Dixie died . . . and that's
how I met Colonel Ashby again and had just about two of the best weeks of my
life before I got caught by Captain Francis W. Pegram from London, England.
But I should stay consecutive and tell you about the weather and how the spirits
left me.

Lucy and I must have been in that cave for some time because the sun was
low and lighting up the mountains when I got out. Once I caught my breath, I
walked back through the woods and didn't stop until it got so dark I couldn't
tell the spaces between the trees; and all the while I wondered about Lucy and
wanted to see her, but I couldn't make myself go back. It was like she had
become a spirit when she killed those deserters and would be attached to that

cave like they were . . . all of them except Jimmadasin, who followed me for a while when I ran out of the cave, but then just all of a sudden went quiet; and that was the last I ever heard of him. Not a proper goodbye or anything. I guess that was my punishment for leaving the baby Jesus without even seeing Him and running out on Lucy and the spirits.

You left Jesus, you'se on you' own now, you don' deserve nobody.

That wasn't Jimmadasin I was hearing. That was just remembering, but Jimmadasin was right: I didn't deserve him or Lucy. So I just lay my head against the crook of a big oak, wrapped my jacket around myself, closed my eyes, and then woke up in the kind of shadowy light that comes into the woods when the sun is up and there's no clouds in the sky.

I could hear the booming of cannon, but it was hard to tell exactly where it was coming from because the noise echoed around the mountains like thunder. I got up and just started walking, keeping pretty much to the edge of the woods, taking my time, resting when I got tired, eating from the forage I'd saved—a piece of sausage, a bit of bacon, and what was left in the bottom of my pocket of the dried cherries I stole from the niggers—and getting back the strength that the ague had taken from me.

Outside of the woods it was muddy and the fields were brown with some spots of snow left; but the sky was a faded blue like the mountains and hills, which were all around, like they'd go on forever, up and up and up, and it was almost as if they were clouds and you could imagine them as all different shapes.

By afternoon it got so hot that I took my jacket off and tied the arms in a knot around my middle. But I didn't care about the heat, and I kept sneaking out from under the trees to sleep; it was like the sun was making me strong, and I could feel it burning my face and filling me up with light and squeezing out the sickness. My head was itching again, even though I washed it in a creek.

I stayed away from towns and farms and cabins; I didn't have any feeling to see people. But that cannonading was a familiar, almost comforting sound; somehow when I heard it, I didn't feel so much alone. It seemed like it was all around me, whispering through the trees and fields and around the mountains, saying the same thing over and over, and it sounded like the thunder I sometimes heard in my head before I was going to cry. And every once in a while I'd just start to cry, and I don't know why because I didn't feel sad, just tired, maybe; and then I'd sleep, and eat, but by the time I'd eaten all my forage, I knew where the skirmishing was. I'd been circling closer and closer to it for two days, like I was being drawn to it, and I could see the smoke and hear the crack of musket that was like firecrackers going off. I thought I was just keeping to the edge of the woods, but I found out later that I was walking through Short Mountain Gap; and out beyond the meadows and fields and the North Fork of the Shenandoah, which was flashing in the sun like a mirror, was the town of Woodstock. The tracks of the Manassas Gap Railroad went right through it. But the cannonading was going on way north of the town. It looked like a real fight because thousands of bluebelly soldiers were crawling down the pike; and they were also marching around the rolling countryside east of the river like squiggly lines of ants. But I could see our own Confederates too, although they weren't anything in comparison to the Yanks.

I should have kept ahead of all that fighting and marched my ass down in the direction of Edenburg, which had a little white church and a gazebo; I remembered that because I went with Poppa to a meeting there once. But I was drawn to the fight because I just had to see what was happening inside all the smoke and noise; it seemed to hurt the inside of my head to try to imagine it, and like I said before, I didn't feel empty and alone and sad when I was near the skirmishing. Maybe it was the comfort of the noise and being near the spirits that always stayed around after the soldiers were killed; and even though I could feel that the spirits had left me and that I probably didn't belong with them anymore, I still felt like I was more a spirit than anything else.

I stayed right away from Woodstock and came up through the woods on the other side of it. Like I said, I was feeling alive again, not sick at all. My heart was beating hard and the sun was shining down on my face as I lay on the edge of the woods where I could look out past fields and meadows into the woods way over on the other side. I listened to the musket and cannon and watched a few Confederate cavalrymen ride across the meadows, and waited.

The skirmishing was along the line of the woods, northwest of Woodstock.

I should have gone along and got out of here, but I figured I was safe enough if I didn't move around. And if there was anything to see, I'd see it. After a while, though, the firing stopped, and I just figured I was wrong about getting to see anything. Every once in a while there'd be a shot, but it didn't seem like any of the skirmishers were serious, or maybe they were all just having lunch. I couldn't imagine that the bluebellies would stop for long. Neither could I imagine how the Confederates would be able to hold them back. It seemed like there were ten bluebellies for every Confederate. Where was General Jackson's army anyway?

I felt suddenly hungry, but I'd eaten everything I'd foraged, and so I figured it was probably time to get some more food. I considered moving south along the pike where, likely as not, I'd find a farm that hadn't been foraged clean by the bluebellies. I also considered hanging around and getting some food from the soldiers that had been killed. I wasn't afraid of getting killed by a minié ball or grape or anything like that because I'd probably just change into a spirit. What scared me was getting wounded, or cut up with a bayonet, or losing an arm or a leg, or getting beat and plugged up the ass by somebody like Private Eurastus. I remember when Poppa was burning up in the Big House, he was screaming for Mother because he was worried about her, not about dying.

But those sonovabitches who hurt her . . .

Private Eurastus, I'd kill you again and again, you damn diarrhea sonovabitch, you would have killed Mother and burned up Poppa, you would have killed Jimmadasin and Sergeant Dunean and Doctor Zearing and Mammy Jack and Lucy and Cow and everybody; and I wondered if he was still killing everybody, killing spirits, killing them all over again, again and again, and I wondered if you could kill a spirit and—

Then I figured I must be having a vision or something because all of a sudden I saw what looked like a company of twenty or thirty Confederate cavalry riding along the edge of the woods and coming right toward me, and riding right in front of them—big as life—was Colonel Turner Ashby. He was riding with several men—who were probably his officers—and a boy who didn't look like he was more than ten. The boy was riding a little sorrel, but Colonel Ashby was riding a huge white stallion, probably the biggest I've ever seen. I remember he had a white horse when he came to church in Winchester. I wondered what he was doing riding with that boy. Maybe it was his son. But I don't remember that Colonel Ashby was ever married. Anyway, I figured he was reconnoitering to find out how far the bluebelly lines were stretched or something because he pointed this way and that and called out to his men and put them in position just where he wanted them along the edge of the woods, and I was glad I was here behind Confederate lines. He certainly looked a sight on that stallion with his long black beard and white gauntlets and white plume in his hat, and it gave me a thrill just to see him. And he had black hair like me, and brown eyes like me too; I remember all that from church.

He rode right by me, close enough that I could see the flies buzzing around his horse's muzzle, and then I heard the crack of a rifle. It sounded like it came from right behind me. I jumped in fright and surprise. If that shot was fired by a Yankee sharpshooter, he wasn't very good because instead of hitting Colonel Ashby he hit the boy's horse right through the eye, and the horse went down and the boy fell off and rolled on the ground, and then jumped to his feet to run, and then there was shooting all around me, and Colonel Ashby's men were riding toward me with their sabers out and firing their pistols and carbines, and I could hear minié balls flying around like bees again, and I was in the middle of it. I just couldn't imagine that I'd been sitting here like no nevermind and didn't know that there were Yankee sharpshooters all around me.

Now, even though everyone was scattering every which way and shouting and shooting, Colonel Ashby didn't seem at all discomfited. He sat right in his saddle, like he was posing for a daguerrian artist, reviewing everything, even though he was the target; and as the boy ran toward him, he waved him back, saying, "Dixie, go back and get that saddle off your horse. Quickly now." He waited while the boy fumbled with the cinch.

Now, although I was seeing all this, I was taken over with panic because I had the Seventh Cavalry shooting at me with their muskets and shotguns and carbines and pistols, and there were bluebellies firing and moving all around me like maggots on a cow. I couldn't see them, but I heard one of them shout and another breathe out when he got hit, and I stayed where I was, afraid to move, which was probably smart, but just as Colonel Ashby made his horse drop to the ground for Dixie, which I thought was a wonderful trick, one of the bluebelly sharpshooters shot Dixie—just out of meanness, I guess. Dixie just fell on top of the saddle he was carrying, and his butternut vest, which had brass buttons and four little pockets, was covered with blood.

Well, the colonel started screaming like he was hit himself and pulled his horse upright and rode over to Dixie; and that's when I ran out of the cover, ran right toward the colonel, and I could hear bullets buzzing around me, and I don't know why I put myself in such danger, but I did. One minute I was frozen to the ground and watching and listening and being invisible, and the next minute I was running right toward the colonel and his horse, and just then that horse looked like it was a mile high. I didn't know what I expected the colonel to do, but I heard him say "Good Lord" and he rode right at me. I thought he was going to cut me in half with his saber, maybe thinking I was the enemy or something because even then I realized what I was doing was damned stupid, but like I said before, sometimes I just don't know what I'm going to do, and that was one of those times. I remember, though, that for maybe a second, while I was looking up at him and his horse, I could see every detail about him: how his mustache fell over his lips, where it was wet with perspiration, how dark his complexion was, the tiny craters in his cheeks, the stains on his jacket, and how his hair curled forward below where he parted it; and his horse was sweating and steam was coming off its flesh like it was an engine, and I could smell that horse and the musty odor of the colonel's uniform and the sharp smell of powder that caught in my throat, and I could taste it like I'd swallowed sand or something; and then it was like when Private Eurastus caught me because I felt myself flying through the air, and then I was holding on to the colonel as we rode along the edge of that line of trees, and the skirmish was over as quick as it began.

We BURIED DIXIE RIGHT THERE WHERE HE FELL.

Colonel Ashby sent his officers back to the skirmishing line below the hill and asked them to send back a burial detail and an extra horse for me. In less than five minutes four men returned with a bay and white stallion that was almost the size of the colonel's, and they dug Dixie a real grave, even and square and deep and everything, while Colonel Ashby kneeled on one knee beside Dixie. I waited to see if the colonel was going to put pennies over Dixie's eyes, and I kept my own eyes peeled for Dixie's spirit to come out of hiding and watch the proceedings. I figured it would come out of his eyes, which Colonel Ashby had closed. Now, maybe that's why the niggers had put those pennies on top of Sweet Grandy's eyes: to keep her spirit from getting out and just walking around wherever it felt like.

Colonel Ashby was talking to a dark-haired man with a brown mustache who looked like he'd never laughed a day in his life. The colonel called him Jedediah. I didn't think this Jedediah was an army man; he wasn't dressed in anything that looked like a uniform. Fact is, he looked more like a preacher than an officer. He kept asking me questions, as if he was speaking for Colonel Ashby. Colonel Ashby just kept looking at me real queer, like he'd seen a ghost or something, and I figured it probably was because he could see I was a spirit. Anyway, whenever Jedediah asked me something, I just nodded or shook my head and tried to appear polite as I could. He figured out quick that I couldn't talk but could understand.

"You got family here, son?"

I shook my head.

"You know who this gentleman is?" He nodded toward Colonel Ashby. I nodded.

"Ah. Then you know Colonel Ashby."

I knew that was a trick question, and I was heading for trouble. I shouldn't have even nodded at all when he asked me the first time, but I figured that everybody knew about the colonel—at least anyone from the Valley. So I kept my head down and watched my shoes and glanced over at Dixie to see about his spirit.

Then Jedediah asked, "Can you write? You want to write your name down here on this pad for me, son?"

At first I wasn't interested in writing down anything to give myself away, but when he turned over a new page for me to write on, I could see that he had pictures or something on the other pages, and I thought that was real interesting. So I took his pad and flipped through those pages. Of course, he grabbed it back like it was his family's secret treasure, but I'd already seen that there were all kinds of sketches in that pad, maps of the Massanuttens and North Mountain and Rude's Hill and one of the entire Valley, and everything was neat and tiny and perfect in those maps: the squiggles of the north fork of the Shenandoah, little crosshatch lines that showed the winding tracks of the Manassas Gap Railroad and the Virginia Central and the B&O. Just looking at those maps, even for a second, made me think of my vision of *Private Newton's War in the Air*. In my vision I was hanging from a rope ladder under a balloon, and everything way below me—all the buildings and streets and monuments—looked perfect, like they were all made out of thin lines and dots.

"Son, just write your name like you were asked," Colonel Ashby said in a quiet voice, like he'd never raise it against anybody; and I was so surprised that he had said something to me that I took the pad from Jedediah again and started to write my name with the pencil he gave me. Now, I figured I could still write; but when I tried to write "Edmund McDowell," I just couldn't remember whether I was supposed to write it from the left or from the right, and then I got scared because I knew it, I knew my name, and I knew the letters, but I didn't know how to write them down anymore. So it was true I'd become a spirit, and I supposed if I just held my breath right then and there I'd probably turn invisible or something, but then I just did something crazy again, like I'd done when I ran out to Colonel Ashby because I didn't want to lose him, I wanted to stay with him because I felt . . . safe. It wasn't that I was afraid of anything, but—

I don't know. I just had to stay with him if I could, so I started to draw on that page, and I looked over at Dixie and just started drawing him. I never had any particular talent, but I was drawing real fast, drawing him even though he was upside down from where I was standing, and I drew him like I was drawing one of Jedediah's maps, drawing with lines that crossed over each other like railroad tracks, and I put pennies over Dixie's eyes and drew a halo around his head, and I suddenly knew that I was drawing the baby Jesus, even though I had run away without seeing Him, and I thought that maybe this would bring Jimmadasin back for a look, but it didn't. I handed the pad back to Jedediah, who had a funny expression on his face when he looked at the picture. Then he passed it over to Colonel Ashby, who said, "It's a sign," and he looked over at me, and all I could see was sadness in him. It wasn't that he was feeling sorry for me, but it was like he probably felt it was his fault that Dixie and everybody else died; and then the soldiers were finished with the grave, and Colonel Ashby said a prayer about how the bluebellies could murder little children but would never conquer the Southern people, and that we—all of us—were instruments of God, we were the sabers and muskets of God, and we would condemn the enemy and execute them and make a fire of them or something; and what he said must have been true, about there being signs and everything, because the soldiers hadn't just covered the grave with dirt than shells started dropping all over like they were devils coming right up from hell. Those Yankee shells howled dreadfully, and when they burst, you could feel it like something was breaking your bones from the inside out. I couldn't help but think that the next one was going to land right where I was standing. Everyone ran for their horses, except for Colonel Ashby, and I stayed there with him.

The colonel just stood by the side of the grave and looked down at the ground like he had lost something in the dead grass. I could see his lips moving, but I couldn't make out what he was saying. Then he put his hat on and nodded at the ground. Maybe he could see Dixie lying under there and was talking with him or something. After that he took hold of my arm—but he didn't squeeze it tight to hurt me—and we walked away.

Jedediah had our horses ready for us. He was stroking their muzzles to calm them down, and I couldn't help but wonder what old Jedediah would do if I stroked his long, horsey face the same way; he looked as nervous as the horses. A shell exploded, ripping out a tree, and branches and clumps of dirt were coming down like they had fallen out of the sky. For a while it was hard to hear, but I just followed Colonel Ashby and Jedediah. Now, with all the noise and pieces of trees falling all over, I didn't have time to get excited that I had my own horse; but I could feel its muscles against my legs, and the smell of horse and leather made me think of being home, and it felt strange just seeing everything exploding and not being able to hear anything but a swooshing sound that sounded like it was miles away; and it almost seemed like I was dreaming about riding that bay and white horse; and I imagined that the clouds of dirt and smoke were the purest, whitest clouds under Heaven, and I felt like the horse was part of my legs, and I was just getting taller and larger and stronger, and that minié balls or shot or grape or canister couldn't hurt me, and it was such a long way down to the ground that if I fell, I'd probably have time to sing the first verse of "Annie Laurie."

We rode out to the skirmishing line where the bluebellies were pushing back the First Virginia battalion on both sides of the turnpike, and, of course, Colonel Ashby's cavalry was harassing the enemy and charging into their front ranks without any fear at all while the infantry soldiers huddled amongst themselves with their bayonets pointed this way and that and waited for the fighting to come to them. I guess they wouldn't have long to wait—I couldn't imagine anything but General Jackson's whole army, and probably Johnson's too, could stop all those Federals in their baggy blue uniforms. But Colonel Ashby didn't seem at all discomposed, even when the bluebellies started screaming "Hurrah!" which was their pitiful version of a rebel yell, and charged. Then everybody was screaming and muskets were popping and minié balls were buzzing like bees, and I saw a 'Federate soldier get so excited he pulled the trigger of his musket before withdrawing the ramrod and sent it flying into the Yankee ranks like an arrow, and a Yank was looking straight at me like he was scared to death, and I saw that he'd been shot in the chest; a second later he fell to his knees. I felt the hair tingle on the back of my neck, and my heart started pounding, and I remembered the pile of arms and legs in the church where Doctor Zearing and Sergeant Dunean were cutting up Yankee soldiers, and I remembered the Confederate soldier who'd lost his eyes and nose and was so polite when I washed his face, and I felt like running and screaming, but it was like I was just watching myself, like I wasn't me because I felt calm and dead and I couldn't have screamed if I'd wanted to anyway. I looked around for Jedediah, as if he were Jimmadasin or something, but he'd disappeared into the fighting; and then Colonel Ashby shouted something to one of his officers—but I couldn't hear what it was—and then just rode off into our own ranks where it was safe, and for a hot second I thought maybe I'd gotten everything all wrong, and that he was a coward and the bravery of his men covered up for him and fooled everyone in the Valley who respected and admired him and expected him to be a hero, or something like that; but I followed him, almost falling off my horse, which seemed to know where it was going before I could even set the reins; and we rode right into the thundering cannon of Chew's Flying Battery, which was probably as famous as Colonel Ashby's cavalry because nobody had ever thought to mount guns on light wagons drawn by riding horses before.

There were only two rifled guns here, and they were working so hard they were red hot—a ten-pounder and down a ways a twenty-pounder—and the artillerymen were doing their jobs and concentrating, and they didn't seem to be paying attention to each other, or looking up to see what was going on around them. A sergeant who looked like he'd never washed his clothes or his face shouted "Commence firing!" and a gunner shouted "Load!" and an artilleryman sponged the barrel while another passed along a round and another put it in the muzzle and rammed it down, and then the gunner sighted the cannon and shouted "Ready!" and an artilleryman tore out a cartridge bag while someone else fussed with the opening on top of the barrel and stuffed something into it and then covered the hole with his hand, and then the gunner shouted "Fire!" and after the blast the cannon was run back up, and everything started all over again. We weren't there for more than a minute before an officer rode up to Colonel Ashby and saluted like he was on a parade field, and he didn't look much older than me, or probably I'd be more accurate to say that he didn't look much older than Lucy.

Turned out he was Captain Chew himself. He was tall and skinny and clean-shaven, and there was a bump in his nose like it had been broken; and he seemed like he was out of breath. If you didn't know who he was, you'd probably just figure he was a private wearing odds and ends clothes from home because he wasn't wearing shoulder straps. He wore a felt hat that had hardly any shape to it and a blouse with a lay-down collar. Anyway, while Colonel Ashby talked to the captain, I kept out of the way and watched the gun crew going through their motions, but I didn't have to wait long because at a command from Captain Chew everyone started packing up.

We were going to retreat, no doubt about that.

Colonel Ashby rode away without giving me a signal, and I thought he probably intended to leave me with Captain Chew; but I was determined not to be left behind. I felt like I was really invisible now, but it wasn't because I was a spirit or anything; I just wasn't important enough for Colonel Ashby or Captain Chew or anybody—except maybe Jedediah—to pay any attention to. Colonel Ashby went back for Jedediah, and then we retreated back to Woodstock with most of the cavalry, leaving the infantry to retreat as best they could. The Yank cavalry pursued us, but they were no match for the men that Colonel Ashby left behind to harass them. Everything was dust and the pounding of hooves and the pop and thunder of guns and cannon, and it's difficult to explain, but all the officers and cavalry soldiers around me seemed excited and sleepy at the same time. That's the only way I can describe them, like they were dreaming or were far away or something, and even though we were riding hard, retreating like cowards who couldn't get away from the fray fast enough, it *did* feel like a dream. It was hot, but you could hardly make out the sun because of all the dust being kicked up around us, and I was riding alongside of Colonel Ashby, who just stared straight ahead, concentrating on something no one else could probably see, just like when he was looking into Dixie's grave; and it was like we were all spirits, spirits riding down the pike with the entire Fifth Army Corps of bluebelly Yanks behind us. Nothing but the entire Army of Northern Virginia could stop them. Or that's what I thought, anyway. I only looked back once, when we were on top of a hill where I could see Woodstock ahead of me a ways, but I turned around, and I could see the bluebelly line stretched back along the pike and in the country to the east and west of it; they were stretched out forever, it seemed, and I imagined I could hear them like thunder as they marched.

I didn't look back again. I practiced being like Colonel Ashby, and I stared straight ahead into the distance, and it seemed that as long as I looked at something way up front, nothing could hurt me, like my spirit was up ahead pulling my body along and protecting it from everything. Like in a dream, as I said; and I had another vision right there riding alongside Colonel Ashby, as we charged down a hill right into Woodstock like the enemy was ahead of us instead of behind us. All of a sudden I remembered the deserter burning and glowing and smelling like hay and burnt leather and chicken and running toward me when I was in the cave; and the reason I know it was a vision instead of just a recollection was because a few minutes after I thought it, the whole town of Woodstock seemed like it was on fire.

I'm getting ahead of myself, but not by much.

We rode into Woodstock, and townspeople were hanging out of windows and waving to us from doors and running out into the street to welcome us, and they were waving Confederate flags and handkerchiefs and bringing out jugs of water and cake and bread, and my stomach rolled and my mouth watered just thinking about food; but the officers were shouting at them to get inside and stay there where it would be safe, that the Yanks were going to get a surprise, and not to be afraid. It wasn't hard to figure out what the surprise was going to be:

Chew's battery had planted several pieces right in the middle of the street at the southern end of town. They must have gotten here well before the cavalry, and now we were riding toward them with our infantry right behind us, and chasing the First Virginia was the bluebelly advance guard and guns were firing and minié balls were flying all over the street and striking houses and pinging off stones; and with all the townspeople watching, we ran and retreated, riding toward Chew's guns, riding past the courthouse, and the town hall with its green dome, and the gabled houses and shacks and there was a building with NEWS EXCHANGE written on a white board over the door—it was probably a tavern— and long granaries along the railroad tracks, and in the distance I could see the Lutheran church and the weeping willows that stood over the graveyard next to it. The First Virginia was in a rout behind us, and Colonel Ashby disappeared. I was looking for him when Jedediah found me and grabbed the reins right out of my hands.

"Son, whatever your God-given name might be, you're not going to ride with the colonel." He said that like he was my father or something, and although all I could think of was to get away from him and find Colonel Ashby, I knew he didn't mean me any harm. Then he said, "I won't have anyone else end up dead like little Dixie, may God bless his immortal soul. Now I'm taking you where it's safe and where people will care for you properly." But I wasn't going to have any of that, even though I didn't have any idea where he thought he'd be taking me; and if he took me anywhere, anyway, it would be like he'd be deserting Colonel Ashby and the cavalry and the army, and they could hang him or shoot him for that. So I nodded like I understood, of course—I'd go with you wher- ever you say, Mr. Jedediah—and even though it didn't seem like he intended on letting go of the reins, I pulled them away when an enemy shell exploded right by us and struck the courthouse. Shingles rained down on us. But I was away from Jedediah, who probably wasn't God-blessing me anymore, but I saw that he wasn't hurt, and I rode away, through the soldiers running and retreating, and then I found Colonel Ashby, who was parading around on his horse and showing off for the citizens who were still running around in the street and looking out of every window and door; and it was like this was a town full of ghosts who weren't afraid of bullets or anything, although there were people screaming and crying. Well, Colonel Ashby was waving his hat around because a minié ball had passed right through the brim; it was a miracle that he didn't end up like that poor Confederate soldier I tended in the church. But Colonel Ashby didn't think anything of it, except as an example to make fun of the bluebellies.

He was defying Banks's entire army, as if he was going to take on every soldier single-handed. I saw there were bales of straw and rubbish piled all around him and his horse, but I didn't see how that could protect him. I rode through the rubbish right up to him, and he didn't shoo me away; he probably didn't even notice me. Maybe he did. But I knew right there that he was a spirit, that he was different from all his men and all the townsfolk. Like I was. And if he wasn't a spirit, then he was just plain crazy. I could see the wildness in his face, although I couldn't tell you exactly how. It wasn't just one thing like his eyes or his expression or anything like that. It was just that I couldn't help but think that he was somehow on fire, like he had seen something terrible and couldn't get away from it, and now he was enjoying the crying and shrieking and pounding of wheels and hooves and the shot and the shells exploding and tearing into gables and stone walls. A shell hit the jail and did just that; I saw it break through a wall, and more shingles rained down on the street; but it had hardly started, and I started feeling wild, like I was Colonel Ashby too, and I got close to him, and he looked over at me and smiled, like he had just seen me for the first time and we were going to share something wonderful. The Confederate soldiers were behind us now, behind Chew's guns, and for what seemed like a long time (but I knew was just a second or two) the main street was empty and full of smoke. I don't know why, but the smell of rain suddenly reached my nose, that damp, fresh smell that comes off the streets and fields, a smell that ends with a tingle like cold metal. Now, I don't know why I should have smelled that because it hadn't rained all day.

Townspeople were hiding inside their buildings. I couldn't see them in the street or in the windows, and it seemed just like the quiet before a storm, and maybe that's what it was—and maybe that's why I smelled the rain—because Colonel Ashby raised his arm, as if to greet the Yank cavalry, who were brave now that the main street was empty. Suddenly bluebelly riders and foot soldiers were rushing into town, crowding into the streets like every bluebelly soldier had suddenly taken it into his head to be the first one to get close to Colonel Ashby.

But when Colonel Ashby lowered his arm, Chew's pieces began firing, and shells flew over our heads, hissing and shrieking like snakes and spirits, and suddenly my heart was pounding and I felt my skin tingling on my face like it was shrinking or something, and I thought, Dear God we're going to die right here, and then I didn't care and then I didn't think anything could hurt us inside the bales of hay and piles of rubbish, and I wanted to ride out there and cut and shoot and kill the bluebellies, and I would be the saber and musket of God, and I would condemn the enemy and execute them and make a fire of them. Chew's shells dropped into the midst of the Federals, and the explosion threw soldiers into the air, tore off arms and legs, and wherever a shell hit, after a second, I could see the Federals clearing a space, and all I could think of was that this was like skipping stones in a pond, that when the stone hit the water, it would make a ring; and I thought of the soldiers like they were the water; and then Colonel Ashby shouted, "Get ready, little brother," and it seemed that only the two of us were out here on the street, and the bluebellies were coming for us, screaming their Yankee yell, and they were probably crazy with anger and fear and just wanted blood, and I could understand that because I would have liked to kill every one of them for Poppa and Mother, even though they had nothing to do with what happened at the Big House; and when Colonel Ashby lit those bales of straw and garbage with a match, it was like I couldn't have dreamed it better. And when that straw caught fire, and our horses started to go crazy with fear, I remembered the farm going up in flames, and I remembered being with Poppa every spring to help burn brush and dead leaves and anything else we could find; and then everything was burning and smoking. I've never seen so much smoke, and it was all around us like fog laying on the mountains, except it was swirling, and my eyes burned, and I was coughing, but I wasn't going to run until Colonel Ashby was ready; and then we were riding under the cover of all that smoke. I guess you could call it retreating, but we'd won, even if we had to leave the town to the bluebellies, even if we couldn't kill every one of them, or even most of them; and I imagined that Poppa would have been pleased, even if Mother would have probably thought that any killing would be wrong. But Poppa understood about being a saber and musket of God and making a fire of the enemy, and that's just what Colonel Ashby did, and I understood about being a nigger and feeling God pushing all over you inside and out so that you can't help but scream "Hallelujah!"

I certainly heard the thunder in my ears and was probably making the "ha" sound, and I saw a black dog dart across the pike; and though I wasn't sure, I figured it was the spirit dog, and if I could have I would have screamed "Hallelujah!" because I thought maybe that was a sign that Jimmadasin and the baby Jesus and the other spirits had forgave me for leaving them in the cave; and I couldn't imagine anything better than riding down the pike ahead of the infantry with Colonel Ashby. We burned three bridges, one above Woodstock and two around Edenburg, and we tried to burn the railroad bridge over Narrow Passage Creek, but the bluebellies came at us and we had to retreat again, but we held the line at Stony Creek, on the other side of Edenburg.

This was the most wonderful day of my life.

Hallelujah.

It seemed to go by in a second, and it wasn't until we made camp and cooked up some pork over a fire that I got sick and vomited and then fell right asleep sitting up, and all I can remember was Jedediah's face real close to mine, and he smelled like tobacco and bad meat, and he pulled me up from where I was by the fire, all the while he was arguing with Colonel Ashby. . . .

Dick is dead, leave him be—

The boy was given to me, Jedediah.

I know a family near Riles Creek.

You, of all people, know that. You saw—

I'm taking him there in the morning.

And I'll have you court-martialled for disobeying a direct order.

Then you'll just have to do that.

Or maybe I dreamed that, but in my dreams I remembered things. I remembered Colonel Ashby calling me Dixie when we were riding and burning bridges, and I remember smiling back at him and after that he named me Dixie, and when I woke up the next morning, Jedediah wasn't anywhere to be seen.

IN HEAVEN WITH GENERAL JACKSON
AND ABE LINCOLN

Possum put on an overcoat,
Raccoon put on a gown,
Rabbit put on a ruffled shirt,
All buttoned up and down.

SONG BY
HENRY GEORGE
GENERAL WASHINGTON

*J*HAVEN'T EVEN GOT TO THE PART ABOUT CAPTAIN FRANCIS W. Pegram from London, England, yet, but there's probably time enough for that. Anyway, he wasn't any different from most of the other officers who figured that niggers and servants didn't have souls or anything. Course, there are always exceptions, like Colonel Ashby and Jedediah and, of course, General Jackson (who was probably even more religious than Jedediah, if it came to that).

Now, it's been my experience that niggers will do most anything to get into a church and feel the presence of the Lord and sing hallelujah and all of that, but I also know that some were never taught anything about religion, and if you haven't been properly taught about religion, then you'd probably rather drink corn juice or applejack with a bunch of other niggers in the village than sit up in the rafters and listen to sermons about sin and responsibility and the proper order of things.

But before I get ahead of myself talking about religion, and who was the most religious and who wasn't, I probably should get back to telling you how I rode with Colonel Ashby and had just about two of the best weeks of my entire life.

Now, while General Jackson and most of his entire army were resting up in their camp on Rude's Hill about three miles south of Mount Jackson, Colonel Ashby and me and the Seventh Virginia Cavalry and Chew's Battery were doing all the fighting against General Banks and his army of Federals. We were on one side of Stony Creek, and they were on the other because that's where Colonel Ashby decided to hold the line. Of course, Stony Creek was only about ten yards wide, which was about how close we were to the Yankee outposts; but the Federals couldn't get across too easily because Colonel Ashby had burned the bridge, and all the streams and creeks and rivers were swollen from rain and melting snow. And General Banks couldn't get at General Jackson unless he crossed the bridge over the north branch of the Shenandoah by the pike, and Colonel Ashby was guarding that bridge and skirmishing and annoying Banks from Strasburg to Columbia Furnace.

For a while Captain Chew's guns were mounted on a hill behind Stony Creek, and the Federal guns were on a hill just behind Edinburg, and when we started dueling, the shot and shell would fly over that town like fireworks on the Fourth of July. Those shells when they came over would howl like devils and then burst with a terrific noise; and I should tell you that General Jackson did send some of his infantry and artillery over to reinforce Colonel Ashby's boys, and sometimes the soldiers would get in the way of the Federal cannon and we'd find bits of them in the trees. I climbed more than one tree, I can tell you, to throw down arms and legs so the soldiers could be buried with all their parts all together. And those Federal shells were *long*; they must have been fifteen inches at least. Now, I also know that Captain Chew was trying out his own special shells that would put God into the enemy, as Jedediah always said. They were some kind of fancy percussion shell that came from England or someplace, but most of them were duds and didn't explode, although Chew fairly well exploded himself when he took one apart and found out it didn't have a percussion cap. He said it was treason by the Yanks or something, but, of course, we blamed most everything that went wrong on the bluebelly bucktails.

Except it seemed that General Jackson blamed everything that went wrong on Colonel Ashby, but that's another story and it was because the Seventh Virginia had probably doubled in size in the past few weeks, and sometimes it did seem like a party around the camp. Most of the new recruits pretty near worshiped Colonel Ashby and just wanted to ride with him and be heroes too, but they didn't have proper uniforms or anything, and some spent their time riding all over and imposing on the citizens and creating havoc and drinking themselves dumb, while others got right in there and kept the Yanks busy. Anyway, most of them were on detached duty, whatever that meant; and the fact was that Colonel Ashby didn't care much about rules and organizing and training and writing up reports. He mostly just had heroic adventures and listened to the spirits and the dead, who talked to him, and I guess they told him when to fight and where. I know he talked to the dead because I heard him, and I'll tell you about that; but no matter what anyone said about how Colonel Ashby didn't have discipline, it was because Colonel Ashby was too busy with artillery brawling and picket stalking, as he called it, to be training in new recruits. While General Jackson was resting up at Reverend Rude's house on Rude's Hill, like I said, Colonel Ashby had to hold the line along the creek and confound Banks's troops, which were just about everywhere. So Major Funsten, who was second in command, took care of most of the organizing.

Anyway, Colonel Ashby couldn't sit still for a minute; he was always getting on one of his stallions and riding off to do reconnaissance and burn bridges or pull up railroad tracks and twist the rails around trees, and once we burned a bridge with the cars still on it, and they were piled one atop the other in a narrow gully below, all bent up and broken and blistered, and you could look right inside those fine iron cars and still see the coals burning red and hot like they were in a cozy fireplace. Colonel Ashby rode around all day harassing the enemy, and there were always different soldiers riding with him. I figured that one or two companies would take a rest so the others could have their turn; but Colonel Ashby, he hardly rested or slept at all, and when he did, it was mostly in the day.

Although everyone respected him and treated him like he was the baby Jesus or something, he didn't have many friends, except for me and Jedediah, but he and Jedediah got cold to each other after they disagreed over what to do about me. Jedediah wasn't having any of that business about me being a sign from the Lord or having something to do with Colonel Ashby's dead brother, Richard, or anything like that; and he and Colonel Ashby had a fight in the camp because Jedediah spoke to General Jackson about my situation. I heard

Jedediah tell Colonel Ashby that he wasn't right, and I never did figure out whether he meant that Colonel Ashby was wrong about something or that there was something wrong inside of his head. I guess he probably told General Jackson the same thing, and that's what started the argument, even though "argument" probably isn't the right word because they hardly raised their voices; but when I walked in on them by mistake I could tell they were probably ready to kill each other. Colonel Ashby would get that same look on his face when he'd talk about how the Yanks murdered his brother Richard by running a bayonet through his stomach after he'd already been shot six times.

I wondered if Jedediah and Colonel Ashby had had these arguments about Dixie, but after we buried him no one ever mentioned his name. It was like he never existed at all, and I felt sorry for him, especially if he'd turned into a spirit and was hanging around and listening and wondering why everyone had just forgot about him like yesterday's breakfast. But if he was a spirit, I figure I would have seen him, unless being around Colonel Ashby and Jedediah and the Seventh Virginia had clouded over my vision so I didn't have the second sight anymore. Now, part of that I knew was true because I didn't *feel* invisible, and everyone who came around to see Colonel Ashby saw me. Colonel Ashby had his headquarters in an old, run-down cabin beyond Stony Creek that belonged to a soldier called Argenbright, and the men would all talk to me, and sometimes they'd give me food or coffee or a little sugar, and if they had to wait around, they'd tell me just about everything that had ever happened to them; I imagine some of them just came over for the company and to hear themselves talk about themselves. I'd just listen to them and think my own thoughts, like when I had the ague and the spirits just talked away at me.

But I was mostly out of the camp with Colonel Ashby, and after a while my ass stopped being sore from riding all the time, and I learned to sleep right in the saddle, which was probably a good thing too because on April 17th General Banks's army started their advance at three-thirty in the morning and pushed us back from Stony Creek, and I guess Colonel Ashby figured he'd have to stop them all by himself. He was shouting "Drive them, boys, drive them," even though we were retreating, but we were fighting for every inch of ground; and he seemed half crazy when he found out that Captain Harper's company of cavalry had been surprised and captured somewhere between Mount Jackson and Columbia Furnace. He told everyone he saw that we were going to create hell for the bluebellies everywhere they marched, and in the cold of the night we rode and burned whatever bridges and railroad property we could, and while

General Jackson was probably having his breakfast at headquarters and packing up for his retreat, we were skirmishing and falling back; and even though we were getting pushed back, and we could see that there were so many Federals that it made you wonder how they could ever be stopped, I felt that nothing could hurt us because we were spirits riding through the night; it was like we were two brothers, like I was his brother Richard who he talked to when he was having visions; and with all the bullets and case shot and grape and canister buzzing through the air and cutting bushes and trees and soldiers into splinters, and with all our men riding and skirmishing and retreating from General Banks, I felt that this was where I belonged; this was wonderful, this was my vision, and it was better than Private Newton and his war in the air, and every once in a while Colonel Ashby would look over at me and laugh like this was the best joke he'd ever heard and we both knew that we were just going to ride on forever and forever and stir up the Federals and sneak up behind them with Chew and his battery and shoot them back to kingdom come and the United States of America.

I should probably explain real quick that there were two Colonel Ashbys, only I was the only one who knew about that. During the day, he would always ride his white stallion and dress real fine, like he was the Knight of the White Prince or the Knight of Hiawatha in one of his tournaments that he always talked about; but at night, when he usually had his heavenly visions like Paul on his way to Damascus, he would wear his plain gray pantaloons and a loose-fitting jacket and would only ride the black stallion. When he rode at night, with a company or sometimes just him and me and a few officers and troopers, he'd talk to his brother Richard in a low voice, sort of like he was singing, but I could make out what he said, and it was sort of like he was asking for directions; and once, when there was just the two of us, we stopped to rest and chew on some hardtack and sip whiskey behind an enemy outpost, and he told me that he always saw Richard when he was fighting and that Richard knew everything that was going to happen and always helped out Colonel Ashby, and that when it was time for Colonel Ashby to get killed, his brother would just let him know, so until then Colonel Ashby didn't have anything to worry about. Sometimes he would be so preoccupied with talking and listening to his brother that he would ride right on through the enemy pickets without even firing at them, leaving his men to do the fighting while we kept riding like we were following the spirit dog.

Well, that's just how it was the night that Banks started his advance.

Colonel Ashby was riding this way and that along the front, following his brother, giggling, whispering, talking to him, and shouting "Drive them, boys, drive them," to his men until he was hoarse, and just after dawn we rode right through the Federal skirmishers, and he was probably thinking he was in one of his tournaments again because he was waving his sword all around as if it would protect him from the minié balls that sounded like bees, like I told you; and I guess his brother Richard knew what he was doing because Colonel Ashby rode right at a Federal soldier who was taking aim at him and took his head right off with his saber. I heard the saber cut through the air like it was singing, and then the Federal fired his musket, and I expected that he'd just killed Colonel Ashby, but nothing could kill Colonel Ashby because he was under the protection of his brother, and although no one else saw it, Colonel Ashby had taken hold of that bluebelly soldier's head and rode around holding it by its red hair like it was a lantern or something, but then it got to be dawn and he threw the head into the woods like it was nothing more than a baseball, even though it was more the size of a cannonball. I wondered if that head was still having thoughts, and I remembered seeing a soldier's head roll right in front of Allan McSherry's foot at Kernstown, and I remembered how its lips were still moving like it was saying its prayers or a spirit had gotten into it or something. This head hadn't tried any talking, although it certainly bled enough—mostly all over Colonel Ashby, who didn't seem to mind at all.

Colonel Ashby talked to his brother Richard while we rode back to the cabin one last time so he could change horses and clothes, and change into his other self.

Now, before I get ahead of myself again, I should also tell you that Colonel Ashby didn't talk to Richard half as much in the daytime as he did at night. He didn't remember most of what we did at night, except for what he wrote down in a little diary he always carried. He'd write in that diary sometimes when it was so dark you could hardly see your hand in front of your face. Sometimes he gave the diary to me to carry, just in case Richard was going to tell him it was his time to get killed. I tried to read that diary once, but I couldn't, even by trying tricks like squinting up my eyes and staring at the letters until they danced around; and I figured it was because he was writing in the secret language of the Masons or something. He told me that because he'd been initiated into the Mason fraternity at Martinsberg, he knew about secret things; and that all the codes of honor and the true Virginia spirit of valor and patriotism and heroism and godliness and everything like that were all part of being a

Mason, and that I would probably be a Mason and understand them one day; but in the meantime he couldn't trust me completely, and I knew he didn't trust me because he kept telling me that General Jackson had an army as large as Banks, which everyone knew wasn't true. It hurt my feelings that he probably thought I was a spy like in my vision of Private Newton's war in the air.

Anyway, Colonel Ashby would read his diary every day and smile like he'd been having his own joke. Once he asked me what it felt like to ride with him through his dreams.

Even if I could talk, I wouldn't have answered him because just talking about such things would probably bring bad luck.

Even though I understood exactly what he meant.

I RESTED MY HORSE WHILE COLONEL ASHBY WASHED UP—HE WAS ALL smeared with blood—and trimmed his beard and put on his fancy uniform. While he dressed, he talked to Lieutenant Sandy Pendleton, who was General Jackson's assistant adjutant general. Lieutenant Pendleton was one of the soldiers who always gave me sugar or a bit of coffee when he came to see Colonel Ashby, and he was written up in the *Spectator* because he carried a lot of wounded men off the field in Kernstown, which made him a hero just like his father, Colonel Pendleton of Rockbridge.

One of the troopers saddled up Colonel Ashby's white stallion, which, as I probably told you, was as big as the black one; and when Colonel Ashby was done talking with Lieutenant Pendleton and got on his horse, he looked like a picture out of the Bible or something with his black beard and white gauntlets and high-top boots and a white plume in his hat, and with his special bridle and saddle and pistols and his saber polished clean of Yankee blood. And he smelled like violets or something, and so did I because although I didn't need any washing up, I stole some perfume from his little blue bottle and slapped my face to bring out the flowers, just like Colonel Ashby did.

But that was about as far as we got because as soon as we got mounted, Jedediah appeared like bad luck. Now, I know I told you that Jedediah probably wasn't an army man and that he looked like a preacher—which he did—but he was General Jackson's own private mapmaker, and he was an engineer and a captain, and he was always going on errands and doing things for General Jackson, and, like I said, he was just about as religious as General Jackson and was always giving Colonel Ashby his *Central Presbyterian* newspaper after he'd finished reading it. Colonel Ashby was always polite about getting the *Central Presbyterian*, but then he'd throw it into the fire because he didn't believe anything but the Bible itself, and maybe his own diary. Maybe it was because he'd been up all night making maps or fighting the Federals, but Jedediah looked all worn out. His eyes were bloodshot, his beard wasn't trimmed and seemed to be growing all over his face every which way, and his skin, what you could see of it, looked the way dead people's does when they're laid out in the casket so everybody can get a last look.

"The general been working you hard?" Colonel Ashby asked Jedediah.

Jedediah's horse was skittish and kept shaking its head and pulling away, but I'd seen that happen before; most horses got nervous around Colonel Ashby's white stallion.

"No more than usual," Jedediah said after he got his horse back under control. "I came to see if you wished to accompany me over to the flank of the Massanuttens to get a look at how Banks is deploying his troops. Get a bird's-eye view from over on Mount Airy. The general's already moving his men off Rude's Hill, as I expect Sandy's already told you." Jedediah and Sandy Pendleton looked at each other real quick, as if they both knew they'd be meeting here and didn't even have to say hello to each other.

"I wouldn't mind getting a look at the enemy's position," Sandy Pendleton said. "I'll take back any message you might have for the general."

"No sense all of us going," Jedediah said.

"Well, if Turner goes with you, I go too," Lieutenant Pendleton said. "General's orders."

"I don't need to climb a mountain to see where the enemy's deployed. I *know* where they are. Now, you go and tell the general that I'll make sure he knows everything when there's something to know."

"My orders are to stay with you, Colonel, and to remind you to stay out of harm's way."

"How can a soldier stay out of harm's way, unless he's a coward . . . or an assistant adjutant general?"

Lieutenant Pendleton grinned at Colonel Ashby. Nothing fazed Lieutenant Pendleton; he was probably the most good-natured officer in the Confederate army. "General Jackson feels that you'll not escape death for very long if you continue to expose yourself needlessly to the enemy."

"None of my actions are needless, Lieutenant. And I'm not afraid of minié balls, even when they're aimed directly at me because they'll always miss their mark. And I'm quite sure that when the Lord decides to take me, it won't matter whether I'm standing in the open or sitting behind a barricade. So I'm ordering you to go and communicate that to the general. That's *my* message."

The lieutenant laughed, but Colonel Ashby wasn't having any of it and ordered him to ride his ass over to General Jackson so Colonel Ashby could get back to kicking the asses of the Federals.

"*You* may not fear minié balls and grape, but what about the boy?" Jedediah asked. "Isn't it about time to have a care for him?"

"His name's Richard," Colonel Ashby said, looking fussed, like he'd been caught out at something. "And he's all done with being a boy." Colonel Ashby looked at me gentle but steady, like he expected me to say something.

I nodded and suddenly got all hot in the face, like I was embarrassed and sad, although I didn't know why. Then I looked down at the ground as if to escape everyone who was looking at me, and I thought about my name. I surely was done with Mundy and had become Richard; and even if Jedediah didn't know it, everybody else in the camp did because they were calling me Richard or Ritchie or Dick, and skinny Captain Chew called me Dick-boy, which always made everybody laugh, and his beef-brained artillerymen who had nicknames like Breakfast and Wasp and Rabbit would call me Prick-boy, but I didn't care because I was mostly out of the camp with Colonel Ashby and out of their way.

"Any more news from home?" Sandy Pendleton asked, changing the subject.

I looked up and saw he was talking to Jedediah.

"I can only wait and pray," Jedediah said. "But the Lord God Omnipotent reigneth, and He will do right."

"What's happened?" Colonel Ashby asked. His voice was low and full of compassion like a minister, and it was as if Lieutenant Pendleton had already left because Colonel Ashby was just paying attention to Jedediah now.

"My Nellie's sick with fever," Jedediah said. "The general had given me permission to do some reconnaissance around Bull Pasture Mountain, just so I could return to Loch Willow and see my family, but with Banks on the move, I know better than to even mention it."

"Children are strong, especially your Nellie; they can survive a fever," Colonel Ashby said. "You survived typhus with nothing worse than a headache."

"I pray God gives her nothing more than a headache," Jedediah said. "But she's got scarlet fever."

Colonel Ashby got that strange, faraway look, and I thought he might start talking to his brother Richard right then and there in front of everyone, but he just said, "You needn't worry about your babies, Jedediah. I can assure you they'll all be fine."

"I wish I was as certain as you are, Turner."

"Faith," Colonel Ashby said.

Jedediah just nodded and said, "Faith," like he was an echo.

MAYBE IT WAS BECAUSE HE FELT SORRY FOR JEDEDIAH—OR MAYBE, AS I figured it, his dead brother gave him some sort of a warning—but Colonel Ashby let Jedediah take me with him. I tried to kick up a fuss, but Colonel Ashby told *me* to take care of Jedediah, who had a better grip on the reins of my horse than I did and was leading me off like he was my father. So Jedediah became my responsibility, and I listened to him talk about his family as we rode out to the flank of the Massanuttens and around to Mount Airy; and as we were going toward those mountains, I couldn't help but think about Jimmadasin and how I had failed him by running off and leaving Lucy all by herself in the cave of the baby Jesus with the dead deserters and Cow and Armarci, who were dead too, and I wondered about Lucy, and how I could make everything right; and Jedediah went on and on telling me about how he and his wife had bought a farm between Franklin and McDowell and turned it into the Loch Willow Academy to board scholars, as he called it, and how they even joined the Union Church because they expected to stay there forever, and last year they had fifty-four students and a total revenue of over seventeen hundred dollars; but when Virginia seceded, one of his teachers organized an infantry company and took all the scholars, and there wasn't much Jedediah could do except join too, especially as his brother, who also worked on the farm, was for the Union and left to fight his own people. So now Jedediah and his wife belonged to the Union Church and didn't have any students. I figured she probably did the best she could with farming. He told me her name was Sara Anne Comfort, and I imagined her looking like a white Mammy Jack, big and fat and comfortable.

"You could do a lot to help her," Jedediah told me.

I didn't turn toward him or make like I was listening while he told me about his daughters, Anne and Nellie, who were five and seven, and although he didn't talk about Nellie being sick with malignant fever, I imagined her sitting all alone on red sandstone flags in front of a pretty white farmhouse while blood gushed out of her eyes and nose, like she was crying it all up. By the time Jedediah had told me about how he hated his brother Nelson, who was a Unionist, and went back to explaining how I could help his wife, Sara Anne, keep the farm going and be the regular man of the house and get an education into the bargain, we were high enough up the mountain to see Banks's army deploying near Mount Jackson on the northeast side of the North River.

Jedediah said there were probably twenty thousand bluebellies milling around over there, and I could see miles of white tents and what was probably a thousand wagons crowded onto the turnpike, probably all carrying supplies and ammunition; and there were enough ten- and twenty-pounder Parrott guns to blow our army clear to Zion. It seemed that we could see everything because the air didn't get in the way like it usually did; there wasn't any mist on the ground and only a few clouds in the sky, and it was warm and brown and green, except for the mountains, which looked pale blue, like they were just floating way out there. But I could see patches of snow that hadn't melted, and I wouldn't bet that the rain and hail and cold were over yet, even though everybody seemed to think that spring was here.

We stopped so Jedediah could draw maps and make notes in his sketchpad for General Jackson. While he drew, he talked to me like I was a baby, which reminded me of the way Sergeant Dunean had talked to me at Kernstown, except Jedediah was talking again about how I could have a family and my own bed and be safe and be the man of the house if I lived on his farm.

But while he was talking and sketching and pretending about me living with his family, I just rode away. He was so occupied with his drawing and thoughts and everything else that by the time he noticed I was on my way, it was too late for him to catch up with me. He tried, though, and he shouted at me, and I remembered Lucy shouting at me, and all I could think of was to get back to Colonel Ashby.

And I remembered what Jimmadasin had said to me.

You left Jesus, you'se on you' own now, you don' deserve nobody.

For a while, when I was with Colonel Ashby, I thought he was wrong; but it turned out that he was right.

I FOUND COLONEL ASHBY BY THE NORTH RIVER BRIDGE. IT WAS STILL spirit weather, so by the time I got down there, gray and black clouds had rolled in and squeezed out the sky, and the temperature dropped, and it started raining,

but not hard, just enough of a drizzle to make you cold, sticky, and uncomfortable. I haven't told you this before, but I was feeling uncomfortable anyway,
probably because I'd been in the camp too long and caught the lice, which
everybody calls graybacks or gray jackets. Although nobody talked about it
much, everybody had the creatures. When Colonel Ashby or Jedediah would
boil their clothes with salt, they'd make me put my shirt and pants into their mess
kettle too, but that didn't happen too often, and so mostly I'd just go "skirmishing" or "knitting," as everybody called it, and pick the bugs out of my clothes,
and you can't imagine how those little tiny sonovabitches itched—worse than
the ringworm, which was nothing by comparison; and I figured that my mother would know more about how to cure me of the graybacks than all the army
surgeons put together; she'd probably make up a medicine with silver nitrate
and vinegar or something and kill those little itchy bastards dead.

Anyway, it was probably just dumb luck that I found Colonel Ashby at all
because if I'd have come down any earlier, he would have been off somewhere
with his troopers resisting and harassing the enemy, tearing up track and burning bridges, locomotives, supply wagons, and destroying anything else that
might be useful to the bluebellies. But it was easy to find General Jackson's
army, which was marching in fine-looking ranks and columns in the direction of
Harrisonburg, and just follow it back, so I guess you could say that while General Jackson was retreating—or retiring, as Jedediah called it—I was advancing; and of course Colonel Ashby's cavalry was the only thing between our
army and the enemy. The bluebelly cavalry was pressing hard on Colonel
Ashby, but I have to give credit to General Jackson's artillery boys, who held
their ground on Rude's Hill and tore up more than a few of the advancing Federals with grape and canister. The cannon on both sides sounded like thunder
rolling back and forth across the mountains, and the grape was flying like it was
raining down out of the dark storm clouds and withering everything it hit as if
it was a curse from Ezekiel or someone in the Bible, and you could smell the
storm and powder and fuse; but Colonel Ashby wasn't fussed by any of it and
was patient while most of his men got across the North River Bridge along with
the rest of the army. Of course, I didn't know then that Colonel Ashby had been
surprised and outflanked by the Federal cavalry, but you wouldn't have known
it to see him there on the bridge with Captain Koontz. There were three other
troopers with them, and they had dismounted and were getting the combustibles ready to turn that bridge into a regular conflagration over the Shenandoah and stop the Federals dead in their tracks. It was a hot moment, and I could

see the Federal cavalry riding hard toward the bridge, and some of Colonel Ashby's troopers tried to stop me from riding toward him, and they called to me "Come out of there" and "Come away from there," but I rode right through them and would have rode over anyone who'd got in my way; and it's strange the kind of things you think about when you are probably just about to get killed: I saw Colonel Ashby, who looked up and saw me coming and just nodded like he expected me or something and then went back to his work like it wasn't anything much, and Captain Koontz looked up at me and hollered for me to get back, and I could see the Yankee cavalry. They were almost on the bridge, and they were all finely equipped, and it looked like they were all wearing new uniforms—that's how clean and polished they looked, as if they'd just been in a parade or something; and they started firing on Colonel Ashby and Captain Koontz and me and the other three men; and everything seemed to slow up and I felt I could just move this way or that to escape minié balls, and I was making the "ha" sound, but I was silently calling to Colonel Ashby's dead brother Richard and to Jimmadasin and Lucy and Cow and even that bastard Eurastus and the baby Jesus too, because it was like I was riding in God's light or something because I just felt good and pure, and I knew exactly how Colonel Ashby felt to know that nothing could touch you until you got the word from the Lord that it was time, and just as I stopped beside Colonel Ashby, he lit his combustibles, and it was just like we were back in Woodstock when he said "Get ready, little brother," and it was like we were all alone, and the bluebellies were coming for us, and it didn't matter a shit because we were going to make a conflagration, only this time, to tell the truth, I don't think Colonel Ashby realized I was there, and I figured that his dead brother Richard had told him to keep away from me or something, but if that was so, dead Richard was wrong this time because although Colonel Ashby lit his rags and straw, they didn't catch properly, and those vedettes were right on top of us with their muskets and pistols and sabers. I could feel the heat from the straw, though, and smell it strong in my nose like when we burned brush and dead leaves and vegetation on the farm, and Colonel Ashby shouted "Mount up" to Captain Koontz and the other men, but it was too late because those Federals were all around us, and a bluebelly sergeant who had a fly crawling right across his forehead told us, clear as day, to surrender, but Captain Koontz shot the poor bastard right in the throat, and the fly flew away as the sergeant made a terrible coughing sound and fell, and our troopers shot two more of the bluebelly vedettes, and then in the blink of an eye we were riding right through those Federals, and we only lost one trooper. He had red hair, and he was shot right through the eye; and I figured right then and there that it was an eye for an eye sort of thing because of what Colonel Ashby had done before to that red-haired bluebelly soldier; but it wasn't over yet because Colonel Ashby's beautiful white stallion was shot through the lungs, but that horse kept going, going right over the North River Bridge, and the cannon fire had been so loud that my ears just felt hollow, and I couldn't hear anything but soft thunder, which was probably why everything seemed to be going slowly. Well, we must've rode a mile, if anything, and the bluebellies were right behind us and firing, but Colonel Ashby's horse was slowing down and foaming from the heat and being shot, so Captain Koontz said, "You go on ahead, I'll ride over to the side of the pike and shoot the first man, get his horse, and we'll make our escape," which I thought was a stupid thing to do, but Captain Koontz shot a bluebelly and caught the bridle when the man fell, so all Colonel Ashby had to do was hold on to that bridle and jump into the saddle. Maybe Colonel Ashby was listening to dead Richard again, who probably told him not to do it, or maybe Colonel Ashby just couldn't leave his stallion behind because he had such a particular fondness for it, but anyway, it was too late because Captain Koontz got shot, and it wasn't more than a minute after that but Colonel Ashby's stallion gave it up and died; and it was a good thing that I was riding beside him because he just climbed over onto my horse and almost knocked me to the ground, but I didn't blame him. It was dead Richard's fault. For all that that spirit was supposed to be keeping Colonel Ashby alive, I knew it was going to be the death of him, and I figured dead Richard was just setting Colonel Ashby up, and I had a revelation, just like Mammy Jack told me I would; and that was that the spirits don't talk to you unless they want to take you away, and I figured right then that I was pretty lucky that Jimmadasin had decided to quit talking to me or I probably wouldn't be here now.

And of course, I figured that when I started seeing the spirit dog again, it would be my time.

So Colonel Ashby and me and dead Richard rode right away from the Federals in the advance, and we made our escape and joined General Jackson's army somewhere around Rude's Hill, and it turned out that Captain Koontz wasn't killed, and when he joined his company he was bleeding and faint and almost falling off his horse, but he still had hold of the reins of the dead bluebelly's mottled horse, which Colonel Ashby gave to me because he decided to keep my stallion to replace his own. That caused some bad feeling among the men of the Seventh Virginia because when a trooper lost his horse it usually meant he'd be demoted into the infantry. And there I was with another horse, and I wasn't even a soldier.

To tell you the truth, I would have preferred the infantry to where I was going.

COLONEL ASHBY HELD THE REAR WHILE GENERAL JACKSON FELL BACK up the Valley to New Market, and then to Lacey's and Big Spring, which is near Harrisonburg; and although General Jackson stopped and rested his army, Colonel Ashby and his cavalry just rode and skirmished, rode and skirmished all over the front of Banks's army, and we burned the bridges near Mount Crawford and Bridgewater after General Jackson's wagon trains had crossed the North River, and this time the bluebellies weren't there to put out the flames. We rode for two days, and I slept in the saddle and slept when we'd stop to eat and whenever else I could until it got so it was hard for me to tell if I was awake or dreaming because I'd dream I was riding or eating or even sleeping; and sometimes I got separated from Colonel Ashby, but I'd always find him again because as Mammy Jack would say, "It's supposed to be," and Colonel Ashby changed horses after dark as he always did and kept his diary and talked to dead Richard, but I guess dead Richard got angry with Colonel Ashby and was fed up with me because after we reached McGaheysville everything seemed to start going wrong. I should have probably known that everything was going to go bad because it had been raining hard for two days, and everything was mud and stink and mist and discomfort, and I kept thinking I could see the spirit dog and Jimmadasin in the spirit fog that settled over everything.

Anyway, it all started in earnest when Colonel Ashby ordered Captain Jordan and Captain Sheets and Lieutenant Mantaur to take their companies and burn the Columbia and Red bridges, near Honeyville, and the White House Bridge, which was further on down the Shenandoah; and it wasn't hardly past nine o'clock in the morning when we caught Captain Jordan and his men drunk on turpentine whiskey and malingering at the Shenandoah Iron Works "just to get out of the weather"; and then, around noon, when Captain Sheets and about fifty of his men tried to burn the Columbia Bridge, the bluebellies chased them down and they scattered like rabbits; and it seemed like the entire cavalry was drunk because they broke ranks, and Colonel Ashby tried to rally them and get them deployed with his own men to meet the enemy, but they just kept scattering everywhere and wouldn't fight. Some of Captain Jordan's men were in such a rush to retreat that they dropped their guns and threw away their coats and blankets and ran off into the woods.

After all that, only the Red Bridge got burned; and Colonel Ashby torched that one himself, with the Federals running close behind him, just like when he lost his prized white stallion.

But it was later in the night that the *real* trouble started, at least for me.

I knew something was wrong because Colonel Ashby wasn't talking to dead Richard, and he forgot his diary, and he was nipping from the same green bottle of turpentine that he had taken away from a corporal in Captain Jordan's company. I remember the man—he used to hire out to do farmwork around Winchester—and Colonel Ashby had told him that if he didn't give over his bottle he'd find himself deranked down to what he called a high private in the foot cavalry.

It didn't take Colonel Ashby much time—or much liquor—to get himself inebriated, and it didn't take Jedediah much time to find him . . . and me.

I'd never really seen Colonel Ashby on a bust, although he'd sip corn juice a few times a night, and, for that matter, so did I. It struck me as strange, but when he got really drunk, he became sober. There was none of his talking to dead Richard or looking through everything to see if there were spirits ahead of him; he talked to me and was courteous to all the boys who stopped in to see him where we were encamped, which was by Miller's Bridge near the town of Conrad's Store. We were on our way toward the Blue Ridge Mountains, and we'd turned off the macadamized road we'd been on.

I can't explain it, but seeing Colonel Ashby like that made me sad, although I wished he could have been that way all the while I knew him. I guess getting drunk turned him into a regular Mason or Knight of Hiawatha or something because he made me feel like I was more important than any of the officers who came to visit him.

Now, although it seemed like it was in the middle of the night, it probably wasn't much past eight o'clock. We were sitting in Colonel Ashby's wall tent, which we'd taken from the Federals, and since we had a stove, and Colonel Ashby's men set it up for him, I figured it was better than accepting the hospitality of strangers and having them watch everything you do, which is what most of the officers did—especially General Jackson, who, like I said, stayed over with Reverend Rude and slept every night like he was right at home. But Colonel Ashby liked to stay by himself so he could "commune with God" or talk to dead Richard or try to figure out his diary or read the Bible, which he liked to do; but most of the time he was out riding anyway, and it was always better to be away from the farts and snoring and talking and laughing in the camps. And all that noxious effluvia, which was what Colonel Ashby called it, would make you ill.

So there we were, Colonel Ashby, Jedediah, and me, all sitting on stools around a hardtack box that was our table. Colonel Ashby didn't try to hide his bottle, neither did he offer any turpentine to Jedediah, who was too religious, as I said, to ever drink it.

"You need sleep, Jedediah," Colonel Ashby said. His words weren't slurred at all; he spoke softly and beautifully and probably should have been a teacher to teach people how to talk properly. Colonel Ashby smiled and asked, "And isn't it rather late for a parade?" Jedediah wasn't dressed like a civilian or a minister. He was wearing gray trousers, a felt hat, and a brown coat with captain's bars on his collar, and he didn't have his sketchpad. He looked so clean I suppose he could have been going to a parade. He certainly looked tired, though, dead tired; but I just figured that he looked like that all the time, except now it was probably worse because of his daughter Nellie, who was sick and probably dying and everything.

Of course, I didn't know if she was dead yet, I just figured so.

"If the general decides he wants a parade, then that's what we'll give him."

I got excited by the idea of a parade, but that wasn't what they meant.

"What's the general want?" Colonel Ashby asked. "And what do you want?"

Jedediah looked at me, and I looked at the floor. I thought about just getting up and leaving and going outside, but I didn't move. Sometimes I want to do something, but I just don't, and I never know if it's because I don't really want to or can't. That was one of those times.

"What the hell have you been telling him?" Colonel Ashby continued, but he said that as if he was saying "Good day," as if he could say "sonovabitch bastard" or "suck my arse" like it was the sweetest greeting in the world. I thought that if I ever remembered how to talk, I'd try to talk like that, soft and smooth, and I suddenly got scared because I couldn't talk, and I thought that right then and there I'd have to try, have to say something, even if it was just "ha," and my heart started pounding and I felt myself getting hot in the face, but all I could do was sit there, and Colonel Ashby said, "Richard, are you all right? Why don't you go out and take some air?" But I just looked down at the ground, at the stones and dirt and weeds and at the turned-over hardtack box with upside-down writing on the side, and I just stared at a spot and tried to get invisible because I didn't want to go out, I wanted to hear whatever was going to be said because Jedediah never was up to any good when it came to me, and I guess it worked because I felt a hand patting my neck, and I didn't know if it was Jedediah or Colonel Ashby because Colonel Ashby sometimes patted me like I was a dog.

I looked up again when they started talking.

"It's not what you think, Turner," Jedediah said. "The general isn't discussing reorganizing the Seventh Virginia, if that's what you're worrying at. I'd know it if he was. You're too important to him. He won't interfere with your command."

"That's not what I've heard."

"I think I see him a bit more than you do," Jedediah said, and I could swear that he started to smile, but I really couldn't tell. I wouldn't think he ever smiled, and probably wouldn't ever again, now that his family was sick and dying with scarlet fever.

"Then he confides in you, does he, Jedediah?"

"He doesn't confide in anybody. Not that I know of."

"Except maybe the little Corbin girl?" Colonel Ashby said; and I could tell that he was just stirring Jedediah up.

"Janie Corbin was the prettiest thing," Jedediah said. "All that thick, blond, curling hair."

"Was?"

"She died of fever before we left Reverend Rude's."

"I'm sorry to hear that, Jedediah, truly I am."

"She was nothing to me, only to the general, and her poor, unfortunate parents, I would suppose." Jedediah went quiet, as if he was thinking carefully about something, then said, "He certainly worshiped the little thing, though. He cut off the gilt band of that brilliant new cap his men gave him and bound her hair up with the golden threads. She always wore it in her hair after that. I imagine it was buried with her. I saw him weeping when he found out she died."

"His sudden affection for his fellow man didn't extend to the three soldiers who stole away for home, probably to see their own little girls, though, did it? Has he remitted their death penalties?"

"Not that I know of," Jedediah said.

"I thought not."

Jedediah looked uncomfortable, as if he had something he wanted to say but couldn't come out with it, so he said everything else he could think of—like how we caught that spy James Andrews who had his own army and stole a locomotive on the Western & Atlantic and how several hundred Confederates were captured at Huntsville and how the *Ram Virginia* captured three merchant ships last Thursday; but Colonel Ashby wasn't listening to any of that, and after asking about Jedediah's wife and daughters he wanted to know just what the hell Jedediah was really here for—it surely wasn't a social visit.

"I'm here on behalf of the general," Jedediah said.

"Well, what does the general want?" Colonel Ashby asked.

"The boy." Jedediah looked at me like he'd never seen me before, but that only took a second, and then he was looking at Colonel Ashby again. "He just wants to visit with him."

"Ah, like with the little girl, is that it?"

Jedediah nodded, and he looked embarrassed, as if he'd just farted in church.

Colonel Ashby touched the whiskey bottle, rubbing it up and down. "And I would expect you told him all about Richard." He meant me, not his brother, of course.

"He asked me, and, yes, I did."

"Then you'd better not keep the general waiting." Colonel Ashby turned to me, and the light from the stove was all over his face, and it seemed like I could see different faces flickering over him. I wondered if one of them was dead Richard's, and that maybe it was dead Richard who was talking to me and telling me to go with Jedediah to meet with General Jackson, and suddenly Colonel Ashby came back, but it was like he wasn't seeing me anymore because his face got drawn and his eyes narrowed, and I could see he was angry . . . no, not angry, it was that he was listening so hard that he probably didn't care much about anything else.

He was probably listening to dead Richard; that's what I figured, anyway, because Jedediah couldn't get his attention, but when we were just about out of the tent, Colonel Ashby called me back and said, "Here, Richard, give this to Old Jack, but, mind you, don't present it to him until such time as you're alone." He slapped the cork into the bottle of whiskey on the table and held it out to me. I took it and waited for Jedediah to complain about how it wouldn't be sensible for me to give General Jackson a half bottle of Colonel Ashby's turpentine because everyone knew that the general was a strict teetotaller.

But Jedediah didn't say one word.

"And you come back here directly when you're done visiting the general," Colonel Ashby said to me; and then he turned away because dead Richard was probably saying something else to him, and Jedediah came back to take the bottle and push me out of the tent, where Rabbit, one of Captain Chew's artillerymen who had called me Prick-boy, was waiting for us with a haversack, which he called his bureau. I didn't like that sonovabitch because he reminded me of Private Eurastus—he was as tall and fat as Eurastus—but he was polite as could be to Jedediah, and I started to wonder if maybe he wasn't so bad after all. Jedediah had different clothes for me in that haversack, which was stuffed so full that the flap couldn't be fastened over the bone buttons. Rabbit pulled out an officer's jacket—which had brass buttons in the front and knotted braid all over the sleeves—and pants with a stripe and a pair of brogans that didn't have any holes in them, and Jedediah made me change clothes outside Colonel Ashby's tent, right there in front of everyone. He didn't seem to hear the soldiers that were passing by or hanging around; they were all laughing and ragging me out, and even though I didn't have a hat on they were shouting:

> Hey, come out of that hat
> you can't hide in thar
> Hey there's a man in that coat
> no, there's a boy in that coat
> come out of that coat
> get out of thar
> Come out of those shoes
> right now this minute boy
> come out of thar.

I felt the humiliation burning, but, like I said, I thought Jedediah was deaf to everything until he shouted back at the men and asked them when *they'd* been invited to visit General Jackson in the flesh, which didn't quiet them down at all, and I felt like I was being served up for dinner; and those shoes that fat Rabbit gave me were too tight and uncomfortable, but when I tried to take them off, Jedediah scolded me that I had to look proper for the general. Now, I know that General Jackson was next to the hand of God, but it seemed to me that General Jackson was also always mad at everything, so I figured I'd try to get invisible, and maybe he wouldn't notice me much. But that wasn't going to be easy because I'd gotten pretty much visible since Dixie died and I took over his place as Richard.

THOSE BROGANS WERE HURTING MY FEET, THE PANTS AND JACKET WERE too large, and the wool cloth and graybacks were conspiring to make me itch all over, but none of that mattered because I felt like a regular soldier in a parade as Jedediah and I rode out to General Jackson's headquarters, which was near the road that led to Swift Run Gap.

I was also carrying Colonel Ashby's bottle of turpentine whiskey in a small haversack slung over my shoulder.

We stopped in front of a big old two-story log house that had a stone chimney on one side and a one-story addition around the back, which Jedediah called an annex. He told me the annex was General Jackson's headquarters, but the rest of the house was the residence of Abe Lincoln. I suppose I must have looked at him funny because he chuckled and said that this Abe Lincoln was a farmer and had no use whatsoever for the Union. But still and all he was a relative of the *real* Abe Lincoln.

An old woman came to the door and told us to wipe the mud off our feet, and after she looked me up and down like I was going to steal something, she allowed us into the house. We followed her into a dining room where an old man was sitting at a round oak table with General Jackson and Lieutenant Sandy Pendleton and three other officers. There was a candle burning on the table and embers glowing in the fireplace. I suppose everyone knows what General Jackson looks like, but it took me by surprise to see him up close. Probably no one will believe me, but all I could think of was that he looked handsome. I expected him to be old and frumpy, but he had brown hair and a brown beard that was thick as the fur on a dog; and he was tall and thin and wiry and was neat as could be in his uniform, and his lips were tight together like he was getting ready for a fight or was thinking hard about something. But he smiled at Jedediah and me and told us to sit down, although I stood because there weren't enough chairs; and he motioned me over to stand by him, which I did, but I wasn't all that comfortable about it; and I couldn't help but notice his eyes, which were blue and looked hard as stones, but his voice was gentle.

I found out later that he didn't talk often, and rarely smiled, but you couldn't prove that by me.

He asked me if I was hungry, and I shook my head, even though the smells of coffee and bacon and roast beef and hot bread and molasses cakes and eggs all scrambled on a big chipped plate just about made me dizzy. And I couldn't help but notice that the loaf of bread was so soft that it showed the marks of someone's hand who had squeezed it too hard. I figured it had to be one of the officers because my mother never would have done that to bread and I suspected that neither would the old woman who let us in. She was fussing around the table and putting a bit of this and a bit of that on a plate, which she slid right in front of me, even though I told General Jackson that I wasn't hungry. Then she brought over a stool and motioned for me to sit on it, but since the stool was lower than the chairs, I had to put the plate on my lap.

"Coffee?" asked General Jackson, and everyone laughed at that, although I don't know why. I didn't even have to nod, and that bitter stuff that was at the same time sweet just about burned my tongue off, but it was good and it smelled like home, and I started thinking about how I used to always wake up to the smell of Mother boiling up coffee, and all of a sudden I felt like crying, which was stupid because I can't imagine anybody crying over coffee; but then when I looked up at the officers who looked all soft and smooth in the flickering candlelight, I imagined that I was in Heaven, sure as shit, and this was probably why Colonel Ashby had decided to let Jedediah take me to meet "Old Jack."

"It's good to see you, Jedediah," General Jackson said. "We've missed your company these last few days."

"I would have thought you'd seen more than enough of me," Jedediah said.

"Ah, no one would ever demean your talents as an officer, but you should break bread with your friends more often." General Jackson smiled, which I'd heard he never did; and the old woman, who was wearing a bonnet like she was a Quakress, bent over his shoulder to take away the pot of coffee in front of him. It looked to me that she favored the general, and when she came back with another pot and poured another cup for the general without even asking his permission, she asked, "General, you *sure* you ain't a relation to ole' General Jackson? You know, he stopped here, indeed he did."

"Sissy, you must've asked him that a dozen times, now leave it be," Old Man Lincoln said. He was sitting in a chair pulled back from the table, as if to prove that he really didn't belong, even though this was his own house, and he looked like Methuselah or Moses or some Jew rabbi with his long white beard and cap and vest and baggy trousers rolled up above his torn stockings.

"Mrs. Lincoln, you honor me," General Jackson said, "but I can't rightly say whether Old Hickory and I have any common family roots. It's possible now, though, isn't it? And that's a good thought because I've always admired him, and I'm a dyed-in-the-wool Democrat, just like he was." He smiled at Mrs. Lincoln—his smile was fast and accompanied with a nod of his head, so I could understand why some people would think he didn't smile because they'd miss it—and she seemed quite pleased that General Jackson had talked to her.

Mr. Lincoln glared at her, though, like she'd just spilled the coffee or squeezed up a loud fart; and Lieutenant Sandy Pendleton seemed to smooth everything out by asking the old man to go on about the ghost or "goblin damned spirit" that inhabited Wizard's Clip, which was a graveyard for Catholics just north of the Lincolns' farm. I guess it was a good night to talk of such things because the wind had picked up and was whistling around the windows, and although it hadn't been raining when we rode over, we could hear thunder now.

"Well, has any of you been there?" asked Mr. Lincoln. "If any of you has, then you seen that it's all barren. Go see for your own selves, but nothing's growed on any of that old Livingston land since my gramma was a girl, an' to this day the niggers won't go near it—you talk to any of the local niggers, you'll see I'm right."

"I've been over there," said a lieutenant who was sitting beside Jedediah. His name was Henry Kidd Douglas, and it seemed that everybody liked him, just like they did Sandy Pendleton, although Lieutenant Douglas didn't seem as easygoing. He had the same kind of look as General Jackson, like they were both dogs that just saw a rabbit and were concentrating hard. "You can see the excavation of the farmhouse and the barn and its appurtenances, and there's a mound that was probably the stable; but Mr. Lincoln's exactly right— everything's blighted, there's nothing but a crop of shale, not a blade of grass, and even the old pear trees are rotted through. Nothing much left—even the foundation stones are gone."

"Probably carted off by farmers," said another officer, who I found out was Doctor McGuire. He was General Jackson's medical director. He looked about thirty years old, which was probably about the same age as Lieutenant Douglas and Sandy Pendleton, I guess; but it's hard for me to tell anyone's age. I can tell if someone's around my age or really old, but anyone in between looks pretty much the same to me. I'll admit, though, that I'd count General Jackson and Jedediah as old, but not Colonel Ashby, who was probably their age, for all I know. Anyway, Doctor McGuire had thin hair and looked like the sort who would resist any kind of fun. I imagined him as a Eurastus with an education.

"And you certainly don't need superstition to explain what happened to poor Mr. Livingston," continued Doctor McGuire. "All this business of capering spirits burning down barns, cutting clothes all to pieces, killing cattle, and scaring the bejesus out of everyone can probably be attributed to jealous neighbors or somesuch. It sounds to me like nothing more than a vicious prank, a trick."

Well, I don't know if Doctor McGuire meant to rile both the Lincolns at the same time, but he certainly succeeded because Mr. Lincoln stood up and started walking around while he talked, and it was the funniest damn thing, but Mrs. Lincoln walked around with him, like they were possessed by the capering spirits Doctor McGuire was talking about. "Well, young sir, if you seen what we seen over the last thirty years, you wouldn't be makin' fun of things you don't know nothing about. You ever seen a flock of geese fly into a place and then suddenly all lose their heads and fly away just like that? Well, we seen it. And more'n that too. And you stay here every night and you'll hear screaming and wailing and carryin' on. And we seen clothes all cut up and layin' everywhere, 'cept when you go over to try to pick something up, ain't nothing there at all. Explain that, what your own eyes sees, Doctor Soldier."

It started raining hard all of a sudden; and I could see where the wind was pushing the water right in through the side of the window, which was rattling like it was one of Mr. Lincoln's spirits. I remembered how the rain used to sound when it hit our roof, and how when I was a kid I would lie in bed and listen to it and imagine it was raining cats and dogs like Mother always said it did, and I would wonder which was the cats and which were the dogs—and then I felt sad all over again, like I was thinking about coffee, even though General Jackson was patting my hair like Mother sometimes did.

"I meant no disrespect," Doctor McGuire said, and he bowed his head, although it seemed to me he was playacting, and I wouldn't have trusted the sonovabitch for a minute, but Mr. Lincoln sat back down in his chair, and I guess he figured he'd won the argument right then and there, but Doctor McGuire couldn't leave it alone, and he kept explaining how everything was natural phenomena or something until you could see that Old Man Lincoln was going to stand up again. Now, I would have figured that General Jackson would have calmed things down, but he just sat quietly and patted me every once in a while, like I was a dog, as I said.

Sandy Pendleton poured oil on the water, as Poppa would say, by explaining how he had heard it all started because someone who was visiting the Livingstons' farm died there, and he was Catholic, and he'd asked for a priest so he could get shrived, whatever that meant, but the Livingstons went to sleep instead of getting him a priest, and that's why everything got haunted; and that calmed down Mr. Lincoln, who said he'd seen the very ghost of that Catholic, and Mr. Lincoln explained how the spirit made a horrible moaning and didn't wear shoes because no one wore shoes where he came from and told them clear as day that it was because of Luther and Calvin that every Protestant soul would burn in Hell for eternity.

I figured that was bullshit because I knew that spirits wore shoes, and Jimmadasin, who qualified as a spirit as easily as Mr. Lincoln's spirits, didn't make horrible moaning noises, at least no more so than he did when he was alive, but it didn't matter because Mr. and Mrs. Lincoln weren't shaking so much with excitement now, and they explained how there'd be ghosts in that place until the authorities got rid of that Catholic cemetery and put it somewhere else. Course, there would be ghosts wherever you put a Catholic cemetery, but I wasn't sure about whether any of that was right.

After being so quiet and patting me and listening to what everybody else said, General Jackson seemed to wake up. "I think we've all discussed enough theology for one night, gentlemen, and I'd like to extend our special thanks to our hosts for taking such good care of us." He nodded at Old Man Lincoln and his wife, who was standing right behind him like she was a soldier, and she nodded back and took General Jackson at his word because she started clearing the table, although Mr. Lincoln tried to keep up the talk about ghosts and spirits. But General Jackson wasn't listening. He was all business now and ordered Sandy Pendleton to take a message to Colonel Ashby right away.

"I'll be returning the boy to Colonel Ashby just now," Jedediah said. "I could certainly save Sandy the ride," but General Jackson wasn't having any of that, and he sent Lieutenant Pendleton into the storm with a letter that was already sealed and ready. I couldn't imagine what it might be, but I figured it wasn't anything good or he would have allowed Jedediah and me to take it back to Colonel Ashby. I looked to Jedediah then because I figured we'd just go along with Sandy, but General Jackson asked me if I'd like to visit with him for a little while. Jedediah nodded to me, as if all of a sudden he couldn't speak either; and so after Mrs. Lincoln lit a fresh candle for him to carry, I followed General Jackson into his study, which wasn't anything but a room with a bed, a beat-up dresser, and a writing desk and chair under the only window in the room. I noticed that although the desk was open so he could write on it, there wasn't anything on it, not even one piece of paper; so I figured he didn't do very much work there, or, if he did, he probably hid it so spies couldn't get at it. He motioned for me to sit down on the bed, and I figured he'd pull out the chair, but he didn't. He put the candle on the desk and sat down on the bed next to me, which didn't make me comfortable, and he asked me about why I couldn't talk, and that didn't make any sense to me at all because how the hell was I supposed to answer him; and then, just as I should have figured, he gave me a piece of paper and a wooden board to put under it, but he fooled me by saying, "Jedediah explained your affliction to me, son, so I don't expect you to write anything, but he tells me you're quite a wonderful artist, is that true?" I felt my face burning, and I kept my head down and stared at the paper he gave me, which was resting on the wooden board on my knees, and on top of the paper was a pencil, chewed up on the end; and I was shaking like I was as excited as the Lincolns when Doctor McGuire started telling them about how the spirits were tricks, and then I just picked up the pencil and started drawing for General Jackson. Now, I didn't know what I was going to draw, and I thought about those geese of Mr. Lincoln's flying around without their heads, and I thought of Jimmadasin and how I'd draw him as a spirit, and then suddenly, like I was having a vision, I remembered how to write and how to speak, and it was like my hand was moving all on its own, and I was about to write "Edmund McDowell," and I knew I could do it, and I thought that if I opened my mouth at that very second I could say my name as well, and then I suddenly got scared, as bad as if someone was shooting at me or when I heard Poppa screaming in the house for Mother, and I knew— I knew—that if I wrote down my name, everything would change in a bad way, and I'd be back at the farm and Mother would be lying there on the flags and the house would be on fire again, and the spirit dog wouldn't take me for no spirit, he would come after me, and just then I could smell his wet fur and his breath, and it smelled like death and putrefaction, like a pond on a hot day, and I started shaking so that it was like I was angry, and I wanted to throw the paper and the board right through that window, which was black, and that's how I imagined Hell would be, black just like that, like I could just fall into it like it was the mouth of some animal, and there wouldn't be teeth or monsters or anything like that,

just blackness that looked flat at first but was so deep you'd never reach the bottom, and you'd die there in the middle of it, blind and flat, and before I knew it
I was drawing on the paper and General Jackson was leaning toward me and his
arm was against my back, as if he was holding me up or something, and since
that window was in front of me I drew it—not very well, just a square—and
under that I drew the desk with its drop lid folded out and its rows of little drawers and three big drawers underneath, but I kept thinking about the window and
spirits and Lucy and then I remembered what Jedediah had said about the little
girl General Jackson liked, and how she died, and so I drew the spirit of a little
girl in that window who was watching over General Jackson, just like I'd drawn
Dixie, except I'd never seen the little girl that General Jackson favored, but I
thought he'd like a drawing of her spirit, which could probably just look like
any little girl.

When I was finished, he didn't say one word.

He just looked at it for a minute, and he looked at me like I'd seen him playing with himself or something, and then he put the wooden board and the paper
and the pencil on the lid of the desk, and he just stared out that window until I
figured I'd probably insulted him with that picture, and I resolved not to draw
ever again, even if Jesus came to me Himself and asked me to.

General Jackson just stood in front of that desk and stared out the window
and said, "When I look out a window after dark, I cannot help but meditate upon
Heaven, with all its joys unspeakable and full of glory." Then he said something
else, but he spoke so softly I couldn't make it out, and while he stared out that
window and talked low to himself—or maybe prayed, could be—I remembered that I had Colonel Ashby's bottle of turpentine whiskey, and I took it out
of the haversack and waited for him to turn around. When he did, and saw that
bottle, he smiled just a little, but, like I said before, it passed away before you
hardly had time to notice it. "Now, this certainly wouldn't be a gift from Jedediah, may the good Lord protect him. Is this, then, a gift from you?"

I thought about nodding or looking down at my feet so he'd assume I gave
him the bottle, but then I figured that maybe he'd punish me for offering him
whiskey because he was a general who meditated on Heaven and didn't swear,
and, from what I heard, didn't eat much of anything except for lemons, and
didn't even drink coffee, much less rotgut spirits—but I knew better about the
coffee because I'd seen him drink it, unless he was just being polite to Old Lady
Lincoln—and so I shook my head no just to be safe.

"Ah, then it's from my friend Turner, is it?"

I nodded.

General Jackson sat down beside me and took the bottle. He uncorked it and held it up to his mouth, but he didn't just start drinking; he hesitated, as if he knew he was committing a sin and wanted to think about it. Then he took a big swallow and asked Colonel Ashby's forgiveness, and I wondered why he'd want Colonel Ashby to forgive him—maybe because General Jackson was drinking all of Colonel Ashby's whiskey—and after he took a few more swigs, General Jackson explained how all things work together for good to God's children, and that we must trust in our kind Heavenly Father, and by the eye of faith see that all things are right, and how that the clouds come, pass over us, and are followed by bright sunshine, and just the same way God permits us to have trouble awhile, but that even in the most trying dispensations of His providence we should be cheered by the brightness that is a little ahead.

If I could've I would have said "Amen," and General Jackson prayed while he drank, and I bowed my head, and we looked out the window into the blackness, and I wondered if all that falling blackness that I was always afraid of was all the time Heaven itself, and after what seemed like hours of praying and being petted, there was a knock on the door, and General Jackson told me to wait right there on the bed while he talked with Jedediah outside the room, and then Jedediah and General Jackson came back for me.

I knew whatever I was supposed to do, I did it wrong.

I could feel it, and I just wanted to get away from there; and as Jedediah and I rode back to Colonel Ashby's camp in the rain and the damp with our tunics and rubber blankets over our shoulders, I kept thinking about the spirit dog.

I just couldn't stop thinking about him—

And if the spirit dog were a person and could pray and talk and everything, I imagine he would look just like General Jackson.

SANDY PENDLETON WAS STILL AT COLONEL ASHBY'S TENT WHEN WE arrived, and it seemed like Colonel Ashby was drunk and angry because he kept saying that something was a conspiracy against him, and he laughed at Jedediah and said, "So the general isn't discussing reorganizing the Seventh Virginia, is he? He won't interfere with my command, will he? Because I'm too important to him, isn't that what you said, Jedediah? I believe it truly was. And if Old Jack was going to do anything untoward, why, you'd know it, wouldn't you? Isn't that what you said?"

I saw Sandy Pendleton try to get Jedediah's attention, but Jedediah was all taken up with Colonel Ashby and didn't seem to know what to say.

"Well, Jedediah . . . ?"

Then Jedediah turned to Sandy Pendleton, who wouldn't look him in the eye; I guess because Colonel Ashby figured there was a conspiracy between them, and I wouldn't put anything past Jedediah, even though I liked Sandy Pendleton. "I'm sure I haven't the faintest idea what you're talking about, Turner. I've brought back the boy, and in jig time, and he delivered your gift to the general and I suspect gave the old man some solace. This hasn't been an easy time."

"No, I would venture that the general had quite a difficult time writing the letter Sandy delivered to me while you were attending to him with my boy. I guess the jealous sonovabitch bastard just couldn't wait, could he?" Colonel Ashby stood up from the table, and he kicked over his stool, probably by mistake, but he looked crazy, and I was sure he was drunk, although I didn't see any bottles or anything. Maybe Sandy Pendleton had brought him some whiskey, or maybe the whiskey he'd drunk before was just taking effect on him. I was scared, though, because I thought he was going to go for Jedediah, and so did Jedediah, who jumped back like he'd been slapped.

"Here," Colonel Ashby said. "Read this and tell me it's a complete surprise," and that's just what Jedediah did, and he swore he didn't know a whisper about it, and he must've mentioned Jesus fifty times, and I believed him, and I guess after a while so did Colonel Ashby because they all sat back down at the table and discussed ramifications and other things I didn't quite understand, and Lieutenant Pendleton and Jedediah seemed to be in agreement that General Jackson hadn't meant any harm by the letter, and that it was to help Colonel Ashby manage his companies, and Colonel Ashby said that if Old Jack wanted him to drill his men instead of fighting the enemy it was all right with him.

Now, I've got to tell you something crazy because I saw General Jackson's letter on the hardtack-box table and I read it, but I couldn't understand any of the words. It was like I'd lost most of what I learned and was and everything, and I thought right then that I'd probably never be able to speak or read again, and I felt a shiver because I figured that's what happened to you after you died and became a spirit, and I figured you'd just keep forgetting how to do things until you couldn't talk and hear and read and write, and finally all you'd be able to do is float until you just became part of the air and there was nothing left of you; I figured this out because before I was a spirit I could read and talk and I was myself; and I remembered my book called *Private Newton's War in the Air*, which was part of my vision and was probably rotting in that nigger cave on the other side of the mountains; and I remembered my vision and Private Newton, but I couldn't read that letter, for all of that. Yet I saw it and remembered it, and I remember it now. This is what it said exactly, even though I didn't know it then:

THE COMMANDING GENERAL HEREBY ORDERS COMPANIES A, B, C, D, E, F, G, H, I, K, OF ASHBY'S CAVALRY TO REPORT TO BRIGADIER GENERAL TALIAFERRO, AND TO BE ATTACHED TO HIS COMMAND; THE OTHER COMPANIES OF THE SAME COMMAND WILL REPORT TO BRIGADIER GENERAL WINDER TO BE ATTACHED TO HIS COMMAND. COLONEL TURNER ASHBY WILL COMMAND THE ADVANCE GUARD OF THE ARMY OF THE VALLEY WHEN ON AN ADVANCE, AND THE REAR GUARD WHEN IN RETREAT, APPLYING TO GENERALS TALIAFERRO AND WINDER FOR TROOPS WHENEVER NEEDED.

There was a note under the order, which was probably personal from General Jackson, but I couldn't see that one enough to remember it.

"Well, it's time for me to write back to my old friend," Colonel Ashby said, and he looked at me, as if we were going to write this note together. He'd calmed down after talking with Lieutenant Pendleton and Jedediah, but, as I think about it now, it probably didn't have anything to do with them. Colonel Ashby was probably so angry that it took a while before he'd listen to his brother's voice, and I'd bet money that his brother's spirit was telling Colonel Ashby to quit the entire Army of the Valley, which is what he did.

Neither Jedediah or Lieutenant Pendleton could talk him out of it, and I think they probably secretly agreed with him, although I still didn't trust Jedediah.

"Send the general my personal felicitations," Colonel Ashby said to Lieutenant Pendleton as he handed him the letter. "He's treated me very badly, and deserves no better."

So now I figured Colonel Ashby and me would get out of the army, but I didn't have any idea what we'd be doing. It didn't matter. I guess I didn't much care. Once I took off those brogans that Jedediah gave me, I didn't much care about anything 'cause it was such a relief. Colonel Ashby took off his jacket and pants and shirt and folded them neatly on the table and then went to bed. The fire was mostly embers, and I imagined that was what Hell looked like, all those embers that took on the shapes of buildings and mountains and valleys and riverbeds, but it looked cozy, so I figured that maybe Hell wasn't as bad as Poppa thought; it certainly seemed peaceful. I thought about putting a few more sticks on, but it wasn't so cold tonight, and Colonel Ashby called me to bed. Now, that was unusual because unless it was so cold we had to spoon, I usually slept separate. His bed was made up of a few saplings padded out with hay, but I was figuring on just sleeping in my poncho by the fire.

But I did what he asked me to; and when I came to bed, Colonel Ashby put his arms around me like I was a girl or something, and for a few minutes I could tell he was listening for something, and then he relaxed and started snoring. Even though I was facing away from him, I could smell the liquor on his breath, and I could smell his sweat, which reminded me of sour apples, and I could feel that his prick was hard, and I got scared for a minute, but I guess he was just having a dream because he said, "Drive them, boys, drive them," as if we were riding into the enemy, and then he went completely quiet and I couldn't even hear him breathe, and I thought for a second that he was dead.

LOSIN' THINGS

WELL, IT DIDN'T TAKE LONG FOR GENERAL JACKSON TO COME TO HIS senses about dividing up Colonel Ashby's command and everything because if Colonel Ashby quit the Army of the Valley, the entire cavalry would quit right along with him, you could bet on that; and so he and Colonel Ashby had a meeting and probably drank up the rest of that bottle of whiskey and prayed about glory and afflictions and tribulations, and that was that. But it didn't help me at all because while Colonel Ashby rode out with all his best men to harass General Banks and drive his pickets right back into their camps near Peal's, which is a few miles from Harrisonburg, I had to stay with Jedediah; and you would have thought I was a deserter or a traitor or a Southern Union man because Jedediah tied me up to him with a leash like I was a cur dog. That leather thong was fastened tight on my right arm, and the other end was wrapped around his left hand like reins for a skittish horse. He told me there was no way in the world he was going to allow me to run away and humiliate him in front of his God and his men like I had done before (although there wasn't anybody around but him and me and maybe God when I rode away from him down Mount Airy). Even though it made him irritable every time I had to relieve myself, he seemed pleased with himself and would nod to the soldiers when they'd look funny at us, until we became the biggest joke in the camp; but old Jedediah seemed to be enjoying and relishing it all to hell and just went around blessing everyone and talking about the eternal weight of glory.

We stopped at the sutler's tent so Jedediah could get some flour and suspenders and a bottle of ink for his drawing because he'd just about run out of working materials and couldn't very easily get any in the middle of this war, and he said the sutler's ink wasn't nothing but pisswash and would fade faster than steam on a glass, and that he'd probably be better off making his own out of polk berries and oak balls; and after that I figured that pisswash as a word was okay to use and wasn't swearing or Jedediah wouldn't've put it into his vocabulary. Anyway, while we were in the sutler's tent, we could hear men singing outside, although it was coming from another tent because it was raining cats and dogs and probably everybody but us were snug in their tents—at least those that had tents—and not walking around looking for ink and suspenders; and that song we were hearing was originally made up by the bluebellies about President Davis, but the singers had changed it to Abe Lincoln, and I guess Jedediah figured it was still a sin anyway, because after he paid for his ink and suspenders, he pulled me out of the sutler's tent, and we went directly to the source of the singing. Those soldiers sang pretty good and although I didn't let Jedediah see, I couldn't help but smile because the song went like this (although longer, but I'm not going to put it all in here):

> One night as Abe lay fast asleep
> With his wife hugged to his heart,
> A little closer she did creep,
> And chanced to let a fart.

> The fart it smelt so strong,
> And sounded so much louder
> He thought that something wrong must be
> For he smelt the Davis powder.

Hark, hark, says he, yet unawake,
How will I show my spunkey?
And reaching down his gun to take
His fingers touched her monkey. . . .

Jedediah tore right into the soldiers' tent, which was a Sibley and looked big enough to hold a division; and there were probably twelve soldiers sitting around a stove in there, including some of the artillerymen I didn't like—Breakfast and Wasp and Rabbit and a couple of other soldiers whose names I didn't know—and I wondered why they weren't with Captain Chew and Colonel Ashby; but the look of surprise on their faces would have made me laugh, except I just about gagged on the smell, which was so bad and putrid that I couldn't understand how any one of them could stay there of their own free will because it smelled like stale coffee and bacon and sweat and tobacco mixed up with the worst fart imaginable. I thought about how they were probably used to the stink because it was mostly their own, and I remembered how animals love the smell of people's shit and farts and figured it was the same thing here. Well, Jedediah scolded them for singing, and even though he wasn't wearing anything that could be thought of as a proper uniform, every one of them seemed to know who he was, and they nodded and were respectful and promised not to sing songs like that ever again, and I saw one of the soldiers hide a red and white package of playing cards, and the men looked really all contrite and they apologized and proclaimed that they loved the Lord and were only having a bit of fun at the expense of that rascal Abe Lincoln and were sorry it was sinful, but still and all they couldn't help but smile a little, and that was because Jedediah and I were leashed together, and then just as we were about to pull over the tent flap and get the hell out of there and into some clean air, a corporal who was almost bald and missing a tooth said, "Cap'n, you sure got yourself a small mule thar, an' you better not ride on him too fast or you'll squash the poor little thing." Well, everybody started laughing and apologizing all over again and asking why I was all leashed up; but Jedediah didn't pay any attention to them, and he let me go a few hours later, probably because he couldn't get anything done when he was all tied up to me, or maybe it was because of the ribbing he took.

After he was done showing me off and doing his errands, we went back to Captain Harnsberger's house, which was also a carriage shop, where Jedediah was renting a room; and he explained that he was taking away my horse—as if I'd've been able to escape him again and track down Colonel Ashby on my own.

I would have probably tried, though.

But once we were dried off and in his room, which was a damn sight bigger than the room where I had visited General Jackson, I watched him draw up his maps from the sketches he had in his book. I'll tell you about Jedediah's book, which caused me to know him in a different way that I wouldn't've expected; but even though the room had a spindle that was as tall as me and a big fireplace with carving all over it and cabinets with glass doors and a desk that was all closed up, and an oak table with pencils and inkwells and pens and a stack of paper, all neatly laid out like one of Jedediah's maps, the only thing I noticed when I walked into that room was the strangest musical instrument I ever saw. It looked like a big fiddle made out of a fat, square-faced cornstalk, and it was just standing in the corner of the room like it belonged there. The fiddle had notches in it and four catgut strings pulled tight as could be, and there was a thin cornstalk leaning up against it, which was probably the bow.

I almost forgot I couldn't talk.

If I could, I would have asked Jedediah how that fiddle came to be because I don't know why, but for some reason I just loved it, like it was out of a story or something; and Jedediah must have seen me looking because he smiled and said, "That's a bass viol. Some call it a viola da gamba, and a real one made out of good old pine and sycamore cut on the quarter has just about the most beautiful, resonant tone you'll ever hear. Only instrument that used to be allowed in the Congregationalist church back east. When I hear it, I always think that's what the Lord's voice must sound like; of course, the Lord's voice would be so loud and deep and perfect that it's a blasphemy for me even to compare it with anything on this poor earth, much less something I made out of a lowly cornstalk. I whittled my first one when I was a young man, so I could learn how to play. We have a real viola at Loch Willow. You'd like to see that," and then he got a funny look on his face, just like Colonel Ashby did when he was listening to dead Richard; and I felt sorry for him, all of a sudden, and I imagined out of the clear blue sky that he was like Poppa, and that's why he leashed me to him, even though it doesn't make any kind of sense.

I listened to him go on about how he made his own wooden guns and sleds and bows and arrows and every kind of instrument and utensil you could imagine, just for fun; and I don't know what got into me but I walked right over to that viola da gamba like I was going to play it. I didn't know how to, or course, but it didn't matter because Jedediah stepped right between it and me and said no, that it wasn't up to being handled by children, and he picked it up along with the bow, took them over to his chair by the table, and sat down to play it for me; and I suppose I expected to hear the Lord come pouring out of that cornstalk like the ocean itself. I imagined it would be like voices I heard in dreams or something, or how Poppa used to sound when he was giving one of his sermons and preaching the skin off the snakes and I remembered how I'd be almost awake and almost asleep and Poppa's voice would seem to grow and grow until it was just about like God was speaking right to me, except by then I'd either start dreaming about something else or I'd jolt awake and Mother would be giving me one of her ugly looks.

Anyway, that's what I expected, or something like that, but when Jedediah started pulling that cornstalk bow over the strings on that cornstalk fiddle that he was holding between his knees like he was churning butter, all that came out was some hymn or another, and it didn't sound deep or resonant like the Lord's voice, although he didn't play any notes that set my teeth on edge. He played on for a while and watched me, and then he'd close his eyes, and I concentrated on him like I was memorizing him for a picture, but I felt as sad hearing him play that viola de gamba made out of cornstalks as I did after I left Poppa and Mother, and it made me think of that poor bastard soldier who was still taking aim after he was dead, and if I could have, I would have said "Mamma" like all the soldiers did in the fields before they died; and I guess my eyes got wet or something because Jedediah stopped playing and got up and patted me and started talking to me like I was a baby, and I wondered if being around someone who couldn't talk just had that effect on people. Then I felt angry at myself and pulled away from Jedediah and walked over to the big spinning wheel in the corner, and I was just trying to figure everything out because I couldn't understand why I'd cry over some hymn played on a stalk of corn, and it seemed to me that I was disappointed because that fiddle wasn't anything much more than a . . . fiddle.

After that I stood behind Jedediah and watched him draw his maps ever so neatly, as he made little ink roads and rivers and streets and forests and mountains, and it was like he was God and looking down at the world from Heaven; and then the next thing I knew I was all fuzzy-mouthed and sleepy-eyed, and laying in Jedediah's makeshift spring bed, which was like the one Colonel Ashby had in his tent; and even though I take considerable pride in being able to remember most everything, I don't know how I got there. I must have been asleep for a while, though, because it was dark, and Jedediah had a lamp and candles on his table, which was spread out with his maps, and he was hunched over his papers and looking about as happy as anyone I'd ever seen, just sitting there drawing and smiling like he was telling himself jokes. I remembered dreaming about Poppa and Mother, and it was like I was in Heaven with them and listening to Jedediah's viola da gamba, and they all had to go somewhere, and I didn't want them to leave, and I was crying, and then I woke up to see Jedediah, and I must admit I was happy to see him. Well, he must have sensed I was awake because he turned around like people sometimes do if you just stare at them hard enough, and he smiled at me and didn't say anything, as if he couldn't talk either; and it was like I was still having that dream or something.

I guess I just fell back asleep like I was in Heaven—but I couldn't find Poppa and Mother again—and when I woke up I figured out why Jedediah had been so happy.

IT WAS HARDLY DAWN, BUT JEDEDIAH WAS UP AND DRESSED AND FUSSING around his room like old Mrs. Lincoln around General Jackson. He had everything that was going into his haversack laid out on the table, which was lit with a lamp; and his poncho and blanket were hanging over the back of his chair. His sketchbook and diary and inkwell and pens and pencils were all pushed together by the table's edge, and next to them were some drawers, a pair of socks, a white cotton shirt and a black leather cravat, trousers, and a vest; and there was an old dented skillet, some salt pork and hardtack, and some coffee and sugar in a bag tied with a knot so one wouldn't get mixed in with the other. And, of course, there was his Bible. But right in the middle of the table, like they were in the place of honor, were two carved, painted dolls, and they looked perfect— even their eyes were painted blue—and each had a little dress and a bonnet; I figured that he must have gotten one of the servants to make up those little dresses.

All of that is what I saw when I sat up, or jolted up, out of bed. Now, I had been in Jedediah's bed, and I don't know if he'd come into the bed with me during the night, or slept in the chair, or just sketched and packed and didn't bother to sleep. But I knew as soon as I saw those dolls, which he had probably been carving up for weeks, that we were going to his farm, and sure enough he had obtained a leave of absence to visit his family, but that was only incidental because we ended up riding all over Bull Pasture Mountain like we were memorizing it, and Jedediah drew more maps than you could shake a stick at.

I'm getting ahead of myself again. . . .

But I figured out that Old Jack never told anybody what he was going to do, or, if he did, he'd tell them the wrong thing, and so he'd be giving old Jedediah a leave of absence to see his family and sick daughters and all that, but General Jackson was really sending him out to scout out the territory for what would later end up being the battle of McDowell, which I didn't see. But I'll get to that too.

Anyway, even though Jedediah got up before the rooster, we stayed in that room all morning like we were prisoners, and Captain Harnsberger's servant Marriah brought us our breakfast and lunch. Marriah was about the skinniest and most frightened woman I ever saw, but she had perfect white teeth and smelled just like fresh hay, and she wore a big shirttail, which was like a dress that came down to her knees; usually only nigger children wore shirttails, but Marriah certainly wasn't a child. She was probably eighteen or even older. Anyway, that shirttail was torn and dirty gray, and it was the damnedest thing, but she wore a petticoat under it, which fooled you into thinking it might have been a fancy dress.

It had been raining all night, and it was still raining—a hard, windy rain; and it was hardly worth looking out the window because it was so dark it looked like the sun was just setting and it was turning into evening. There was plenty of thunder and lightning, and I wondered how long this spirit weather was going to last, and I was sure that it was a bad omen, and who the hell knew but it might be another Great Flood and we'd all get drowned or something. Marriah certainly thought so because when she came in with our tray for lunch, she was whining that she "wasn't going to go out in that pourin' rain 'cause Lawd da water wuz up to my waist in dose ditches," and she was so scared she was shaking, especially whenever there was a crack of thunder, and Jedediah had to calm her down and explain that if she looked careful for a rainbow that was God's promise that nobody was going to drown in a flood anymore. She smiled at that and left the room, and that was the last time I ever saw her.

I sometimes think about people like Marriah who I saw once or twice or knew a little bit and will probably never see again, and I wonder what happened to them, and if they're alive, or old, and what they look like, but that's not getting me along with this story, so I'll just tell you about how I finally saw what was inside Jedediah's book. I looked into it when Lieutenant Sandy Pendleton came to the door in the afternoon to say that General Jackson was breaking camp, although I didn't know that then because after making small talk and asking me how I was, Sandy Pendleton and Jedediah went outside the door to talk. I could hear them talking low, but I couldn't make out any words, even when I tiptoed right up to the door and put my ear against it. All I heard was something like chewing and the sound of water, so, figuring that this was my chance to do *something*, I looked around that room. I could probably have climbed out the window behind the spindle, and I probably would have, but I saw Jedediah's notebook just inside his haversack, and I saw it because one of the buttons wasn't closed—he had stuffed it too full—so I pulled the notebook out for a quick peep, just to quench my curiosity, and then I was going to leave and find my horse, or any horse, and ride off to find Colonel Ashby before dead Richard directed him to stand in front of a bullet because it was time. I figured that dead Richard didn't like me around Colonel Ashby because when the colonel was paying attention to me he wasn't listening entirely to dead Richard, and so I'd probably be saving his life.

It would have been easiest and fastest just to grab Jedediah's sketchbook and some of the food (I would have left Jedediah his bag of coffee and sugar) and climb right out that window. But that would be stealing, and although I've proven myself at being decent at foraging, I wasn't going to steal from Jedediah.

It would have been like stealing from Poppa.

But I forgot all about escaping when I saw that first drawing in Jedediah's book. It was like I was back in the cave of the baby Jesus and was seeing the baby Jesus Himself. It was like I was having a vision—one that Mammy Jack would have probably approved of—and I wasn't disappointed like I had been when I heard Jedediah play his viola da gamba because that first drawing was like it came right out of my own mind, or my own dream, or something; and although I couldn't see her face because it was turned, I knew that the angel floating in the air was my mother. That was Mother's figure, and I ought to know because I'd seen her naked before, but I don't want to think about that. Anyway, in the picture she had a sword in one hand and a snake with long fangs and what looked like an upside-down candlestick in the other, and running below her with its mouth wide open and its tongue hanging out like it was thirsty for blood or something was the spirit dog—the very same one that I had seen; and there was writing on the page next to it, but I couldn't read it and didn't even try, but on the next page was a drawing of Jedediah with his horse behind him, and Jedediah had his sketchpad on his lap and was drawing something, but I wouldn't know what it was because he was looking straight out of the picture—maybe he was drawing me! And on each page after that were drawings of his daughters and his wife and "scholars" and two old slaves and his farm and fields and outbuildings, and all the places he'd seen, like the Camden Street depot in Baltimore, and drawings of soldiers and women in railroad cars, and houses, and boats on the Potomac at Point of Rock; and looking at those sketches, turning the pages fast, one after the other—there must have been a hundred—was like nothing I'd ever experienced before; it was like I was remembering seeing all those places and people and soldiers cooking coffee or walking down Church Street, and it seemed like everyone I'd ever seen was in there, only the drawing of Colonel Ashby looked wrong; he didn't look like he was alive; he was too calm and his eyes didn't have anything in them, and that scared me, like Jedediah had seen something I hadn't; and I turned back to the pictures of his daughters to see if they looked dead too, but they didn't; and then the door creaked open and Jedediah caught me red-handed, and I realized that I'd been just standing there when I could have taken it with me through the window. But Jedediah waited until I was finished. I could feel him staring down at me because the back of my neck was getting hot like there was a ray of sun coming through the roof and hitting me right there, but before I closed his diary, I flipped the pages back for one last look at Mother floating above the spirit dog, and I wondered how Jedediah knew about such things. He must have seen the spirit dog too, because he said something about the sketch being about Bellona, the spirit of war, who was screaming her cry of horror (and even though I couldn't read what he had written under that picture, I remembered the writing and can tell you that old Jedediah was telling the truth). Even though I couldn't see her face, I knew it was Mother; and because of that I figured it was a sign from the Lord or something that I should go along with Jedediah, even if it meant leaving Colonel Ashby and the Army of Northern Virginia and catching the fever from his daughter Nellie and learning Latin and Greek and Smyth's algebra—whatever that was.

But I wondered about the spirit dog.

I SAW GENERAL JACKSON ONE MORE TIME BECAUSE SANDY PENDLETON and Jedediah and I rode back to the camp to see him; and on the way we saw the damnedest thing; we saw the Third Brigade and the Stonewall Brigade marching up the river toward Port Republic on the same road we were on, which was unpaved and so muddy that the cannon wagons were sinking in it right up to their axles, and horses were slipping all over and throwing their riders, and the soldiers were slipping too because nobody could get their balance. It was like walking or riding on ice. Now, Jedediah and Sandy Pendleton and I were in the same predicament, but I guess we were lucky to have good horses that found their way through the slippery spots because although our horses foundered, they didn't fall once, which Jedediah said was positively a miracle. Soldiers pulled the heavy wagons out of the mire and put stones and brushwood in the road to get some purchase, but from what I could see, none of that did any good; and I just figured that this was probably what Hell was like because it was, like I said before, raining cats and dogs; and with the wind, it seemed like it was raining sideways. I was drenched, even with my rubber poncho and blanket and everything else. It was no use because the wind would push that rain right up your legs and down your neck, and we could hardly see where we were going because a mist had fallen so it was like walking through the clouds or being on top of a mountain, and you could hardly see what was ahead until you were practically there, but I glimpsed the river, which was roaring; it was so overfilled with rainwater, and the fields were so soaked with rain that there were pools all over like lakes, and I remembered what Jedediah had said to Marriah about the rainbow and how God promised there wouldn't be another flood. I looked around hard but couldn't find any rainbow, and I thought that maybe Marriah had good reason to be nervous.

I guess everyone going past me felt as rotten as I did. They surely looked uncomfortable. I couldn't imagine that the solid column of soldiers would ever end, but I could surely believe that this man's Army of Northern Virginia was the Army of God, and that we would have a hundred 'Federates for every one of Banks's bluebellies, and we wouldn't ever lose again, but if I was also right about this being like Hell, then I was, of course, just fooling myself because most of those creatures going by me with their muskets and blankets and bare feet looked like they hadn't eaten in weeks and were made out of the mud that was splattered all over them; and I must've looked the same, a mud spirit, and suddenly I was so hungry that my stomach rolled, even though I'd eaten a few hours before, and the rain was burning me because it felt so cold, and it was mingling with the lice and I was itching and burning and feeling generally like I wanted to pull my skin right off; and right there and then I wondered whether I'd be better off being a spirit or a person, and although sometimes I yearned to be a spirit, I figured that the one was as bad as the other. But there was certainly something to being a spirit and just being able to pass right through everything if I wanted and not feel a thing, and then I thought about the damnedest thing: I wondered if it hurt fireflies to be swallowed by frogs and get turned into lanterns, but it felt nice to think about how the frogs glowed in the pond after they'd swallowed fireflies.

The grumbling and talking and shouting and ordering of the men seemed to take up everything, until even the rolling of thunder seemed to be just part of that column of soldiers marching through the mud and snaky-snaky mist, and men were calling out to each other and to us—

> *Your mamma know you out?*
> *Up yer arse.*
> *Captain Hotchkiss, where we goin'?*
> *Hey, Lieutenant Pendleton,*
> *where we goin'?*
> *Captain Hotchkiss, we goin' to Richmond?*
> *Answer me that.*
> *We shod be goin' the odder way,*
> *not out of the Valley.*
> *Retreatin'.*

And someone shouted "Halt!" and the marching stopped and the wagons stayed mired in the mud and everybody waited and grumbled until "Forward!" was passed down the line, and they'd start marching again; but after seeing all those men filthy and ragged, some of them without shoes and some without socks, well, I couldn't believe my eyes when I saw a company that looked like they'd just come out of their tents for a parade because they were all dressed in new uniforms, and even though those boys were splattered with mud, and their shoes were covered with the muck, they stepped smartly like they were practicing close-order drill, and they all looked well fed and . . . happy, like they'd be happy to march through Hell if they were told to, and there wasn't an old man among them—except one; and Sandy Pendleton and Jedediah waved to him, and he was superintendent of the corps; and all those bright and brassy new soldiers were cadets from the Virginia Military Institute, which is where Poppa thought I should get educated, but Mother, of course, hadn't agreed.

When we left them behind to disappear into the mist, Jedediah made clucking noises and told Sandy Pendleton that it was a grievous shame that such boys were being taken before they were ripe, but Sandy disagreed and said something about fields of honor and the humiliation of being a slave to the North, and how "honor maketh men," and then Jedediah patted my head like I had something to do with it, and neither one of them spoke until we reached the camp.

By that time it was hailing, and the spirits must have been joyous just stirring up the weather like that; and with all the rain and wind, I guess I just figured that anything could happen, that Jimmadasin or the spirit dog or Poppa or Mother or Cow or the baby Jesus might just appear out of the mist, or that anything could be expected . . . and so I wasn't surprised when I saw that General Jackson's camp was full of soldiers—'Federate boys—and it didn't seem like any tents had come down, but for that second, though, I wondered if maybe I'd been really seeing spirits marching past me, as if all those scarecrow soldiers wearing homespun were spirits that had been growed out of the mist.

But I hadn't been seeing spirits, and I wasn't seeing spirits in the camp; I was seeing General Ewell's army, which was probably as big as General Jackson's. They came up the river from Port Republic, and I figured that something must be up, and that nobody would know except General Jackson, who was having a meeting with General Ewell in a big Sibley tent, which had a stovepipe coming out of the top of it; and it must have been hot in there because that pipe was belching up enough smoke for twenty soldiers. As we arrived, General Ewell came through that tent flap like he'd just escaped from a cage or something, and he was making the air blue with cursing and calling to his staff, and he had a funny way of making a "th" sound with some of his words; but he seemed happy to see Sandy Pendleton and Jedediah, like they were old friends, and he had a loud laugh and slapped Sandy on the back and told him to "dry yourthelf off"; and then he went about his business, and after the guard announced us and General Jackson said "Enter," we went into the tent, which, as I thought, was hot and dry from the stove. But it didn't smell bad, and thank goodness it didn't smell like a fart. We were soaked, of course, and it's funny how when everything gets wet it smells more like itself, if that makes any sense, but I could surely smell the rubber on my poncho, and the old-lady smell of wool from the blanket, and leather, and the earth smell, which reminded me of home and some other things I didn't want to think about, and I guess that was the strongest thing about that tent: the smell coming up from the ground.

The tent was empty, except for a table, which wasn't anything more than a hardtack box with legs, and a few stools. General Jackson turned around to greet us, and it seemed to me that he had just been standing there staring at the tent canvas. His uniform was specked with mud, but it was dry and wrinkled, and he looked nervous as a cat, as if he was trapped inside this Sibley tent with only that table and two stools to sit on while the rest of his army was going on to glory.

"Captain Hotchkiss and Lieutenant Pendleton reporting as ordered, sir," Sandy Pendleton said, and he held his hand up by his hat in a smart salute until General Jackson returned it. I didn't notice that Jedediah saluted, though, and so I figured that only lieutenants had to do that, or that it was all right for Lieutenant Pendleton to salute for everybody.

Well, General Jackson didn't give Sandy Pendleton time to do much more than salute because he asked him about how far the troops had advanced, and when Sandy told him, General Jackson told him to go back and check the ordnance and division trains. I figured that General Jackson probably just wanted to get rid of him for a time. I'd heard stories along the way about how General Jackson would send his officers on errands over and over again, or order them to find out information he already knew; and I heard how he would never bend the rule of law, even if it meant executing a man, and how he'd blamed General Garnett for retreating at Kernstown and put him under arrest when everybody knew that General Garnett was the best officer he had, except for Colonel Ashby, and was just saving the lives of his men, but General Jackson wouldn't hear any of that, and his old brigade didn't cheer him for three weeks; and I'd heard how he wouldn't allow his men furloughs even when their wives or babies were sick and dying; but then, here we were, and Jedediah was going to go home and see his family, and probably none of those stories were true, anyway, unless, of course, maybe the general would change his mind and send Jedediah on a different errand.

Lieutenant Pendleton didn't look too happy about going right back out into the rain, but he didn't argue; he only asked if we could know where we were going, and the general got a sly look on his face, which I suppose was the way he smiled, and asked, "Sandy, can you keep a secret?"

Lieutenant Pendleton surely must have known he was being set up, and probably regretted asking such a dumb question right there and then, because he looked around at Jedediah, as if Jedediah could tell him something, and then General Jackson said, "Well, so can I. Now attend to your duties."

Sandy Pendleton left, and I figured that we were probably all in trouble, but General Jackson just asked, "Have you heard further news of your sweet daughter, Jedediah? What *is* her name? Ah, Annie, isn't it?"

"That's my youngest daughter, General. My eldest daughter, Nellie, was taken with fever. I have just received a letter from my wife telling me that she's fully recovered, thanks to the Lord's intercession, and Doctor Berkeley's excellent ministrations. You have our heartfelt gratitude for sending him to us."

"The Lord permits us to have trouble awhile, but then all things work together for good," General Jackson said like had been reading that right out of the air, and then they just stood there, thinking about God, I guess, before General Jackson went on. "Doctor Berkeley has reported to me that the child is well, and no doubt explained to you that she was misdiagnosed."

Jedediah nodded but didn't say anything. Then General Jackson looked over at me and that sly smile look came over him, and he reached into a haversack and pulled out an orange, which he gave to me. I don't know what I said or did because I was so excited over that damn orange, but I peeled it right then and there, and although it was sticky and the juice spit out all over my shirt when I pulled the pieces apart, it was delicious; in fact, I can't ever remember anything tasting so good. As I ate those stringy little sacks that just seemed to burst when I bit down on them, I thought about the river all bloated over from the rain and imagined it was thick with orange juice, and that if anybody fell into it they'd at least drown in sweetness; and I figured that General Jackson was probably the only man in the Army of Northern Virginia, or probably the entire Confederate States of America, to have an orange.

And I just ate it.

Well, that eating was like praying or having what Mother used to call a reverie, and I listened to General Jackson explain about how important it was to get some scabs for vaccination, and how crusts from children were the most desirable because syphilis and smallpox could be somewhat the same, and you weren't going to catch the clap from children; and Doctor Berkeley—he was the regiment surgeon—believed in protective medicine and didn't believe any of that guff about obtaining vaccine from the udder of a cow, which was unnatural—and General Jackson went on about how Jedediah had to scrape off whatever crusts were left on Nellie's skin and how he had to vaccinate himself and me with one of them, and that he'd better not come back without being properly vaccinated. I didn't want to think about scraping off Nellie's crusts and sores, and I figured I'd be long gone before Jedediah would get his chance to stick one of her scabs into me.

Now, I wondered, as I said, about why General Jackson was being so easy about allowing Jedediah to go home, and I figured it out that General Jackson needed Jedediah to make him some maps of Sitlington's Hill, and he knew that old Jedediah would just sneak home anyway and probably bring some fever or another back to the camp, so this way General Jackson got to kill two birds with the same stone.

After General Jackson was finished talking about all that, he asked Jedediah if he could have a moment alone with me, which didn't make me comfortable, and I'm sure that Jedediah wasn't too happy about it either because it meant he had to go out in the rain. Well, maybe he could go back and look around the sutler's tent some more, if it was still there.

Anyway, as soon as Jedediah left, General Jackson pulled the two stools close to the stove; and we sat there just feeling the heat and listening to the wood hiss and crackle.

"I've saved your drawing," General Jackson said. "But if I burned it, would you make me another one?"

I couldn't imagine what he was getting at, so I pretended I didn't hear what he said.

"It's a sin to be drawn to the things of the flesh, unless perhaps if it be to further God's will," General Jackson said. "That's an important lesson. I was drawn to a little girl who died, a lovely little thing who made me think of everything that was good and innocent and pure. I was also drawn to the sculpture and magnificent buildings in Florence, but that was so long ago, and I shall never see such marvels again. If I allowed myself, I would long to be there; and that would be a sin. Do you know why?"

I just kept staring at that stove because I figured that it would be dangerous if I did anything wrong. I don't know why I felt that way, but whatever it was that General Jackson had to say to me, I didn't care to know; and as I felt the heat all around me, I tried to get as invisible as I could, but it wouldn't work; I knew it wouldn't work because General Jackson had me in his sights as if he was aiming a pistol right at me.

"Because my duty is here, and my reward will be in God's hands. I'm also drawn to you, son, and do you know why? It's because I sense that you have become a consequence." He laughed at that. "But that makes no sense to you, does it, son? None whatsoever. It wouldn't, unless you knew a certain maxim. Have you heard this: 'Duty is ours, consequences are God's'?"

I shook my head; and I don't know why, but I felt scared, like when I saw Cow and Armarci lying dead in the cave.

"Now draw me another picture," General Jackson said, and he told me to wipe the stickiness from the orange off my hands, and then gave me a piece of the whitest paper I ever saw and a pencil and a board. But I just sat there with the board on my lap and stared at the paper until General Jackson put some more wood into the stove, and I saw all those red embers flickering and crumbling and sparking, and I thought about Poppa's exhortations about Hell and damnation, and I remembered the deserter in the cave of the baby Jesus; I remembered him running toward me with the fire all over him like he was the Devil himself, and I thought of Poppa burning up inside of the Big House, and I guess I saw what should be on that pure white piece of paper, and I thought that Jedediah would probably pay everything he made for paper such as this, and although I saw the picture inside my head, I couldn't draw it. It was like I forgot how to do it, or couldn't do it, or didn't want to do it, I don't know which.

Whichever it was, I couldn't draw anymore.

So I just stared down at that white paper and thought about God and Poppa and the deserter, and I tried to imagine what it would be like to be a spirit like Jimmadasin and how if I was a spirit I'd be invisible and could come and go without getting hungry or tired, and I figured that the graybacks would stop itching once you got to be a spirit, although it would be hard to think about the maggots crawling around on your corpse, even if you didn't need it anymore; but all the while I could feel General Jackson watching me, and it made me feel cold, like I had the ague or something. I felt like I was in church, and I was going to have to sit there for a long, long time, until General Jackson patted me like a dog and said he was sorry, although I never did figure out what he was sorry about; and he called for Jedediah.

Jedediah didn't look like he'd been standing around in the rain, so I figured he probably found General Ewell's tent and dried off by the fire like I was doing.

"Can you deliver this to General Johnson tonight?" General Jackson asked, and he handed Jedediah a small envelope.

"Yes, of course," Jedediah said, and then Jedediah gave General Jackson a speech by his wife to thank him for Doctor Berkeley and his mercy, and they talked about the fall of New Orleans and how it wasn't a surprise until General Jackson got a look on his face like he was just hearing his own thoughts.

Jedediah said goodbye.

General Jackson nodded.

And I just felt bad that I couldn't draw him anything.

BEFORE I TELL YOU ABOUT JEDEDIAH AND ME, I SHOULD TELL YOU ABOUT how General Jackson fooled everybody. Now, I knew that Old Jack was up to *something*—like I said before—but I didn't know what. Of course, I didn't find out the exact story until later, a while after I got lost in all the smoke, and I'll explain about that when I get to it. Anyway, everybody figured that General Jackson was abandoning the Valley to Banks and Milroy and Schenck and Fremont and the rest of the Federal generals with their bluebelly soldiers who were overrunning everything. They already had Winchester and Strasburg and Front Royal and New Market and Harrisonburg. Only Staunton was free. Everything else now belonged to the Federals, and they invaded farms and villages and foraged everything bare, especially cattle and anything left in granaries. Now, I know that some Southern Union men still say that the bluebellies behaved like gentlemen, but they probably wouldn't be saying that if the bluebellies had been robbing *their* houses and barns and everything else. I guess I just figured that everybody at one time or another just got spells and had to kill people, like those men who killed Poppa and Mother. Even Colonel Ashby, who rode around that day with the Yank's head like it was a rabbit's foot or something, got those spells. Now, I had probably gotten the same way when I killed Eurastus, and I guess I would kill him again, if I killed him at all; and sometimes I just felt like I wanted to kill everybody in sight, but mostly, mostly those soldiers who had burned our farm and killed Poppa and laid on top of Mother, which killed her too. I imagine they were bluebellies, even though I couldn't tell what they were, but I could get my heart beating fast and the anger burning in my throat just by thinking about them. And when I thought about the bluebellies, I imagined those soldiers burning the farm; and it's funny, but I can't remember any of their faces. I imagine them all looking like Eurastus, which made me hate him all the more, even though he was dead. I imagine he'd be a dangerous spirit, and I felt sorry for Jimmadasin if he ever had the misfortune to meet up with him.

But I'm digressin'. Damn. I was telling you about General Jackson's plans. His army only managed to move about five miles in that spirit weather, and I heard that he called on everybody to help with the guns and wagons because of the mud being so terrible and the road so bad, but he didn't expect his men to do anything he wouldn't do, so he carried stones and timber right along with everybody else. They were heading for Port Republic, but General Jackson turned them around and instead of crossing the Shenandoah, he took Brown's Gap into the Blue Ridge Mountains. Of course, everybody, including the Federals, probably, thought General Jackson was leaving the Valley and heading over to protect Richmond; but he fooled them all by putting his troops on the Virginia Central Railroad and going right back into the Valley where he met up with General Johnson, and together they chased and vanquished the hell out of the Federals at the battle of McDowell.

Which was pretty close to Jedediah's farm and school at Loch Willow.

IT TOOK US ALL DAY AND A GOOD PART OF THE NIGHT TO REACH GENERAL Johnson's camp near Staunton and deliver General Jackson's letter.

We were both of us feeling sick by then because of the rain pouring down and the general miasmas of the night. It was like riding through fog all the way; we could hardly see anything, and that night was so dark that I couldn't see my arm in front of me. I don't know how the horses stayed on their feet, much less how they followed the road, but they did; and it was like coming into Heaven when I saw General Johnson's campfires on the hills behind West View. It had finally stopped raining, and those fires looked like big, fuzzy, twinkling stars, especially since you couldn't see any stars in the sky, just blackness that seemed to be pressing right down on top of us. I don't know how they got the wood to burn, but they did; and we could smell it damp and sharp before we could even see the camp. I imagined green wood spitting and crackling, and suddenly I remembered my mother's face, like she was staring at me out of a tintype picture, but that was only for a second, and my mouth watered just thinking of bacon with grease bubbling all over it, and hot, soft bread. I was just dreaming about the bread, but it wasn't impossible to imagine getting a piece of bacon down there in that camp. Especially as I was with Jedediah, who might be skinny but surely wasn't going to starve.

General Johnson had made his headquarters at Dr. John Lewis's house, and there were tents and campfires all over his lawns, and all the talking of the soldiers seemed to blend together into a kind of water noise, except when someone would say something loud or laugh, and you could hear that clear above everything else. We passed some soldiers playing "hot jackets," just like they were home and cutting up with their friends, all of them attacking each other with hickory switches and fighting and laughing and shouting like Christmas. Jedediah and I were tired and wet, and I just wanted something to eat and some sleep; but Jedediah seemed more awake than anybody I'd ever seen. He was nervous, and I wondered if he was going to try something stupid like trying to ride up to Loch Willow in the dark, trusting the horses and God to find the way. I was thinking about escaping and maybe staying here in General Johnson's camp for a while, but once I met General Johnson, I wanted to get as far away as possible.

It looked to me like General Johnson and his officers had pretty much taken over Dr. Lewis's house. The general received us in a big living room, and he was sitting at a dining table that was round at the corners, and the light from a lamp on the table put shadows and lines into his face, and I'd have sworn he was a spirit sitting right there, even though he was dressed up in his uniform and making some sort of strange wheezing sound whenever he breathed in or out; but his eyes were like glass, like a cat's, and he just looked hard, like you couldn't break that face even if you smashed it with the butt of a rifle, and it looked narrow and reminded me of an ax, and the general had a mustache that was greased and shiny and covered up his mouth. But it was his eyes that got me. I figured they had to be spirit eyes; not like Jimmadasin's, but like the mean spirit that looked like him and had me thrown down into a hole in the ground. Now, anyone else would have probably been fooled by the general because he was talking and nodding and telling us to sit down and asking us if we were hungry—which I was!, but Jedediah just shook his head politely—and asking us about General Jackson's health; and it was easy to see the general didn't mean any of that small talk, but old Jedediah smiled and nodded to him and told him about his wife and how Old Jack had sent Doctor Berkeley to save the life of his daughter Nellie; but it seemed to me that Jedediah was just twisting the truth around a little to make it sound better.

I looked around the room while they talked because I guess I didn't want General Johnson to catch me with his eyes, and I knew better than to look into the eyes of a spirit, and it occurred to me right then that it wasn't Jedediah who was vulnerable; it was me, because the general probably saw right off that I was part spirit myself, but there wasn't any way I could make myself invisible to him or close up my thoughts. If the general was a spirit, he'd be able to see right in; and so I concentrated on looking around the room, which was big but wasn't much. It had probably been pretty once, but there was mud all over the floor, and in the cracks of the floorboards, and behind the general was a big four-poster bed, and there was another bed on the other wall with newspapers spread all over it, and the wallpaper and ceiling looked all yellow like it was old and had seen a lot of weather; but just looking around the room made me think of my own farm and Poppa and Mother, and although I tried to stop thinking, my mind just went on giving me pictures, no matter that I was trying not to think about them, and I knew right then—in fact, I knew when I first saw General Johnson—that everything was going to go bad after that, at least for a while. I could feel it, but I regretted thinking it right away because just then the general looked over at me like he had heard that thought, and he smiled at me as if he was telling me he knew all about everything. Then he turned back to Jedediah, who gave him General Jackson's letter, and while he read it, Jedediah just stared at the lamp on the table like all of a sudden all the life had gone out of him.

"Well, thank you for this, Jedediah," General Johnson said after he finished the letter. "I know what an imposition this must have been. This night's not fit for man nor beast. But it's God's will, which we question only at our peril." He smiled—I guess that thought pleased him—and folded General Jackson's letter back up and turned it over and over, each time tapping its edges on the table. "I've heard about your boy here. Jack says he's almost as good as you with a pencil."

Jedediah looked over at me, and I could see his cheeks were a little red. "I'd have to agree. General Jackson showed me the drawing he did for him."

"Well, maybe one day you'll do one for me," General Johnson said to me.

I tried to be invisible, even though I knew that wouldn't work, and even though I had forgotten how to draw.

"All you have to do is nod your head, and I'll be a happy man." General Johnson was smiling, and I knew he was making fun of me. It felt like an hour was passing, and my arms and head and legs were aching, that's how still I was standing because if I nodded Jedediah would hound me for a drawing to give the general.

"Come, now," Jedediah said. "Give General Johnson your respect."

I nodded, but it was a lie. I'd forgotten how to draw, and I wondered what

I'd draw if I knew how, and I thought about Mother, and I remembered how she combed and cut my hair and talked to me about how she went to dances when she was a girl, and I remembered her singing hymns to me—her favorites were "All Hail the Power of Jesus' Name" and "Just as I Am, Without One Plea" and "There Is a Fountain Filled with Blood"—and fussing with the weights of her mahogany clock, which she said was all she had left of the life of her girlhood; and I remembered how she'd read me tracts like "Come to Jesus" and "A Model Boy" and "The Whiskey Erysipelas" and "The Scoffer Rebuked," to convert me surely to the Lord; but in all that remembering, remembering Sunday dinners and church and tending the garden and how she'd tuck me in and kiss me good night and her particular smell that was nice and yet always made me glad when she left . . . I remembered all that, but I couldn't remember her face. I shut my eyes tight and tried to see her, but I just couldn't; and I knew right there and then that General Johnson, who was a spirit like I said, had taken her from me.

And right there in front of Jedediah and the spirit I made the "ha" sound. But it was no use getting all upset. Getting to be a spirit meant you had to lose things.

Not then, but later on, I wondered what General Johnson had lost.

WELL, WE DIDN'T GO HUNGRY THAT NIGHT BECAUSE JEDEDIAH FOUND us a place in camp, and we slept warm and dry in a nice barricaded tent with a wall of logs right next to a well. It was noisy, though, because soldiers were talking and laughing or fighting to get to the bucket; you'd think that well was filled with tangleleg whiskey instead of muddy water, but I had my bacon and a hardtack cracker, which Jedediah called a white-oak chip because it was like chewing on a tree; and a nigger who was probably around my age came calling; he was selling pies with apples and sugar in them, and Jedediah bought two of them from the scamp. There wasn't any sugar that I could taste, or crab apples neither, even though they looked like pretty good buckwheat cakes. No, all they tasted of was rancid lard, but we ate them nevertheless, and they filled us up as if we'd been to table for a real dinner. Of course, a few hours later when we were supposed to be asleep, Jedediah got up maybe five times to leave the tent, and he was groaning and praying, although it sounded more like swearing; and I figured he must have had a bowel complaint from those "mighty nice" pies we ate. I was feeling a bit of the ague too, but I only got up once, and that was after I had this dream, which made me all sweaty and sick feeling. I dreamed of General Johnson, and I was watching him laying on top of my mother on the red sandstone flags by the Big House, only those flags were glowing like coals, and both him and Mother were burning like they were logs on the fire; and I dreamed that Mother put her arms around the general like she loved him more than Poppa, and I screamed because I could scream in my dream, and I was as loud as the Lord, and General Johnson lifted his head toward me, and his eyes and everything were on fire, and he got off Mother, who wasn't anything more than a pile of ashes now—ashes that looked like they'd been damped with water and left to make a lump like cow droppings or something—and the general came for me, burning like the deserter in the cave of the baby Jesus, and I felt the heat coming off him, and felt myself starting to burn, and I was scared to death and angry, angry at Mother for what she'd done with the general, and it served her right to be a dungpile of ashes, and then I felt so hot that I woke up, but instead I was in another dream; and there was Mother again, exactly like the drawing in Jedediah's sketchbook; she was flying naked in the air like an angel and the spirit dog was running below her on the ground, and I was running with the spirit dog too, and I tried to get over to the other side so I could see Mother's face, but she kept turning it away from me so I would never be able to remember what she looked like, and I screamed and ran after her as fast as I could, ran right through her shadow, which was moving over the ground, and my screams turned into the howls of the spirit dog—until then I hadn't known he could howl—and then Jedediah was calling to me and shaking me, and there was an explosion of red light like when someone punches you in the eye, and I figured I must've just been hit by a shell and was finally and properly dead.

A spirit like Jimmadasin . . . or probably more like Eurastus.

But it was only Jedediah holding a lamp and waking me, and I couldn't tell whether it was still the middle of the night or near morning. Jedediah looked like death; he was pale and his beard was flattened on one side of his face and his hair was sticking out. "Time to get moving," he said. "Come on, hurry, now," and it seemed we were sneaking out of General Johnson's camp, which was fine by me—I was pleased to be finished with that dream, and with General Johnson—although I didn't much care for the idea of riding in the dark. I was still feeling sick in my stomach. Jedediah had our horses all saddled and ready to go, and he wasn't wearing anything that could be taken for a uniform and he looked like a dirt farmer down on luck, which most everybody was, so I just figured we were going to spy on the Federals, which is sort of what we did, but I didn't realize at the time that the land from Monterey and McDowell up north to Franklin and Petersburg and Moorefield was thick with Federals. I'd bet money that Jedediah knew, though. I hadn't thought of Jedediah being brave like Colonel Ashby, but I guess he'd do anything just to get home, even for five minutes. We weren't riding for much more than an hour when the sky started turning gray on the edges, and the stars got dimmer and dimmer; and although there was a chill in the air, everything was clear and sharp and fresh, and I imagined that spring and summer were hiding under the chill. I was right too, because when the sun came up, it was a fine, sunny, spring day.

Jedediah was following his own route, which was out of sight of the Staunton and Parkersburg turnpike, although we took our chances and went back to the road to cross the Big Calf-Pasture River, which was swelled up from all the rain. We kept to the fields and edges of the forest where we could, and the farmers were out planting their corn, and the sky was empty except for the sun, and I was sweating in my dirty shirt and as itchy as if I'd been sleeping naked under my woolen blanket. My crotch hurt from riding, which meant I'd been falling asleep on my horse—every time I did, I'd somehow inch up on the saddle and sit on myself, which is a nice way of saying what I mean, and then I'd wake up quick like I'd been kicked right between the legs; and sometimes I'd dream that I was caught by the Federals and they were torturing me and squeezing me with iron tongs right over my crotch, and then I'd wake up and swear on every Bible in the world that I'd never do that again.

We rode through pasture land, and Jedediah didn't pay any attention to me; he was just having his own thoughts, I guess; and then we were riding right up Bull Pasture Mountain, and I was scared looking down because although it was flat up at the top and green as you could imagine, just as if we weren't in the mountains, when I looked down from the edge into the deep gorge that separated one part of the mountain from the other, I could see the turnpike and the river way down at the bottom and dead trees hanging right from the side; and I could see boulders down at the bottom too; and all around me, everywhere I looked, were hills and mountains and woods, everything green and dark from the spirit weather, and I got dizzy just looking around from the edge, and Jedediah called me away from there, and he sounded angry, or scared, and he asked me if I wanted to show myself off to the Federals. I was looking but couldn't see any Federals. Of course, that didn't mean anything. So we rode around Sitlington's Hill, which was mostly pasture land, and I started feeling relaxed and sleepy and comfortable and cozy. I remembered walking around checking the gums on our farm, and I imagined that there were gums all around here, and in each one a rabbit fat as a hen would be trapped, and I'd kill those rabbits quick so they didn't have any pain and drop them just as quick so I wouldn't have bad luck and die before my next birthday, although it probably wouldn't matter now. I figured I was getting close to being a spirit, and I had a nice time daydreaming about whether I'd get a nice funeral like the one those niggers gave to Sweet Grandy, and I remembered all the jars of preserves and plates of chitlins and chine and the dried fruit and the smells of all those niggers pressed together and how I wished I could've just stayed there with them, and I could even imagine myself lying on a table with all those niggers standing over me and smiling, and Uncle Isaac and Mammy Jack would be there too, and I'd be staring up right through the big copper pennies they'd put over my eyes, and I'd see Poppa and Mother, but all those thoughts were making me uncomfortable, so I just followed Jedediah, and I was so quiet and invisible that I practically wasn't there.

Jedediah just kept making drawings in his book and riding all over, but he wouldn't let me get off my horse and just look around myself; he seemed to be getting more nervous by the minute, and he kept telling me "We're almost done, we're almost done." We must have covered every inch of that place, and Jedediah must have drawn it all too, until he finally found what he was looking for, which wasn't anything more than a mountain track that came around the mountain to the northwest and over the river and ended up on the road somewhere between McDowell and Franklin. We got down the mountain fine, and over the river too, but then all of a sudden someone shouted, "Halt, who goes there?" and before I knew what hit me, Jedediah was shouting at me to follow him, and although I heard shots, and heard one buzz right past my head, I never turned around once, and I couldn't tell you if there was one bluebelly or twenty. I followed Jedediah through some woods and was almost knocked off my horse by a branch, and got myself all scratched to hell in the doing, but we lost whoever was firing at us; and I've got to tell you, I started wondering about Jedediah. He'd certainly fooled me because I never figured him to make an escape. I'd have thought he'd try to talk his way around what we were doing here, but instead we rode around in a big circle and spied on the bluebellies camped near McDowell. Weren't near as many as I would have thought; and then when Jedediah'd had his fill of that, we went up toward Franklin, riding through rough country where we'd be hard to spot. But since we'd spent most of the day riding around Bull Pasture Mountain, it was soon dark. Jedediah found a safe place to camp behind a screen of woods, and we each ate a hardtack cracker. The chill of winter came back after dark, but Jedediah wouldn't light a fire, so we shivered all night. But it wasn't all night. Maybe three hours was all because he got me up in the blackest of the night.

By dawn, we reached Loch Willow; and, I don't know why, but my heart was beating so fast that I thought it was trying to choke me.

But when I saw the house with its big chimney and shade trees and the barn and cabins and all the outbuildings, I knew I couldn't belong anywhere again.

LISTENIN' TO THE
SPIRITS FIGHT

Now I lay me down to sleep,
While graybacks o'er my body creep;
If I should die before I wake,
I pray the Lord their jaws to break.

REBEL PRAYER

W E'D BARELY TAKEN TWO STEPS UP TO THE PORCH WHEN JEDEDIAH'S
wife opened the door and came out to meet us. I don't know why, but I was trying not to look around too much; I just knew I didn't want to see Loch Willow
yet, and so I only allowed myself to look at certain things and certain places, and
it was like the whole world was narrowed down to only where I was looking.

And right then I was looking at Mrs. Sara Anne Comfort Hotchkiss.

I remembered her name because Jedediah told me, but he forgot to tell me
that she was skinny as a rail and as tall as he was, and that her hair was so blond
it looked white, so when I first looked at her I couldn't tell if she was beautiful or just a tall, skinny old woman. She was old—probably as old as Jedediah,
anyway—but I guess I thought she was beautiful when I first looked at her; and
I wondered how Jedediah could have such a beautiful wife because everyone at

camp always laughed at him, and you'd have thought he didn't have anything on his mind except maps and reading and preaching the Bible. I guess I was surprised, though, that she wasn't big and fat like Mammy Jack. I would have liked her better that way.

As it was, I didn't like her at all; and I don't know why I disliked her when she came out on the porch because that was before she—

I'm getting ahead of myself before I even start.

Anyway, she nodded to Jedediah like he was the minister coming for a Sunday meeting, and then they hugged each other and stayed together like that long enough for me to walk down the stairs, get back on my horse, and ride back to find Colonel Ashby; but I didn't do any such thing.

I guess I just didn't think of it.

I was just looking at Mrs. Sara Anne and seeing every little part of her face and hair and even the loops of lace on her dress—some of those loops were yellow from age and a few were torn, or undone; and then I couldn't help myself but I started wondering what she looked like under that dress. I tried to imagine her breasts, if she had any, but she probably didn't, she was so skinny; and laying on top of her would be like laying on a piece of wood with knots on it, and I wondered what she smelled like up close and imagined kissing her and smelling her and touching her between the legs and I thought about Lucy, and then I stopped thinking about Mrs. Sara Anne that way because for some reason I started thinking about Mother, and I felt bad and dirty for thinking about Mrs. Sara Anne that way; and I knew it was a sin just to think about putting it in somebody else's wife; and then Jedediah let go of her, and they started talking fast, but I could hardly make out what they said, they were talking so softly, like they were afraid for me or anybody else in the world to hear them, and then Jedediah introduced me as "Young Richard," which is what Colonel Ashby named me, except he just called me "Richard," and I bowed to Mrs. Sara Anne Comfort Hotchkiss just like Mother had trained me, but all the while I was looking at her, I was still thinking about kissing and smelling her, and I was also thinking at the same time about what Colonel Ashby's brother dead Richard looked like, although I imagined he looked like Colonel Ashby, and I wondered if maybe he didn't look like me too.

I heard a bird singing behind me, and it was getting brighter out, and I thought I could smell smoke in the air, like someone was burning the fields of broom sedge, but it wasn't the right time of the year. I must have just smelled smoke in the chimney, but for a second I could remember burning away that dried broom with Poppa and the nigger children, and the recollection was so clear I almost fell down just remembering it; but even so I didn't look up at the sky because then I'd be looking around at everything, and I was afraid to do that almost as if I'd see our own farm, our barn and lumber house and schoolhouse and the old nigger log cabins and the smoke house and corn house and ice house and, in fact, I was sure I'd see something like that, but then I wasn't thinking about anything except getting away . . . which is what I should have done when I had the chance.

Everything happened so fast I don't remember it happening. It was like I remembered it after it was all said and done. Not that it was as terrible as watching the Big House burn or being in Kernstown fields with all the soldiers crying for their mammas, but it was terrible enough. It was like I was dreaming or something because all of a sudden I heard—or remembered, I don't know which—Jedediah's wife say, "Surely he can't come into our home wearing those clothes—just look at him, Jedediah, he's filthy and I imagine the lice are crawling all over him. No, we've got to get him out of those clothes."

She was speaking so softly I could hardly hear her, but at the same time she was giving orders like Colonel Ashby, and then she called out to Cornelius Rumtopum, a light-skinned nigger who appeared behind us like he had been waiting there all along; and he was surely as skinny as Mrs. Sara Anne, but not as tall, and he wore a big-brimmed hat that was once white but was now dingy gray and it looked like charcoal had been rubbed into it—and the nigger walked right over to us like he was marching in the army, and then he stood on the porch steps and waited; and as I was still trying to keep control of what I was seeing, I looked in a narrow way and could see as if I was using a glass that he had big hands pale as pancakes underneath and two big chipped teeth right in the front of his mouth and his face had craters in there like he'd dug the skin right out. Mammy Jack would've thought him handsome, though, I'm sure about that—probably because he looked strong minded and had a good chin (Mammy Jack told me she just loved a good chin); and while I was looking right at him, Jedediah kept on talking to Mrs. Sara Anne about the children, and how he was dying for them and for his rocking chair and his fire, and "Thank the Good Lord that He spared my little babies," and he God-blessed Doctor Berkeley and Old Jack and Mrs. Sara Anne and every other goddamnbody, except himself, and then when he was good and ready, he asked after the nigger.

Well, it seemed the nigger had become a regular part of the family, to hear him—the nigger—talk, and I'll tell you what he said, but before he said anything more than "Mornin' Missus an' mornin' Marster suh," Mrs. Sara Anne looked over at me and in her quiet, polite little voice told me to take off everything I was wearing. Of course, I had no intention of doing that, and I thought for a minute that Jedediah was going to help her see reason, and I guess just because I couldn't talk they figured that I wasn't any more civilized than a creature in a side show and would walk around naked in front of anyone. I knew right then what I had to do, but that skinny nigger swept me up in the air as soon as I had the thought to run, and he was as strong as Jimmadasin or that bastard Eurastus, maybe even stronger, and he was telling me "dat liddle boys should do as dey're tol'." He held on to me while Jedediah told me to do what I was told, that Mrs. Sara Anne was in charge of me now and I wasn't any better than the niggers, and if I wanted to get an education and get fed and make myself right with God and take my proper place as a man and all of that, I'd better take off every stitch this very minute.

So, in the end, I had to take off my clothes.

I could feel myself burning like I'd put my face too close to a stove, even my eyes were hurting, and Mrs. Sara Anne, instead of turning away from my humiliation, she was watching me like a hawk, inspecting every inch of me like I was a nigger on the block, and I was holding back the "ha" sound and wondering why she wouldn't let me undress in private, but she was inspecting me for marks and scabs and "papules" and blisters so I wouldn't "infect the family in the house." She didn't trust Jedediah to know what the clap looked like, so I couldn't even keep my drawers on. It was the nigger who pulled them down and laughed and said, "You ain't hung yet," but Mrs. Sara Anne gave him a strong look and he apologized, and then she put her face right down by my crotch and slapped my hands when I tried to cover myself.

"I can't make out any pustules, but it looks like he's full of every kind of bug," Mrs. Sara Anne said, and then she looked at my head. "And I always said where there's bugs there's clap."

Then she talked to Jedediah and the nigger so as I couldn't hear, and then Jedediah said to the nigger, "Don't let the boy out of your sight, that's your primary duty," and they went inside, leaving the nigger to drag me out to the creek behind the house and make me wash up with soap and compound of calomel, which burned my skin terrible, worse by far than Mother's silver nitrate medication for the ringworm. And although the creek just about came over my ankles, it was so cold it burned, and I felt like I was being scalded by the water and soap and calomel.

"Marster ain't the boss, Missus is," the nigger said while he stood over me in the creek. I almost lost my breath when he made me rub that ice-cold water all over myself, and I couldn't stop shivering, and all I wanted to do was get out of there; but the nigger didn't seem to mind standing barefoot in the creek and holding me down in that water; and he explained that although he'd only met Jedediah on two occasions, he'd surely got to know the missus, who was soft and white and quiet as a cat, but she was a hungry cat, and he could tell "at first sight phew! phew! phew! who makes de law just by the smell of her, an I'se right because she don't treat niggers right or you right or da marster right." That's just what he said, but then he turned everything he'd just told me around and said that she didn't work him to death and fed him same as her own little girls, and he explained about how he came here, and how he'd been on his own since the epidemic of yellow fever in 1852, exactly ten years ago, which was a sign foretelling the releasing of the niggers from bondage, and he told me how all the white folk had died of fever, and how he buried them one after the other, and once he buried "one dumb white fuckah only he was live an' allasudden screamed his head off, but he was cold before long, but me I don' never get sick or die," and so he walked off that farm or plantation or whatever it was, healthy as the angels, and ever since then he wasn't 'ceptible to fever of any kind, and he was one sought-after nigger, and he went here and there and everywhere, and it was the Lawd's will that he came to Missus Sara Anne to farm and take care of everything and clean up the kitchen and the bedrooms and keep the children safe from conjurin', which "is da cause of eve'y disease dat kills you."

I looked at the little holes in his face and figured he'd had fever—yellow fever or scarlet fever or typhoid fever or smallpox or maybe all of them—but he cured it and probably had a walkin' boy hidden away somewhere, and it seemed to me just then that it was probably good sometimes not to be able to talk, and he must have heard that thought because he said, "I knows you can't talk, little marster, but if you ever learned you can call me Rum—dat's my secret name nobody knows but niggers. It's f'om a song, you wanna heah't?"

I nodded, even though I was shivering in the stream and burning from the calomel. All I wanted to do was get out of there; and he took the bottle away from me and said, "Dat's shit, youse burnin' skin, but youse burned enough to satisfy the missus." He pulled me away from the creek, and while I put my arms across my chest to get warm and stood in the meadow by the edge of the creek, he sang his song off-key, and even though I was hurting and burning and

freezing from that calomel and soap and the creek, I couldn't help but smile a little, and he smiled back and nodded. . . .

> *Keemo, Kimo, dar you are?*
> *Heh, ho, de rum to pumadiddle,*
> *Set back penny wink,*
> *Come Tom Nippy Cat,*
> *Sing song Kitty,*
> *Can't you carry me o'er?*

Rum sang some more verses that all started with "Uppity darky's haid so
po'," and then told me, "You'se the onliest white folk to know that song 'cause
it's about a cat roamed 'round the slave row, an' that cat give me my name,
so it's a powerful song, an' dangerous too," and then Jedediah came from the
house and brought me some drawers and a shirt and pants, which one of his
scholars must have left behind.

But Jedediah looked uncomfortable, and when I saw the scissors and razor
he was holding I knew why, and as I couldn't just run away naked, I tried to grab
those clothes he was carrying, and I figured I'd put them on when I got far away
from Loch Willow, but Rum was quick as a cat himself. He caught me again, and
that surprised me because I was thinking he'd let me have a second to get away;
but he was working for Mrs. Sara Anne first and being nice to me second. So I
had to just give it up and squat in that meadow while Jedediah apologized and
told me how this was all for my own good and how neither he or Mrs. Sara Anne
or the nigger would hurt me for anything. Meanwhile Rum was holding me
down and Jedediah was snipping away and my hair was falling all over me and
getting in my eyes and tickling me, and even though the sun was out and there
weren't any clouds, it was cold; and I figured Mrs. Sara Anne and Jedediah and
Rum had everything backwards, and they should have cut my hair and then
made me wash; but I guess I had been thinking too fast because when Jedediah was finished, Rum took me back out into the creek—but I didn't feel much
of the cold this time because my feet were all numb and I was shivering so hard
I couldn't tell the difference—and he shaved my head until it bled and then
rubbed calomel over it, which burned so much that I almost got away because
I punched at that nigger and bolted, but he caught me around the neck and
everything looked red for a second and I heard Jedediah shouting something
about hurting me or maybe not hurting me, and then Rum almost drowned

me washing off the calomel, which certainly burned out the ringworm and the lice.

The next thing I knew I was sitting at Mrs. Sara Anne's kitchen table and having my breakfast like nothing had ever happened. Of course, I was dressed in the clothes Jedediah gave me, and they smelled like the air does after a storm, and I was as bald as Mammy Jack's husband, Uncle Isaac.

And shivering like I'd never get warm.

But for all of that I was hungry and I had fresh eggs and bacon and real coffee, and I felt the heat from the stove and smelled the green wood that whistled and snapped in the fire. I wondered about Jedediah's youngest daughter, Annie, but it seemed she was sick too, and while I was eating, Jedediah was visiting his girls and giving them their dolls; and Mrs. Sara Anne sat beside me and watched me eat, as if she'd never seen anybody have breakfast before, and Rum stood behind me like a guard.

"My Jedediah tells me you're quite the artist," Mrs. Sara Anne said, and it seemed that was all white people ever asked me about, and I was waiting for her to shove a piece of paper in front of me, but thank goodness I'd forgot how to draw, although I kept seeing Jedediah's drawing of my mother and the spirit dog. Mrs. Sara Anne kept talking to me like I was answering her, and she leaned over to pour me some more coffee, and I got a smell of her, and she had the smell of death that grew on old people. Mother had the same kind of smell, and it made me dizzy and a little sick, and I don't know why, but it also made me angry, especially when I tried to remember Mother's face again and I couldn't, even though I knew what she looked like—I just couldn't *see* her in my mind anymore—and instead of being able to remember her face I remembered the old Sweet Grandy lady who I'd seen laying dead on a door with pennies in her eyes. Now even though she was dead, she didn't smell bad; she didn't smell at all.

Mrs. Sara Anne was still talking to me about planting corn and hard work and working the farm and chores and study, and she asked me if I could write and I shook my head, and that wasn't a lie because I'd forgot how to write just like I forgot how to draw and remember Mother's face, but I remembered about farming, and suddenly I was remembering cradling wheat in the field with Uncle Isaac and the niggers. Harvest was one of my favorite times, and sometimes Poppa would let me work a cradle with Uncle Isaac and the other niggers, but I couldn't keep up, and there was serious rivalry about who was the best, and Uncle Isaac always won because he could cut into the wheat faster than anyone in Frederick County.

I could smell the fields and the sweat, and I could remember everything, it seemed, even the sound of those cradles cutting into the grain and how the niggers swung the cradles from right to left, and how the wheat fell on the curved fingers of the cradle neat as you could imagine, and back and forth and back and forth the niggers would swing and step and swing and step, and they'd just talk because it was too hard to swing deep into the wheat and sing, and they'd taunt each other with "Nigger, you ain't stayin' in front of me," "I'm goin' beat off youh ass," "You done takin' dose little mouf 'fuls?" But there was one time when a young nigger just about beat Uncle Isaac; he kept right up with him, swinging and cutting, and he dropped the wheat off the fingers nice and neat, and Uncle Isaac was sweating—the drops were flying off him and he was sniffing like he had a bad cold—and there was a fight, and the other nigger got fired and everyone declared that Uncle Isaac won, except Poppa was ugly and mad because he didn't want to lose Isaac, and so he had to lose the other nigger; and then, after all that, he lost Isaac anyway when he ran away, so there you are and—

Then I was done eating and Mrs. Sara Anne was done asking me questions I couldn't answer, and I was thinking about Poppa and trying to remember his face, but shadows kept getting in the way and I kept seeing other faces on Poppa, even though I knew it was supposed to be Poppa, but instead he was Uncle Isaac and Jimmadasin and even Eurastus, and after that I had to stop thinking about any of that; and Rum and I followed Mrs. Sara Anne down a narrow hallway, which was dark and smelled like mold. There was a big room at the end, which had a bed and fireplace and a spindle, just like in Jedediah's room in Captain Harnsberger's house, except this room smelled like stale milk and one wall was filled with drawings and maps and paintings, and I knew they were Jedediah's because they all looked somehow the same.

Old Jedediah was sitting on a stool beside the bed, and in the middle of that big bed, which had curtains pulled open and a canopy on top, was Jedediah's daughter Nellie, who was seven years old, and she had hair like her mother and eyes that were black as an Indian's. She looked sick, of course, and her face was puffy and had what looked like blisters on it, but not that many, although there were reddish splotches and sores that would probably look like the pocks in Rum's face, but I couldn't see any scabs, although I couldn't see anything except her face and hands. For all I knew, she probably had scabs all over her body, but Jedediah seemed beside himself, he was so happy, and he called her "Nellie Nellie," as if he was stuttering, and that's how he introduced her to me, and

Jedediah laughed, which was the first time I ever saw him do that. I was wondering about where Jedediah and Mrs. Sara Anne had put all her scabs, and I looked around for a glass bottle or a porcelain jar but didn't see any. I should probably get on about the scabs and vaccination, but after standing in the creek and burning with the soap and calomel, being rubbed with a scab just didn't seem very important—of course, like most things, I was wrong about what was going to be important.

Nellie was holding her doll, and she looked at me in a way I've seen older people do when they raise their heads so they're looking down their noses at you, but I've never seen a child do that, and I figured that little NellieNellie took right after her mother; and I figured right there and then, sick or not, that she didn't like me at all, but she mumbled something like "Pleazetameetyuh" and then looked back at Jedediah like there were only the two of them, and Mrs. Sara Anne and Rum and me weren't even there. Rum wasn't there for very long anyway because Mrs. Sara Anne told him to get back to his chores and the planting, and he wanted to take me along with him, but Jedediah said, "There'll be enough time for that once he's settled in and part of the family," and Jedediah nodded at me when he said that, and I could see that he was proud of himself and wanted me to think he was proud of me too; and I guess I liked old Jedediah. Rum bowed his head a little to Jedediah the same way Uncle Isaac used to bow to Poppa, which Mammy Jack told me was a way of keeping respect and giving respect. But Uncle Isaac hadn't given Poppa or Mammy Jack any respect by running off.

Rum winked at me and went off on his own, and I imagined that if he was smart, he'd be doing just what Uncle Isaac did, although I hoped he wouldn't.

Then Nellie looked at me and asked, "Can you remember when you were born?"

I didn't expect such a dumb question, and I shook my head, but I did try to remember; the earliest thing I could remember was waking up in the night when I was a baby and making a claw out of my hand and scaring myself so much that I started crying. What came into my mind after that, though, was Poppa and Mother taking me for a ride in the carriage, and Mother was wearing a white shawl, and she smelled like wildflowers, and everything was so bright it hurt your eyes, probably because it was summer and noon, and I figured that I was probably remembering a dream about Heaven or something.

"Well, I can," Nellie said.

"You little fibber," Mrs. Sara Anne said, and she stood behind Jedediah and put her hands on his shoulders, and all I wanted to do was get out of that room. "Now, *I* remember you being born, indeed I do, and so does your father and Mrs. Grace."

I figured Mrs. Grace must have been the midwife, but could be she was just a friend or a neighbor or a servant or a schoolteacher.

"I 'member choking, and you were praying to God to save me," Nellie said.

"Little pitchers have big ears, now don't they," Mrs. Sara Anne said to Jedediah.

"Well, I *do* remember, no matter what you think. And I remember before I was born too. Do *you?*" Nellie was looking at me again, and I shivered, although I knew it was from being in the creek, and I thought that I would have been better off helping Rum with his chores. Then she turned back to Jedediah and asked, "Poppa, why can't he *talk?*" and I felt my stomach jerk, just hearing her say "Poppa," and I stopped shivering then; it was like I had just become a spirit again or was invisible, and as I looked around the room, I could see myself in a mirror in a fancy frame that looked like Mother's pewter cups that she was so proud of, and although it scared me at first, when I looked at myself in that mirror I knew that I was somebody else, and suddenly I remembered everything, just like Nellie was asking, and I remembered Poppa's face and Mother's face, and I guess it was like drowning: Poppa once told me a story about how you see everything that ever happened in your life in one second when you're drowning, and that's the Lord giving you a chance to see all the errors of your life before He takes you up—or throws you down—but I don't know how Poppa would've known about that because he didn't drown, although I wondered if the same thing happens when you burn, and, yes, I figured that was so, and that Poppa saw his whole life all in one second when he burned up in the Big House, and all the time he was burning and seeing everything that happened in his life, I was right there, sitting in the woods just beyond the front yard, watching those diarrhea bastards hurting Mother and burning the house; and I didn't do anything, I should have done something, but I couldn't, I just couldn't, but I knew that was a lie because I should have tried to kill those soldiers or deserters or whatever they were, I should have tried to save Mother or go into the house and get Poppa, and it would've been better if I had just gotten killed and gone to Heaven with them; but I lost my chance, and I figured that the most I could hope for now was to continue turning into a spirit and find the spirit dog and Jimmadasin.

So I guess it was like drowning because I remembered all sorts of things, tiny things like how Poppa would tell me stories about the catnippers and ogres, and then, probably because he had sinned by telling me all those stories, he'd tell me stories from the Bible about snakes and plagues and pharaohs, and I remember him telling me about Samson and Delilah, and I remembered exactly how he sat by my bed just like Jedediah was sitting by Nellie's bed—I figured Nellie was just using Jedediah's and Mrs. Sara Anne's room because she was sick— and I remember Poppa telling me that story about Samson, I remember every word, and so I figured this was all a sign, and Mammy Jack would have to agree; but that revelation left me all empty. Looking into that mirror, I couldn't tell if I was a spirit or a person. I wasn't anything. The only thing I knew was that hair was everything, even though I'd never thought about it before, but the Bible understood about all that, and it was enough to make me want to pray, but I didn't.

I heard Jedediah tell Nellie that he'd already explained why I couldn't talk, and I wondered about that. Maybe he knew things I didn't about that, but it was difficult to keep little Nellie's attention, and she was looking right at me again and saying, "There's lions and tigers all over the farm, and they'll probably eat Cornelius—and *you*."

"What's all this?" Jedediah asked.

"It's all my fault," Mrs. Sara Anne said. "I asked Cornelius to sit with her for an hour last night before bedtime, and he filled her head with stories about some lions and tigers that escaped from a menagerie in Richmond, and now she thinks that the farm's infested with wild animals. She says she won't ever go out of the house again, so I suppose we should thank Cornelius for that." Mrs. Sara Anne tucked Nellie in and straightened out the covers. "But there aren't any animals on our land except our own . . . or what we have left of our own," Mrs. Sara Anne said to Nellie. She gave Jedediah a meaningful look, and I figured that the bluebellies must have been through and taken what they wanted; but I also figured that Mrs. Sara Anne should count herself fortunate to have anything left, including her life and children and some livestock and Rum, if he was even there then.

"Lions could get in here," Nellie said. "Through the window."

"Hush up," Mrs. Sara Anne said. "There aren't any lions."

"Even tigers could get through the window."

"All the windows are closed," Jedediah said. "But young Richard and I will stand guard and protect you."

"Doesn't matter," Nellie said, as if she understood all there was to know about wild animals; and maybe there *were* wild animals out there.

Niggers would probably know about that sort of thing, if anybody would.

But Mrs. Sara Anne gave Jedediah a scornful look, and I wondered if they were going to have a fight over the lions until Jedediah looked over at me and said, "Well, I think it's time for you to meet Nellie's little sister—my Annie Bluebell," and then Nellie started having a tantrum, probably because she didn't want to be alone or didn't want her poppa seeing her sister instead of her. Mrs. Sara Anne shut Nellie up quick, but Jedediah seemed happy about her having that tantrum, and he nodded to me, man to man, and so I followed him out of the bedroom and down the hall into a small room that had two beds and a chair.

Of course, Mrs. Sara Anne followed us.

Annie Bluebell was fast asleep in the bed farthest from the window; the other bed was beside the door and made up like new, and the doll Jedediah made for her was sitting right on the pillow like it was alive and staring at us. Annie was wearing a faded yellow nightdress that was soaking wet from sweat and fever, I guess, and it seemed to be pulling at her neck. I figured she had the same fever her sister did, and I guessed I'd probably get it too, no matter how many times I got vaccinated with Nellie's scabs. Annie looked like her sister too, only younger; she had the same blond hair, and although there was only one scab on her face that I could see, her skin looked red and blotchy, and then she moaned and turned over in the bed, and Jedediah said, "Now now, Bluebell, now now," and tucked her in and wiped her face and patted her hair; and after he watched her sleep for a bit, he motioned me to get out of the room, and so we left Mrs. Sara Anne to tend Annie and watch her sleep and went back into the kitchen, which was where I should have looked for the bottle of scabs in the first place because it was sitting big as life on a shelf across from the stove, although I couldn't have seen into it anyway because it was an apothecary jar that had been stolen from the Federals. It was white, and when Jedediah brought it down I could see there was writing in blue lettering and a picture of an eagle and a snake.

"Well, we might as well get the inevitable over with," Jedediah said, and he took a little knife out of a black leather case that Doctor Berkeley probably left for him, and he wiped the blade off with his fingers to make sure it was clean. "Sit down, and it'll be over before you know it." I sat down and looked around for Mrs. Sara Anne. I figured that Doctor Berkeley must have vaccinated her and Annie, but it didn't seem to have took on Annie. Jedediah pulled the cap off the jar and set it down on the table and told me to look at the door and count to five, but I didn't trust looking away from anybody, counting or not. I suppose I should have gotten up right then and ran for the door—after all, Rum was out doing chores and probably wouldn't be able to catch me—but I guess I'd got deeper into being a spirit because I fooled myself by just sitting there like nothing mattered about anything; and Jedediah pierced me on my arm with the tip of his knife and then took a brown scab out of the jar like it was a stamp, and he put it over my skin, but it didn't soak up any of the blood. "You see, nothing to it," he said, and he wiped off the knife, rolled up his sleeve, and pricked himself. He slid another scab out of the jar and pasted it on his skin, and I wondered how many scabs were in that jar, and sitting there with Jedediah and looking at Nellie's scabs on our arms made me think about stamps, which were pretty much as good as money, although they'd all stick together and usually the only way to separate them was to soak them, but then they'd get so sticky that you had to heat them up on a griddle to dry them off.

"Well, I've kept my word to Old Jack about protecting us from the smallpox," Jedediah said—more like he was talking to himself than to me—"and a man's word is his bond."

That gave me a fright because Poppa used to say that, and being here and sitting in this kitchen, I could almost get mixed up; but this wasn't the Big House and Jedediah wasn't Poppa, and Mrs. Sara Anne certainly wasn't my mother, and so I just sat still and waited; and after a time she came into the kitchen, and sniffed when she saw Jedediah and me sitting at the table with Nellie's scabs on our arms.

"Jedediah, why didn't you wait for me, for goodness sakes? Doctor Berkeley showed me exactly how to use those scabs, and there's no reason to allow them to sit on your arms like that so they lose all their potency and can't be used by anyone else. Now that's just pure selfishness—I promised him everything you took back to him would be fresh." And while she talked she picked up the scabs from Jedediah and me, wiped them off in a cloth, and dropped them back into the porcelain jar.

"I just wanted to make sure it would take," Jedediah said.

"Doctor Berkeley said it just needed contact, one quick rubbing would have done it. I just pray you didn't make yourself and the boy sick by leaving it on for too long."

"I'm sure we didn't, Mother."

Now, I thought it was strange for Jedediah to call his wife "Mother," and I never heard that before, but she seemed to like it because she smiled at him, and they suddenly started laughing, and I had no idea what they were laughing about. I must admit I was perplexed, especially as Mrs. Sara Anne decided that Jedediah needed a nap and that I should be helping the nigger with his chores, and that Jedediah didn't need to worry about Nellie because she was now sleeping in her own room with her sister, and they were happy as lambs. Then Jedediah explained to me how he was never going to tie me up again like he did when we were camped near Conrad's Store because a man's word is his bond, and "You're never ever going to try to run away again, isn't that right?" And I nodded, even though none of that applied to me since my head was all shaved and I was more a spirit than anything else. But Jedediah went on anyway and explained that it was my responsibility to protect the family and help out because I was the man now, and if I tried to escape Cornelius would come after me like Hell's own hounds, or I would get killed by bluebellies, or any number of terrible things would happen to me; and so I was left on my own to find Cornelius Rumtopum or steal back my horse and ride back to find Colonel Ashby or just sit under one of the big shade trees in the back yard and figure things out.

So I just walked out of the house, and to tell the truth, I didn't know what I was going to do. I could have just as easily stole away from Loch Willow as anything; but somehow it was like everything was conspiring to make me stay there. The sun was up, and it was already warm, and it felt like a pure spring day, like the heat was inside of everything and working its way out, and for a few minutes I guess I got confused because this place suddenly felt like home, especially with Jedediah and Mrs. Sara Anne and their girls hidden inside the house.

Of course, none of that explained why I ended up standing under the window of Jedediah's and Mrs. Sara Anne's bedroom . . . just standing there like I was another tree or grass or the fence, standing there and listening as hard as I could, listening over the wind and the birds and the shuffly, leafy twig-snapping sounds of rabbits and squirrels, and I could hear Jedediah laughing and Mrs. Sara Anne saying something like "No!" and "Oh!" and I could hear the bed creaking away, and I stood even closer and heard slapping sounds, and I just couldn't help myself, but I stood on some dead wood that I packed tight so I could get high enough so I could just see through a space in the curtains into their window, and I saw them all tangled up together with Jedediah on top and pumping himself into her like he was the Devil himself, and I shivered because I was looking at something nobody should see, I was committing a sin by seeing

Jedediah and Mrs. Sara Anne screwing each other like animals, only animals were different, and then Mrs. Sara Anne pulled herself out from under Jedediah, who seemed like he was taken by surprise and didn't know what he should do next, but she was holding his thing, which surprised me because it was so big, and then she put it into her mouth, and he made moaning noises and struggled around until he had his face right in her crotch; I never saw anything like that—never even imagined it, I swear—and I could see Mrs. Sara Anne plain as the sunny day, and I was right about her having only little bumps for breasts, she looked like a young girl, not like Lucy, and I couldn't help but think about Lucy while I was standing there, and at any moment that dead wood could shift, and Jedediah would know I was out there, and even though this was probably another sin, I was pushing myself right up against the house like it was Lucy and surely if I was going to act so stupid I deserved to get a splinter in my dick or something, even though it was buttoned inside my pants and—

Something slapped me, and I slipped and was caught and sonovabitch if it wasn't the nigger Rum, who was grinning at me and holding me tight, like he was Eurastus, and I considered that maybe he was trying to test me to see if I could talk. But he let me go right away and stood to the side of the window and watched them, and I guess he forgot about me completely because he started doing something to himself that humiliated me, and I wasn't going to watch *that,* so I ran off before he got any ideas about me, and I don't even know if he looked to see me running away because I didn't look back once; and that's when I probably should have gotten my horse, but instead I stopped and leaned against one of the big plane trees and felt the sun on my face—even though it was warm, I was shivering—and then I humiliated myself again, but it seemed like everything was out of my control now, and I was thinking about Lucy and remembering her breasts.

But I'll explain about Lucy later. . . .

It didn't occur to me until after Jedediah left to go back to General Jackson that there was no viola da gamba at Loch Willow, and I searched everywhere, when I could. I figured it would be in the living room where Jedediah liked to sit in his rocker and read the Bible or newspapers or his religious tracts. He had collected Bibles and old issues of *The Soldier's Visitor* and *The Soldier's Friend* to take back to his men, and he'd sit in that rocker for hours and read, so as he'd know every word in every magazine. He didn't seem to talk much to Mrs. Sara Anne or spend a lot of time with her, and I figured that once you get married you just do your chores and have family discussions when something had to be decided. Jedediah and Mrs. Sara Anne acted pretty much the same way Poppa and Mother did, except I could see that Mrs. Sara Anne was in charge, like Rum said; but as I thought about things, I guess Mother was in charge too. I didn't think it mattered much anyway, but I couldn't imagine Mother and Poppa fucking the way I saw Jedediah and Mrs. Sara Anne. I thought about what it would be like to be married to Lucy, and I thought about having her do what Mrs. Sara Anne did to Jedediah because I had a lot of time to think once Jedediah left.

Mrs. Sara Anne insisted that I work with Rum all day, but I didn't mind because although he talked a lot when he showed me what to do and explained my chores and where I was going to sleep, he liked being quiet; and we would spend hours working without Rum saying one word. I should tell you that as soon as Jedediah left, Mrs. Sara Anne told me that I was to sleep and take my meals with Rum in the shack where the scholars used to be boarded, and that I wasn't to come near Nellie and Annie, not for anything; and if she caught me in the big house, she'd have Rum whip me raw lest I infect them with whatever I had.

I got a shiver when she called her house the big house, and most every day I was going to run off, but I just couldn't seem to get myself ready to do that, surely not during the day—it would be too hard—and with those few sunny days and everything coming into bloom and turning into summer, I just seemed to be having trouble planning anything on my own; and so I did my chores with Rum and we took our meals together as Mrs. Sara Anne said, and it was as if I were living with Rum on my own farm, except I had to stay away from the big house.

But after a few days I got the ague again, and I figured it was probably from the scab, especially since the place where Jedediah had cut me turned all festered and I couldn't touch it because it seemed to burn from the inside. Rum made me stay in our shack, and he put calomel on my vaccination blister because Mrs. Sara Anne instructed him to, but he shook his head and said, "Just ain't goin' to work for dat," and then before I knew what he was going to do, he pressed on my arm so hard it squeezed the pus right out, and the pain was so sharp that I made the "ha" sound and my whole body was shaking like I was having a fit, and then he put up a liniment of tansy leaves, egg, vinegar, and turpentine. He made me pee over it and smear it on my arm, which he wrapped up with a bit of flan- nel cloth, and after telling me this remedy worked every time, he left me alone to sleep; and that's when I had the dreams about lions walking around our farm and chasing the deserters or bluebellies or renegades or whatever they were, chasing them around the red flags in front of the Big House where Mother was lying dead, and when those lions and tigers caught those men, they tore off their arms and ate their faces and legs and private parts; and it was hot, so hot that I could hardly breathe, and then I realized those lions were made out of fire, and they were running wild, and setting everything alight, but then I was in the house with Poppa, who wasn't dead, and we were in the sitting room, and I was playing Jedediah's viola da gamba, but not the one made out of cornstalks, this was the real one, and it was the most beautiful wood you could ever imagine, smooth and dark as an old piece of leather, and it was so shiny that it might as well have been a mirror; and I played the viola, and Poppa sang a hymn, and the angels heard everything and appeared in our sitting room until it was so full of them that you could hardly find a place to sit; and then, with all those angels around us, we waited for the fire to come in, which it did, like snakes crawling and rolling along the floor and ceiling, and then Poppa started screaming, but I couldn't, I could only wonder why Poppa would scream with all those angels flapping their wings like birds and touching each other and floating around the room, and I heard wood snapping and cracking as everything started burning all around me, and Poppa was snapping and cracking, although he had stopped shouting and was dead, and all that snapping and cracking sounded like grape and canister and I could hear minié balls buzzing all around me, and then I was outside again and Mother was sitting up as if she was all right, except she didn't move, and I could see she was like that soldier who had died holding the gun, and she was looking right at me . . . even when I woke up shaking and shivering.

"It's all right, Richard," Mother said, and she patted my shoulder. But it wasn't Mother; it was Mrs. Sara Anne. I must have jumped because she held on to my arm like I was going to run away.

I could hear artillery and gunfire, and I figured there was a fight going on in the cornfields where Rum and I had been planting.

"Cornelius and I have been looking after you since you took sick, but you're going to be just fine now. It was the vaccination that made you sick. It made my daughter Annie sick too, but I was afraid that you were going to break out in blisters with the variola, just like my Nellie did." I didn't know what "variola" meant, but I guess it was just another way of saying "fever"; and I looked right at Mrs. Sara Anne, who looked all disheveled: her blond hair was pulled back into a bun, but she probably needed to redo it because most of it had come undone, and with the light coming through the window behind her she looked like she had a halo around her head. Her face looked shiny and all pulled tight, and she had that death smell. It was familiar, though; I smelled it at Kernstown, and, for that matter, I smelled it on Jimmadasin before he got killed, when he first found me on Kernstown field and started hugging me and cooing at me and saying in that high voice of his, "Dem soldiers gone, young marster's safe wid me."

I guess I did feel safe with Jimmadasin.

I certainly didn't feel safe *here* because suddenly there was a terrific pounding, like shells were dropping right beside us, and I figured there was nothing to do but get out of there as fast as I could, but Mrs. Sara Anne didn't seem afraid at all and said, "Don't pay that noise any mind because everything echoes through these mountains. General Jackson and his troops are fighting the bloodybones Yankees over on Bull Pasture Mountain, and, God forgive me, but I pray that our boys smash every single one of Milroy's coarse, rude Teutons into our good earth."

I knew where they were fighting because Jedediah had staked out Bull Pasture Mountain and Sitlington's Hill and made maps of all of it for General Jackson, and I wondered if Jedediah was in the thick of it up there and figured he'd be coming back to see Mrs. Sara Anne and his children, and I wondered how long I'd been sick and figured it must've been a few days, at least, and Mrs. Sara Anne was right about Jedediah leaving those scabs on for too long, and then I wondered if maybe he was sick too and wasn't up there with General Jackson and Colonel Ashby and Captain Chew, but Captain Chew would have a hard time getting his guns up Bull Pasture Mountain, and I looked out the window and could tell that it was getting late in the afternoon. I looked around the room, quick and without even thinking about it, but Rum wasn't there. It was quite a large room, and there were more beds than Rum and I could sleep in, and an old stove and table and a few chairs, but it wasn't much better fitted out than some tents I've been in. There were shelves all along the walls, but there wasn't anything on them, not even one book, and as I lay there with Mrs. Sara Anne pushing her hand against my shoulder and the sun coming in and swirling up the dust, I wondered if Jedediah had just got over the fever too, and maybe he was somewhere between here and Staunton, and I suppose that Mrs. Sara Anne was also worried and maybe she was caring for me and pretending I was Jedediah. I wondered where Rum was, although I'd've bet a penny that he would have hightailed himself to someplace safe and far away, but I didn't have to wait long to find out because Mrs. Sara Anne said, "I can't find Cornelius anywhere. That noise would give anybody a fright, so I guess all we can do is wait for him to come back. I can't understand it, though, because I've explained to him how sounds get magnified in these mountains. He's been all through the fields, and he knows as well as I do that everything is safe here."

But Mrs. Sara Anne didn't look too sure of herself when she said that.

So she said a prayer over me as if I was laid out like the old Sweet Grandy lady and said she'd be back with some soup, and I was to stay just where I was and would I promise, and then she was gone, and there were no angels filling up this shack, although there were plenty of shelves and two other beds where they could sit, and as I listened to the guns firing and shells exploding, I figured that in one, maybe two minutes, a shell would hit the shack and I'd finally be a spirit because I knew what it sounded like to be in the middle of a battle, and that's what it sounded like. Maybe if I was just hearing the artillery missiles (which sounded like a hundred locomotive whistles screaming all at once), I could have convinced myself it was just some kind of echo; but I was hearing the pop-pop of muskets, which was like thunder, and men screaming and crying, and I heard our boys yelling like banshees as they were probably charging the enemy, and I heard the sounds of metal clanging and I heard clear as could be:

"Fire low and give it to them"

"Coward"

"You lie"

"Adjutant"

"Forward, Eighty-second"

"Hold your ranks"

"Close up, men, close up"

"Guide center"

"Halt, you sonovabitch"

I knew those men were all around me, but even so, I couldn't get myself up out of that bed, and so I laid there and listened until the same angels I had seen before started filling up the shack, floating in the sunlight coming through the window and sitting on the shelves, and the noise all around me was sort of a comfort, and I just floated along on it and looked for Poppa and Mother and Jimmadasin, and I guess I was hungry because all I could think of was soup.

It was so close I could smell it.

But I could also smell something else.

The spirit dog.

FOLLOWIN' THE SPIRITS THROUGH

THE SMOKE

De fire mus' burn an' de dross be burnt up,
an' de lan' mus' go froo de fiery furnace,
an' den bimeby all de people will go free.

FROM A BOOK BY
THE BLUEBELLY SOLDIER
JESSE BOWMAN YOUNG

*N*OW, I SHOULD TELL YOU THAT MRS. SARA ANNE WAS WRONG about there being no spirits, but she was right too, because I learned later from Uncle Randolph why the battle of McDowell—where General Jackson and General Johnson routed and humiliated the bluebellies—sounded like it was happening right at Loch Willow. Uncle Randolph said we could probably hear everything so well because of what he called an acoustic shadow, which was caused by the woods all around us and "the vicissitudes of the weather"; and since we were right in that acoustic shadow, we could hear what was going on at that battle better than people who were right there. I don't suppose Rum would have believed any of that anyway, and I probably don't either, but that's just how Uncle Randolph explained it, and he would know because he's an artillerist and an engineer, and he worked for the Ordnance Bureau and helped build the

gunpowder mill in Augusta before he turned into a black snake Federalist traitor, which is what Poppa called him.

But, like I said, I didn't know about acoustic shadows then, and I didn't
know who was winning or losing at McDowell. All I knew was that *something*
was happening all around me, and so I just lay there feeling the fever burning
behind my eyes and under my cheeks and in my neck and listened to what the
bluebellies and our own boys were saying—they were calling to each other and
crying and giving out orders:

"Captain, Captain, over here!"

"Don't let a man through your line."

"John, where are you? I can't even see you."

"Is that you?"

"Come back, you stupid sumbitch, all you stupid sumbitches!"

"Keep your position, you, come back heah."

"We din' come all this way to Virginia to run before Yankee cocksuckers."

"Water, please."

"Don' move."

"Close those ranks."

"Water, please, wa—"

And I heard laughing, crazy laughing, and it kept up like it was never
going to stop, like it was the biggest joke in the world, and it turned into our own
rebel yell, which was so loud and so close and so clear that I thought it was coming right through my chest, and then there was more laughing, like everybody
was hearing the joke again; and I knew what it all was, the boys were just going
crazy with the fighting and the buzz and hiss and thunder boom of bullets and
grape and canister, and then the shouting and shooting would suddenly stop and
then start again, and sometimes it would get real faint and faraway, and then the
voices and gunfire would get loud again, like the army was coming closer and
closer and would be overrunning Loch Willow in the next minute; and it all went
on and on like that until after it got dark; and as the shooting stopped and started, I'd wake up and fall asleep, wake up and fall asleep—and once I sat bolt up
in the bed because along with the noise of the battle all around me, I heard a song
coming from the big house, and Mrs. Sara Anne or one of her girls was playing
the piano, sweet as you could imagine, probably to cover up the cannonading,
and I must admit I thought for a minute that I'd been taken right up to Heaven
and all the angels were playing and singing "All Hail the Power of Jesus'

Name"; but it all became a swarm of bees, the crackcrack of muskets and shouting, and I could hear everybody calling out, and it was dark now, and the window reflected the lamp and the fire burning in the fireplace. I must have been
sleeping when Mrs. Sara Anne fixed up the fire for me, and though it was burning hot in the room, I could feel the cold coming in like smoke through the cracks
in the window and under the door and through the walls, and for some reason I
imagined it was like snakes coming in through those cracks, but when I woke up
again there was the brightest daylight I ever saw coming through the window,
and the fire was out, and it was bitter cold, like winter had come right back (but
then again I should have known better because I knew all about spirit weather),
and I could see that the big oak tree outside the window was sparkling and shining and covered with ice, and it was so bright and quiet and cold that if I wasn't
shivering I'd have thought I was dead.

MRS. SARA ANNE CAME AND GOT ME, AND SHE MADE ME STRIP NAKED AND
wash up in a white basin, and I had to do that right in front of her without even
a fire to take away the chill; and although I was humiliated, I pretended I was
Jedediah and that I was married to her so it would be all right, but she called me
a very nasty boy with a terrible dirty mind and slapped me hard and sudden on
my private, which shriveled right up, and I made the "ha" sound because it hurt
and I turned away from her and my face was all hot and I thought to run out the
door, but, of course, I was naked. After I finished washing, she pointed to a pile
of clean drawers and trousers and shirts (which all must have belonged to Jedediah); and she smiled at me like she understood that it was only natural for me
to be full of lust for her. Even though I could hear the wind rattling the window
and whistling through the cracks, Mrs. Sara Anne looked as fresh and tidy as if
she'd just combed her hair in here. Her hair was pulled back into a bun; there
wasn't a hair out of place, and she wasn't wearing a bonnet, just a big gray frock
over her dress, as if it were Sunday and she was coming to get me for church. I
wondered if it was Sunday, because as I'll tell you, we prayed just like it was, but
I found out it was only Friday the 9th of May.

My birthday.

She gave me a piece of rope to tie up the trousers, as she'd figured that
Jedediah's pants would be too big for me, and then took me back to the big
house, and I guess for one perfect day I was the man of the house. Now, this

didn't mean that I felt any different about her than when I first met her. Well, maybe it did. Some. But that might be because I was in a different position of responsibility all of a sudden, being, like I said, the man of the house.

Of course, as you could probably imagine, this wasn't going to last, but I sat in Jedediah's living room with Mrs. Sara Anne and NellieNellie and Annie Bluebell, and they were all in white dresses with ruffles on the sleeves, just like it was Sunday; and I don't know why, but I was hearing the soft thunder in my ears like I always did when I was going to cry, but I didn't cry, and even though I could have, I didn't think about Mother and Poppa or my birthday because, like I said, I was all emptied out; but ever since I looked in Mrs. Sara Anne's pewter mirror and saw that I was somebody else, I could remember and read and probably, if I wanted to, I could draw too. I knew I could read because I read the calendar in the kitchen over the shelf where Jedediah had kept the white bottle of Nellie's scabs. The writing on the calendar told about "E. T. Babbitt's Pure Concentrated Potash," which was warranted double the strength of common potash and superior to any saponifier in the market—course, I couldn't tell you even now what a "saponifier" was. But even though I could remember now and read and everything else, I still couldn't speak.

And even if I could, I probably wouldn't anyway.

So we all sat through the day, mostly in the parlor, which was a room right out of Heaven, and I could understand why they'd kept me out of that room before so I couldn't see what they had in there. There were big, stuffed chairs that looked like they'd never been sat in and a sofa with flowers painted on the parts where you rest your back, but the piano, which wasn't all that big, seemed to take up most of the room, probably because it looked so heavy, like it had been built right there because no one could have gotten it through the doors. There was a little stool, where Mrs. Sara Anne sat when she played the piano and sang, and above the piano with all its rounded edges and curlicue legs was a painting of what looked like a tower with sails on it, and just by looking at that painting I could tell it wasn't any of Jedediah's work. There was a blue sky behind it and blurry hills, and I just wanted to climb into that little picture like it was a window, and just live in there. I imagined it would be quiet, except for the wind, maybe, and it would never get dark.

I sat on one of the cushioned chairs all day like a king, and Mrs. Sara Anne said, "We're going to treat this day like the Sabbath and pray for our boys and especially for our own husband and father, Jedediah, may the Lord bless him and keep him safe for us, and young Richard will rest with us and gain back his strength so he can continue the planting." Now, it was the strangest thing because although she was looking right at me and talking to me, she was pretending that she was talking to someone else; and, I guess, maybe she was right, because after looking in the mirror I knew I wasn't Mundy anymore, and I might as well be young Richard.

But I surely knew something was wrong about Nellie and Annie because I don't know how they could sit there so quiet on that couch, just sit there with their dolls on their laps, as if they were dolls holding dolls, although I know that probably doesn't make any sense; and they listened to Mrs. Sara Anne like perfect little girls, and they didn't fidget when she lectured us from the Bible from Deuteronomy about the eagle stirring up the nest and how God is the eagle stirring up our nest to make us understand about how our duties are more important than our comforts, and how Job found that out and so did David, and Absalom too, who started the great rebellion, but I didn't know about Absalom; I liked thinking about that eagle, though, and then Mrs. Sara Anne played the piano, and her girls sang hymns with her, and I knew all the words to most of them, such as "Rock of Ages" and "Amazing Grace" and "When I Survey the Wondrous Cross," and then Mrs. Sara Anne turned around on the piano stool and asked me if I thought Cornelius Rumtopum would be back tomorrow so we could get on with the planting, and I guess she was just talking to herself and looking at me, but I nodded anyway, just to make her feel better, and I guess she did because she left us "children" to sit together in prayer while she made Sunday dinner.

Of course, as soon as she left the room, the girls started fighting over their dolls, but real quiet; and it wasn't up to me to mind them, even though I was the man of the house, but then Nellie smacked Annie Bluebell hard on the face and hurt her scab because it bled onto the neck of her dress, and Annie started crying and screaming like all her skin was being pulled off, and even though she was younger and smaller than Nellie, she got Nellie's doll and tore the head right off it, quick as a flash. Mrs. Sara Anne ran into the parlor, and Nellie screamed, "Look, Mamma, look what Annie did, she killed my doll!" but Mrs. Sara Anne wasn't hearing any of that because Annie was bleeding and crying, and breathing like she was coughing and had the hiccups.

Then Nellie tried to blame everything on me.

But Mrs. Sara Anne wasn't listening. She dragged Annie kicking and screaming out of the parlor to clean her up and "get some respect back into this house" and she told Nellie to act her age and stop whining like a baby and clean up the stuffing that was all over the couch and the floor; but as soon as they left, Nellie patted her hair and pulled on the sides of her dress to make it look bigger, I guess, and then sat back down on the sofa. She was still making crying hiccup noises and breathing funny like her sister. She brushed the stuffing from the doll off the couch; it was just bits of rag and sawdust; and then she looked at me like she did when I first saw her in Jedediah's and Mrs. Sara Anne's bedroom and asked, "Are you a ghost?"

Before I could think about it, I nodded. I was looking at her close, though, and could see that her eyes were blue and her teeth weren't straight. She had four pink sores on her face where the scabs had probably dropped off.

"I thought so," she said, and seemed happy about that. "But the lions and tigers, they're real, and they're *still* out there." She looked out the window and then back at me. "I heard them."

I nodded again to keep her happy. I could hear Annie crying and Mrs. Sara Anne scolding her, and then I heard a slap and yowling and then after a minute it was quiet. Nellie listened too; she just sat where she was and smiled like her mother, just a faint smile like she was nodding and saying "That's right, that's right."

"I heard dogs barking. Did you hear them?" Nellie asked me, and that's when I remembered smelling the spirit dog when I had the fever and was listening to the spirit voices coming from the acoustic shadow on top of Bull Pasture Mountain in McDowell. I shook my head. I hadn't heard the spirit dog, only smelled him, and he was probably here, waiting for me to come along; but I wasn't coming along yet because Mrs. Sara Anne was cooking fried salt pork with potatoes and Sunday baked beans, and the sweet-sugar smell of that food was all over the house, even in the parlor.

And it was my birthday.

"Well, I heard *everything*," Nellie said. "I did too."

AFTER ALL THAT, I WENT BACK TO THE SHED TO SLEEP, EVEN THOUGH there was a small bedroom all fitted out for guests down at the end of the hall across from Jedediah's and Mrs. Sara Anne's bedroom. I figured that if I was the man of the house, I should have been in the house to protect everybody, but, to tell you the truth, I was glad to get out of the way, and I was a little afraid of sleeping in the big house. It was enough that I'd had my birthday sitting in the parlor, which didn't look anything like the parlor of my own house, but after a while it made me feel dizzy and a little sick being in that room; and after what Nellie had said about hearing the spirit dog, I knew that was just the spirit dog's way of telling me that it was time to go.

I wasn't afraid, or anything like that, and although the variola from Nellie's scab had given me a bit of the ague, I'd be strong enough to get on my way and march from here to kingdom come. There wasn't anything more to do than wait for a sign.

I slept and dreamed about planting corn, and in every furrow where I planted a seed, a soldier grew right out of the dirt instead of a cornstalk, and those soldiers were bluebellies and 'Federates, and they were all wearing uniforms that looked as new as the ones I saw on those boys from the Virginia Military Institute, and those cornstalk soldiers didn't waste any time before they started fighting and shooting and waving their muskets and bayonets in the air, and grape and canister were flying all over and the cabins and barn and lumber house and the shack where I was sleeping all burst into flames, and it seemed like they were hit by lightning because after the flash I'd hear a roll of thunder, and then the big house got hit, and everything was on fire, and there'd be the boom of thunder each time, but that's all the noise there was, just the roll of the thunder, and even though soldiers were fighting and killing each other all over Loch Willow and burning everything, it was still quiet and peaceful, except for the thunder, which was the sound, like I told you, that I heard when I was sad and going to humiliate myself by crying; but even though I heard the thunder and probably felt like crying in that dream, I didn't mind any of it, and my heart wasn't pounding because I was scared or anything, it was just that everything terrible had been changed into something good, and although Mrs. Sara Anne and Nellie and Annie and probably Jedediah and Cornelius Rumtopum were all screaming and burning up, I couldn't hear them, so it was all right, and the fire was warm and cozy and I saw the angels coming out of it, their wings made up out of the flames like butterflies, and there was an angel behind each soldier telling him what to do, making sure he'd get killed so he could rise up to Heaven, and I saw the angels take the soldiers up, and there were bluebelly angels and 'Federate angels, and pretty soon Loch Willow and the sky and everything was on fire and full of angels, and when I woke up, shivering, which didn't make any sense, since I'd been dreaming of all that fire, it was Saturday, and the rooster woke me up, even though it should've stayed asleep because the fog was coming in like steam pouring all over everything and making the trees look like they'd got caught in the clouds. But, dark as it was, I could feel that it was going to be a warm day, and that spring would be settling in now too. There wasn't even an ember in the fireplace, and although the shack was cold, it didn't feel like the wind was blowing the chill through the cracks. I waited for Mrs. Sara Anne to come and wake me up proper, but when my stomach started growling and making me burp and she still didn't appear, I walked over to the big house.

I looked around in the mist for the spirit dog; he wasn't anywhere that I could see, and I expect that I would have seen him if he was ready to be seen, but the windows of the big house were all yellow and inviting, and Mrs. Sara Anne had made breakfast for the girls; and I knocked on the door polite as can be because no matter what Jedediah said, I knew I was a visitor, and so did Mrs. Sara Anne, but she invited me in and made a fuss about how I was up at a proper hour, not like some wastrels she could speak of who had forgot all they were taught at Loch Willow and spent all their time shirking their duty, and she went on to say that she didn't mean the nigger Cornelius Rumtopum either, although there were surely enough darkies around here who couldn't be bothered to attend their services on Sunday and instead stuck around with each other swearing and fornicating and taking their tobacco and whiskey. Well, Mrs. Sara Anne went on, as if she were talking to herself, and having a good conversation at that, while she put up some coffee and bread and milk for me. I sat down at the table, and Nellie and Annie were asking Mrs. Sara Anne questions about me, as if I wasn't even there, and then Annie leaned toward me and said, "I'm not supposed to talk to you because you'll carry me away with you and—"

Mrs. Sara Anne shut her up and ordered Nellie to take her sister into the parlor to play quietly and practice their hymns, but to leave the piano alone because if she heard so much as one note, she'd send them both outside to play, and that set Annie to shrieking, although Nellie didn't say anything, and I figured that she was afraid to go outside because of the spirits. Nellie had probably put the fear of God into her sister about how if they so much as went outside, lions and tigers and ghosts and spirits would come after them and probably eat them for breakfast.

Maybe the fever from the variola allowed Nellie to see the spirits, and that's probably why she thought that *I* was a spirit.

She was the only one who ever saw that.

By now the sun had come up and burned off the fog, just like I thought it would, and Mrs. Sara Anne said, "You go out and get the horse and plow ready, and when I'm done here I'll meet you in the back field where you and Cornelius were planting. We'll show Jedediah what we can get done on this farm, and we'll put Cornelius to shame for staying away when his chores are here and waiting for him."

It turned into a perfect spring day, and Mrs. Sara Anne's peach trees were starting to bloom, and although Loch Willow didn't look much like Mother and Poppa's farm, it felt good being in the open and feeling the sun baking on my neck and hearing Nellie and Annie laughing and shouting, and it reminded me of the nigger kids that always used to be around during planting and especially harvesting. Mrs. Sara Anne was wearing a straw bonnet, just like her girls, which I figured she probably made, and an old dirty apron over her dress; and she was perspiring in the heat, just like I was, and I've got to hand it to her, but Mrs. Sara Anne, skinny as she was, worked as hard as any nigger I've ever seen, and while she was working and sweating she was talking about niggers too—I guess because she was mad at Rum for running away from the spirits that infested Loch Willow, but probably because she just liked to talk and probably talked to herself as much as to her girls or anybody else; and that woman ought to have been a preacher like Poppa because she did seem to love it so, and she preached at me, probably practicing for what she'd teach her girls on Sunday.

"Cornelius said not to trust you with the horse, now why would he say that?"

I could feel her looking at me, but I didn't look up. I wasn't thinking about what she was saying because although it had been a sunny day and just about perfect, as I said, there was something suddenly wrong about it. Now, it was still sunny, and the sky was still clear and blue and tied up with those silky, stringy kinds of clouds that seem to crisscross each other, but I was smelling something like burning; and it *was* burning, and Mrs. Sara Anne smelled it too because we both stopped working and looked around, and she sniffed at the air and looked worried and said, "Must be Mr. Roland Jeffries burning off some of his sedge. Can you smell it, Richard? I certainly can."

But that wasn't sedge we were smelling; it was too thick, and I remembered that smell so deep I'd never forget it, and I knew that, just like in my dream, everything was on fire, we just couldn't see it yet; and I was right because behind me in the east there was black fog, only it wasn't fog, it was smoke, and I looked around at the hills and mountains that were blue and gray and shimmery and all around us like the backsides of giants or something, and I figured it was only a matter of time before we'd see the fire and feel the heat and hear the crackling of trees and boards and things would explode, and the fire would be like snakes shooting forward on their stomachs faster than you could run; and the smoke was getting thicker by the minute, and I guess we were back in the acoustic shadow again because I could hear voices and the pop-pop of muskets, only now it sounded far away and muffled, like the smoke was choking everything up, and it didn't take very long for Mrs. Sara Anne to decide we should all be getting along back to the big house right quick, and she didn't want to even bother with the plow, just leave it where it sat, and so we just took the horse and her girls, and Nellie decided she wasn't afraid of being out in the fields and didn't have to go in, and the way Mrs. Sara Anne had to chase after Nellie and Annie, I was reminded of old Jimmadasin trying to grab on to me and Harry and Allan McSherry in Kernstown field, but Mrs. Sara Anne didn't lose either one of them, and she held on to the reins of that old horse too, like her life depended on it, and dragged her girls through the fields and wouldn't stop even when Annie fell because her legs couldn't keep up. Hell, I could barely keep up with Mrs. Sara Anne, who might not have thought much of her nigger Cornelius Rumtopum because he was low and barbarous and full of superstition, but she wasn't going to give me a chance to take her horse, and I got so disgusted with it all that I just let them get ahead of me, and then I snuck away and let myself get invisible and settled down behind an old stone wall that was broken up but went quite a ways across the field; and I sat there behind the wall and remembered how our men got killed fighting the bluebellies who were protected behind that stone wall at Kernstown field, and I closed my eyes tight and put my thoughts into a little narrow place and tried to see the spirit dog in my mind, sort of getting ready to see him when he was ready; and I waited for Mrs. Sara Anne to call me, which she did, but she did more than that, she came back for me with her girls, and then I did something that I knew was wrong. I ran back across the fields, and if she was going to catch me, she'd have to let go of her girls and get on that horse of hers, or pull the girls up on the horse too, but I didn't think she'd bother going that far, and it made me sad because she didn't swear at me or call me a nigger or anything like that, she just called me back, and I thought of the Big House being on fire, and I thought about Poppa being with the angels and watching me again, and I remember seeing Mother and the men and the horses, and right now I could smell it all again, and so I ran, sonovabitch, I ran and ran and made the "ha" sound, and Mrs. Sara Anne probably wouldn't've been able to get me even if she came after me on the horse because it wasn't far to the woods, and I was in there and breathing that moldy smell of leaves and dirt before you could say "Jack Robinson," and I stopped right on the edge of those woods, and I could hardly catch my breath, and I was dizzy because all that running brought the ague right back, and then it was all quiet and perfect, and I think I fell asleep for a minute, but when I woke up, I prayed for the spirit dog to appear now so I could follow him because it was time.

It wasn't real praying, of course, but I guess conjurin' is about the same thing, only without the Bible.

But the spirit dog didn't appear.

I sat back against an oak tree and looked around. I could see the fields and hills and the chimney of the big house and the mountains way off that were like walls, all gray and bluish and shadowy; and then I looked up at the sky, looked straight up where it was blue—but real blue, not like the mountains—and I picked out one cloud, which was shaped like a bonnet with a ribbon going all around it, and I was looking for Poppa up there. I figured if he was there he'd look down to watch and see what I was up to, and he'd see that I had my chance to do the right thing and be the man of the house and all that and protect the women, and it wasn't even as if I'd seen the spirit dog or anything, or that I was afraid of everything catching fire because I wasn't afraid, I *wanted* everything to catch fire, although I didn't want Mrs. Sara Anne and her girls to get killed or burned, but it didn't matter now because I'd left them all alone, and even though I was staring up through the crack in the clouds as hard as I could, I couldn't see Poppa. He was probably disgusted with me; hell, the spirit dog was probably disgusted with me; and while I was thinking about Poppa and the spirit dog, I heard noises coming up from the ground like something was echoing right under my head, and so I left Poppa to do whatever he was doing up there in Heaven and put my ear against the dirt, and even though I couldn't hear talking or yelling like when I was under the acoustical shadow, I could hear pounding and scratching, and I thought that maybe the ground was full of insects or something, but it wasn't that, it was footsteps . . . thousands of them.

That pounding and scratching was a sign. All I had to do was get up and walk back to the big house, and I could protect Mrs. Sara Anne and the girls, just as I promised Jedediah, and Poppa could watch me from Heaven and tell Mother, and they could both look down on me and be proud, especially if I got killed protecting Mrs. Sara Anne and the girls, and then an angel could just carry me to Heaven, and I'd be done with all this down here; but even though I had every intention to do just that, to march myself right back to the big house and be the man of the house, I found myself walking toward Franklin Road, where the woods were on fire. The smoke was making everything heavy and dark, and the darkness was spreading over across the sky, and I shivered just seeing it because it was as if the sky was disappearing or something. Maybe I walked into the smoke and darkness because I *wanted* to run back to the big house and protect Mrs. Sara Anne and the girls. But as you already know, sometimes I set out to do one thing and end up doing another, which Mother figured was just a flaw in my character. As I said, I wanted to go back, but I never even took a step in that direction.

All that smoke and darkness were calling me, just as if it had a voice, and I started running toward it, which was as foolish as when Dixie was shot, and I ran out to Colonel Ashby with all those minié balls buzzing all around my head.

I guess I figured that the smoke and darkness would swallow me up, if it didn't choke me first, and I'd find Rum in that darkness, or maybe Jimmadasin would forgive me and show himself and maybe even talk to me. I could see trees snapping as they caught fire, and the flames would come up and then disappear, and I heard voices and thought I saw the spirit dog—I thought I saw those eyes of his glowing in the smoke like hot coals—but I was deluding myself about it all. I didn't see the spirit dog, and Rum wouldn't be anywhere near fire and soldiers, and Jimmadasin was probably still in the cave of the baby Jesus and cursing me for running away from him and Lucy and Cow and Armarci, who were all spirits now, except for Lucy. But it was all a sign; and I can prove it, now that I can finally tell you about Captain Pegram.

Because it was on account of Captain Francis W. Pegram that I found Lucy.

The power of roots

W'en a feller comes a knockin',
Dey hollar Oh, sho,
Hop light ladies,
Oh, Miss Loo.

SUNDAY SCHOOL
SONG

*I*GOT CAUGHT BY CAPTAIN FRANCIS W. PEGRAM FROM LONDON, England, in that smoke, but I could have just as easily been caught by the blue- bellies, who were retreating from McDowell up the Franklin Road.

The bluebellies were setting everything on fire to confuse General Jack- son, who was pursuing them, which is just what you'd expect, of course. I didn't know it was the Federals that were marching up Franklin Road, which runs in a northeast direction along the South Fork of the Shenandoah, but since that's where the fire was, I kept going west to get out of its way. I know that probably doesn't make sense, considering I just told you about how I was run- ning to get right into all that smoke and fire and see if there were any angels and such, but I found out quick that it just couldn't be done, unless you wanted to catch fire yourself. I tried to push myself into that heat, but it took my breath away, and I guess I wasn't ready for angels because I ran from the heat and fire as hard as I could. I should tell you that I wasn't alone because there were snakes and deer and every other kind of animal running from the heat too, but it was the snakes that scared me the most, and I remembered my dream and how I thought the fire was like snakes crawling fast, and it scared me something terrible when I saw those snakes slithering along the ground like they really were the fire, and for all I know, maybe they were. I thought about all those snakes and animals heading for Mrs. Sara Anne's big house, and then the fire would be following, but after getting near the fire, I knew I wasn't ready to give myself up to it like Poppa did, and Poppa couldn't save Mother, so I figured I couldn't save Mrs. Sara Anne and her girls either.

It seemed that the whole world had got dark, and it was cold, and the burnt smells and ash were everywhere so that it hurt to take a deep breath. I figured it was night and that time had gotten away from me; and there was an orange haze in the sky, which scared me because it looked like something bad from the Bible or something. But I figured I was safe because even though I could hear cannonading and gunfire echoing all around me, it sounded like it was coming from far away. I hoped that the Federals were retreating and that General Jackson was shelling them every chance he got, although it could have just as easily been the other way around.

But I kept telling myself that I was out of it now. I was a spirit—Nellie had seen that—although I would have to do some foraging because my stomach was growling like I hadn't eaten in a week; and, of course, I didn't have time to steal anything to take along with me. I considered trying to find some bacon and hardtack—the dead soldiers, if I could find any, wouldn't be needing it; but it was too dark, and I couldn't tell where the cannonading and gunfire were coming from anyway.

All I could do was wait until the sun came up, if it was ever going to come up again. Poppa had once told me that in the Last Days the sun wouldn't come up, and all the evil people would get their comeuppance, and all the good people who prayed and lived proper lives would ascend right to Heaven—or maybe Mammy Jack or Uncle Isaac told me all about that. I thought about the Last Days and getting carried up to Heaven by the angels, and I wondered if spirits could be angels and maybe if I could get back on Jimmadasin's good side, he'd take me up to Heaven with him, and I wondered how it worked for niggers in Heaven, whether they'd have their own place and like that; and I suppose I fell asleep listening to the thunder of those twenty-pounders, which sounded like logs crashing and rolling down a hill, but when I woke up it was still dark, and everything smelled like wet ashes. I figured that it wasn't ever going to get to be day again, and I'd better just start walking; and since there were Federals and our own boys all over, it wasn't long before I heard voices.

"Ain' that sumbitch ever goin' to let us stop and rest?"

"If you mean Gen'l Jackson, I'll break yoah legs an' dig you a hole for to rest."

"Didn't mean nothin' except I'm tired."

"Everybody's tired."

" 'Cept Old Jack, he don' need to sleep, an' when he does, he does it on the sorrel."

"Least he ain't walkin'."

"Maybe he is, you don' know that. You don' know nothin'."

I could hear coughing and the rustle of clothing and branches cracking, and for one crazy second I imagined girls dancing around at a party in crinoline dresses all stiff and starchy and making just that noise, and I stood still; it wasn't hard to be invisible in the dark, but the trick was to try not to breathe very much, even though my heart was beating so hard it made me dizzy; and hearing all that coughing gave me a tickle in the throat and I had all I could do not to start coughing myself; and then they were gone, and it was quiet, quieter than you could imagine; there weren't any bird or animal sounds, and even the wind died off. I listened, expecting the sounds to come back any second, and I wondered if I had suddenly gone deaf or something; and then after what seemed to be an hour, but was probably maybe only a minute, I heard voices again, but they were too far away to make out. I kept walking, but I didn't come upon our boys or the bluebellies.

I guess I had been hearing spirits.

It started to get light, but I couldn't see much of anything through the smoke and fog. I almost tripped over a dead bluebelly, who must have been laying there in the woods for a long time because his face was all blue and swollen, but the maggots hadn't gotten to him yet, and so I rifled through his haversack and found some bacon and hardtack and a little bag of sugar and coffee all mixed together. I was so hungry for that sugar that I ate the coffee right along with it, and of course the bacon and hardtack too, which all gave me a stomachache and made me sick, and I guess I should have gotten along on my way, but I stayed there with that dead bluebelly for a while, maybe because I felt bad about stealing from him, even though he was dead. I could smell his odor, which was like the sickest fart you could imagine, but it didn't make me sick like it would other people because I just put it out of my mind. I didn't expect to see angels come down and pick him up or anything like that (I supposed they would have done that already, if they were going to, because he was too bloated up and heavy now), but I couldn't help myself because all of a sudden I wanted to know about him, so I went through his pockets and laid everything out on his blanket like I was getting it ready for one of Jedediah's inspections, which all the men hated because this was supposed to be a war and not some sort of beauty and neatness contest.

His name was Robert K. Worsham, and he was in the Twenty-fifth Ohio. I found that out from a letter, which was mostly smeared from being wet, and I wondered if he had peed on it or something; but inside the letter was a good ambrotype picture of someone who could have been Robert K. Worsham, and he was sitting with a woman and their arms were one over the other, like they were locked together, and he was wearing a cravat and his face wasn't puffed up and she had braids and a ring on her finger and she was looking out of that picture so hard that it seemed she was going to ask me something important.

I tried to read the letter, which was from him to Rebecca Forget Me Not, and it was about a grand cotillion party in the Yankee camp right in front of Robert K. Worsham's tent, and how the music was excellent and the boys were going to the right, promenade all, and that one of the soldiers, "who was a broth of an Irish boy, was calling another soldier 'Jane' and swinging soldier Jane around and shouting 'Come around, my big tall girl,' " but the rest of the ink was smeared, and some of it had got onto the photograph. I tried to picture all that he was writing about in my mind, and I remembered footraces and hurdles and sack races and wheelbarrow races in the camp, but I couldn't remember ever seeing our own boys dancing with each other at a cotillion, although everybody talked about the whores and asked me if I wanted to dip my wick, but I never did, even though I met some of the whores, who were very polite and pretty and all painted up like Jedediah's dolls. I don't know why, but just then I remembered how Captain Chew's artillerymen Wasp and Rabbit put the powder from a couple of cartridges into an empty canteen and threw it into the fire, and sonovabitch that canteen made a considerable noise, and Wasp and Rabbit got into trouble for wasting ammunition and waking everyone up. They tried to blame it on me, but everybody knew they did it.

I heard the cannonading again, and I wondered if maybe I started it by thinking about that canteen, but that was just foolishness, so I went back to looking through Private Worsham's belongings, and he had more things hidden than you could shake a stick at: I found a pocket knife and a white linen shirt, which I put on, and even though it smelled of the damp, it was the cleanest clothes I ever wore. I found a white glove and wondered what he'd be doing with that—he wasn't an officer; I just figured that bluebelly officers wore white gloves. Jedediah made white glove inspections, as he called them, but he never wore white gloves, and I couldn't imagine what he'd wear them for anyway. I found a half-full canteen, which was probably what made me think of Wasp and Rabbit, and I found a pen and a bottle of ink. That man was carrying more than a sutler. I didn't want to touch him, but I felt like it was my duty or something to go through his pockets, and I found a little bag tied with a leather thong; inside were cheese and nuts and one piece of candy. I ate the cheese and nuts and candy, but I laid everything else out along the blanket, and I figured it would be perfect if I could have laid him on the blanket and put his belongings all around him, but, of course, he was too heavy for that. I tried to imagine how it would be talking to him, and I guess I did talk to him a little about how he was dead and better off being a spirit anyway, and I remember some of what we said.

Now, you should understand that you don't have to move your mouth to talk to the dead. Spirits can hear what you say in your mind just like talking. Course, like I told you, I just imagined this all, anyway.

"Is that you in the picture, Private Robert K. Worsham?"

"Sergeant."

"You ain't got no markings."

"Don' need them when you're dead."

"If you were a sergeant, they'd be on your uniform."

"Don't matter, I'm a sergeant."

"Is this your wife?" I held up the picture and the letter all in one hand.

" 'Tis."

"She's pretty."

" 'Tis."

"Is that you?"

" 'Tis."

"When are the angels taking your spirit up to Heaven?"

"I thought this was Heaven."

"This here?"

"You see the address on the envelope?"

"Yeah." Only part of it was blurred, but I could see it was addressed to William M. Buck's store in Front Royal.

"Take my letter there and tell Rebecca, Forget Me Not."

"Tell her what?"

"Forget me not."

Well, just then he farted, and I thought a musket had gone off or something, and you can't imagine how terrible the smell was. Even out in the open it made me sick; it was worse than the smell of dead horses and mules that had got spicy from being out in the elements.

I got up and ran away from there as fast as I could.

I didn't know you could fart like that after you were dead, and I figured it was a sign, and I considered throwing away the shirt and what I had left of the hardtack and bacon.

But I didn't, of course.

It was probably midmorning, and most of the smoke had cleared, although everything still smelled like wet ashes. The cannonading had stopped again, and that awful quiet came back. I don't know why, but even though it was light and I could see pretty well into the fog laying in the woods, I was scared and shivering like I'd just discovered that I was dead or something and that everything had stopped and all the animals were dead, even the snakes and the birds and the insects, and I didn't care but I wanted to see Mrs. Sara Anne or Jedediah or *anybody* that was alive, and so that's why I started back to Loch Willow to do my duty as the man of the house, and I was near the Franklin Road when I found our own rebel skirmishers, except they weren't really skirmishers because they were following up the rear, and they weren't much older than me or Harry or Allan McSherry.

Now, everybody knows that Colonel John Preston and his cadets from the Virginia Military Institute were left to guard the bluebelly prisoners at McDowell—I found out all about that later. But no matter what anybody says, I saw some of those cadets bringing up the rear. I recognized them by their uniforms, and they surely looked different than when I saw them with Jedediah. Come to think of it, the last time I saw them, there was a fog covering everything too, only it wasn't from fires like this one. Those boys had looked perfect in their new uniforms, marching around, but it seemed that all changed because their uniforms were all dirty and torn and piecemeal just like what everybody else wore; but they looked like soldiers now. When you see soldiers who've been marching for a while, they get a funny look, like they're just looking straight ahead but aren't seeing anything, if you know what I mean. The Institute cadets had that look, and they were dragging their asses to keep their ranks closed. I could hear them talking as they passed, about how they weren't ever going back to school, and about Emma Binghaven, who had a big cunt, and about how Gag got it in the belly and there wasn't going to be anything any doctor could do for the poor bastard, and someone was deathly sick and someone preferred to be buried in Tennessee than up here in Virginia, and then the guns started firing and I was alone again like I'd just dreamed that up in the fog, or that those cadets from the Virginia Military Institute were all spirits, and probably those cadets were all dead but since General Jackson used to teach there, they would follow him forever.

So after all that I wasn't even sure those cadets were alive or just spirits, but I wasn't taking any chances, even though I knew I was acting stupid by following them, but follow them I did because, like I said, I was scared of being alone with just dead people, and I was going to find out, one way or another, whether I was following spirits or soldiers; and so although I kept to the woods, I kept those boys in sight as they walked along the wood road, and then I heard a whoop, and I thought it was a rebel yell and that fighting was going to break out all around me. I went farther into the woods, but curiosity got the better of me, and I sneaked up on the cadets, who'd stopped marching and were all crowded around an older cadet or a soldier—I just couldn't tell—who was waving a paper from General Jackson himself, or that's what he said, and then he read it to them in the middle of the road.

"Soldiers of the Army of the Valley and Northwest: I congratulate you on your recent victory at McDowell. I request you to unite with me this morning in thanksgiving to Almighty God for thus having crowned your arms with success and in praying that He will continue to lead you on from victory to victory until our independence shall be established, and make us that people whose God is the Lord. The chaplains will hold divine service at ten o' clock A.M. this day, in their respective regiments."

I could tell by the sun that it was later than ten o' clock A.M. this day, but after that they marched even harder to close up ranks, and I kept following them now that I knew they weren't spirits. I felt better being around them, and even though I considered going back to Mrs. Sara Anne, I didn't do it. I didn't want to see Loch Willow ever again, and I figured it was probably burned up, which wasn't my fault, even though it felt that way. I could still hear musket fire, so I suppose everyone wasn't celebrating the Lord's day, which I found out was

Monday because General Jackson had declared it so, and I guess generals could make Sunday any day they wanted.

I should tell you that I kept my eye out for the spirit dog while I was following the cadets, and if the spirit dog were to appear and give me a sign to leave, I would have done so. Fact was that I felt like a dog sniffing after the army. It was humiliating, but I felt safe when I could hear talking and footsteps, even though I knew I was in danger. But I kept remembering that dead soldier farting, and how I thought he was going to explode, and—

I can't make sense of it, either.

But I felt better sniffing around here than being alone without the spirits. Hell, I couldn't even find the spirit of the dead soldier whose things I'd laid out on his blanket.

The cadets joined up with the regiment I guess they were attached to and camped with them in a field near the road, and I wondered about the Yankees all getting away and General Jackson's troops just sitting around having prayer meetings by the campfires and playing cards. It was cool, but not cold, and the smoke still hung in the trees and in the sky and everywhere, and everything still felt dead and wet, and I stayed away and kept to myself for the rest of the holy Monday. I didn't pray, but I tried to hear the cadets talking and I thought about the dead soldier, and what I had said to him. I know it sounds crazy, but I did talk to him, like I told you.

I reached into my pocket and felt the letter and thought about Rebecca Forget Me Not looking out of that picture at me.

I guess she'd be wanting her letter back.

IT WAS DOGS THAT FOUND ME, THREE BLOTCHY BROWN HOUNDS ALL YIP-ping and yapping and howling, and a nigger had them harnessed and tied up, and for a second I thought it was Rum, but it wasn't, just another nigger without any shoes. He was dressed up in baggy army pants and he had on a torn shirt that was exactly the color of piss, and I must admit, surprised as I was at seeing him and those dogs—and scared too, I guess—I just couldn't get over the color of that shirt. Must have been some kind of special dye. But I didn't have time to think about that very much, and I figured if I ran off he'd loose the dogs on me, but I was in trouble whether I ran or stayed because if somebody in the regiment thought I was a spy, he might shoot me dead right there. I'd heard about spies getting shot or hung onto the nearest tree just as quick as if they were deserters. Well, those dogs were barking and straining against their straps, and that nigger just looked at me like he wasn't at all surprised to find me hiding in the woods, and all of a sudden my head started itching again, which it did since Rum had shaved my head, and I wanted to scratch it, but sometimes when I did it would bleed, and I was afraid that if I moved the nigger would let the dogs loose on me.

"Who go dere?" he asked. "An' what's da password? Go on an' give it up or I'se goin' to—"

"Baxter, what have you got *here?*" said someone else in the damnedest voice I've ever heard. It sounded like he was speaking out of his nose or something, and all his words sounded all sharp and precise like they were all cut out; and I couldn't help but think that they sounded flat too, like there was nothing inside them. Probably doesn't make sense, but that's what he sounded like to me, anyway. He appeared out of the woods like another spirit, and the dogs looked happy to see him because they jumped all over him until he said something and they quieted down just like that.

Although it wasn't sunny, there was light coming into the woods; and it was gray and smoky and patchy. These woods were full of shadows, which made you wonder what kind of things might have been hiding in them—like Captain Francis W. Pegram from London, England. He didn't introduce himself, but I found out soon enough that's who he was. Seeing him there came as much as a surprise as when I first saw the cadets from the academy because this Captain Francis W. Pegram was all dusted off and dressed in officers' clothes: He had on gray trousers, a jacket that was decorated with all kinds of gold braid on each arm and bars of gold lace on each side of his collar, and he was wearing a woodpecker cap with even more gold braid. He had more gold braid on him than anyone I've ever seen, and I found out later that he had two beautiful black geldings that Colonel Ashby would have loved, a broken-down mule that was the skinniest and boniest and meanest animal I ever saw, and, of course, the broken-down servant who found me. Baxter. Although I couldn't imagine that was his real name. But you could never tell with niggers. I wish that Poppa and Mother had given me a better name, something more like Cornelius Rumtopum, or maybe an Indian name, but I guess it didn't matter.

Since I wasn't Mundy anymore, I could give myself any name I wanted.

It was strange, though, because the name that came into my mind was the dead bluebelly, Robert K. Worsham, and I remembered the letter I had in my pocket to Rebecca Forget Me Not, and I wondered if I'd fart like that after I was dead.

Course, I wasn't daydreaming, but I was thinking about what I just told you while Captain Pegram questioned me; and I shook my head and waved my arms until he finally understood that even though I couldn't talk I could hear, and all of that. They both talked loud to me, and spoke funny, like I was a baby or something, which I suppose is what people have to do when they meet someone who can't talk. After a while, though, they lowered their voices, and Captain Pegram told Baxter to bind me up, and though I considered running, I decided against it because I knew sure as I was standing there that Baxter would like nothing better than to loose those dogs on me; so I let him tie a strap around my arms and chest like I was just another one of Captain Pegram's dogs. I guess Jedediah had figured that I was a dog too; and I knew that if I could talk, it would be different; but I figured I could probably find Jedediah or Colonel Ashby or even General Jackson, although I was entirely wrong about that too. I suppose it was maybe because of losing my hair, although my head was getting all prickly like the skin of a peach, but Colonel Ashby wouldn't have recognized me even if I walked in front of him. Of course, he'd have figured it out when he saw I couldn't talk, but it wasn't that easy, I found out—I might as well have been in Georgia or Tennessee; and I never did find Jedediah, or Colonel Ashby, for that matter.

So Captain Pegram and Baxter took me through the woods to their camp—they were attached to General Johnson's brigade because the Twelfth Georgia was all around here, and everybody respected them because they'd fight you even if you had a musket and a pistol and a bayonet, and they only had their fingernails. Like I said, I figured Captain Pegram would report me, and I'd see Sandy Pendleton or General Jackson, but if Captain Pegram had planned on reporting me the next day, he was too late. I guess in London, England, they take their sweet time about everything.

Well, as Poppa used to say, "Everything happens for the best"; but I was having trouble believing that at the time because I didn't want to be anywhere near General Johnson. I'll never forget how his eyes and face looked all hard and spiritlike when Jedediah and I visited him on the way to Loch Willow, and I was relieved when I found out that he had been seriously wounded at McDowell.

But you never know with spirits, and General Johnson was surely a spirit. I figured it would take more than a bullet to kill him.

Camp was set up on the edge of the woods, and on one side was hills and on the other was the side of a mountain, so it was sort of like being in a ravine. There were fires everywhere, and a few white tents were up, probably just for the officers like Captain Pegram, but it didn't matter much because it was a warm day, and the soldiers were just laying around on the ground like cattle before a rain; they were cooking and playing cards, and I saw two soldiers dancing, just like in Private Worsham's letter that was in my pocket, and some were shouting and playing Hot Jackets, just like I saw the last time I was in General Johnson's camp, and even though it was Monday, General Jackson had proclaimed it was Sunday, and even though the army was only given a half day to pray and give thanks and celebrate and like that, we didn't break camp until the next day. I guess that General Johnson was around *somewhere*, though, because the spirit weather came back.

It was colder than a witch's tit that night, and it was so windy that the sleet was blowing sideways. All you could see was the sleet and the campfires; and the embers flew all around in the wind and reminded me of the spirit dog because his eyes were red like that; but I'd figured by then that I wasn't ever going to see the spirit dog again. Of course, there were other things I never figured to see again that fooled me, but I'm not going to get ahead of my story.

Anyway, it was fine for Captain Pegram and me because we were protected in the tent. The pig stove made cracking noises like it was going to break, and the neck where it connected with the pipe was red hot, and I felt sleepy sitting in there with all that heat, and I was a little worried about Captain Pegram, whether he was going to try anything like Eurastus did, especially since he kept watching me and had me strapped to the stove on the bottom where it wasn't so hot, I suppose; I didn't let on, but I could have escaped, and as soon as he fell asleep, that's what I planned to do. But all he did was talk in that funny way of his, through his nose, like I said. I should probably tell you that I was a little afraid of him because he was as big as Eurastus, but he seemed soft all over, and his face was always red like he was embarrassed or had just come in out of the cold. He had a big belly, but I wasn't fooled by any of that.

I just figured he was probably strong and dangerous.

Mostly, though, I think he was homesick or something because all he did was talk about how his great-grandfather was called the Honorable Black Jack Brixton—which, of course, made me think of Mammy Jack—and that he never read anything but tracts and the Bible, and how old Black Jack sold birds in Poplar and Limehouse and Blackwall and lived near the Jews' burial ground, and he caught larks and linnets and goldfinches and sold them to go to Port

Philip and sold them to the captains of the sailing ships that went to the West Indies; and then Captain Pegram talked about how his father had to live on nothing but a penny loaf of bread and never had a shilling plate of meat like we did.

Now, I didn't understand half of what he was talking about, although it sounded strange and interesting to me, even though I didn't believe that Black Jack Brixton was his grandfather because I couldn't see any nigger in Captain Pegram's red face, not even a little bit. Well, from the way he told it, his grandfather made a lot of money and got to be a Lord or something, which probably was because he was so religious, and Captain Pegram told me how he and his father helped the poor and how he knew the back streets of London like the back of his hand, and he knew the costerlads and costergirls and all the tricks of the costermongers, and he knew the cheap-johns and Jew-girls and the cigar-end finders, and, as I told you before, I didn't understand hardly anything about what he said—it was more like he was talking to himself, like he was asleep or something—and all I knew was that we didn't have a shilling plate of meat, whatever that was, but I sure as hell was hungry.

Hungry as I was, though, I forgot all about it when he explained about how there were consart rooms, which were the same as cock-and-hen clubs, but I didn't know what either one was, except that he talked about the street-fire king who was called Salamander, and that Salamander would put sulphur on a plate and light it and put it under his nose like it was the sweetest perfume, and after that he'd eat it up with a fork while it was burning, and he'd put gunpowder in the palm of his hand and explode it, and he explained how he tried it himself once and came away with seven shillings and sixpence, which I guess was a lot of money; and he knew all about how to eat a lighted link, the kind you can purchase at oil shops, except I never heard of an oil shop, and Captain Pegram said you won't burn the inside of your mouth, but if the pitch falls outside, well, then you're in trouble, and he told me that you just hold your breath when you put the fire in your mouth and it goes out quick as anything, and you get spit all over the link and tuck it in your cheek like chewing tobacco.

Captain Pegram told me that all you needed was confidence, and that could have come right out of the Bible he said because that's just about all you need to know, and now he'd told me, and I wouldn't have any troubles for the rest of my life, unless I tried something foolish like running off when he fell asleep, but he said he never slept, he just closed his eyes and thought about things. Now, I didn't believe any of that, but in a way I guess I did believe it, and I couldn't help but think that Captain Pegram was the wrong person because he just didn't look like the way he talked, but the more he talked the more I could see he was dangerous, and although I'm getting ahead of myself, I'll tell you that was the most he ever talked to me, and, like I said, he was probably homesick or something or just talking to himself.

I figure he was talking to me like he'd talk to one of his dogs, although I thought it was strange that he didn't keep any of his dogs in his tent. They were probably outside, guarding it, and if I escaped they'd probably be after me like a shot; but after Captain Pegram was all talked out, he finally got around to cooking, and he made the most delicious food I could imagine; he cooked up beef, which he called "the sinews of war" because it was so stringy and tough, and he made up a sauce out of bacon fat and brown sugar, and although he ate most of it, he gave some to me to eat right out of the skillet; and then he went to sleep—or closed his eyes to think about things. He had that old oven stoked up high, and I guess it didn't bother Captain Pegram, but I was sweating and feeling weak from all that heat, seeing that I was tied up to the leg of the old pig oven; and there wasn't anything for me to do but sit while Captain Pegram thought about things, and I heard noise outside, and it must have been closer to morning than evening, but General Jackson's and General Johnson's armies were on the move again, swearing and marching and sounding like horses clack clacking on a wood road, and I could hear teamsters shouting, and wagons creaking, and canteens and sabers clattering; and Captain Pegram got up and pointed his finger at me like he was going to tell me something solemn, and he went outside and called for Baxter.

I don't know why, but when he called, "Baxter! Here boy, now," I thought about the street-fire king Salamander and figured that would be a good name for me 'cause I certainly knew most everything about fire.

When Captain Pegram finally returned, he was fit to be tied because Baxter had deserted and took a horse and the dogs.

"Bloody hell! I'll have that horse-thieving pickaninny bastard sold down to Georgia. Steal *my* horse. . . . Bloody black bastard could have at least left me my dogs."

But I figured if they were really Captain Pegram's dogs they wouldn't have gone with the nigger.

WELL, I FIGURE THAT THE PICKANINNY BASTARD TOOK OFF LIKE HE DID when he saw me because like I probably told you niggers can see things nobody else can; they know how to see into the world of the spirits and like that, which is how they know about dreams and conjurations and putting pennies over dead people's eyes and the virtue of roots.

Now, Captain Pegram's nigger, Baxter, must have known a thing or two because he had special black roots that looked like little twisted men, and they had arms and legs and everything; and they were supposed to protect him from being killed or beaten by white people. I knew that was true because I found his roots along with his ropes and brushes and a bag of feed all tied up for the horses and the mule, and I remembered what Uncle Isaac had told me about the virtue of roots, which was that as long as you carried them always on your right side, you'd be safe from white marsters, unless they knew the special nigger tricks of conjuration, which wasn't very likely.

You see, niggers understand that mostly people get killed by trickery, and I figure that was pretty much right; at least it seemed so to me after seeing all the soldiers dead in the fields. It was a trick that some got killed and some didn't, and Colonel Ashby knew about that, which is why he could ride into the enemy with his dead brother Richard, and all those minié balls would go right around him like he had a bad smell or something. Course, the spirits could help you, just like Richard helped him and Jimmadasin helped me, although I was entirely on my own now. Except I didn't know what I was. Sometimes I figured I was more spirit, and then sometimes, when I was so hungry I could faint and my scalp was itching and the graybacks were crawling all over me like maggots on a cow, I figured I was just like any of the other soldiers, sweating and stinking of their own shit.

Anyway, what I was trying to say is that Baxter quit the camp faster than a jackrabbit because he probably saw that I was mostly a spirit, and he was too smart to stay around. Now, I suppose I was just guessin' about the roots and him seeing me to be a spirit, but I took those roots of his and carried them on my right side, which is probably why I didn't get killed. I don't understand why he left them, though. Maybe he had better ones, or maybe he was just so scared at seeing me that he forgot to take them. Of course, I also considered that he left them there to conjure me, or maybe Captain Pegram, but I figured that a root is a root and that it didn't matter what Baxter thought he was putting on those roots, they'd still protect me from harm. But I also figured there wasn't any sense taking chances, so I thought I'd put one of Mammy Jack's vision blessings on them, but all I could think of was a song she used to sing when she was angry:

Jackass rared.
Jackass pitch.
Throwed ole Marsa in de ditch.
Jackass stamped.
Jackass neighed.
Throwed ole Marsa on his haid.

I guess it worked, though, because I still have those roots protectin' me.

I FIGURED AT FIRST THAT CAPTAIN PEGRAM WAS A SPY BECAUSE HE didn't seem to belong to anybody, and maybe *that's* why his nigger ran off because if Captain Pegram got caught, they'd hang him and his nigger from one of the nearest trees. I hadn't seen that happen, but I knew it was true.

I figured that I was probably in trouble too, but it wasn't even dawn when Sandy Pendleton came to see Captain Pegram. He came right into the tent, and he looked at me like he'd never seen me before, and he told Captain Pegram to get me moving to light the stove and provide some warmth, and that he'd been hoping for a bit of English breakfast. Captain Pegram apologized because I guess he didn't understand that Sandy Pendleton was making a little fun at him; and it didn't seem that Sandy Pendleton could see that I was tied up to the stove—the rope probably wasn't that noticeable.

He told Captain Pegram that Old Jack wanted to see him about something, and that it was urgent and he'd better be prepared to ride; and then he left, and I don't know why, but I was shaking all over like I was more scared than I'd ever been before. I didn't know it then because I hadn't come across Captain Pegram's little brass mirror or looked into a basin of water to see my reflection, but I had blotches all over my face like I had the variola, except it was only pimples, and my hair wasn't thick, it was short and prickly; and I guess I wasn't anything like I was.

Captain Pegram untied me and said, "Light the fire. I'll be right back. Do you understand that?"

I nodded.

"Be warned, the cadets will be watching your every move, and my own men will be watching, and I'll be *right* back."

I didn't think he had any men, but I nodded; and he said, "Best for you here. You'll be safe, you'll eat, you'll be warm."

I was surprised that he said that, but then he must have had another change of mind because he grabbed hold of me hard and said, "If you do the least little thing wrong, I'll ..."

I nodded again, and I figured that he was just getting nervous leaving me here with all his possessions; but maybe he thought I was scared because of how I was shaking after Sandy Pendleton left.

Fact is, I guess I was still shaking.

CAPTAIN PEGRAM DIDN'T COME RIGHT BACK.

In fact, I didn't think I was going to ever see him again, but I was wrong about that because he appeared five days later at Mount Solon with General Ewell, who everybody called "Old Baldhead"; and then it seemed that he brought the entire Louisiana regiment to New Market to meet General Jackson. Captain Pegram had turned into one of the Louisiana Tigers, which were supposed to be the meanest and most terrifying soldiers in the entire Confederate army. They were all Irish and Catholic, and I don't know if he changed his religion or something, but he changed his uniform to a red cap with a blue tassel and a red shirt and striped pants that looked like they'd never seen any dirt; and those pants were tucked into polished boots that looked like they'd never seen mud. You wouldn't know if he was an officer or an actor or someone in the circus, but all the Louisiana Tigers were like that, and they only followed orders from God and General Jackson, and no one ever laughed at them, not if they wanted to live.

I'm getting way ahead of myself again, but that's because I still can't help thinking about those uniforms. It seemed to me those bright colors were about as perfect as God.

Anyway, I took good care of Captain Pegram's tent and his mule and all the rest of his possessions while he was away. Well, I took care of everything except for that stove, which was too heavy to lift onto that mule, so I left it behind. I just loaded that old skinny mule up as best I could with Captain Pegram's tent and stores and blankets and whatever else I could get over that mule's back without getting kicked or bit; and I followed along with the cadets, and they all figured that I was Captain Pegram's servant and that everything was legal and proper. So I had a job in General Jackson's Army of Northern Virginia, and, for a while, I guess I was part of his foot cavalry, because I couldn't ride that mule, not with everything piled on top of him. I figured I had it worse than the regular soldiers because they didn't have to put up with getting bit or kicked or waylaid in the wrong direction because mules never do what they're told, and I got so I hated that animal because sometimes the only way to get him to move was to crack a strap over his ears, and then sometimes he'd sit down right on the ground and probably twenty men pulling on him wouldn't be able to get him up—all that's natural for a mule, which is why Poppa used to call them "a stubborn fact"; and sometimes he'd bolt forward, and everything I'd tied on to him would come shaking loose, and that mule would make the damnedest noise; it sounded something like a screech and also like an old man groaning; and no matter what, that sound would always make me feel bad, like I was Eurastus or something and attacking a poor, defenseless beast.

I can't describe the sound the mule made any better than that, but the first time I heard it I thought of Poppa screaming in the fire and the soldiers dying in Kernstown field. And even though I fed him all the oats Captain Pegram had, he always looked half dead and starved. Course, he ate most anything he could find, especially brush. I never even gave that mule a name, not that he could have heard me or understood even if I did; and most every night I considered taking enough of Captain Pegram's food and possessions to keep me going and just running off on my own. But I didn't. Truth to tell, I didn't want to be on my own, and I didn't want to be a spirit anymore, either. But I still kept myself pretty invisible, which is probably why none of the cadets or the foot cavalry paid me much attention, except when the mule did something stupid like sit down in the middle of the road, or throw off all of Captain Pegram's possessions, or kick me good in the stomach, which he only did once.

I carried my share of Captain Pegram's possessions, and my pack was as heavy as anyone's; but, like I said, I kept out of everybody's way, which is the only way to stay out of trouble. I did make one friend, though—a soldier who everybody called R. W., as if all he had were those initials and no first name. His last name was Waldrop, and he was a corporal in the Twenty-first Virginia, and he came over to visit Captain Pegram's tent and "borrow" a little of Captain Pegram's stores, usually a little sugar or flour or tobacco.

I discovered that being a servant wasn't so bad, as long as the marster was gone and there was enough food to eat, and Captain Pegram had quite a heavy store, which is probably why the mule was always acting ornery. Corporal R. W. Waldrop didn't take advantage, though, and if I thought he had stealin' bones, as Aunt Hanna would say, I would never had given him anything. But I could tell things about people, and so could Corporal R. W. Waldrop; he certainly could tell things; and if I could have asked him, I imagine he would have told me. He had no trouble seeing me; and I guess he liked to talk to me, probably because I couldn't say anything back to him.

He was taller than Jedediah, and his uniform was so ragged and baggy that he looked more like a scarecrow than a soldier; and if I didn't know better, I would have figured him for a spirit like Jimmadasin, probably because most of his fingers on his left hand had been shot off. He had only a thumb and a pinkie, and for some reason all I could think of whenever I saw that hand of his was a spider. His pants were so long that he had to roll up the legs like the niggers did in the cornfields, and he used to complain that even though his regulation Virginia-issue uniform had pockets, he couldn't get anything in or out of them; but most soldiers wore uniforms that didn't fit, so that was nothing unusual.

But I couldn't help but stare at his Adam's apple because it looked like he'd swallowed something and it had got stuck right there in his throat. I always imagined it was a piece of hardtack cracker that just wouldn't go down because I could almost see where the side of the cracker was pushing out in his throat; and Corporal R. W. Waldrop had holes in his face like Mrs. Sara Anne's nigger Rum, and he told me that he used to have pustules all over his face just like me when he was young and that I'd be getting over that soon as I had a woman, and he said he could tell that I never had a woman just by looking at the pimples on my face, and I wondered if all the other soldiers knew about that too. I figured that everybody in the camp probably knew. Those pustules were terrible, I suppose, and they just seemed to appear all of a sudden like a scourge on my face or something, and, frankly, thinking about them makes me sick, and except for being a signpost that I never had a woman, they weren't important to anything.

But I guess it was a combination of my pimples, Corporal R. W. Waldrop, and Captain Pegram that brought me to Lucy.

I DON'T MUCH LIKE TO ADMIT IT, BUT BEING WITH GENERAL JACKSON'S army was something like being a baby and knowing that Mother and Poppa were in the next room. I know that probably doesn't make any sense, but that's what it felt like to me.

I should also tell you about how the foot cavalry worked. Everybody joked that Old Jack always marched at dawn, except when he started the night before, and sometimes we'd start at three in the morning or even earlier. The way it worked was that everybody had to march something called the "route step" in the first three hundred yards. I didn't know what that meant, but everybody would start off marching like they were on a parade, with the officers shouting commands and saying something like *"hiphup"* and walking alongside everybody to make sure they kept up.

Well, we'd march like that for most of an hour, then stack arms for ten minutes; and then the officers would start shouting, and everyone would start swearing and groaning and pissing and moaning, and we'd start again, and then rest, and then eat lunch, and then march and rest and march and rest; and the first day, which was May 14th, we marched eighteen miles, and the next day we marched fifteen miles, and when we got outside of Lebanon, which was on the 16th, the officers declared a fast day, and we didn't march, which was a good thing because everybody was broke down and straggling and trying to sleep while marching, which, of course, is impossible.

I know that because I tried it.

We were marching so long that a soldier from the Twenty-seventh got desperate enough to untie Captain Pegram's gear from the mule, and he was doing pretty good riding that broken-down animal. There wasn't anything I could do about it because I didn't have my Colt .44 revolver, and Captain Pegram didn't leave me a musket; but after everybody was done laughing, an officer who was marching alongside the cadets told that private that he'd "shoot his fat, foolish, malingerin' ass off if he didn't stop harassing that poor animal and get back up front into line," and that was that.

I went back along the road and picked up Captain Pegram's tent and extra saddle and blankets and uniforms and his little wood stool and almost all the stores and whatever else I could find laying out there in the dark that the soldiers hadn't stoled; and the mule groaned and screamed and kicked and made a fuss when I loaded him up—I guess he figured he was going to be free as the spirits after that soldier got off his back.

Anyway, we all got up the next day and marched until Sunday; and by that time we were all broke down and straggling again, but it was warm and sunny, and we were all encamped by the North River across from Bridgewater. Some of the cadets went over to listen to Reverend Doctor Dabney preach over at headquarters, which was on Castle Hill, to the west of Mount Solon, and when they came back from his service they were talking about how Captain Pegram and "Old Baldhead" General Richard S. Ewell had come from Conrad's Store to visit General Jackson; and everybody was talking about Old Baldhead like they knew him firsthand, and they talked about how his head was shaped like a bomb and that he looked like a woodcock because of the way he cocked his head when he talked, and how he swore like a sonovabitch and had a lisp and would always say "What do you thuppose President Davis made me a major general for?" and the cadets laughed at that and made funny motions like they were girls or something, and they said he only ate hulled wheat and corn and egg yolks and raisins, but that was because he had ulcers eating at his stomach, and I figured that if I ever got ulcers that's what I'd eat.

I remember meeting Old Baldhead when I was with Sandy Pendleton and Jedediah, and I suppose he did remind me of a bird or something; and I could understand why Old Baldhead would like Captain Pegram because it sounded like they were two peas in a pod, as my mother would say.

Captain Pegram came over that Sunday after services to take a look at me and make sure that I hadn't stoled his mule and his tent and everything else, but he didn't bring Old Baldhead with him.

Now, I know I got ahead of myself before, when I told you about how Captain Pegram changed to wearing a red shirt and a blue tassel and stripey pants; but when we were camped across from Bridgewater, Captain Pegram hadn't yet converted to being a Catholic Louisiana Tiger; and he was still just aide-de-camp to Old Baldhead. Captain Pegram was wearing all his braid and his gray trousers, and he inspected his mule and his tent and his stores, and he told me to lay everything out for him, so he could count his rations; and I was thinking about running away because of how I had to leave his stove behind, but he didn't say anything about it, as if he figured it was only natural—of course, it was warm and maybe he just forgot about it; and then he saluted me like I was Old Baldhead himself, and I didn't know what to do, so I saluted him back, and he said he'd be seeing me soon, which turned out to be right, and then he rode off.

Course, as soon as he was gone, all the cadets started laughing; but I went into the tent. I was too humiliated to stay out there in front of them, but I could hear what they were saying, and after a while they got sick of laughing at me and Captain Pegram and they talked about the evacuation of Norfolk, and how the *Ram Virginia* got blowed up, and how the bluebellies were twelve miles away from Richmond and they'd probably set it all afire, and I remembered Poppa giving a sermon, and saying something about "Depart ye wicked, into the everlasting fire," and I figured that was a stupid thing for me to be thinking because the bluebellies were the wicked ones, and they should be the ones to go into the fire, but Mother and Poppa went into the fire, and probably Mrs. Sara Anne and her daughters too, and then I thought about the deserter who caught on fire in the cave of the baby Jesus, and it seemed to me that the fire was waiting for everybody, whether they were wicked or good, it didn't matter; and then, I don't know why, but I started thinking about the book I had lost and how I dreamed I was Private Newton, only sometimes I was the traitor and sometimes I wasn't; and then I stopped listening to my own thoughts and heard the cadets talking about how the river was deep and Old Jack was going to have to construct a bridge if we were going to get across it.

Which is just what he did.

But before I get to any of that, I should get on and tell you about what else happened on that Sunday when Reverend Doctor Dabney preached at headquarters and Captain Pegram came to inspect me and his mule and his tent.

It surprised me more than anything in my life, I can tell you that, and it was Corporal R. W. Waldrop who led me to it.

R. W. CAME OVER TO VISIT ME IN CAPTAIN PEGRAM'S TENT AFTER DARK, and he said that it was time for me to lose my pimples and become a man, and I must admit that surprised me a little, that he'd stashed a woman somewhere out here in the camp; and, to tell the truth, I didn't want to go anyway.

I'd seen Jedediah and Mrs. Sara Anne doing those terrible things to each other when I sinned by looking at them through the window, and I still couldn't get it out of my mind how Mrs. Sara Anne took Jedediah's thing in her mouth like she was going to eat it because—Lord Almighty!—how could she put that in her mouth if she was a religious woman because Jedediah peed out of it; and I suppose it was a sin even to think about it, but I wondered if maybe that's just what happened, and it half made me sick. Anyway, I'd already been touched by Lucy, and I'd touched her breasts and humiliated myself by coming all over in her hand like I did, and I could've put it in, and then I would've become a man right then and there, and I suppose the pustules would never have grown out of my face and neck and shoulders.

I had one behind my ear that hurt like a sonovabitch.

Anyway, R. W. wouldn't accept that I didn't want to go, and since I could only shake my head, he figured I was foolin', and so he dragged me out of the tent. I could have fought him or pulled away. I don't know why I didn't. Maybe I didn't want to hurt his feelings, or maybe I wanted to go after all; and it was probably the most beautiful night I'd ever seen. The stars were all over the sky, and I could see the Big Dipper and Orion's belt, and the insects were making a constant buzzing noise, and it was warm, and there were little tickly breezes that smelled of leaves and perfume, which made me think of Mother. I could see campfires everywhere I looked, and with all the tree branches waving around in the wind, the fires blinked on and off like they were fireflies or something.

Now, since this is my own diary, I'll admit that I was scared. I don't know why, but just thinking of doing what Jedediah did to Mrs. Sara Anne made me want to run off and hide, and yet whenever I thought about Mrs. Sara Anne, which I guess I did a lot, I'd get excited and want to pollute myself; and I got the same way whenever I thought about Lucy.

I imagine if Lucy just touched me anywhere, I'd get myself all wet and sticky, but I wasn't getting excited as I walked through the camp with R. W. and then through the woods, and for a minute I thought he had some way of getting us over the river to Bridgeport, but no, we practically marched over to Old Jack's headquarters, and in the middle of campfires and tents and lean-tos there was an officer's tent, or that's what I thought it was anyway. All R. W. told me was that these tents belonged to Colonel Taliaferro's brigade, and I remembered something Jedediah once said about how Colonel Taliaferro was always on General Jackson's left side, whatever that meant; and we walked to the officer's tent, and R. W. stuck his head inside the tent, said, "He's here," and then pulled me into the tent, which was pretty much empty, except for a blanket thrown on the ground and an overturned hardtack box. There was a Remington musket on that box and caps and cartridges too, but none of that was important because R. W. got out of that tent as fast as he could; and there I was looking right at a soldier who was standing right in front of me, and I thought, What the hell kind of game was R. W. playing, and I'll tell you I got really scared then.

Only it wasn't a soldier. Well, it was, and it wasn't.

It was Lucy, which you've probably already figured out; but I wouldn't've known that until she said, "Dan'l Onions, as I live and breathe. You little sonovabitch bastard, you left me with it all in the cave, didn't you?"

Course, I couldn't say anything, but I couldn't move either. Lucy—if it really was Lucy—was wearing baggy pants like R. W.'s and a shirt that you could put three people into. Lucy's hair was short, and it looked like she'd had it shaved off like mine, only hers had more time to grow; and even though I was standing right there looking straight at her, I still wasn't sure; she could have been anybody; except for the smoothness of her face, which looked dirty, she could've been R. W. or anybody, like I said. Of course, she didn't have an Adam's apple like his, but I've never seen anybody else with one like that either.

"Seems you ain't done so good on your own," Lucy said. "You look a sight. R. W. was right about you needing a fuck. Christ Almighty, you got more pimples than everybody in the army put together. That's what you came here for is a fuck, ain't it, an' don't try to escape." She looked over at the rifle quick and said, "Remember when you tried that before?" Lucy smiled, but I could feel my face burning, and all I wanted to do was get out of there, yet I felt this wonderful happiness just seeing her; it was like Jedediah and Mother and Poppa and everybody had come back to life or something, and so there I was with my face burning, and I was feeling humiliated and happy at the same time. It was like I didn't know where to put my hands, and they were shaking, and even though I told you how happy I felt seeing Lucy right there in front of me, I still wanted to get out of there.

I know that doesn't make sense, but that's the way I was feeling.

Probably because I'd run away and left her and had humiliated myself.

I remembered how she had caught me polluting myself, and I remembered her breasts, and how they felt sticky in my hands; and then, like she knew exactly what I was thinking, she unbuttoned her shirt and said, "You need more proof than this?" And I could see them; they were strapped tight with a piece of muslin or something, probably so they wouldn't move around; but I didn't get stiff or anything; I was backing away from her like I was as scared as when Sandy Pendleton came into Captain Pegram's tent.

I don't know why I was scared then, and I don't know why I was scared seeing Lucy's breasts, but I was, and she laughed; and then she did the damnedest thing: She just stood there and looked down at the ground like she was ashamed or something, and I thought that maybe she was crying; but I couldn't move again. I just stood there like I was thinking, and I couldn't get out of the tent or give her any consolation, although I don't know why she'd be crying.

After Lucy was done looking at the floor, she said, "I knew it was you when Robert told me about you."

I wondered who "Robert" was, but I figured out that it had to be R. W.

"If you think I'm just a whore, think again, Dan'l Onions. I fought my ass off like everybody else. I can shoot a musket truer than you, that's for fuckin' sure. I couldn' even count how many bluebellies I killed over at Bull Pasture Mountain."

I just looked at her and nodded. I guess I was so surprised by it all that it was like seeing God or an angel or something. But even though I knew now that it was Lucy, even though her shirt was open and I could see she was a girl, I still kept seeing a man or a boy, and I just couldn't make it out right to myself.

"You know, I always wondered what you were thinking. I'd make up conversations with you, ain't that stupid? I don't know why, but there you are. I did that even after you left. I still do it some." Then she laughed. "Now I can do it while you're right here, can't I."

I nodded.

"I ain't got too much time left in this man's army. Remember how I told you I was goin' to make my money? Well, that's what I'm doing. I told you I'm goin' to buy pretty clothes and eat fancy and go to Richmond, and that's where I'm going to have my—" She stopped right there and then started again. "That's where I'm going to have my baby." She looked hard at me and put her hand on her stomach. "It's in there, and it'll be a boy, I know that, and I can tell you right now I'll have enough money—all I need, anyway. But I ain't so stupid as to show you where, but you can't tell nobody now, can you?"

I shook my head.

"Well, you want to finish . . . ?"

I could have run out right then, but I already ran away from her once, and so I sat down on a rubber poncho that was laid out on the ground, and I figured that maybe if she was going to have a baby, I'd go with her or something; but she kept talking to me and trying to trick me by telling me she had the clap and would I still want to do it to her if I knew that; and she paced around that poncho, and I thought I probably made a mistake by sitting down on it, and she said that she really didn't want to have a baby, that she didn't know anything at all about babies, and that she wanted to stay here in the army and fight the bluebellies and keep making money, but that she was going to start showin' soon, and did I want to see, and I nodded again, although I didn't know what to expect; and she took off her shirt and the muslin and her pants, and I couldn't tell anything, except she certainly was no soldier; and then all at once I felt something hot in my crotch, like graybacks, only different, and I knew that was probably the most sinful thing I could feel; and she must've sat down because we just lay there together, and she touched my dick and moved it around and pushed it between her legs, and it felt scratchy and it hurt and then everything felt oily and warm and tingling and clean and I heard myself making the "ha" sound; and I couldn't help it, but I kept thinking about Jedediah and Mrs. Sara Anne and how she put her mouth on his thing, and I wondered if Lucy ever did that with the soldiers, and I imagined her doing it to me, but while I was thinking about that

I felt myself coming, and it felt like I was getting all sucked through my thing, and I guess I was shaking and twitching and everything else; and then it was over, and I remembered that Lucy just lay there quiet the whole time, and when we were done and I was sort of laying on top of her, she looked at me like she had to find something.

I just lay there and figured I was a man now, and the pimples would probably just disappear, and Lucy and I would go anywhere we wanted together with her baby; and I guess I fell asleep because all of a sudden there was swearing and smashing sounds and names were being called out:

"Danks."
"Goodgame."
"Hatley."
"Imboden."
"Jenkins."
"Jones."
"Madill."
"McIntosh."
"Owens."
"Proctor."
"Williams."

And everyone answered *"Present, sir!"* and there were more names and more answers and it was dark and Lucy was gone.

Puttin' money in
the bank

The rose is red
The grass is green
The days is past
That we have seen!

PRIVATE
R. G. HUDSON,
CONFEDERATE
STATES OF
AMERICA ARMY

*W*ELL, MY FIRST THOUGHT WAS TO GET OUT OF THAT TENT AND GET AS invisible as I could and get the hell out of there, but once I was in the woods where I couldn't be seen, I looked around hard to see where Lucy had gone to. She should have been in ranks with the other soldiers, but it was too dark to tell much of anything. I heard everyone complaining and swearing and saying "Oh Lord" and "Oh God" and "Lord God Almighty" and "Sweet Jesus" and "Jesus Savior," just like they'd been shot and were dying in the road; and behind me the leaves rustled in the wind, and there were animal sounds that would've probably scared me once but don't now; and all of a sudden as I was looking for Lucy I wondered if the spirit dog was out here in the woods, which was unusual 'cause I hadn't thought about him for a while; and I figured it was going to rain because when I looked up I couldn't see the moon or clouds or stars, just shapes of blackness, one swallowing the other, and I felt something on my face and brushed it away and imagined it was the walkin' boy, and I remembered how much I hated spiders; and I remembered how Lucy had saved me and how I'd run away from her; and right in those woods it came to me like the voice of the Lord speaking to Moses or something that I should marry her. Mammy Jack would've understood that because it was like a vision, even if I didn't see anything except those dark swirly shapes like I told you.

The soldiers were moving down the road and the officers were saying "hip" and "hup," and I imagined Lucy would probably soon be fighting the bluebellies like everybody else and lying dead and bloating up and farting like Robert K. Worsham, and I had to stop thinking like that and being a coward because just then I figured that I could walk around wherever I wanted and nobody would take any notice or bother me probably because I was Captain Pegram's servant and part of this man's army, but since I couldn't talk to tell them who I was, they'd probably think I was a spy and shoot me dead or hang me from the nearest tree.

Well, I'd been a coward twice on Lucy, so I took my chances and ran along the edge of the woods where it touched the road and caught up with what was probably Lucy's company, but I didn't know which one it was; she could be in the Tenth or Twenty-third or Thirty-seventh or, for all I knew, she might not be in any of them. She might have just been visiting. Anyway, it didn't do me any good trying to find her because, as I said, it was too dark.

But nobody looked at me or said "Halt and identify yourself " or anything like that, and I was walking along bold as could be. I considered that I might be invisible, but Lucy could see me and Private R. W. Waldrop could see her, so it was sure she wasn't a spirit; and although I was worried about where she was and how I was going to find her, I also figured that I was a man now and probably wouldn't ever be a spirit or anything like that again, and that my pimples would probably dry up and fall off like variola scabs, or maybe they would just go back into my skin and disappear like warts do sometimes, but I have to admit that Private R. W. Waldrop was right: I felt entirely different. I had done it now and couldn't ever go back to being anything else, and maybe being a boy and being a spirit were close to being the same thing, although Jimmadasin wasn't a boy, so maybe I was just thinking foolishness, but I can't help thinking that I was right.

Anyway, after all that thinking and worrying about being married and finding Lucy and wondering too if she really did have the clap—and if she did, then I probably had it too, and, to tell the truth, I wondered exactly what it was—I went back to Captain Pegram's tent; and, as I expected, the cadets and the Twelfth Georgia were all astir and I suppose I should consider myself lucky that nothing had got stoled. I broke down the tent quick as I could and loaded everything on the mule, which was kicking and trying to get his head around to bite me if I got too close; and the foolish thing made that sad noise like I was torturing it or something; but I knew better than to feel bad because that mule was just starving to bite or kick me; and I followed the Twelfth Georgia and the cadets.

It was probably three o'clock in the morning, and we were marching fast with that route step, and there must have been thousands and thousands and thousands of us because all the complaining and hiphups and boots and wagons and everything sounded like a waterfall, and I imagined that there were waterfalls all around us—all that water crashing and bubbling up white and foamy around the rocks—and I couldn't help it but I thought about Lucy and how she found me in the cave, and I remembered the noises of the stream near the cave where Lucy caught me polluting myself, and I remembered seeing Lucy's breasts for the first time and fighting with her for my Colt .44 revolver; and suddenly I felt all knotted up because maybe I'd never see her again, and I kept thinking of her being with other soldiers, and maybe she'd go off with Private R. W. Waldrop or someone else and have her baby; and I felt hot all over my face just thinking about how I was a coward and ran from that tent to protect myself even though I didn't need protecting, and Lucy probably did, although she was probably just marching in ranks like everybody else; but I kept thinking about what I saw Mrs. Sara Anne do to Jedediah, and I imagined Lucy doing that to other soldiers, and then I got too close to the mule and it kicked me in the stomach and made me puke.

I guess I deserved it, but I was still thinking about Lucy and getting married when I got moving again and caught up with the Twelfth Georgia. I watched that mule careful now. Everybody knows about how a mule can kick you with its hind legs even when you're standing by its head. I guess Captain Pegram's mule was just reminding me. Anyway, we crossed over the North River at Bridgewater; and that was the damnedest sight I ever saw because it was just a bunch of wagons pushed across the river—every kind of wagon, but mostly big four- and six-horse wagons—and there were planks resting on them making a bridge. But those planks bounced around quite a bit, which you'd expect, and the mule didn't like going across at all; and to tell the truth, if the damned animal fell in the river and drowned, I wouldn't've felt bad, except that he was carrying the tent and food stores and ponchos and blankets and everything else.

We crossed that bridge just after dawn, and everything looked gray and sorrowful and uncomfortable, but when the sun came up, the sky cleared and looked blue like mountains do when they're far away; and there wasn't any haze anywhere, but it was hot and sweaty weather nevertheless. Mother always used to say this was boiling weather, although I never figured out exactly why. Maybe because the sky looked like water or something, but I never saw the sky look like it was boiling unless there was a storm coming on, so I don't know. You'll have to find Mother's spirit and ask her, I guess.

That's what I plan to do anyway.

And I guess while I'm at it, I'll ask Poppa why he called our rabbit traps gums.

The soldiers were dropping back and resting in the woods where it was cool, and the officers were swearing and threatening the malingerers with their sabers; and after a while it was like nobody could speak; it got so quiet there was only the sounds of marching and breathing and birds and the long whistle of the bugs that meant it was going to get even hotter. Mother said you could measure the temperature by the sound of the bugs.

All I knew was that it was going to be boiling weather.

WELL, IT WAS THAT—BOILING WEATHER, AND IT DIDN'T SEEM LIKE IT was ever going to cool; and we marched all night and all day, with only an hour for dinner and maybe two hours for sleeping and then it was marching and grumbling and swearing and officers giving orders and threatening malingerers and then we'd stop for fifteen minutes and stack muskets, and march and stop and stack and march and stop and stack and do it all over again and again, and I saw soldiers falling on the road—even the regular boys and cadets would slip into the woods for a nap and maybe they'd come back and maybe they wouldn't; and if I wasn't looking for Lucy, well, I'd have tiptoed into those woods myself and got away from this man's army, and even if I didn't take Captain Pegram's supplies, I could've foraged around for food and drink and been just fine.

But I was looking for Lucy, like I said.

That mule served its purpose too, because when I dropped behind and was marching with another company, nobody even knew I was there; they all probably figured I was an officer's servant, which, of course, I was; and so I pushed forward, and in the time it took us to go from Bridgewater to Harrisonburg, I figure I must have walked through a few brigades searching for Lucy until I finally found R. W.

I suppose it was pure luck, although I figure I'd have to find him or Lucy sooner or later; I just wished I'd found Lucy instead of him. He dropped out of ranks when he saw me, which showed he wasn't no coward because if an officer saw that, R. W. would have been in trouble. R. W. wanted to know what I was doing up here and all that, and, of course, I couldn't tell him, but he knew that, I suppose; and I walked along with him with Captain Pegram's mule, and he asked me if I had any salt pork or beef or anything because "I'm so hungry I could eat the wood off my shoes," and the mule was too tired to kick at me, I guess (or else it just forgot), but I got some bacon out for R. W., which he ate raw and kept walking.

Now, I tried to ask him about Lucy but could only make the "ha" sound, and I got so mad at myself that I wanted to punch my own face, but all I could do was make motions with my hands, which he understood when I drew Lucy's body in the air; and he grinned in a way that made me want to hit him, but I guess I deserved that because the only way I could make him understand was to make dirty motions in the air, and when I got him to understand he patted me on the back with that spider hand of his and smiled and his Adam's apple went up and down like he'd got something caught in his throat again, and then an officer started yelling at both of us for breaking ranks. "And what the hell are you colludin' over, anyway?" And R. W. explained that I was Captain Pegram's servant, and, of course, the lieutenant didn't know Captain Pegram from a hole in his shirt, but he respected rank, and since Captain Pegram was Old Baldhead's aide-de-camp, he ordered me back to my unit. I guess he didn't care where that was, as long as I was out of his sight.

I was sure that R. W. knew where Lucy was, and I figured I'd get back to see him later, but like most things I figure on, they don't happen quite the way I expect.

I saw R. W. again, and I'll tell you about that; but, like I said, nothing happens the way I expect, and everything happens the wrong way, like my vision about Lucy and hearing the voice of God sayin' we should get married and everything.

I know this is probably blasphemy, but even though I know there's a God because of my visions and all and what Mammy Jack told me, I figure He doesn't think much about who gets shot or lost or anything like that because they can just become spirits or angels and not have to worry about eating or following orders anymore. And I suppose since He's the Lord and can do just about whatever He pleases, He can also lie, if it pleases Him, which it probably does.

Least that's *my* experience of 'ligion.

Anyway, I looked and looked for Lucy. Until I turned into a coward again.

I'll tell you about that so I can get it over with, and then maybe I won't have to think about it anymore, although I never could forget much of anything.

MOTHER USED TO TELL ME THAT THE APPLE DOESN'T FALL FAR FROM THE tree and that everything terrible I got from her—like her good memory, which she said was a curse, except for remembering the Bible. Now, since I can't remember hardly anything from the Bible—yet I can remember most everything else—I figure I'm probably cursed, although I don't know why. Even before I killed Eurastus and became a coward and all that, I couldn't remember the Bible.

I know I probably should have prayed to find Lucy, but it just didn't work out. I tried, but every time I did I knew I was just fooling; and to tell you the truth I figured I'd just get myself in more trouble because every time I tried praying I'd get angry—I don't know why, but I just did—and I'd imagine to myself that God was like Eurastus or something.

Maybe that's why I hadn't found Lucy.

I found Captain Pegram, though—or, rather, he found me, which is what I really can't understand. There were all those thousands of soldiers, and they were all crowded together, and there was a band playing a waltz, and soldiers dancing around like we'd just won the war; only we hadn't won the war; and there I was with the mule and my feet aching and bleeding and I was itchin' everywhere, just like everybody else, and I figured that I was about as invisible as one man could ever be in a swarm of soldiers. It smelled terrible, like sweat and farts; it didn't bother me because I was used to it, but I can tell you that the stink was thick.

We'd got to New Market, which is about thirty miles away from where we started at Mount Solon, and we were camped in the fields of wheat and clover on both sides of the Valley Pike, when out of the clear blue an army of our own boys appeared, and they were marching right along the pike like they were on parade, and it must have been about five o'clock because the sun was dropping into the mountains, and everything looked like there was dust in the air; and there were these soldiers all marching in a column at right-shoulder shift in their fresh uniforms and white gaiters, and their bayonets were flashing like mirrors and there wasn't a straggler among them, even though it was hotter than bacon on a griddle; and then I saw the Creoles. It was they who were playing instruments and waltzing around like they were at a cotillion, and I heard some of the cadets talking, and that's how I knew those dancing soldiers were Creoles from Louisiana, and that all their caperings were evil devices and snares, and I wondered if being Creoles meant they were Catholics; but, evil or not, I thought it would be surely wonderful to be waltzing around in those bright, clean uniforms.

I also knew from listening to everyone around me that this new brigade was part of Old Baldhead's army, and it was being led by General Taylor, who was the son of President Zachary Taylor and the brother-in-law of President Davis, so I guess he was in a good position to lead most anybody; but I didn't see him. What I saw was the Louisiana Tigers with their red caps and red shirts and striped pants, and seeing them all like that, you could imagine that they'd dyed their uniforms in bluebelly blood or something, and they were as neat and clean as those gaitered Creoles that they followed; and the soldiers all around me cheered the Zouaves, but nobody seemed to like those dancing Creoles and called them niggers—that "They are nothin' but niggers, that's all they are."

I wasn't sure about whether they were niggers or not because maybe Lucy was a nigger, and they didn't look so dark to me, although with all their commotion and dancin' and playing "Bonnie Blue Flag," they could've been niggers with light skin; and I would have been a damn sight better off dancing with the Creole niggers than standing in the clover with the cadets and the Twelfth Georgia boys because all of a sudden Captain Pegram was right in front of me; and he was a Zouave now with a cap and a tassel and a red vest like I described to you earlier, and he was sitting up there on his horse and looking down at me like it was the will of God.

Only he wasn't Captain Pegram anymore; he was Major Pegram.

I guess I should have stayed back in the field, and maybe if I had, Major Pegram wouldn't've seen me and maybe then I would've found Lucy marching along in the ranks, and I would've married her, and then I would have been the father of her baby, and we'd go into the woods and live up in the Massanuttens like cave niggers, and maybe Jimmadasin would come back and forgive me and—but, of course, all that was nothing but foolish thinking because Major Pegram would've probably found me, no matter what.

But I was right about one thing, at least, because Jimmadasin did come back.

"Well, lad, come along," Major Pegram said to me. "You don't have to stay with these good soldiers any longer. I'll show you *real* fighting soldiers." And I thought that the boys around me were going to pull him right off his horse and beat him senseless for saying that; and it got quiet for just maybe one second, and then the Twelfth Georgia boys started swearing all at once, so it was hard to make out the words, they were so jumbled up.

Stick it diarrhea sonovabitch
up where the sun don't shine corn-holer
come and get it you limey sonovabitch
big mouth fat bastard go back where
shoot your fat ass off
you belong

And I thought you could get shot for saying all that to an officer, but maybe it was different because he was a foreigner, and I knew that soldiers sometimes killed their officers, so maybe Major Pegram was going to get his turn for bragging and being stupid, but he just turned around and rode a few steps, turned around again and waited until I followed, and everyone was jeering at me; and then I was in the middle of those Louisiana Tigers, and the mule was getting stubborn and confused and started making its screeching and groaning noises, which always meant trouble; and I figured if the boys from the Twelfth did anything untoward to Major Pegram, the Zouaves would probably just go on a killing spree and dye their uniforms new again with Georgia blood.

But the Twelfth didn't have to do a thing because the mule did it for them; all of a sudden it seemed to go stark raving mad, and it started kicking with its hind legs and then its front legs and jumping and tossing like someone had set it on fire; and it caught Major Pegram's horse and broke its leg, just like that, and the horse made a terrible noise and just collapsed, with Major Pegram still riding it; and I think Major Pegram's leg got broken too, because the horse fell right on him; and Major Pegram started screaming like he had the colic, even though he was wearing his red cap and tassel and a red vest and the striped pants that proved he was a Louisiana Tiger and a Catholic; but that mule wasn't finished because it kicked a Zouave soldier and probably broke his bones too; and then there was the crack of a musket, and the mule was dead, shot right in the eye, which was an ugly thing to see; and then I thought I heard Jimmadasin's voice, I heard it speaking right in my ear like he was whispering to me, like he used to do when he got to be a spirit, and right then I didn't know to be scared or over-joyed, but I figured it was all right and that he wasn't the spirit who looked like him and had threatened me with the walkin' boy, and I was so happy to hear Jimmadasin that I didn't think about why he'd come back, but there were all the red-shirted Zouave Louisiana Tiger soldiers around me, thick as suckling pigs around tits, and then before I could even figure out what was going on, the Twelfth Georgia boys were right in the middle of those Louisiana Tigers, and they were brawling and kicking and punching and swearing; and, truth to tell, I don't even know if those Tigers knew what hit them at first, but somebody hit me, and I couldn't tell if it was a Georgia or a red shirt, but my jaw got numb and it was sort of like lights flashed and then it got dark for a second, so dark that I thought I was dead, and then I could see a little and everything was gray, and that's when I heard Jimmadasin sayin' "Run, Marster Mundy, is youah time to go now, wha'd you get yourself into here?" And even though his voice sound-ed like wind or thunder or all the noise made out of the men fighting and swear-ing, I could hear that Jimmadasin was under it all, and so I listened to him, and ran, but he told me to pick up the haversack that had flew off Major Pegram's horse, and I did what he told me, and I ran through the fields and meadows until I got to the safety of the woods, and by the time I could think about anything it was already getting dark, and I could see the lights going on in Middletown over to my left, and I could see the campfires of General Jackson's army, and I knew that Lucy was somewhere in there, and Jimmadasin kept whisperin' to me, whispering whispering, and the side of my face was pounding, and it was like I could hear Jimmadasin speaking in that pounding, and he said that it was the Georgia boys that did something to the mule, and "ha ha dat horse prob'ly breaked Major Pegram's leg," but Jimmadasin felt sorry for the horse, which was probably already put down by now; and I watched the camp and the forest and the hills; and Middletown seemed like it was all wrapped up in haze, and I listened to the animals scurrying in the woods, and I could hear voices, and barking and howling like all the dogs in the world had got crowded into Middletown.

I wondered if the spirit dog was out there with them, but I didn't ask Jimmadasin about that; I asked him about the walkin' boy, though, and the spirit that looked like him; and Jimmadasin laughed like it was the funniest thing he'd ever heard.

WELL, THE REST OF THIS, I GUESS, IS ALL ABOUT FIRE AND REMEMBERIN' and how I changed my name; and I'm going to tell you all this as quick as I can to get through it, and maybe you'll see why later.

I spent the night in the woods with Jimmadasin, and it cooled down a bit and campfires were lit all over the fields, and it was so clear that everything seemed too close. I opened Major Pegram's haversack, and, sure enough, Jimmadasin was right because that haversack was just about stuffed full of hardtack crackers and bacon and coffee and sugar, and there was some beef and a piece of cheese that looked all cracked and yellowed and molded over, and there was a medicine bottle of whiskey, which Jimmadasin told me to drink up 'cause I'd need the strength, and there were some biscuits that were so stale they'd break your teeth, but I ate them anyway. There was also a Colt .44 revolver and cartridges and caps, and I imagined that Jimmadasin was helping me replace the one I lost.

"I guess you forgived me then."

"You foun' Lucy, an' I come back. Dat don' mean nuthin', you still left the baby Jesus, now get youh ass up—"

I woke up sick from drinking Major Pegram's whiskey, and bits of the bacon I ate before kept coming up my throat, and every time I swallowed, my chest burned like I was still drinking that whiskey.

It was dark, probably three o'clock or something; and I listened for Jimmadasin, but all I could hear was the soldiers bitching because General Jackson was getting them ready for another one of his marches, so I figured that Jimmadasin had probably left again because I left the baby Jesus and deserted Lucy, and I figured he'd just come back for a while to torment me like devils; but I guess he took pity on me because I was so sick, even though it was him that told me to drink the whiskey, because I heard him whispering again like he was scared someone else would hear him or something, and he said, "We goin' to find Lucy, an' den maybe we all live in da Massanutten like I tole you," and, sick as I was, we followed General Jackson's foot cavalry, all the while looking looking looking for Lucy, and so we had to move even faster, but we had to keep out of sight; and it felt like I had the variola or the ague or something because I felt all hot and weak and dizzy, but Jimmadasin kept pushing me to keep going.

He said I was just sick on the whiskey.

THE TROOPS DIDN'T ACTUALLY MARCH UNTIL THE SKY STARTED GETTING gray, and then Old Jack fooled everyone again because instead of going on up to Strasburg to fight the bluebellies, the column marched into New Market, turned right at Cross Street, and headed out to the New Market Gap, which is in the Massanuttens; and Jimmadasin and I followed along, even though I still felt sick, and it was hot and there'd been no rain, so the grass started getting brown; but once we were up in those portals of Heaven, which is what Poppa called any mountain he happened to see—probably because of Moses getting the Bible on top of a mountain—once we were up there, I felt like Jimmadasin and I were both spirits.

If it wasn't that we were looking for Lucy, I would've just stayed up in the mountain because it was so clear and bright; and you could see so far out across the Valley that it was probably like being in Heaven with sunlight all around you and everything. But Jimmadasin wouldn't have any of that, and he marched me along like he was Major Pegram; and we marched all day, Old Jack's troops keeping to the road, of course, while Jimmadasin and I stayed in the woods, which were so thick that if you got lost in them you'd probably never get out. Which was okay by me, except I thought I could find Lucy, and then it would be fine to get lost in the Massanuttens, and we could dig us a deep cave and put a cover of dirt and leaves and timber over it and never get found even after the fighting stopped forever.

Well, I *was* going to get to what I told you I'd tell you, and here I am talking about diggin' caves and living in the woods, so, anyway, we followed General Jackson and General Taylor and the Zouaves and the Creoles, and I wondered if Major Pegram was riding with them, or whether they left him in Middletown with a broken leg. It didn't matter to me because although I told you that I couldn't be a spirit again because I was a man after I did what I did with Lucy, I was just plain wrong.

Maybe it was being in the mountains with Jimmadasin, but I could feel myself getting more and more invisible, pretty much with every breath I took. It was like the air was getting into me everywhere so much that I was turning into it; and now I wasn't a boy and I wasn't a man; I was just air like Jimmadasin, but if I could have found Lucy, now that would have changed me into a man forever.

Jimmadasin kept talking, and it was like listening to water running and the wind blowing through the trees, and it was cool and dry-smelling like leaves after summer—cool in the woods but still boiling weather out on the road; and we looked and looked; we watched those troops, and looked into the faces of the men; and Jimmadasin and I were both calling Lucy Lucy Lucy, but no one could hear us, except each other; and there was nothing but that and marching, and my feet kept bleeding because I had walked right through the canvas shoes I'd stoled from the dead bluebelly soldier, which probably showed that I was still a man and not entirely a spirit; but I asked Jimmadasin about that, and he showed me his feet, which were bleeding too, so I just don't know; and we probably marched another twenty miles that day.

We went through Luray, and where the roads intersect we went through Thornton's Gap and then north to Front Royal.

Now, there was fighting and killing all through the boiling weather of the next days. We outnumbered the bluebellies, and there were so many of them dying all bunched together that you wouldn't give it no never mind after seeing them and their wagons piled all over the road. But I finally did right by Sergeant Robert K. Worsham and his poor wife, Rebecca Forget Me Not. You remember him probably; he was the dead soldier who farted and scared the life out of me, and it was his spirit that told me "Take my letter there, and tell Rebecca Forget Me Not."

I made things right the day our troops marched down what was called the Snake Road, which no one ever used to get to Front Royal because it wound around so much that it seemed you were always going back to where you started; and Jimmadasin and I had sneaked through the woods right up to the front of our troops, and it was afternoon and so hot that I thought I was going to die of thirst; and buzzards were flying around in circles way up in the sky behind me, and the bugs were whistling that it was going to get even hotter, and the mountains looked all hazy, like they were made out of water. There was an overgrown field in front of me with stone fences going this way and that, and I could see the town of Front Royal on lower ground down to my right.

The skirmishing had already started.

As soon as I heard those muskets and those minié balls buzzing like the bugs announcing it was going to be boiling weather, I felt all excited and comfortable at the same time, like I was thrilled and just happy, even though there'd be a lot of killin' and screaming and everyone calling for their mothers; but none of that mattered as long as you got to be a spirit and the angels would find you and take you up to Heaven straightaway, just like I told you about, although I wasn't ready to get killed yet. I don't know why, though. Maybe I was just afraid of gettin' shot or something.

Anyway, while all that was going on, I saw a woman waving her bonnet over her head and running across an open field in front of us, and it seemed that the Federals were firing right at her; in fact, an artillery shell exploded right by her, and I thought she was surely dead because she fell to the ground, but then she got up and ran through those high weeds and climbed over the fences like she was a boy, or like Lucy could have done probably.

Jimmadasin and I got closer, but not so close that I could see who she was talking to, and Jimmadasin was talking on and on without stopping about what was in Sergeant Robert K. Worsham's letter to his poor wife, like he'd read it himself, even though he couldn't read, but I guess spirits just know about everything you know, and Jimmadasin said:

"*If you gets killed, den all's be fine wid da baby Jesus an' you.*"

"*And if I don't?*"

"*Den you better find Miss Lucy.*"

So we sneaked through the woods so we could catch up with the woman if she was going to run back across that field, and I know it doesn't make much sense, even to me now as I think about it, but I wasn't at all worried about getting blowed up or shot by a musket. Now, I suppose I could have sneaked into town later and given that letter to most anybody, but I just felt like I had to give it to that woman who'd run across the field, and that no one else would do. It was like Sergeant Robert K. Worsham had told me that he wanted me to give his letter only to that woman, even though he didn't. But I just knew that's who I had to give it to, and so did Jimmadasin because he didn't make a fuss about it.

Now, I understood that she might not want to be going across that field again, and I also figured that she could be a spy or something too; and if I ran out there after her, it was sure that our own soldiers would probably try to shoot me.

But when I saw her running across that field in her blue dress and white apron, I guess I must have had a vision or something because even though she had to run across the field and climb fences, and even though she fell down when the shell exploded, I figured she was a spirit, or had one inside her; and I thought about what it would feel like to have Jimmadasin or Cow or Eurastus inside me like blood or something, and that gave me a bad shiver.

Anyway, I guess I figured she was an angel, although I learned later on from Uncle Randolph that her name was Belle Boyd, and that most everybody in Front Royal knew her; Uncle Randolph knew her Aunt Fannie or somebody, who owned the hotel there, but I don't know much about that. Well, Jimmadasin and I waited, like I said, until she was ready to leave, and I saw her kiss her hand to an officer, only this time she didn't just dash across the field like she was running with her eyes closed and prayin' that the bullets would go around her. She must've gotten smart because after she waved to the officer, she ran into the woods. She was smart because once you got into those woods you could stay hid forever.

Jimmadasin and I ran too, and we surprised her, as you can imagine, because spirits hardly make any noise at all, and she was unsuspecting that we were following her. "What do you want?" she said. "I'll scream, I swear, and our boys will—"

She just didn't finish what she was saying.

Maybe Jimmadasin gave her a shock or something, but I waved my hands to calm her and got out Sergeant Robert K. Worsham's letter to Rebecca Forget Me Not. I held that letter out to her, but she backed away from me like I was Eurastus coming for her; and I made more motions in the air until finally she said, "Can't you talk?" and I shook my head, and she seemed less scared and finally took the letter.

She looked at the envelope, front and back, then opened it, all the while looking up at me and Jimmadasin like we were going to rush her and beat her; and I was shaking, even though I wasn't scared, and I guess I should confess that I was looking at her dress and wondering what she looked like under it, and how her breasts didn't seem much bigger than Mrs. Sara Anne's, and I thought about Mrs. Sara Anne putting Jedediah's thing in her mouth, and I thought about this Belle Boyd doing that to me, although, of course, I didn't know her name then; and I knew well enough that I shouldn't be thinking such thoughts and that Jimmadasin would know what I was thinking about, but I couldn't help myself; my face felt hot all of a sudden, and I felt my thing getting hard, which was humiliating and a sin, and I also thought of Lucy, and I remember how pretty she looked naked even with all her hair cut off, and that I was going to be the father of her baby and live in the Massanuttens with her like cave niggers, and how I'd run away from her because I was a coward; and I thought about Lucy putting R. W.'s thing in her mouth, and my face got even hotter, and then Miss Belle Boyd said, "I'll give this to my friend Lucy Buck. She'll know who your friend's

Rebecca Forget Me Not is. Although I've never known the Bucks to have any truck with Yankees. No offense, but you're a Yankee, aren't you? You're a deserter, isn't that right?"

Now, I don't know what possessed me, but when she said that to me I just turned around and ran through those woods like the bluebellies were chasing after me, which, of course, they weren't; and Miss Belle Boyd must've thought I was a coward, and she was probably right because I have no excuse for running away like that. It was as if she'd said something terrible to me or something; and maybe she did because I deserted everybody—Lucy and Mother and Poppa and Jimmadasin, except he found me and forgave me, or that's what I thought anyway. I was wrong about that too.

So I never did find out if Sergeant Robert K. Worsham's Rebecca Forget Me Not ever got his letter, but I delivered it the best I could.

You can't ask more than that, Sergeant Robert K. Worsham.

Now I'll tell you how I saw R. W. get killed and get it over with.

I've been trying to get to it, but it just seems to keep slipping away from me like a piece of shell on the bottom of a bowl of raw egg.

LIKE I TOLD YOU, I RAN THROUGH THE WOODS, AND THEN I FELL ASLEEP, and then I listened to muskets and cannonading, and you probably know all about how there was a fight near the hospital by the Front Royal courthouse, and how the Louisiana Tigers went right through the town and killed and chased the bluebellies, but I kept out of the town, and Jimmadasin was quiet for most of the time, except when he was pestering me to *git on mah feet and move mah arse*, and it's a wonder that I got to fall asleep at all after I ran through the woods.

Now, even though Jimmadasin told me that I was just sick on the whiskey, he was tricking me about that because I was sick with the ague all over again, which just came upon me with its fever, and, of course, it brought me Jimmadasin, or maybe Jimmadasin brought me the ague, I don't know which, even as I think about it now; but I felt hot and dizzy and weak, and I kept having to pee, even though there was nothing to pee, and when I could, it burned like a sonovabitch; and I don't know how I kept going, walking along with Jimmadasin, who was saying "hip hup hip hup hip hup" like he was in the white man's army, and I should also tell you that he started talking again in that high-pitched voice of his like he was scared of something. I wondered what a spirit would have to be scared of, and I asked him, but Jimmadasin only answered when he felt like it; but Jimmadasin liked to sing, and when he sang he didn't use his high, screechy voice, but he sounded like he was in the choir and singing for God Himself, except he was singing:

> *Keemo, Kimo, dar you are?*
> *Heh, ho, de rum to pumadiddle,*
> *Set back penny wink,*
> *Come Tom Nippy Cat,*
> *Sing song Kitty,*
> *Can't you carry me o'er?*

And only Mrs. Sara Anne's nigger, Cornelius Rumtopum, knew that song because it was his, not Jimmadasin's or nobody else's; and I asked Jimmadasin how he come to know it, but, of course, he didn't answer, just went on singing; and I smelled burning and saw smoke filling up the sky because the bluebellies were trying to burn down the North Fork bridge and the railroad bridge, which were the only ways to get across the river and out of Front Royal to Winchester; and they almost got the railroad bridge before the Louisiana boys rushed in and chased them out, but that bridge wasn't too steady; I know that because I crossed over it too, but not until later.

I remember the bugle blowing and how the bluebelly camps were burning and chimneyfulls of smoke and ash was settling down over everything like black snow; and that was because the bluebellies were putting everything to the torch, and I remember an explosion that lit up the whole sky when some stockpile of shells caught fire; and so anyway Jimmadasin and I followed General Jackson's army and looked for Lucy and called out her name, and I remember that Jimmadasin carried me over the railroad bridge, even though I know that was impossible and that I probably just walked, and I remember how the river was churning and angry and swollen like it would have liked more than anything to have drowned me; and the volleys of cannons and muskets were like music, the way they would stop and start, and Jimmadasin was singing, and I could hear a band playing "Maryland, Ain't You Happy"; and when I got over that bridge, I slept, and I walked marched followed our boys and looked looked looked for Lucy. *"You'se goin' to fin' her yah yah yah. You'se goin' to fin' the baby Jesus.*
   "Eye in de cave.
   "Eye in de cave.

"Keep yo' eye in de cave.

"You gwine fine Jesus p'otectin' de night.

"P'otectin' lil' white Mundy dere in de night.

"You left Jesus, you'se on you' own now, you don' deserve nobody and—"

We were going back to Winchester by way of Cedarville and then to Middletown, but it's hard for me to remember how each thing happened one after the other because it was like everything was all happening at once, and one minute I was sick and the next minute I was peeing and the next minute I was keeping pace with General Jackson's army and feeling the heat of the sun and feeling wonderful like nothing could hurt me and that marching just like this in the heat was like being on fire and going to Heaven, and I thought of Poppa and Mother, and I knew that I was going home.

I could feel that I was going home, although I wouldn't've believed it then; and, like I said, everything was happening at once, even music from the bands because I remember hearing "Oh, dear! What can the matter be?" and the Federals were playing that; but the Federals were retreatin', and leaving behind their supply wagons and sutlers' carts and everything else you could imagine: muskets, bluebelly uniforms, boots, tents, chairs, cattle, mules, mirrors, brushes, bacon, flour, salt, sugar, coffee, hard bread, molasses, cheese, canned meat, butter, sweet cakes, whiskey—even Bibles; there was a wagon with what must have been a hundred holy Bibles stacked in it, all black with gold letters on their fronts and smelling like the pews in church. And our boys took everything they needed, and some rode off and became deserters so they could take their prizes back home, but the Federals tried to burn everything they owned so Old Jack wouldn't get it, and one night as Jimmadasin and I followed our boys, we could see most everything by the light coming off the bluebellies' wagons, which were burning like campfires all over the road; and our bands were playing like they were on parade, and the boys were singing, and everywhere along the road and behind the stone walls in the fields on either side of the pike were the knapsacks of the bluebellies who were probably intending on fighting but decided to run off instead.

It got freezing cold that night because it was spirit weather; it didn't bother me, though, because the fever was keeping me warm enough. It was like having your own fire. I don't know how Jimmadasin and I kept up with the troops, and we probably didn't because by morning our boys were asleep all over the pike as if they'd all been killed in a battle, but Jimmadasin said dey weren't no spirits; and, like I said, we stayed to the woods, which was good protection, and Jimmadasin kept pushing me on so we could find Lucy, and, like I said, it was on account of him that I found R. W., although I didn't know it was him at first.

There was more fighting, of course, and the sky got dark, but that was mostly because of the spirit weather; and there was skirmishing and cannon volleys, and everything echoed around the mountains; and I imagine we were somewhere past Middletown and probably pretty close to Winchester because General Jackson wasn't going to stop until he chased the Federals right into the Potomac, where General Banks's army would drown like they were the Egyptians out of the Bible.

Anyway, somewhere between Middletown and Winchester and off the Valley Pike, Jimmadasin and I saw the damnedest thing.

Well, before we saw that, we saw everybody get killed on the pike, and I watched it from behind a fence in the field.

The Federal cavalry was running from one of our volleys, and there were shells tearing everything apart in the road, and the dust rose up off that road so it was practically impossible to see, and there was a terrific volley of musket fire, and when that dust started to clear, I could see I don't know how many bluebellies all tangled up together with their horses, and then more bluebellies were riding right into them and I guess none of them could rein up because they all rode right into the pile; and everyone was screaming and groaning, and more bluebellies were riding into the pile, and even the horses were making terrible whinnying noises, and the soldiers were shrieking; and then our own foot cavalry were running towards all the screaming and groaning bluebellies; and when the dust settled, like I told you, I looked up at the sun and figured it was around noon; and as cold as it was at night, it was just that hot in the day, stifling, sweaty hot; it was boiling weather and spirit weather all mixed up together.

I could feel my sweat dripping inside my shirt, and I could taste salt on the corners of my mouth, and I watched our boys taking everybody prisoner, except for a few bluebellies that managed to ride off, but there weren't many, and even from where I was hiding in the field I could smell the stink of the horses and the men, and they all smelled like a fart, and I considered that maybe we all smelled like that inside, and when anybody got hit by a bullet that smell came out, just like when you fart, like old dead Sergeant Robert K. Worsham; and you wouldn't smell only if you were all dried out like the old Sweet Grandy lady or the bluebelly whose shoes I stoled.

But what I got to tell you didn't happen there on the Valley Pike.

It was in the woods by a railroad embankment; and after we watched all those bluebellies ride into each other and get killed, Jimmadasin and I sneaked out of there because our own boys might take us prisoners right along with the Federals. Course, they probably wouldn't've been able to take Jimmadasin prisoner as he was a spirit, but I wasn't completely a spirit, or a man, or anything, for that matter, so they'd probably see me, and that would be that.

I don't know why, but I didn't want to leave. This probably seems terrible and is probably the greatest sin imaginable, but I didn't want to leave that field and the dust and those dead men. Fact is, I wanted to see it happen all over again because hearing all that screaming and praying and cannonading and musket firing, and seeing all those bluebellies riding like they could ride through anything, and then seeing them crashing into all those dead and wounded horses and soldiers—all that thrilled me.

I felt like everything was perfect, even the heat—especially the heat— which could burn everything; and it would be perfect if everything burned, that's what I wanted, that's what I was waiting for, although I know it doesn't make any sense when you think about it, but I probably wanted those soldiers to keep killing themselves over and over again because then everyone would get paid back for killing Poppa and Mother, and I guess I also wanted to wait and see if the spirits would come out of those dead soldiers like maggots or something.

But Jimmadasin wouldn't let me.

Neither would he let me use Major Pegram's Colt .44 revolver and just shoot those bluebellies, and I guess he was right because I don't know what got into me; I just got happy like Mother probably used to get in church, and I got angry at the same time, and for a few seconds everything—the Valley Pike, the soldiers, the woods, the air, the trees—all turned red, or maybe more like pink, like sometimes happens when you shut your eyes hard and see colors, and all I wanted to do was empty out that Colt .44 revolver, and I thought that if I could get those bullets out, everything would be better, and I wouldn't ever think about Poppa or Mother or Eurastus or anybody again, but, like I said, Jimmadasin wouldn't let me be until we got out of there.

So as I started telling you, we walked and walked and walked until we came to a railroad embankment. It seemed there was skirmishing all around us, but that was because musket and artillery were echoing all over the mountains, so for every cannonade there'd be a faint one right after, which, like I said, was comforting; but none of that mattered because there were musket shots real close by.

We followed after those shots and found dead bluebellies laying dead near that embankment, and I could see that their hands were just about black because they'd been digging into the black soil of that embankment, and there was good Confederate money laying around everywhere and flying up in the air with every breeze; and there were two of our own soldiers gathering up that money, pulling it right out of the ground like it had been growin' there like grass or trees.

I knew better than to get any closer and lose the protection of the trees 'cause I figured those two Confederate boys would just as soon shoot at me as whistle, what with all that money they were harvesting out of the embankment, and I knew what was going on because I'd heard the Twelfth Georgia boys discussing how some bluebellies had gotten caught burying Confederate money, and how they finally confessed it was counterfeit; and the Twelfth Georgia boys called it "puttin' money in the bank" and said they wouldn't care if it was counterfeit or not, they'd spend it anyway; but I've got to confess to you that I didn't know what "counterfeit" was, and I thought it might have something to do with getting sick and having fits, but I couldn't understand what that would have to do with Confederate money.

It took some getting closer for me to figure out that one of those soldiers taking the bluebellies' money out of that embankment was R. W.

Well, I got so excited when I saw who it was that I started running over to him, right over the rocks and stones and timber and twisted-up rails that were piled all around the embankment.

Jimmadasin was shouting "Get back heah, don' look, hide yoah face," and, sure enough, bluebellies must have just come upon us because I heard shots and saw R. W. fall over like he was nothing if not surprised he was hit right through the chest just like Colonel Ashby's boy Dixie and the blood was running out of him all over his vest and pockets and this is the part that just won't stay in my mind it won't stay in my mind no matter how hard I try to keep it there the soldier he was with got shot too, in the face, *and God O God, I knew who it was I knew who it was and even though it wasn't Mother it was Lucy I kept thinking Mother Mother Mother like the soldiers did when they were dying and*

I saw everything in the instant before I embraced the dirt, which was what the soldiers called it; and I guess I didn't even know what I was doing because I don't remember having Major Pegram's Colt .44 revolver, but I did, and before I realized what was what I was firing at the bluebellies, or where I thought they were, which was in front of me and to the right of where R. W. was laying.

I was crying and firing that Colt .44 right from the ground, and Jimmadasin was shouting "Run run run" right in my ear like he was right there and he was sayin' "Don' look don' look don' look" over and over, and while I had the red madness and was firing I could forget what I had just seen and put it right out of my mind, and only think about what was happening now right now right now, and I heard someone make a funny sound, and I saw that I hit one of the bluebellies, and he didn't look much older than Harry McSherry, who was about fourteen; in fact, he looked like Harry, but it couldn't've been him because Harry couldn't stand to be a bluebelly, and anyway, Mrs. McSherry wouldn't have allowed him to fight, even for General Jackson or Colonel Ashby; and I figured I should be prayin' and saying something about going through the shadow of death and the Lord is my shepherd, like that because there were probably more bluebellies all around me, and maybe they'd already shot me and I hadn't heard it, and maybe I was already dead, but there was nothing on fire, and if I was dead then everything would be on fire, I knew that, and although everything was pink and sort of tinted, it wasn't fire, and my heart was beating hard in my throat probably just like R. W.'s Adam's apple, but that wouldn't be moving now 'cause he was dead.

I was glad to be dead, I wanted to be dead, and it got quiet, as if the rest of the bluebellies had just disappeared or something, or maybe there had only been the one, the one I shot, the one who looked like Harry McSherry.

I thought about the bluebelly I'd killed, and I concentrated on thinking about him and nobody else, but then I looked around for angels because I was in a hurry to get away from here, to be dead and be a spirit and get to Heaven quick as I could; and Jimmadasin was still shouting at me, and then all of a sudden I couldn't help it but I remembered everything all over again.

I could see her and just looking made me sick and made my chest hurt.

Jimmadasin, I found her, I found her, you sonovabitch diarrhea bastard nigger—and I stood up, I stood up straight like Mother had always taught me, and my voice came back like God decided I should have it for a minute, but nobody shot me, and I looked around, and there was only the bluebelly I'd shot, and I'd shot him right through the eye, and there was nobody else, not R. W. or Lucy or anybody; and it was calm like everybody in the world was dead, and I tried to make a sound again, but I could only breathe.

I listened for Jimmadasin, but he'd gone too, and the Colt .44 was gone, and then I realized that I had closed my eyes, and I opened them and I looked right at the bluebelly I'd shot, like he was mine, like he was something I'd found in a knapsack or a wagon, and I didn't look anywhere else, and I tried to talk to his spirit.

I'm sorry I shot you dead in the eye you sonovabitch bastard, but there was no sound, just my breathing and the insects and the cannonading; and then the red went out of the air, and I couldn't even hear my own breathing, and I figured I *must* have been shot, even though I couldn't feel anything or see any blood, because I'd said "Mother" like the soldiers did when they were dying, and I felt thirsty and had to pee, and I peed myself right there, and then I ran like a coward, even though I was a man because I'd killed somebody and I'd dipped my wick with Lucy and now Lucy Lucy Lucy I saw you Lucy, and all I could think about was running, even though the ague had taken me over as punishment, but I knew only one thing—

I was going home.

Mother.

Poppa.

The portals of heaven

Sun, you be here an' I'll be gone,
Sun, you be here an' I'll be gone,
Sun, you be here an' I'll be gone.

'MANCIPATION
SONG

WELL, I DID PEE MYSELF, WHICH IS HUMILIATING; IT'S EVEN MORE
humiliating to write it down, but it was because of the peeing that I gave myself
a new name, even though it didn't work.

I was dirty filthy anyway, but I just couldn't stand myself, maybe because
when I was little I used to wet the bed sometimes—not often, but sometimes—
and Mother wouldn't waste any time washing my clothes. She'd start washing
them and my sheets at three o'clock in the morning, if that's when she discovered my "accident," and she wouldn't come near me or look at me or talk to me
sometimes for hours, although it never seemed to bother Poppa because he
probably had the same problem when he was little.

If he did, he never said anything about it, though.

But Poppa never talked about himself or how he was when he was young.

It was like he was always a minister and was born wearing a black vest and car-rying a Bible. He was never without his Bible, even when we were planting or bringing in the harvest. He'd always read everyone the Bible on Hog Day before he'd let anybody eat the hog livers, which smelled so good and sweet it makes me dizzy just thinking about them; and he'd always have his Bible wrapped up in a canvas bag with laces so the elements couldn't get at it when we were in the fields; and we'd pray when we took breaks, and I remember, I remember thinking—probably because I'd always lay down flat in the meadow and look upwards to Heaven—that it was our prayin' that was driving the clouds across the sky, and that those clouds were the mysterious words of the Bible, and that if I had the proper understanding of religion like Poppa did, I'd be able to read the Bible just by looking up at the sky.

I know this probably doesn't seem to have much to do with me wetting my pants, but it does because although I was on my way home—I was going home, even if I wasn't thinking about it or admitting it to myself—I knew I had to get washed, as if Mother and Poppa would be waiting to inspect me or something. But I was never far away from General Jackson's army, which was pretty much everywhere, and I could hear the troops walking and marching if I stood still and listened. It was like hearing a faint drum, all those feet stepping along; but most of the time you couldn't hear the marching because there was constant skirmishing and cannonading, and every once in a while, I could hear shouting and screaming. I didn't know if our boys or the Federals were just shouting for joy, *Hallelujah,* or screaming for help or for their mammas before they died or something.

By now I was skirting along the Valley Pike, but as I told you before, I stayed away from the roads as best I could, but with my pants all sticky with pee and filth and stiff like they needed tanning, I got back on the road to get some new clothes from the wagons. I told you this too, I think, but there were wagons overturned and smashed and burned all over the pike. General Banks's troops just ran and left them and sometimes they burned them. I'd seen piles of uni-forms all folded neatly in a wagon earlier, but now that I was looking for clothes, I couldn't find anything, so I just found a Federal soldier who wasn't too bloated or full of maggots and I took his pants—now, that wasn't as easy as it seems because most of the soldiers had already peed or shit their pants before they died, but I finally found one who I guess had been empty when he got shot. He was bald and had big splotchy freckles and a thick mustache, and he looked familiar, like I'd seen him somewhere before in Winchester, but it seemed that everybody I saw looked familiar, like every dead soldier was from Winchester. Course, at that rate, there wouldn't be anybody left in that town by the time General Jackson got there. Anyway, while I was getting my clothes from that dead soldier, I figured while I was at it, I'd also find a pair of shoes; and I tried on a few before I almost got caught by our own boys while I was being foolish and lingering there on the pike, so I left without getting any shoes, which I really didn't need because it was warm now.

But I wanted them because my feet were still bleeding and full of pus.

You probably remember that Jimmadasin's feet were bleeding too; and in case you're wondering about him, I should tell you that he left again, and this time it was for good. It took me a while to realize he'd gone because sometimes Jimmadasin just gets quiet, but after I saw R. W. and—

After I ran away, Jimmadasin just stopped talking to me, and I waited and waited and gave him time. I tried talking to him all afternoon and all through the night, even when I was dreaming. I dreamed Jimmadasin and Lucy and I were in the cave of the baby Jesus again, but I had to pee so bad I could hardly control myself, and so I left them there in the cave and went outside, but Jimmadasin was angry and he yelled, "You left Jesus, youse on you' own now, you don' deserve nobody," and then I dreamed I was watching the deserter or soldier or whatever he was hurting Mother, and I heard Poppa screaming, and the whole forest was on fire and I had to get out of there, but I couldn't leave Mother, except it wasn't Mother that the deserter was hurting and laying on top of anymore; it was Lucy, and then I could see that she was dead, and it was R. W. who was laying on top of her, and he was dead too, and it was because everyone was dead; and then when I woke up I had to pee; and I knew Jimmadasin was gone.

The ague had come on during the night, and when I peed it burned so bad I could hardly do it. I slept while General Jackson and his foot cavalry were on their way to Winchester; and I felt a little better by morning, but, like I told you, I knew Jimmadasin had gone; and it was like *all* the spirits had gone, or something.

Everything still felt like it was dead, just like it was in my dream, even though it was harvest time and the wheat was high and ready to be bound and toted to the shocks and then pitched into wagons and carried to a stack, and then after all that it would end up on the threshing table; and how I wished I could bring all that back again—working with Poppa and Uncle Isaac and all the hired niggers and getting more tired and hungry and happy than I can ever remember, but, like I said, it was all dead now. All I could smell was rot, like a horse had died, and my mouth tasted sour like I'd slept with food in it; and, of course, a mist just dropped down, indicatin' spirit weather, but this was some sort of spirit weather without spirits. It was quiet, like after a fire, except in the distance, of course.

If I listened I could hear the drums, except they weren't drums, just cannonading and musket fire, which were all coming from Winchester, I figured, although it was hard to tell because of the mountains, which turned everything into an echo. Or maybe I was in another acoustic shadow like when I was at Jedediah's farm.

So I just walked and remembered. The ague was good for remembering, and I thought of things that made me smile, like how the niggers always demanded whiskey for harvest work, didn't matter who they belonged to, and they'd work hard all right, but after dinner there'd be dancin' and playin' and shouting and laughing and stories, and I guess my fever was like whiskey too, because I could almost see it all happening, like those niggers were dancing in the trees and in the air and on the road and way off in the distance in the hills, and I remembered the long table Mother always prepared for the servants, and how she always set it up under the shade trees by the red sandstone flags where those diarrhea deserter sonovabitches killed her, and Mammy Jack would be running in and out of the house and putting every kind of comestible (that's what Mother called food) you could imagine on that table: corn pone, boiled bacon, cabbage (which I hated), thick milk, jam, hot bread, coffee, black-eyed peas, and potatoes. And sick as I was, I could smell all that comestible food—spirit food, I guess it was—and I wanted more than anything to hear Poppa reading his Bible (he always read his Bible before he'd let anyone take even a bite) and I wanted to see Mother in her Sunday dress with her brooch and her bonnet with the white bow, and I knew that the ague surely had taken hold of me again, but walking seemed to burn it out; and so I walked and walked and walked, and I had visions, and it was a good thing there was no one else around because I kept crying over nothing like I was a baby, and an old song kept running through my mind from Hog Day, and it was as if I was being pulled along by that song and its smells, and I remembered the words just as the niggers sung them:

Oh, gimme little shortlin' shortlin'
Oh, gimme little shortlin' bread
Run here, Mammy, run here quick,
Shortlin' bread done made me sick.

And I remembered Mammy Jack and how she could throw those playing cards in the air and catch them and make them look like snakes being throwed up in the air, and how she got her vision; and I suppose I was having visions right along because of the ague, but I slept and then walked and slept and walked, and I got sick some, just like in the song, and for a time I could smell bread everywhere; and I got closer and closer to the cannonading until it sounded like a thunderstorm crashing in the mountains, or maybe it was more like hail coming down on a roof, and the weather suddenly got cold—spirit weather, like I said—and the next night I shivered and there was frost on the grass; and now I'll tell you how I saw Mammy Jack, except, of course, she might have just been a spirit.

But I don't think so.

WHEN I GOT BACK HOME, THERE WAS FIGHTING ALL AROUND WINCHESter because that was one of General Jackson's greatest victories, when he pushed General Banks and his Federals right out of there, pushed them down Loudoun and Braddock and Market streets, and then right on down the Martinsville Pike; and those Federals probably knew that the only place they'd be safe was in the Potomac.

Now, I didn't see the battle, even though I felt drawn to the noise, and there was a lot of it. I could hear muskets and the crashing of shells and soldiers crying, and once I heard the rebel yell, and it was like it came from right inside my chest or something, and it sounded like it would rip everything apart; and instead of running toward the battle and maybe drawing my Colt .44 revolver and doing my duty, I just kept walking home like nothing had ever happened.

I walked through the fields, and the wheat was up to my waist, and everything smelled new and fresh, and there wasn't the smell of death anywhere; only the noise remindin' me that everyone was getting shot and wounded and killed; and when I was near the road, I could see the bluebellies rushing everywhere with their wagons, and whole families of niggers were trying to get out with them so they wouldn't have to be servants anymore and then they'd be equal to white people.

That's why Uncle Isaac left Mammy Jack and Mother and Poppa and the farm, and Poppa hated him for that and took it out on Mammy Jack more often than not, but Uncle Isaac had said "Ain't no more blowin' dat fo' day horn," which Mammy Jack explained to me meant he was going to be free no matter what, but that she was going to wait for him because he was only goin' to get caught by the paddyrollers or the soldiers, and then he'd be coming back home to her, but he didn't; and so Mammy Jack ran away to find him.

Well, I guess all the niggers escaping with the bluebellies weren't going to be *blowin' dat fo' day horn* anymore, but I'd heard stories that the bluebellies would just work those niggers to death; and they called them "contrabands," 'cause they escaped. I figured that's what happened to Uncle Isaac. He was strong and wiry, and so he probably got to be a contraband nigger in the North; only it seemed to me it wouldn't make much difference where he was 'cause a nigger is a nigger and a white man is a white man, and, as Poppa told me, that's the way the Lord planned it out.

I figure he would've been better off with Poppa, except those deserters that killed Mother and Poppa would've probably killed him too.

WHEN I REACHED THE EDGE OF OUR FARM, I THOUGHT I HEARD A DRUM roll; but it was just the hot part of the battle when everyone goes crazy for fighting and killing. It's the red madness when everything gets perfect, and you want to stand right there and shoot, and those minié balls and grape and canister become nothing more than maybe a strong wind blowing around; and even though I wasn't there, I knew exactly what was happening, and I could feel the thrill of it even without being there, but when I came to the stone fence where I'd let that rabbit go on that Sunday when Mother and Poppa got killed, I knew I couldn't go onto my own land without cryin' and humiliating myself.

So I waited, as if I expected the spirit dog to show up any minute. The spirit dog never did show up, but I was trembling the same way as when I saw him the first time; and it was hard to breathe, and I had to pee again, which was humiliating because it was so bad and so sudden that I almost did it in my pants again, but I didn't, thank God; and then suddenly, right out of the blue, I knew what I had to do.

I just had to change my name, is all.

It was, of course, a vision, and I figured it out in a second, and after that the shaking stopped, and I breathed regular, and I remembered what Major Pegram had told me in his tent about the street-fire king who was called Salamander, and how that Salamander would put sulphur on a plate and light it and eat it up while it was burning like it was no nevermind; and so I figured if *I* was Salamander I could go right up to the Big House and nothing could hurt me. It wouldn't even matter if it was on fire 'cause I'd be protected—I know that doesn't make sense, but I had the ague, after all; and I'll tell you the truth that even though I washed the piss off me and changed into the dead bluebelly's clothes, I still felt dirty, like the dirt was inside me or something, and I remember Poppa giving sermons about being unclean and odious, and I guess he was right because I couldn't get rid of the dirt inside me, except maybe by getting rid of myself; but once I had that vision I didn't feel I had to pee, and I didn't feel filthy-dirty anymore.

I suppose I didn't feel anything, which was a relief.

So I climbed over the wall, and even though I was now Salamander the Fire King, I remembered everything—there was the gum trap I left in the woods after I let the rabbit go free, there was the elm tree that I fell out of and broke my foot when I was little, there were all the familiar fields and meadows and hills stretched out in front of me, and it was like I could put my arms around the whole farm; but everything was different, everything had gone wild—there should have been corn ready for thinning, but the old fields were dug up and burned or overgrown or brown like everything was dyin'—and even though I knew the land and where everything was, it didn't feel like I was back on the farm; and I guess that was because I wasn't Mundy anymore.

The sun was going behind the mountains and everything was shadowy and blue-colored, and I felt like I wanted to cry, and I heard thunder, even though it wasn't going to rain; and I knew I should be shaking and being scared because everything looked blue and shadowy and perfect just like this when I came back after the battle of Kernstown and heard Poppa screaming out for Mother while he was burning up in the house, and I saw Mother getting dragged around and around and killed and fucked and—

Sonovabitch I didn't have to think about that, and I wasn't shaking one little bit because I'd cured myself, and that was probably just as powerful as Mammy Jack's vision about the Ship of Zion loaded up with all the angels and seraphs and everything; and I figured I could probably talk if I wanted to now, but when I tried, I could only make the "ha" sound. Now, that surprised me some, and I figured I'd never get out of being myself completely, but maybe it was just that Salamander the Fire King didn't talk neither, but I knew I was just faking to myself; and the ague must have weakened some because I started thinking that I couldn't be a spirit or the Fire King or Private Newton, who was a traitor anyway; and I started shaking again and feeling weak and scared and unclean because Jimmadasin was right, I left Jesus and Lucy and Mother and Poppa and even Mrs. Sara Anne and her children; and then I was walking past the barn and the lumber house and the schoolhouse, and they were all burned. Part of the schoolhouse was still standing, but the roof was gone and so was the back wall, and it was all black, and I could still smell the fire; that smell, which was like wet ashes, was all over here, and I wished I had run into the fire that the bluebellies had set back near Loch Willow, and I was getting more and more scared, although there was nothing here to be afraid of, except what I was rememberin', and in a minute or a second I'd probably just turn around and run, but I didn't, I kept on walking, and there were the nigger quarters, which were log cabins, and quite a bit down a ways was Mammy Jack's cottage, which had been bigger than all the others but was burned down now; and there was the hen house, and when I looked inside there weren't any hens in it, of course, and the smoke houses were as empty as the hen house; and it was getting dark and I didn't want to keep walking on because I'd get to the Big House, which was just over the hill; and I didn't want to see that, I didn't want to see it ever again—and why did I come back here?—and I listened listened listened because I was suddenly scared that the deserters or whoever the men were that killed Mother and Poppa were still out there by the house. I heard rustling and scratching, and I figured it was the deserters, but it wasn't anything, just night noises.

It got dark quick, like it always did when the air took on that blue color.

I started feeling sick, really sick, and I threw up and peed myself, and I don't remember anything, not even falling down or sleeping, just being filthy, until I woke up and found myself in a one-room cabin, and it was cold, and there was only a candle burning and the windows were all covered over, and there was a skinny old nigger woman standing by the bed I was laying on, and she was watching me and watching me and watching me.

It couldn't be Mammy Jack, but it was.

NOW, FOR A SECOND I IMAGINED THAT I WAS SUFFERIN' THE FEVER FROM being vaccinated and that I was still at Mrs. Sara Anne's in the shack where the scholars used to be boarded at Loch Willow and that Mrs. Sara Anne was standing over me.

I could hear the cannonading, or maybe thunder, and I figured I was back in the acoustic shadow; and I was thirsty and my mouth was dry and I had to pee again—God, I hated having to pee, even when I was feverish or delirious or whatever I was—and then I remember falling or something and dreaming about being Private Newton and Salamander the Fire King at the same time, and I remember being hot, and I was walking into the fire, where I could be perfect and happy and find Mother and Poppa, and I imagined that was probably what Heaven was like, and that the Bible and everybody had it wrong about it being like that in Hell, and then like a twig snapping I woke up and looked at Mammy Jack, who was skinny as her long-gone husband, Uncle Isaac. Like I told you.

"You're goin' to be fine, Marster Mundy, don't be scared, it's only Hannah, yas, yas, I know I lost some of my sides"—and Mammy Jack laughed at that—"and maybe some of my front, but I'm still me, jus' like you're still you."

But I wasn't still me, even though I couldn't tell her that; and I tried to get myself off that bed, but I was too dizzy, and I had to accept her help just to pull myself up so I could lean my back and head against the wall.

"Still a poor frog," she said. "I can't imagine what you been through, but you'll tell Hannah all about it when you're ready."

I nodded, and looked around, and I knew this wasn't her cottage 'cause that had burned down, so this must be one of the nigger cabins Poppa rented; they were too far away from the Big House for the deserters to have burned them down; but this old deteriorated cabin didn't look lived in, at least not by Mammy Jack, who always said that "everything in the worl' has its own place," and this place was dirty and smelled like sweat and old eggs. There was a table with a broken leg and two chairs and a cupboard that had once been on the wall but was now on the floor, which was dirt.

"I figured you was a ghost when I saw you layin' by the Big House, an' you was all curled up like a baby, but you was shakin' like you was havin' a fit or a vision—was dat it, Marster Mundy, was you havin' a vision? You tell Hannah if dat's what it was. You can't imagine how worried I was about you after I heared what happened." And then Mammy Jack stopped talking and she looked all sly like she was thinking up something bad, and maybe it was because her face had got so skinny that she looked like that, and I wondered what she would look like if she was herself again and fat; and she said, "Your Mamma and Poppa . . ." She looked hard at me like she was expecting I would finish up for her or something. "Do you know what happened?"

I nodded, and she started crying, and she was holding my hand so hard it hurt, and she said, "Tell me where you been, how you 'scaped, you poor baby," and after a while, of course, she figured I couldn't talk, and she made a fuss about that, and she told me that "it jus' weren't our time yet," and that when the Lord's will came down terrible on Mother and Poppa, she was on her way back home because she couldn't find Uncle Issac; and then she did the damnedest thing for a nigger: She lay down on the bed and put her arms around me and pushed my face into her bosom, even though there wasn't much of that left on her, and she cried and rocked back and forth, and she prayed for Uncle Isaac to come back to her, and thanked the Lord for bringing me back to her, and then she said we were going away, that she jus' couldn't stay no longer, and we'd go up north and find my Uncle Randolph, who was a good man and would take care of us, and he'd help us find Uncle Isaac, and we'd all be free and happy and all that.

Now, I had no intention of becoming a bluebelly, but I guess Mammy Jack's crying and wailing was catching, like a cold or something, because I started crying and shaking for no reason at all, and then I started remembering things about Mammy Jack and Mother and Poppa and how Poppa and Uncle Randolph almost came to punching each other because Uncle Randolph was a traitor and Poppa hated him for it, but all that crying and shaking I was telling you about was all happening inside me because outside I just lay there like a stone or something, and I figured that was because I'd become Salamander the Fire King and maybe a little of Private Newton the traitor; and I breathed in Mammy Jack, and smelled eggs and sweat, and I just wanted to stay there forever and breathe her in; and I remembered Sweet Grandy the dead lady with the pennies over her eyes, and I imagined having pennies over my eyes instead of being covered up with Mammy Jack's bosom; and I listened to the cannonading and cried for Mammy Jack and Uncle Isaac and Mother and Poppa, but my eyes didn't get wet, and it was like all that crying and feelin' empty and sad was all far away from me, and I heard a terrible echoey sound all around me, like Mammy Jack was crying all over her body, but it was only me making the "ha" sound.

I SNEAKED AWAY FROM HER WHEN SHE LEFT ME ALONE IN THE SHACK.

It was early morning, although there weren't any roosters to make any noise, and there wasn't no bird noise at all that I could remember. I guess Mammy Jack was getting everything ready for us to elope over to the North. I hid out in the woods because I wasn't done here at our farm yet, and I felt terrible because Mammy Jack was beside herself when she didn't find me, and she must have walked over every acre calling me and begging and pleading with me to come out, that there wasn't no time, no time at all, that she'd waited too long because of me and I certainly owed it to her to come on out and show myself and be a regular man and how everything was going to be better in the North and that there wasn't anything here for me, nothin' at all, and that we'd have a new life, and then she must've left because I was alone with nothing but the wind and trees and the insects; and Mammy Jack was right, I didn't want to be alone, and I cried for her going away because, although I didn't know it, but that was the last time I ever saw her, and I love her, I still do, but I had something to do, and I was going to do it, and I was going to open up the Gates of Heaven, Poppa told me you could do that with prayer, but I knew what would open the Gates of Heaven, and it was matches, and I didn't wait, but I set everything on fire.

I started with the trees in the woods, and then I burned all the buildings on the farm, and I imagined they were talking to me as the fire caught at them, especially the barn, which wailed like the wind; and after I set all the nigger shacks afire, I walked down to the Big House and lit what I could and then there was nothing to do but wait for the fire and the angels to come across the field like snakes and take me up to Mother and Poppa—or maybe the spirit dog would finally come out and take me to wherever it was he came from.

I guess I just didn't figure it was going to be such a long wait.

Afterword

My nephew Edmund McDowell came to live with us on June 6, 1862, which, coincidentally, is the same day his hero General Turner Ashby died in battle. My dear wife, Rebecca Cowles McDowell, and I will be eternally grateful to the Reverend Doctor A. A. H. Boyd, pastor of the Presbyterian church on Loudoun Street in Winchester, who recognized Edmund when he was found at the site of the second fire at my late brother's farm. It is due in large part to Doctor Boyd's bold efforts that Edmund was reunited with his family. He also tried to help us locate the servant Hanna, of whom Mundy was so fond. Our efforts, alas, were unsuccessful in that regard. We will always be grateful to this man of the cloth who believed so fervently in a cause diametrically opposed to our own.

But it is with extreme sadness and disappointment that I must report that Edmund left us the summer after he completed this diary. We have exhausted our resources trying to locate our nephew, to no avail. May the Lord God in His mercy protect him.

Edmund left us only the following note inserted in his diary:

"Can't wait anymore. Gone to find the spirit dog."

LIEUTENANT COLONEL
RANDOLPH ESTES MCDOWELL (RET.)
SEPTEMBER 29, 1865
SCRANTON, PENNSYLVANIA

A NOTE FROM JACK ÐANN

Once, when asked to contribute an essay about one of my favorite books, I wrote:

Some books are read; others seem to become part of our own, private experience.

Perhaps it's a function of youth, just as the music we hear during adolescence and early adulthood remains part of our intensely evocative experience. Yet I find something like that still happening: even now certain books become my own. Perhaps art enables us to overcome the ennui and cynicism of "maturity" and suspend our disbelief. Thus we become innocents once again, opening ourselves to life.

The Painted Bird (by Jerzy Kosinski) still burns in my memory, perhaps more brightly than any of the others. It is still an experienced nightmare, a waking dream, after fifteen years. I discovered the book when I began to write fiction, when I was crossing that bridge from being reader to writer. The initial horror I remember experiencing when I first read the book has transformed itself over the years into a sensation of numinal perfection, of something magical and yet terrible, something so incandescently pure and frightening as to be insidious.

So when asked to recommend my favorite novel, I went back to my library to re-read *The Painted Bird*.

And there I found *The Silent. . . .*

In Kosinski's introduction to a new edition of the book, he wrote that old school friends "blamed me for watering down historical truth and accused me of pandering to an Anglo-Saxon sensibility whose only confrontation with national cataclysm had been the Civil War a century earlier, when bands of abandoned children roamed through the devastated South." When I read that sentence, I was electrified. It was the shock of recognition. I knew, as soon as I read Kosinski's words, that my next major work would be about the Civil War. My experience has always been that the material chooses the writer.

That's what happened with my last novel, *The Memory Cathedral*.

And that's what happened here. . . .

As soon as I read Kosinski's lines, I glimpsed the thoughts and dreams and fears and obsessions of my protagonist: a fourteen-year-old boy, mute from the horrors he has witnessed, chased by demons real and imagined, seeing the tragedy of the Civil War through a child's eyes where reality, folk superstition, magic, and history have become incandescent. I set out to portray the personal and secret world that exists within familiar textbook and popular history.

When I read Kosinski's comparison of *The Painted Bird* with the experience of children during the Civil War, I remembered how I had felt when I read *Lord of the Flies*, and I compared that experience to reading Kosinski's own *The Painted Bird*, Twain's *The Adventures of Huckleberry Finn*, and Salinger's *The Catcher in the Rye*. I could *hear* Mundy's voice whispering to me; and in that instant of "recognition" (for want of a better word), I knew how *The Silent* had to be shaped. The story required a close-focus immediacy, and it had to be told from the most personal of viewpoints: first person.

I wanted the reader to experience the greatest, most cataclysmic and influential period in our history through the eyes of a child. *With* the eyes of a child. I wanted to disclose the small details not found in traditional histories and bring this period to life through the *experience* of personal, emotional history. Mundy conflates fantasy and reality as he tries to make sense of his experiences; and as he finds imaginary friends to guide him and make sense of the world, *The Silent* becomes peopled with ghosts and spirits that are as capricious as the living. But they, too, betray him and turn away from him. Although there might be those who consider *The Silent* "magical realism," my purpose was to create a *heightened* reality. I wanted to convey the terrible bliss of combat and the irreal sense of compression and excitement and horror that occurs when the familiar world breaks down. A Yankee civilian wrote that the Civil War "crowded into a few years the emotions of a lifetime." For Mundy, the experience and emotions of a lifetime were crowded into a single year.

I drew from diaries of the period, in the same way that I fleshed out the characters and background in *The Memory Cathedral*. I believe that fiction lives in the details, and diaries and reminiscences are the best sources. Just as *The Diaries of Ibn Battuta*, Lucca Landucci's *A Florentine Diary*, and Leonardo da Vinci's notebooks shaped *The Memory Cathedral*, so did firsthand reports help me discover the form and narrative thrust of *The Silent*—recollections such as Cornelia McDonald's *A Woman's Civil War*, Luther Hopkins's *From Bull Run to Appomattox: A Boy's View*, Francis Dawson's *Reminiscences of Confederate Service*, Jedediah Hotchkiss's *Make Me a Map of the Valley*, Jesse Bowman Young's *What a Boy Saw in the Army*, John S. Robson's *How a One-Legged Rebel Lives*, Lucy Rebecca Buck's *Sad Earth, Sweet Heaven*, and Henry Kyd Douglas's *I Rode with Stonewall*, to name but a very few. The Hopkins and Young books were especially revealing, for they depict the experiences of teenage soldiers in the Union and Confederate armies. Although I found many interesting details about the war in books such as *What a Boy Saw in the Army*, some of these old soldiers were more interested in relating incidents that emphasized patriotism and heroism rather than the indelicate details of the horrors and idiocies of war. But I have always found that the most interesting and revelatory "bits"—the material that ends up driving the novel—can be buried in the most unlikely text.

So in the end—and as always!—there was no choice but to try to read everything I could—books on the sexual mores of the period, such as Thomas P. Lowry's excellent *The Story the Soldiers Wouldn't Tell: Sex in the Civil War*, chapbooks published locally in very limited quantities on subjects as diverse as Civil War ghosts and women soldiers who disguised themselves as men, letters published by regional organizations such as the Winchester-Frederick County Historical Society, monographs on the geology of the region, texts on Civil War medical equipment and surgical procedures, texts on munitions and uniforms and railroads, folklore journals, newspapers and magazines of the period, and the endlessly fascinating (and alternatively numbing) eighty-volume *War of the Rebellion* series, published by the Government Printing Office. The *War of the Rebellion* series includes military correspondence, logs, hearings, maps, and casualty figures from both sides of the conflict. (The author was fortunate that only about seven volumes were relevant to Mundy's adventures!)

One of the most interesting sources was *Weevils in the Wheat: Interviews with Virginia Ex-Slaves*, edited by Charles L. Perdue, Jr., Thomas E. Barden, and Robert K. Phillips. In 1936 the Virginia Writers Project began interviewing ex-slaves in Virginia, and over a period of a year conducted more than three hundred interviews. Unfortunately, almost half of the interviews have been lost or destroyed, but the surviving reminiscences are a deep look into the period. Although these are "translations" by the interviewers—and some of their notations are quite idiosyncratic—one can still hear the poetry of Negro slave dialect in these songs and stories that have been all but lost; they are precious accounts of faith and joy and despair. It was after I read these interviews that Mundy's voice became louder, more insistent, and I glimpsed new scenes and plot twists as if I were a sailor seeing land through the roiling fog and mist. I also found the sketchbook of artist James E. Taylor invaluable. Taylor accompanied General Philip H. Sheridan during his campaign in the Shenandoah Valley in 1864. Although Taylor would not by any measure be considered a great artist, I found his detailed drawings of the Valley—its people, houses, battlefields, towns, cities, and roads— more useful than the brilliant battlefield and campground drawings and paintings of Winslow Homer or the heart-wrenching battle photographs of Alexander Gardner. While Homer and Gardner recorded timeless moments, Taylor recorded the mundane, easily forgotten details of everyday life. I found those details invaluable because for me a novel comes to life through the small moments that pave the way for the great scenes and epiphanies . . . if, indeed, there are to be any.

Although I glimpsed Mundy and *The Silent* when I first read Kosinski's foreword (and I could feel some of the pulse and rhythms of the book when I immersed myself in the period and place—after I had read diary upon diary, source upon source), I didn't have the blood and bones of the book until I actually walked everywhere Mundy walked. Until I had lived for a time in the Valley and looked through the scrims of the present into the past. The Valley is still alive with ghosts. When I stood stock-still in some of the old graveyards and battlefields, I could hear the whispers of the past, and it was there that *The Silent* came to life. It was in the silent, empty fields, which had once been soaked with blood, that I listened to Mundy and saw the novel as if I were a Peeping Tom eavesdropping on the land itself.

And just as I was eavesdropping on Mundy, so was Mundy eavesdropping on himself, creating this diary as a mnemonic—a means by which he might recapture everything he had lost. Can one come of age and become human without coming to terms with loss? Perhaps that's the central question of the book.

Indeed, does Mundy become human . . . or does he become a spirit?

He left me with the last line: *"Can't wait anymore. Gone to find the spirit dog."*

I leave it to you to decide.

ABOUT THE AUTHOR

Jack Dann is the author of several novels, including *The Memory Cathedral*. He lives in New York and Australia and is at work on a new novel.